OPHRAH'S GATE

JIM LEVER

USA • Canada • UK • Ireland

Note for Librarians: A cataloguing record for this book is available from Library and Archives Canada at www.collectionscanada.ca/amicus/index-e.html
ISBN 1-4120-9446-1

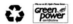

Trafford's print shop runs on "green energy" from solar, wind and other environmentally-friendly power sources.

Offices in Canada, USA, Ireland and UK

Book sales for North America and international:
Trafford Publishing, 6E–2333 Government St.,
Victoria, BC V8T 4P4 CANADA
phone 250 383 6864 (toll-free 1 888 232 4444)
fax 250 383 6804; email to orders@trafford.com
Book sales in Europe:
Trafford Publishing (UK) Limited, 9 Park End Street, 2nd Floor
Oxford, UK OX1 1HH UNITED KINGDOM
phone 44 (0)1865 722 113 (local rate 0845 230 9601)
facsimile 44 (0)1865 722 868; info.uk@trafford.com
Order online at:
trafford.com/06-1201

10 9 8 7 6 5 4 3 2

To My Teachers

Brenda Lever, my wife
Audrey Davis, my mother
John Henry Davis, my dad

Loring and Irene Hembree
Hassie and Russell Rice
Antoinette Jones
Ralph and Birdie Girtman
Dr. Colquitt and Doris Sims
Louise Stamps
Marie Shepard
Sallie Kennedy
Joe Brown
Janet Bowen Cannon
Julian Cannon
Eunice Mixon
Harry and Martha Barrineau
Bill Greer
Frank and Jeanette McGill
Mary Hancock
J.D. Lindsey
Dr. Frank King
Sam Warren
Amihai Mazar
Nava Panitz Cohen
John Camp

Preface

On St. Simons Island, one of Georgia's coastal barriers, Christ Episcopal Church has endured beneath the massive live oaks since colonial times. Across the way from the old church, hidden by garlands of Spanish moss, there is a tabby mix masonry bench. Sitting here for a spell, in the stillness, has the power to transform a life—at least the perspective on that life. And when perspective changes a life can be changed.

But it takes great faith to act on a spiritual flash; it will take time and it may take many failures. An epiphany may also require the realization that much of the promise is not meant for this lifetime; this is the part which requires the most tenacious faith.

From within the wood-frame walls of Christ Church, one seated on the hard stone bench may just be able to comprehend the message spoken from behind the heart pine pulpit. The parable is of one lost and dying of thirst in a desert in the old west, who happens upon a dilapidated ranch house and tack shed. Beside the house is an old well with a cast iron hand pump. There is a crudely painted sign affixed to the pump which says, "You will find a jug of water beneath the piece of tin on the back porch. If you drink the water, that's all there is; if you use the water to prime this old pump there will be water for all."

Faith is not a belief or a belief system; faith is action in spite of doubt and fear. Faith must be kinetic or there is no potential.

OPHRAH'S GATE is a story of shattered hopes, futile pursuits and lost faith and of fanatical devotion and the resulting devastation. But this is more a story of dreams reborn, wonderful discoveries and the three great loves in concert.

The main characters in this book are all fictional. A few incidental characters are real people whom I believe to be well enough published or known so as to be in the public domain. Any words attributed to them are entirely mine, not theirs and I sincerely hope none will find such attributions offensive in any way as I have the greatest respect for them all.

                                        Jim Lever
                                        Tifton, Georgia
                                        January 12, 2006

1

PETER ALDRICH Awoke with a jolt. From the glass front of the building across Hilel Street, the sun's reflection streamed into the drab room. The clamor of the street's night life had kept him awake until a couple of hours ago. Damnable Shabbat revelers, he thought to himself, they seem to delight in keeping the whole town awake. The idiots must be the remnant of Jews who earned God's wrath so often in the scriptures.

Six in the morning, Saturday, the third of April, only three days before the true Christmas Day. Aldrich lay on a padded slab, staring at the ceiling, unrested.

A to-do list began to appear in his mind; he could see the two-tone green lines on the Day-Timer paper as he prioritized the entries.

His clarion call, a sermon from four months before, began to replay itself. He could hear the prophet's voice screaming for a re-deemer to arise:

"The Almighty is waiting. You know who you are and you know He's calling you out just as He called Abraham and Moses, Gideon and David. And you... you know what it is you're called for. He doesn't need your strength; He doesn't need your wisdom; He doesn't need anything you possess. He doesn't need any of your ability... He only needs your avail-ability. He, alone, chooses those who will join His roll of hero saints.

Remember when He called Gideon out... to purge the land of the Midianites? Remember how Gideon answered...? He said, 'God...sure-ly you don't mean me. In all the land, Manassah is the poorest, my clan is the weakest and in my house I am the least'. But God did mean Gideon. And of the thirty-two thousand men Gideon called to arms, God accepted only one out of a hundred. But with that three hundred, so the Bible tells us, Gideon annihilates an army 'as thick as locusts that could no more be counted than the grains of sand on the seashore.'

Friends, listen to what I say. The list of plain, lowly, humble but available people God calls out for greatness, goes on and on and, of course, we believe this list of great saints continues right on into this latter day. But, my brothers and sisters, the greatest in this hallowed hall of fame were never recognized as great in their own lifetime. Fact is, most of the movers and shakers of their day probably never even heard of them...and if they had, they probably considered them lunatics, fanatics, trouble makers or just plain losers. But my, oh my, how God's good time changes all things. Isn't it amazing? Today we name our children Deborah, David or Gideon; Matthew, Mary, Martha, Luke, John, Paul...but what do we call our dogs, even our zoo animals...? Plato, Caesar, Cleopatra, Jezebel, Nero, Ramses, Hannibal.

Don't you see the burning bush? Can't you feel the dew on the wool? Do you dare to answer His call?"

Aldrich could still see the prophet's laser gaze burning across the congregation and straight into his own eyes. The words, the knowing stare, confirmed the voice commanding him to act. God was ordering him to be much more than the developer of Park City real estate and an elder in The Church of Jesus Christ of Latter Day Saints. He would use his wealth and his knowledge of ancient history to restore honor to the faith.

As it had been with Joseph Smith, so it would be now with Peter Aldrich. He was ordained by a direct command and the very hand of God. He needed no sanction from Salt Lake City. After all, was it not those same church leaders who paid Mark Hofmann a small fortune for the prophet, Joseph Smith's Salamander letters, demonic forgeries which brought disgrace to the church? He, Peter Aldrich, was called by God to rescue, to redeem, to glorify the one true church. Now was the time and the opportunity.

The Hilel Tower Hotel was not Aldrich's favorite but it was a safe place to avoid a chance encounter with an acquaintance. The beds were awful, the street noise withering and the elevators a bad carnival ride. On the other hand, the hotel was well located in West Jerusalem, a block from the Ben Yahuda Mall, four from Zion Square and a short walk up from the Old City.

There was nothing he had to do before his noon appointment but there was no way could he get back to sleep; nine time zones of jet lag and his anxiety over the mission made sure of it. He lay still with his eyes closed and tried to review each step of the plan. He was dog tired but too wired to stay in bed. With torpid movements, he got up and started through his morning routine. He brushed and shaved in subconscious mode, still trying to gather his thoughts.

Aldrich paused to stare into the mirror; he hardly recognized the six foot tall figure who stooped to peer back at him. The former down hill racer and Olympic hopeful was only a begrudged memory, a face from the past, now as distant as were Squaw Valley and Innsbruck. And he hated the face that refused to make eye contact; the hollow cheeks, the anesthetic blue eyes and yellowing gray hair, he resented it all.

His eyes felt like shakers of coarse salt. Six drops of Natural Tears didn't do much to help the jet-cabin dryness and stinging. The steamy shower worked better. He could have easily dozed off. He might have slept better standing there under the warm trickle than he had in the torture rack of a bed. Actually, he hadn't slept well since he had stopped taking the Lithium but he must keep his mind clear and open to hear God's voice.

Outside in the hallway he tapped hard on the elevator buttons for the umpteenth time. He moaned in frustration and started to take the stairs but as soon as he turned he heard the dull dink-dink and the elevator door scraped open. He stepped into the dingy closet and pressed the button for the lobby. "Piece of junk feels like it's riding on bungee cords," he muttered to himself.

Downstairs, the lobby was deserted except for a desk clerk behind the blonde ash check-in counter. Oblivious to the world, he shuffled through a sheaf of paperwork. A musk of stale tobacco smoke and spilt beer marked the room. Aldrich walked on through to the dining room. It, too, was almost empty. An old man sat in a well lit corner. He didn't look up from the day old copy of Ha'aretz he held out at arms length.

Aldrich walked over to the serving line. Kosher breakfasts never varied; salads, fish, fruit, dairy. None of it enticed Aldrich. He opted for juice and instant cocoa. Over here, abstaining from coffee was easy, nothing but instant anywhere in Israel, even in the better restaurants. A big commercial toaster stood uselessly against the wall, unplugged and covered as required by religious law. It was Shabbat. He gulped down the too-sweet grapefruit juice and waited for his cocoa to cool down enough to sip. He was too restless to just sit there, he had to move about. He left the full cup on the table, untasted and walked outside.

A quiet, pleasant morning, still cool and the ubiquitous gas and diesel fumes had dissipated. All the shops were closed with either a padlocked accordion gate or steel shutter securing the fronts. Last night's litter garnished the old veneer of city grime which covered the street. A cab waited near the hotel entrance. The driver, neck arched back and mouth wide open, slept snoring behind the wheel. A dozen spry sparrows, well into a new day of foraging, were the only detectable movement – only the sparrows and Aldrich. A street or two over he could hear the unmistakable slams and hydraulic moans of a dumpster truck going through its sequences.

Aldrich walked across Hilel Street and south on Rabbi Akiva past the Italian pastaria where he was to meet the artisan at twelve. Spaghettim was one of few restaurants that would be open anywhere in West Jerusalem until the halakah siren officially ended Shabbat at sunset. His releasing ramble took him through Independence Park and on through the grounds of The Three Arches Hotel, the only YMCA in the world, he guessed, with one hundred and seventy dollar a night rooms. But when compared to the three hundred a night singles at the King David, just across the street, the Y seemed reasonable.

Inside the lobby of the King David, Aldrich paused at the "Scheduled Events" board: nine Bar Mitzvah parties and two wedding receptions. Any one could top a quarter million dollars if the hosts came close to filling the grand ball room or even the terrace gardens with guests. He crossed the lobby and exited the opposite side of the building, actually the hotel's front; King David Street parallels the rear elevation. From the portico he stopped to gaze out across the Hinnom Valley toward the Western wall of the Old City. The activity around the Jaffa Gate seemed light even for a Shabbat early morn.

His moment of meditation was fractured by loud cackling laughter from one of the tables just beyond where he stood. Around the terrace and poolside a number of guests were having breakfast. There was no mistaking the language or their accents, Aldrich recognized the combination all too well. He despised the sound of it.

"Rude, gluttonous, spoiled New York whores."

Aldrich muttered the words loudly enough to satisfy himself without risking being overheard. He defended his deep resentment as righteous indignation, not bigotry. They had earned his contempt. With their ill gotten gains they had damn near taken over Park City's resort properties just as they had in Vail, Aspen and most of the rest in Colorado. There was no trusting them, no such thing as good faith with these scabby crooks. They all seem to have some perverted need to beat you out of something, some kind of twisted game with them, he rationalized. They had rather beat you out of a dime than to make an honest dollar, try to turn every deal into a knife fight but don't want you to have a knife.

His thoughts were locked on target. As if practicing a sermon, he preached damnation to his oblivious congregation with such venom that at times he growled out the words just barely under his breath.

"How dare you revel here, the very place where the Messiah suffered and died. Aren't there enough other places in the world where your lot can party like the feeding pigs you are? You with your kosher slop and fermented swill, you even pollute your breakfast juices with alcohol.

"Look at your table manners. Your children eat like chimps, screaming, reaching and grabbing. And you women, dear God, is there one of you here under two hundred pounds? At least your men have the good sense to be somewhere else.

"You assume an intellectual, cultural and even a spiritual superiority. You arrogant reprobates, is it any wonder the world has despised you for centuries. You have the ignorant audacity to think you belong here, but you don't. The real Jews are up in the trenches on the Golan and manning the bunkers around Gaza. Not one in a thousand Israelis could even afford to eat a breakfast here with... You fat, lazy, 'chosen' sluts."

Aldrich's face was contorted with disdain. He studied the diners who never so much as glanced back. Every fiber in his being craved to scream out his message of condemnation to the decadent Jews just as Jeremiah had done twenty-five centuries before. But he knew that to do so would seal his fate; he was called by God to be a redeemer, not a prophet.

He would heed the lesson of Moses and not repeat the same mistake; when God says speak, He doesn't mean strike. So, for now, he must content himself with scathing them within the confines of his mind and muffled voice but scathe them he would, even if only with whispers.

"The fruits of your shame cover this land like the dust. Your money is your god and your purchased political influence your only hope of salvation. Do the forests of planted trees, the kibbutz swimming pools, the libraries, do they ease your conscience and soothe..."

Aldrich caught himself. Some of the guests had begun to notice either his caustic monologue or his demeanor. One of the waiters approached with a concerned expression on his face.

"Sir, are you okay?"

"Yes I'm fine, thank you. I'm a little jet-lagged.

"Yes sir. May I show you to a table?"

"No, no thank you. I've already had breakfast. Just out for a walk"

The waiter gave him a polite nod and returned toward his station. Aldrich squinted, reached into a pocket for his sunglasses and put them on. Time to walk on: he could bump into someone he knew here at the King David. He didn't want to have to try and explain his presence in Jerusalem right now, especially to any local acquaintances who might remember the encounter later.

Down the slope, just outside the King David's gardens, Aldrich entered the opulent Yemin Moshe neighborhood with its famous windmill. When it was founded in 1892, Yemin Moshe was the first Jewish community outside the old city walls. For the next seventy-five years it survived under Ottoman and Arab control; it was a tough neighborhood to grow up and live in. Since the '67 war, it had become one of the most desirable residential sections of the city. The irony was that the tenacious, long-time residents and their descendants could no longer afford to live here. It had been bought up by rich Jews from other nations, mostly American. Aldrich stood in silence, gazing into the blades of the old windmill simmering over the inequity.

Aldrich spent the remainder of the morning walking taking in the sights, sounds and smells within the old city walls. Here there was little risk of a chance encounter that would be remembered. At the same time he worked through the logistics and the potential pitfalls of the next few days. By the time his loop brought him back to Rabbi Akiva Street and Spaghettim, it was almost noon. He estimated that he had racked up ten miles. An elk and antelope hunter, Aldrich was used to walking miles in high altitudes, but somehow city miles always seemed harder. Must be the concrete, the noise and all the fumes.

An entry walk led through a green tunnel that had been pruned out of an enormous fig. The old tree guarded the entry to the restaurant's garden. Aldrich worked his way over the mosaic of exposed roots and broken pavement to a wrought iron gate. He ignored a conspicuous please-wait-to-be-seated sign hanging on the open gate. His time in country had taught him that to obey a sign here dooms one to a kind of Israeli limbo. He had convinced himself that here the national pastime was line breaking and the motto, it's easier to get forgiveness than permission.

He made his way to a table under an arbor beside a lush hedge screening the stone wall of an adjacent building. Considering the months, long rash of suicide bombings all over the country, the place was crowded; this was one of the few places open.

If the maitre'd was irritated that he hadn't bothered to wait for a table, it didn't show. Aldrich saw him pointing his table out to a waiter who brought over a bread basket and a carafe of water. At the gate, next to the sign, he noticed a small man looking over the crowd, searching.

The description fit, a diminutive man, close cropped beard, gold rimmed, glass-brick thick lens and a blue, needlepoint kippah clipped to his thin hair. The artisan had arrived. Aldrich caught his eye from across the patio. He nodded slightly and the small man moved toward the table.

"Mister Adams?" The apprehension in his voice was apparent.

"Yes," said Aldrich, "have a seat."

The artisan did one of the little half-bow-half-nods typical of the reticent Ashkenazim, pulled back a chair and sat down.

"I am Yoram Perlman."

"Yes, good, glad you could make it. Let me get the waiter back."

Aldrich stood, held his napkin with one hand and summoned with the other. He sat back down as a waiter darted in their direction. Perlman ordered the special, fruti de mar, five kinds of shellfish, not a kosher morsel in the dish. Aldrich ordered the same. When the young man left with their order, it was the artisan who spoke first.

"So, Mister Adams, tell me exactly how I may be of service."

Aldrich had been taught to pause for thought before ever answering a direct question, part of his missionary instruction. The training had served him well in business. Now, before responding to the artisan, he shifted his eyes in the direction of another waiter who approached with a tray of glasses and bottles. After he had served Perlman and left, Aldrich answered.

"As I told you when I called, I'm familiar with your work. You're quite a talented artist. I'm particularly interested in your, what do you call them? Reproductions? Copies? I'm sure you don't…

Perlman interrupted, "If you were about to say you're sure I don't call them forgeries or fakes or imitations, you're correct; I don't. I call my work traditional ceramic art."

Perlman impaled a lemon wedge. He pinched the rind and ratcheted his fork so that the pulpy juice trickled into his water glass.

Now making eye contact with Aldrich, he continued as he poured water from the carafe. "Everything I have ever created is an original. I have never copied another artifact. Each of my creations is an original and, therefore, none, not even one, can be labeled a fake. I have never misrepresented the age of any piece."

Aldrich believed him. He was sure that he never had misrepresented either the age or authenticity. He never had to. The reputable dealers who bought his "originals" were completely willing to do that on their own, which is exactly how Aldrich had found out about the artisan in the first place.

Three years ago Aldrich purchased an expensive scarab for his personal collection. The dealer had guaranteed it and furnished him with a signed certificate of authenticity. Aldrich later discovered an anachronistic hieroglyph and knew he had bought a fake. Nevertheless, the quality of the piece was astounding. It was not so much the artistic style as it was the technical perfection. The piece was beautifully aged, but beautiful aging was not too hard to achieve. What amazed Aldrich was the microscopic surface crystals visible under forty power magnification.

Aldrich had recently read an intriguing article in *Biblical Archaeology Review* on the subject of seal authentication. These tiny crystals take centuries to grow; at least that was the claim of the magazine article. Aldrich now knew this standard had been compromised. And he suspected that he and the artisan might well be the only two who knew it.

"Yes, of course," Aldrich agreed. "I understand. In fact, I may well be the single greatest admirer of your work. I may, just possibly, become your most generous patron."

The artisan ceased chewing and looked up from buttering his third thick slice of focaccia.

"Patron, you say?"

Bingo! Aldrich held a poker face knowing he had hit a hot button. Perlman needed money. Aldrich hadn't expected a Countess Mara tie, but the artisan was shabby, even for Israel. He had expected that Perlman would find the word "patron" much more palatable than client or customer or, god forbid, employer.

"Yes, patron," said Aldrich, "I am prepared to offer you an immediate sum which I think you will find to be a most attractive advance. That is, if you are interested and would be willing to accept a specific commission?"

"Possibly," Perlman said.

The artisan tried his best to sound nonchalant, but his dilating pupils and a pronounced swallow betrayed pretence.

Aldrich nodded. "I've been a customer of our mutual friend for several years now. A couple of years ago I paid him a small fortune for a Ramses scarab which he represented as genuine. It wasn't but it is the best 'traditional style creation' I've ever seen.

Now Perlman was nervous. He wasn't sure that he wasn't being blackmailed. James Adams had led him to believe he was just a collector, albeit one referred to him by his best customer.

At the least, he expected he was going to have to cough up a sizable refund. But he had gotten no angry call from the dealer who bought it as genuine. He might have suspected that the scarab was looted from a dig or even stolen. But he would have never paid what he did if he had doubted its authenticity. Perlman's mind raced to fit together the pieces of the menacing puzzle. Aldrich sensed the artisan's growing stress; he had to convince him that he was safe. He was not in trouble with the law; neither was he about to be exposed by an angry victim.

"Relax, Mr. Perlman, I'm not here to make any demands or threats. As far as the scarab is concerned, it was a godsend."

When Aldrich discovered the scarab was not three thousand years old he called the antiquities dealer intending to confront him. Aldrich learned that a vendor from whom the dealer regularly purchased reproduction artifacts had offered him a small personal collection of scarab seals. The dealer had said that the vendor told him his father had bought them from Bedouins and that they had been in the family for years. Aldrich asked if there might be any more Middle Kingdom Scarabs available from the same collection. The dealer said that he didn't have any more; he thought that he had bought the entire collection. When Aldrich asked how he could contact the vendor directly to get more information on the collection, specifically on the scarab he had bought, the dealer readily gave him Perlman's name and address. Only then did Aldrich believe that the antique dealer must have bought the Ramses Scarab as genuine. He was sure that the dealer was not aware of the artisan's level of mastery. That was when Aldrich realized that Perlman's talents could be worth much more than what he had paid the dealer for the scarab.

"You see," continued Aldrich, "had I not bought your creation I wouldn't know of your skill. Even though I went back to Shihadeh to find you, I never told him that the scarab is not genuine. So, as far as I know, he's still completely unaware of any of this."

"Exactly what do you want from me, Mr. Adams?"

"I want one of your unique creations." said Aldrich. "You will be well paid."

Perlman nodded that he was listening.

"I want you to create a tablet for me. I want it made of vitrified clay. I want it with several lines of inscription; I'll give you the exact inscription. I want it with credible surface corrosion and, finally, I want the same surface crystals that make my scarab so convincing."

Aldrich paused to assess the artisan's reaction to the work order. Perlman gazed through the table top for a few long moments before looking up.

"How soon do you need it? I can not grow the crystals over night. Then there's still the distressing and aging."

"I want it as soon as possible," Aldrich answered, "but it has to be perfect."

Their food arrived at the table; Perlman held his reply. When they were served and the waiter had left, the artisan tucked the red and white gingham napkin into the band collar of his shirt, unscrewed the top from a shaker of fresh grated Parmigiano-Reggiano and dumped half the contents into his bowl. While Perlman tossed linguine, pine nut pesto and cheese with his fork and spoon, he answered.

"I could have it ready in about three months. It would not be cheap. Depending on the inscription and the dimensions, it would cost, probably, 40,000 shekels. I would have to do most of the work in a clean room which I would have to make myself. And then the piece itself would take many hours of microsurgical enhancement."

"Tell you what; I'm going to walk back to my hotel. Why don't you finish your meal and then meet me there. I'm in room 512 at the Tower, just half a block from here. I have the drawings and specifications in my room."

"Aren't you going to eat?"

Perlman looked surprised that anyone could walk away from such a meal. Aldrich didn't bother to even answer him. Instead, he made sure that Perlman had heard the hotel and room number.

"Jerusalem Tower, room 512," Aldrich repeated. "From this point on, I prefer that we not be seen together."

"Yes, I'll be over shortly."

Aldrich pulled a money clip from his trousers pocket and peeled off two hundred shekel notes. He folded them and slid the money under a corner of the ash tray and left for the hotel. Perlman continued with his lunch, all the time staring across the table at the untouched entree. It bothered him that he couldn't figure out any way to take the food without having to wrestle a flimsy container all afternoon. He couldn't very well go up to Adams's room with it. He tried to put it out of his mind while he finished eating.

A few minutes later, Aldrich heard the knock at his door and let Perlman in.

"Sit down," Aldrich said. "First of all, change the price."

"I don't see a way."

"Your estimate isn't high enough."

"I beg your pardon?"

"Number one: I don't just want this to be a priority project; I want it to be your only project. Number two: I want you in a financial position which will insure that you never reveal the slightest detail of our arrangement."

"I would not..."

"I want to be sure of it. So, here's what I propose. In this attaché you will find twenty five thousand U.S. dollars. This is your advance. If you complete it on time and it's perfect you'll be paid another twenty-five thousand.

Within a few weeks after delivery, you will receive documentation along with debit cards to a private account in Banque Baumann and Cie's Luxembourg branch. On or about the tenth of July, each and every year, for as long as you live, fifty thousand dollars will be deposited into that account. You can access the account through any major bank ATM. All the details will be explained in the documentation."

"Are you serious?" Perlman asked. "What do you want me to do?" He fumbled through a couple of pockets and pulled out a worn silver cigarette case. He flipped the top open, removed one and placed it to his lips.

"I would appreciate your not doing that in here," said Aldrich. "Smoking."

"Yes, of course."

Perlman replaced the cigarette inside the case. Aldrich picked up where he left off.

"At some point in the months to come – it could be as long as a year or two, I don't know – you'll hear a lot of news about the piece. So much so that I expect you might be tempted to disclose that you were its creator. So, listen to me carefully, Mr. Perlman; I want you to understand this perfectly. If I ever hear one single word associating you with this tablet, the Swiss bank account will be closed and there will never be another single agorot deposited into it. Are we clear on that?"

"Yes."

"Do you have any questions about your compensation?"

"No, it all sounds acceptable to me," said Perlman. "If I may ask, what kind of news is it that you are expecting me to hear?"

"Mr. Perlman, all you need to know is exactly what it is that I want you to make, what I will pay for it and the conditions as I have just explained them. Whatever I do with my purchase and whatever you may hear of it afterwards is none of your concern, whatsoever. Are we in agreement?"

"Yes, it's just that..."

"Good. I sincerely hope we are. Then, why don't we take a look at the drawings."

Aldrich opened the black leather attaché on the bed. The artisan gaped at the sudden sight of fifty stacks of U.S. twenty dollar bills. Aldrich took out a manila envelope from the case's file section, removed the contents and placed them on the desk in front of

Perlman. It contained a one to one scale drawing, written specifications and an enlarged copy of the message to be inscribed on the clay tablet.

Aldrich unfolded a 16 by 20 sheet of vellum depicting the inscription, seven short lines of text in Paleo-Hebrew script. Perlman raised the full scale drawing and held it within six inches of his thick glasses. The magnification through the lenses gave his eyes a grotesque appearance as he examined the details of the artifact he was to create.

"I see no problems here," Perlman said. "Larger pieces are easier to work with than small ones. But, there is more material to be examined for inconsistencies and giveaways."

Now the artisan lifted the 16 by 20 vellum and held it even closer to his face examining each character of text on the drawing. Aldrich was concerned that Perlman might actually understand the inscription, at least enough of it to know more than he wanted him to, which was nothing.

"Do you read Phoenician script Hebrew?" he asked.

"No," Perlman said, "I only recognize the forms. But I can tell you this. I know there were many forms of the same letter and that new forms are being discovered rather frequently. Some are so different they probably could not be recognized out of context. That could a be problem with your inscription."

"What do you mean?"

"Just that if every letter – not to mention every word – is instantly recognizable, this alone may cast suspicion upon the authenticity of the piece. But enough, already; I don't even know if you care about that degree of authenticity."

Perlman paused to let Aldrich consider the significance of his concern before he continued with a solution.

"I understand," said Perlman, "that I need to know nothing about your plans for this piece, Mr. Adams. But, if you want it to be as perfect as I can make it, I suggest that you allow me to change the form of one or more of the letters which appear in one or two of the most obvious words. I don't need to know what the word means. For instance, show me a letter "mim" or "pey" ('M' or 'P'); I can change its form enough to be unique—and intriguing."

Again, Perlman paused to give his patron time to dwell on the suggestion. Aldrich remained silent. Out of habit the artisan reached into his pocket for a cigarette, remembered and withdrew his empty hand.

"I think you're right," Aldrich said eventually. "Is there any reason that you suggested 'mim' and 'pey'?"

"Yes, I'm aware that there are quite a few variances of these two. What we have to do is pick a word, one about which there will be no doubt by virtue of its context. Then I must change the form of one of the letters and use that form consistently, where ever it appears in the inscription. I can come up with an unknown variation of any letter but you must pick the first word since I am ignorant of the message."

"Okay, let's do it. I'll circle two letters for you."

Aldrich took a mechanical pencil from the attaché case and leaned over the vellum. He circled the letters. "Any problem with these?" he asked. "Yod and mim (Y and M). Yod in the name Yosef and mim in hamizrah and hama'arav (east and west) won't be missed.

"No, none. There are several known variants of the yod, too."

Both men stood silent, staring at the vellum. Then Perlman lifted a cheap, ad ballpoint from his shirt pocket protector and practiced a couple of trial variations of the letters. He clicked the point back inside the pen, began gathering and folding the drawings and returned them to the manila envelope.

Aldrich removed a few personal items from the attaché, took the envelope from Perlman and dropped it into the case. Without even giving the twenty-five thousand a parting glance, he closed the attaché and snapped the latches shut. With his palms upturned, he motioned permission for Perlman to take it.

"I'll call you every week to check on your progress." said Aldrich. "When it's ready, I'll give you instructions when and where to bring it."

"If I run into any problems, how can I get in touch with you?"

"You can't. You'll have to wait till I call. But for what you're being paid, Mr. Perlman, I expect this project to take precedence over any other issue."

"Yes, of course it will."

"Good. Now I'm afraid you must be on your way; I have a plane to catch. I'll be in touch."

2

AIRPORT SECURITY, Especially in the States, was a joke. No security, at all; pure marketing, corporate America style, the perception-equals-reality sales game. The strategy: make the public—the dumb jerks—feel safe enough to buy tickets. Any increased protection is purely incidental.

The inspections couldn't catch the drug mules and they sure as hell couldn't catch the weapons carriers now. Young business flyers were playing their own game: see who can get the Swiss Army knife or nail files through security on the most flights before having it confiscated. A website had appeared where the victors could read and post tales of sneak-it-through intrigue.

The site was a great training manual. What worked with Swiss Army knives and nail files had just worked perfectly with three blasting caps and eight feet of time fuse.

James Peter Aldrich nodded as the TSA officer thanked him and handed back his pair of custom Frank Brothers wingtips. He took his time tying them on and then went back to the x-ray pick up bin to retrieve his carry-ons. He was an imposing picture of a man, 6'4", gray around the temples and dressed in a $1500 Hertling tropical wool suit. And with his poker face, detached air and the business class boarding pass, the whole picture was a fit. The deference of the security personnel was evident, regardless of policy.

A player beat the system with three skills: invisibility, concealment and diversion. Hartsfield – Jackson International, Atlanta. Dark suit, loose tie, carry-on with little wheels and a scarred briefcase. In Atlanta, that was invisibility He'd come in on a charter flight from Salt Lake, spent the night at the Ritz – Carlton in Buckhead.

In Salt Lake he had removed the cordage from the welt of the nylon carry-on and threaded the time fuse back in its place. The blasting caps fit perfectly inside the barrels of Pentel roller balls. The pens, car keys, loose change and sunglasses, bypassing the metal detector and the x-ray machine in the little basket for pocket contents, never got a second glance.

The carry-on with the time fuse didn't interrupt the x-ray operator's glazed stare. In the checked bag, still sealed in its factory carton, was a keyless entry system that would "fit all makes and models – cars and trucks". This was all he had to bring, every other ingredient for the bomb had been easy enough to buy—or pilfer—on his last trip over.

The flight was without incident. Luckily for him, no one occupied the next seat. He could spread out. But the divider wall between his seat and economy class was far from soundproof. And the first row in economy is where women with screaming infants in carriers are always seated.

Aldrich was prepared. As soon as his dinner tray was picked up, he took an Ambien with the last few swallows of Chateldon, blew up his travel pillow and slept through most of the eleven hour flight.

Getting into Israel was tougher than getting out of the U.S. Intense screening of incoming passengers for explosives was unlikely. Nevertheless Israeli security was never predictable. Sniffer dogs were all over Lod and they darned sure weren't sniffing for herbs or fruit.

The way to beat them? Let them find what they're whiffing for, but on someone else. All that took was a stealthy squirt of concentrated, liquid fertilizer from a nasal spray bottle onto another passenger's bags in a different overhead bin. That should get you through passport control if the nitrate dogs were there waiting.

Aldrich was as familiar with Tel Aviv's Ben Gurion as he was with Salt Lake City International. For years he had worked to help the church establish a foothold in Israel and a prominent physical presence in Jerusalem. Most had considered it a near impossible achievement yet there it stood, on prime real estate, atop Mt. Scopus. Jerusalem's new Mormon Center was up and running. And now, after twenty or more trips, when Aldrich's stamped up passport was scanned, the Israeli data banks quickly confirmed his legitimacy and he was not detained.

At the carousel, a couple of more careful squirts on someone else's bags or garments, then follow from a safe distance back and you're right on through customs and outside to the waiting taxis.

Out on the curb Aldrich walked past the first assault of drivers. He took a kind of Mephistophelian delight in ignoring the taxis near the front. Usually he opted for one of the last in line, unless it was driven by some churlish Russian.

This morning he placed his bags in the back seat and hopped the front of a dusty Mercedes C. Both the weathered old Ashkenazi cabby and Aldrich were unconcerned with the barrage of protest from the other drivers. Aldrich noticed the tattooed triangle and number inside the old man's left arm. Auschwitz. Aldrich guessed his age to be late sixties, maybe a ten year old kid when the camps were liberated.

They pulled out and around the incensed waiting line. "Ehfoh?" the old Jew asked.

"Jerusalem; American Colony Hotel," answered Aldrich.

The drive to Jerusalem would take about thirty minutes, then another fifteen through the city to the hotel. Aldrich remembered the old two-lane that took nearly an hour to travel. The new four and six lanes were nice but the highway had lost most of old road's historic appeal. Gone were the turnouts with markers calling attention to Emmaus and the road to it and to Jamnia where the Sanhedrin relocated after the Roman destruction of Jerusalem. And from the new expressway, the old Templar fortress, Byzantine and Crusader churches were indescript ruins that wouldn't rate the second glance of an uninformed eye.

Less than a mile south of the highway Israel's tank museum and memorial to their armored military units stood prominently with multiple white and tekhlet flags flying. Then as the highway exited the coastal plains and began the climb through the Judea Hills, a few ancient thirties vintage junk trucks began to appear. The clusters of twisted metal littered the ravine bottoms and rusted away in obscurity within tangles of roadside undergrowth largely ignored. But these scrap iron armored wrecks were the unsung memorials to the Jewish victors who broke the Arab siege of Jerusalem during the forty eight war for independence. For a generation there had been wreaths and markers and kid's field trips but now they were all but forgotten.

Aldrich remembered a prior shuttle ride and the apathetic

Israeli who knew nothing of the old wrecks' part in making her recent aliyah even possible. He pondered the similarities between states and faiths; the generation that builds remembers; the next soon forgets; and the rest seldom give a damn.

After a few more miles the cab entered the new construction of West Jerusalem. There was no longer a bare hilltop within his sight. He remembered that only a few years ago that had not been the case. And he believed the demographers warnings that within a decade Israel would be the most densely populated nation on earth and there would be no countryside left along the forty kilometers of Highway 1 between Jerusalem and Tel Aviv.

Within minutes they arrived at the American Colony Hotel. After he checked in, he decided to spend a few minutes in the courtyard and have a glass of fresh mango juice. For the next few hours, there was no reason for evasion and it may even help, at some point, if he was remembered as a guest at the Colony.

In the early afternoon, after he had changed into jeans and a polo, Aldrich walked down to the gas station on Nablus Road. It was easy to catch a cab there filling up. The ride up to the corner of Jaffa and Yirmiyahu was only about three kilometers. Then a block and a half walk brought him to a section of shops with rental residences above.

The tiny efficiency apartment was above some sort of electrical parts shop. The other ingredients for the bomb had been waiting here in the tiny room he had leased for this exact purpose over six months ago. Even if discovered, in context with the groceries, cleaning products and his other personal effects, none of the components should trigger any suspicions.

Ammonium nitrate fertilizer? He had made certain that the neighbors could see clay pots exploding with periwinkles and a prolific window box of herbs. And it was only a five-pound bag. Kerosene? There was a small space heater in the corner of the otherwise unheated walkup flat. Nothing unusual about an insulated two-liter thermos, a small spool of 16 gauge automotive wire, a squeeze tube of silicon glue.

Two model airplane engines didn't look out of place sitting on the balsa kit, a Super Ring Master with "42 Inch Wing Span!" Even a seasoned Israeli investigator would hardly suspect that the expensive model airplane kit and the two motors were purchased only for a pair of ten shekel glow plugs.

A canister of methyl bromide could be more difficult to explain. But it had been wiped clean of fingerprints, rolled up in a dish towel and wedged between the back of the sink bowl and the wall. You had to almost stand on your head inside the base cabinet to see it, and it could have been there long before he rented the place.

The most difficult item to find had been the high voltage stun gun. He found one in a kind of military surplus and tool store between Kikar Dizengoff and Rehov Kaplan in Tel Aviv. Probably could have brought one over in the checked bag; he thought it was better to have one from Israel.

Aldrich glanced down at his watch. Time to make the call. He walked out into the unlit passageway, dark even in mid afternoon, careful to lock the door behind him. There was never anyone in the dim corridor or stairwell. Most of the tenants were old—old and poor—and the six flights of stairs down to the street had to be for something worth the effort.

He exited the building onto the jammed sidewalk on Yirmiyahu Street. Dark trousers, a white, band collar shirt from a back street used clothing shop, clear glass lenses in cheap wire frames and a nondescript yarmulke. Now, he was invisible here in the mass of locals. He wouldn't use a pay phone here but another a street or two farther away.

On the next block he entered a small courtyard mall. On the outside wall of a small post office there was a single, orange Bezek pay phone. He inserted a plastic phone card. The LCD display showed fifty credits. He tapped in the number he had memorized weeks earlier. Three rings. An answer.

"I'm here," said Aldrich, "I'll meet you tonight at nine?"

"Yes, where?"

"I'll be at the entrance to Christ Church guest house. Come in through the Jaffa Gate and take the first right."

"On Armenian Patriarch?"

"Yes."

"Up, on the left, maybe a hundred meters, there's an iron gate. If it's closed I'll push it open for you. Follow the drive around the church to the parking area. Try to get a space in the far corner, back in next to the wall. I'll come right on back."

"I understand. And you will have something for me?"

"Yes, I have it all. Nine o'clock."

Back in the flat he began assembling the components, door

locked and bolted, shutters closed, nothing running, nothing on; he must be unobserved and undisturbed. He poured about a cup of the nitrate fertilizer into a plastic mixing bowl and began pulverizing the ice cream salt size granules using a Maccabee beer bottle as a pestle. He wanted the grains as fine as meat tenderizer. That's the size they have to be to become a high explosive when mixed with the kerosene. The job took over an hour, one cup at a time. He pulverized eight cups and thoroughly mixed in one half cup of the kerosene. The ratio must be exactly sixteen to one. Then the oily mixture could not be packed tightly into the thermos or the blasting caps might not initiate the explosion. That could not be allowed to happen; the very future of the Faith depended on it. He would use a triple redundant detonation technique, two improvised electrical caps and one time delay fuse cap.

The glow plugs from the model airplane engines were wired, inserted and crimped into two of the fuse caps. One end of the length of time fuse he crimped into the last cap with pliers. Now he had to time the fuse for this climate and elevation. From the eight foot length, he measured and cut off exactly twelve inches, laid it on the tile floor and lit it. His eyes fixed on the second hand of his watch. Then it was out.

"Twenty-six seconds times seven equals..." Aldrich mumbled the calculations to himself. "Just over three minutes."

He wanted five minutes. Using a cigarette to further delay the backup detonation, he would have it. He had already timed two. They burned one inch in six to seven minutes. He cut the fuse again, on a sharp slant exposing the inner core, and taped a single match between it and one of the cigarettes. It would be better to do this on location but that would be too risky. But, in case this one did get broken, he would put matches, cigarettes and tape inside the backpack with the thermos.

All that remained was to insert the time fuse, wires with the blasting caps through the spout, sink them down into the filled thermos. He screwed on the plastic lid and sealed the spout with a plug of toilet paper and silicon glue. He washed his hands, wiped down the thermos and sniffed it for kerosene. Only a faint odor; the job was done.

He had already wired a twelve volt plug to the keyless entry system's receiver unit. He would wait until the last possible moment to connect the bomb's two wires. When connected and plugged into an auto's cigarette lighter, the little backpack would be instantly transformed into a deadly, remote control bomb with a time fuse back up.

Six o'clock; time to spare but he wouldn't waste it. He should leave for the Old City no later than eight or eight-fifteen. The walk down to Jaffa Street took a minute or two. The twelve bus runs every fifteen minutes, then a ten, maybe fifteen minute ride to the stop across from the Jaffa Gate; five more to walk up to Christ Church. He totaled the schedule. Thirty minutes, forty-five at the most.

He decided to leave promptly at eight. That would get him there in time to check out the gate and the parking lot before his contact arrived.

From now until eight he would check the apartment for anything that could link him to what was about to happen—not that he expected that. The rent was paid for another six months. The landlord knew it was a second home; for weeks at a time there would be no one there. But when he walked out this time, less than two hours now, he would not be coming back.

He placed the plastic mixing bowl and the Maccabee bottle in a plastic grocery bag. The two model airplane engines without glow plugs could be a link; he dropped them both into the bag. Then he took the trash down and concealed his small bag inside another one that was already there. Back up from the dumpster, he slowly inspected every inch of the tiny flat. Nothing unusual, maybe it was even suspiciously boring, he thought, but he could live with that. Until eight, he would sit in the upholstered chair with threadbare arms and rehash every element of the plan…and wait.

He was not as nervous as he thought he should be. He felt a sense of relief; his long wait was finally over and now the operation was in motion. This was one more case of the dread of a thing being worse than the doing.

He passed the time watching a work crew on a roof across the street. They wrestled with a bulky solar water heater that was tarred into place. Aldrich figured that the mounting bolts were either frozen or so covered with tar that they couldn't be removed. He could see that the workers were arguing, over the remedy, he guessed. Eventually, one of the men came back up with a small oxyacetylene torch, lit it and began working on the fasteners.

It was the right solution to the problem, Aldrich thought. The intense heat would either melt away the covering of tar or heat up the bolts so that they were no longer seized up. But if they were still stuck, the flame could be adjusted up and either the bolts or the whole contraption cut off the roof.

At ten till eight Aldrich got up from the tattered chair. He removed the canister of methyl bromide from behind the sink. He placed it and the stun gun inside the lethal backpack and zipped it shut. He scrutinized the shape of it. It didn't look out of the ordinary, no need to pad it.

"Damn," he unzipped it, reached into the pack and removed the little key chain transmitter that would activate the keyless entry detonator. Muttering to himself, he stuck it into his pants pocket.

"That's all I need... to lock the damn thing up in his car."

Before leaving, he removed the band collar shirt. He put on a light blue, open collar, Mexican wedding shirt. He hung a large wooden cross on a rawhide lace around his neck and pulled a wide brim, tan boonie down on his head. Now the perfect pilgrim, he would be invisible inside the old city walls—invisible except to the hundred or so trinket hawkers certain to be waiting in ambush. The walk, a less than five minute wait and the bus ride went without a hitch.

Inside the walls of the Old City it took less than ten minutes to look over the walled campus of Christ Church. The complex included a not so inexpensive hostel and guest house, rectory, a private garden, the church itself. And there was the isolated parking area where he was to meet his contact. He found nothing here that posed a threat. The iron gate stood latched open over the sett stone entrance. There were twenty minutes to spare.

He walked the short distance back to the corner of Armenian Patriarch Road and David Street to a little cafe. He took a can of 7-Up out of an upright cooler and snapped a ten shekel coin on the edge of the counter. He sat down at one of the three tables outside on the elevated sidewalk. From here he would not miss his appointment's right turn up to the Church and left in through the iron gate. He raised the bottle and took a slug of the soda. Wet, almost cool and it came close to tasting like 7-Up. But he was thirsty and it was quenching.

He searched the power poles, the building tops and every conceivable mounting for the Old City's ubiquitous surveillance cameras. He knew the odds were good that he was on screen. He could not appear too preoccupied with the backpack; neither could he let it attract attention by moving away from it. The pack must be as boringly invisible as its pilgrim owner. All there was to do was to wait for the contact to turn the corner.

He was almost relaxed. For the first time since he walked off the bus the sights, sounds and smells of the Old City registered with his senses. It was an amalgam unlike anywhere else in the world. The Old City's social synthesis of ancient, new and timeless presents itself as a seething collage: a perpetual competition of decibels and dialects, seductive aromas and putrid stenches, long corridors of coruscating color and dark back alley dungeons.

A muezzin's recorded nasal squall blared out from the loud speakers atop one of the myriad, unseen minarets. He sounded as if he were chiding a Palestinian teen's lip-sync rap concert on a portable karaoke player. The teasing whiffs of sandalwood and saffron instantly withered before an assault of stale sweat and stepped in shit. A haughty faced Bedouin cropped an overloaded donkey in toward the interior souvenir markets.

Now, in the last minutes of daylight, as if on cue, the shop owners along David Street began retrieving their colorful displays. In their place appeared the drab monotones of steel gray, flat black or dingy blue of iron shutters and accordion gates. Even the sounds and smells seemed to abate as the lambent swaths of color made way for the night.

An old white Renault 19 entered through the Jaffa gate. The color and style were what he had been told to expect. It made the right turn directly in front of the sidewalk table, eased up the street and entered the church grounds. Aldrich gulped down the last swallow of soda and walked off to keep his appointment. When he reached the iron gate he opened the door to the guest house lobby and stepped halfway inside. A young English woman—the accent was unmistakable – was behind the desk attempting to give directions to an older couple. Her preoccupation with the frustrating situation was evident. She didn't notice the door open or the stranger peering in. Neither was she aware that Aldrich backed out and pulled the heavy iron gate across the single lane entrance which was not visible from her position at the lobby desk

When the gate was bolted, he walked on through between the guest house and the church, back toward the rear parking area. Inside the church an unseen virtuoso rehearsed a repertoire of John

Stanley Voluntaries. The English pipe organ's distinctive sub-bass trill caused a rhythmic flickering of a dim porch light at a rear entrance.

Beyond the church, the unpaved parking area was almost empty. Backed up to the farthest wall, the white Renault sat waiting. Aldrich walked on at a stroll but not directly toward the car. His eyes searched for any chance observer. Once satisfied, he turned and approached the driver's window.

The driver appeared the same as he had three months before. Same needlepoint kippah and thick glasses. Aldrich noticed that he seemed quite relaxed, his arm draped out the window and a cigarette between two fingers. But why shouldn't he be? He was doing nothing to be nervous about.

"Mister Perlman," said Aldrich, "you're right on time."

"Yes, please get in," answered the driver. "I'll put this out." He took a deep drag from the cigarette and thumped it out onto the dry ground as he blew the smoke out the window.

"I'll get in the back so we'll have more room," said Aldrich. He opened the door behind the driver and slid across to the other side. He placed the backpack on the seat behind the driver. "Let me see what you've come up with."

"Yes, of course," said Perlman.

He leaned toward the empty front seat and lifted a Steimatzky Bookstore plastic bag from the floorboard. He removed an object from several folds of newspaper. Without unwrapping the contents, he handed it back, between the seats, to his passenger. When it was unwrapped, Aldrich took a small Maglite out of one of the backpack pockets and put on his reading glasses. After a lengthy, silent inspection he refolded the old Ha'aretz around the piece. He sat silently for another few moments.

"It looks perfect; is it?"

"As perfect as I can make it," said Perlman.

"Good. I suppose you're anxious to see what I have for you."

Without answering, Perlman raised both eyebrows, gave a slight shrug of the shoulders and nodded his agreement. Aldrich reached into a front pocket of the backpack. He withdrew a sealed envelope and handed it across the seat.

"It's all there, twenty-five thousand U.S. Count it."

Perlman attempted to tear into the tough Tyvek envelope. He paid no attention to the activity behind him. Aldrich took out the

200,000 volt stun gun and switched it on. Then with one powerful thrust he pressed the charged probes into Perlman's mastoid process. With a wheezing soprano gasp, Perlman's neck contracted in a convulsive arch. Tremors engulfed his entire body. Again Aldrich plunged the synapse scrambling current into Perlman's neck.

With the stun gun ready to hit again, Aldrich reached into the pack and placed the canister of methyl bromide on the seat beside himself. He opened the door and exited the car without taking his eyes off his trembling victim. He jerked open the driver's door and repositioned the stun gun to Perlman's neck. He rolled up the driver's window, checking to make sure the others were all the way up.

With his eyes glued to the helpless driver, he closed the door and reached into his pocket for his knife. Leaning into the back seat he swapped the stun gun for the pressurized can of poison gas. He took a deep breath, held it in, and pierced the side of the gas canister with the knife's awl. Instantly, he tossed it into the floorboard, grabbed the stun gun and slammed the back door shut. He could see the deadly liquid escaping the container, vaporizing and engulfing the interior of the car.

Aldrich paused to check the area; still, there was no one in sight. Now Perlman's convulsive throes swirled the deadly fume cloud and rocked the small car. Aldrich readied himself to keep the door forced shut if his victim recovered enough to attempt an escape but that was unlikely. Yoram Perlman was a small, frail man who couldn't muscle the door open if Aldrich held it shut. And even if he came to enough to try, he would breathe in all the more deeply and succumb to the gas more quickly. Conscious or unconscious, it would take no more than a few more seconds for the intense concentration of methyl bromide to cause death.

For a few minutes there had been no movement inside the Renault. Aldrich caught the first acrid whiff of the colorless gas escaping the car. He backed off aways to windward. Even a trace stung the eyes and burned the sinuses much like a too thick swab of Chinese mustard on an egg roll. He could only imagine what it was like inside the small car. Once again, he visually searched the deserted parking area. Still, nothing. From within the dust covered foliage of a cypress that snuggled the wall behind the car, a drove of palm dove were flushed by the rising fumes. Time enough; he's got to be gone, Aldrich assured himself.

As he neared the car he took in a deep breath and held it,

reached for the back door handle. With his eyes squinted tight, he opened it. Now the front. Again he quickly backed off up wind. He supersaturated his lungs with several deep breaths. Holding the last lungful, he repeated the sequence on the other side of the car. A minute or two in the stiff evening breeze would soon air out the car.

Aldrich rolled down the windows and got in. He was met by Perlman's frozen stare and gaping mouth. Mucus and saliva coated his face, glazing the front of his shirt. There was no carotid pulse.

The body had to be moved to the passenger seat. The lifting and pulling forced some of the lingering gas from Perlman's clothing. Aldrich had to retreat until the fumes escaped.

When he had drug Perlman into the passenger seat, he removed his handkerchief and wiped the wet slime from the face and chin. He tried to close the mouth and eyes but he had to settle for reclining the seat and turning the head toward the driver's side. When he had the body positioned as naturally as possible, he closed the doors, stepped back and assessed the scene. The corpse would have to pass for a sleeping passenger.

Aldrich knew that the whole damn country may all be gawkers but they never interfered, let alone got involved. Confidently, he closed the other doors and crawled in behind the wheel. The acrid fumes were still irritating but he had to get going. He had to get more air moving through the car but first he had to get rid of the empty bromide canister. He spotted a trash bin and drove by, close enough, to toss it into one of the large plastic containers.

At the iron gate, he parked back a bit, lights on bright to blind. He ignored the little sign on the stone wall opposite the hinges asking drivers to close the gate after passing through. Outside the Jaffa Gate he turned right and drove clockwise around the wall. After a turn north on Road 1, he headed directly to a residential area on the hillside just above the Hyatt Hotel.

Aldrich had decided on this secluded apartment parking area weeks ago after several trips to the vicinity. It offered all he needed to successfully dispose of Perlman's body and to slip, unnoticed, into the night. There were always vacant parking spaces in the apartment complex. He drove straight to one near a pedestrian exit. The set of steps climbed up to a one-way turnstile gate which exited onto a perimeter street that wound on around the hillside toward Hebrew University.

He pulled in between two parked cars. One, a Honda, had a stationary jack under the rear axle. A wheel and brake drum were removed; it wouldn't be going anywhere tonight. The other was a small workman's truck which was not likely to be used until morning. Nevertheless, he would have to keep alert for the owners.

He switched off the ignition and sat in the silence as long as he dared. Staring across his shoulder at his dead passenger, he debated whether or not to drag him back into the driver's seat. He convinced himself it wouldn't make any difference, not with as much gasoline in the tank as the gauge indicated.

He reached into the floorboard behind him to retrieve the JanSport pack and then unzipped the large compartment. He removed the keyless entry system control unit and plugged it into the lighter. The LED glowed green. He stretched back to reach into his pants pocket for the key chain remote. He pressed the unlock button and, instantly, the red LED lit up.

Again he paused, focusing on Perlman's pallid eyes. He reached over and placed his hand, palm down, on the crown of the dead man's head. With detachment, but as if he was invoking a divine blessing on an ill or troubled brother in the faith, he prayed aloud.

"O Lord, it is written that it is better that thousands should perish than for a whole people to fall from faith. Into thy hands, O Lord, I commend your lost child, Yoram Perlman, for your forgiveness and restoration. In the name of the Father and of the Son. Amen."

With a slight smile and nod of conviction, he pressed affectionately on the dead man's head as if to assure him that everything would be all right. Suddenly aware that the next critical moments demanded his total concentration, Aldrich glanced around nervously, snatched back into grim reality from the sanctity of his liturgy.

He reminded himself with a whisper, "This is the dangerous part, Peter. One slip now and everything's been for nothing. You'll kill your fool self and fail God, too."

He placed the stun gun and the envelope of cash in the Steimatzky bag along with the wrapped piece. Before making the final connection he got out of the car, walked over to the set of steps. He placed the remote control and the shopping bag against the riser on the first tread.

Back inside the car, he made one final inspection. He removed the wire nuts from the exposed wires on the control unit. The arteries pounded in his neck as he twisted the stripped ends of each wire to its color coded mate leading into the insulated thermos. Now he twisted two wire nuts onto the connected bear ends and tucked the apparatus back into the JanSport except the plug and the end of the time fuse with the cigarette taped to it. It was okay, no need to redo it. His hands trembled. He struck a match, lowered his lips to the cigarette filter and sucked the flame into the tobacco. It was lit.

Of habit, he almost removed the keys from the ignition before he got out of the ticking Renault. His mind raced. He forced himself to move at a deliberate pace to pick up the remote control and the shopping bag. He moved up the steps, through the turnstile and down the sidewalk in the direction of the University.

When he reached the point on the hillside where the sidewalk began to curve around the slope, he stopped before losing his line of sight back to the parking lot and the white Renault. Without taking his hands out of his pockets, he pressed hard on the "unlock" button on the remote. The little car vanished in a swirling billow of fire that lit up the facade of the apartments across the lot. Then the shock wave hit, more of a bellow than a boom, not as loud as Aldrich had expected, but the flames were much more intense.

Aldrich hoped that it would look like Perlman was the victim of a random terrorist bomb. If not, he hoped the entire situation would be so confusing that the police would never agree as to exactly what had happened and why. Why was a local Jewish man with no connection to this area of the city, alone in a parked car, killed by the blast of a bomb that detonated inside the car? Then again, Aldrich knew this would be only one of myriad senseless iniquities that plague the religious center of the Western World. Here there was so much that would never be answered or explained.

Peter Aldrich crossed the street and started down a path that meandered through a playground and park. He walked in the direction of the Hyatt, a slow stroll off into the mystery and darkness of a Jerusalem night.

3

Only the Sound of trowels scraping the dry crust defiled the timeless silence of northern Israel's Beth Shean Valley. A blanket of thick, humid air promised a boiler room of a day. Only 6:30 in the morning and the workers were wiping away sweat with bandanas. Dawn's squadrons of bug-gorging swallows had already retreated to the cool shade of their daylight roosts. A thick morning haze obscured the distant Transjordan; it screened the summer sun more effectively than the black nursery netting tents that shaded the Tel Kefar Archaeological Excavation.

Tel Kefar was unique; it was the largest unexcavated site in Israel and it had remained abandoned and sealed in time ever since its destruction by invading Assyrians. When the young reform rabbi, Jesus of Nazareth, passed by, the tel had already been in ruins for over 700 years. And except for a few Islamic burials and Bedouin trash pits, the site was free of the archaeological clutter that comes with continuous human occupation. The old tel was a rare treasure, a clean link back to the time of the Judges and to the reigns of the Israelite kings.

This integrity and the promise of unprecedented discoveries brought one of the world's great biblical archaeologists to Tel Kefar. Professor Moshe Benjamin of the Hebrew University of Jerusalem was a warrior-scholar and a national treasure, feared on the battle-field, respected in the scientific field. He had authored books on military strategy and had written college texts on archaeology.

This morning the aging professor sat under the break tent. Balanced on an unopened bail of sand bags, he was engrossed in the latest site survey. The binder held graphs of shapes and colors bounced back from a magnetic scan of the tel. He was still awed with the technology. How many abandoned test pits had gone down within centimeters of a historical treasure? With these charts of coded colors, pits could be opened over known anomalies, features hidden beneath the surface of the tel. No longer was directional radar in the exclusive domain of cutting edge navigation; the possibilities were staggering.

The whiff of an old familiar fragrance interrupted Moshe's concentration. Farm workers had begun to mow hay in a field at the base of the tel. Moshe uncapped his water bottle and took a big swallow of orange Kool-Aid; he had loved the stuff since he was a kid. The aroma of the fresh cut bahaia and sweet swallows of orangeade channeled his thoughts back to Kibbutz Ein Gev, his boyhood home. Then, Kool-Aid was something special, for kids, for Shabbat. Mowing hay was special, too, but on the other end of the pleasure scale.

The barrel chested professor held his watch out closer to his focal length and angled it to catch the sunlight. And though his eyesight and receding, gray hair revealed the years, his rugged physique did not. The strong hands, powerful arms and tree-trunk legs were those of a much younger man and the old colonel's endurance was the stuff of legends.

Soon the new arrivals would be coming up for orientation. The second week of the dig season was beginning, fifteen volunteers gone, and twelve new to take their places. Moshe's custom was to personally welcome and orient incoming staff and volunteer workers.

On a project this size, especially this season, he could use twice as many workers. But with the intifada in its fourth year—or was this the fifth – and escalating, he knew he was lucky to have any. Citing liability issues with student travel to the Mideast, most Canadian and American universities had reneged on long standing participation agreements. What saved this year's dig from being canceled was a team of for-extra-credit students from Hebrew, several European grad students and a loyal cadre of older individual volunteers who followed Dr. Benjamin from dig to dig.

Moshe laid the survey graphs on one of the sawhorse tables. He would use them to explain how the exact excavation areas had been chosen. As soon as they hit the raw plywood table top, one of the Palestinian laborers weighted the stack with a basalt stone. He was Moshe's favorite, hired to push wheelbarrows. But over the course of four summers, he had overseen his own evolution into a job description more like Dr. Benjamin's adjutant-valet.

Abbas was a teenager from an Arab village on the other side of the Gilboa Ridge, field rock poor and without a scintilla of resentment in him. He lived for his summer job. And he lived for the chance, one day, to live in America.

In his seasoned Israeli English, Moshe greeted the arriving volunteers. "Ladies, men, please, come in around closer so you can hear." The orientation continued through the usual agenda of information and instruction unique to archaeology; drink lots of water so you don't die; watch for scorpions, especially the small yellows; treat the balks like Holy Ground.

"Balks are the walls of earth between the squares," Moshe said. "Do not walk or stand on the balks. Do not sit or lean against the balks. And I require that the edge of the balks be protected with a parapet line of sandbags. Now, you want to know why I am so hung out" – no could screw up an idiom quite like Moshe – "on the balks?"

The professor explained in explicit detail that archaeology is a destructive science. Once an area has been excavated it can never be excavated again. The walls of the excavation square are the only record of what was in the layers above the bottom of the hole. If a team suspects that it has missed a floor, a roof or some other feature; their only confirmation is in the balk.

"This is why it is imperative not to remove objects from the balk. So now, when the area supervisor screams at you to get the hell off the balk, I hope you understand why they do this."

For the remainder of the lecture Moshe detailed the tedious process of recording, centimeter by centimeter, their progress on a scale drawing called the daily top plan. He covered the mathematical relationship between benchmarks and instrument height and documentation of the exact location of every uncovered feature and artifact.

"Finally, I will stress the need to always drink plenty of water. In the army we have to stop and drink water every ten minutes. Does not matter if you feel thirsty. By the time you get thirsty, it might be too late and you are already dehydrated. How do you know you are dehydrated? You feel very tired, weak and you probably have headache. Then you can not drink enough to not be thirsty and you get shelshool. I want to also warn…"

Several hands in the group shot up.

Moshe pointed to young man holding his hand high, one of seven Japanese Christians who had signed on for the final five weeks of excavation.

"Yes. Dakah Benjamean, please to explain shelshool?"

Moshe paused and then turned to one of his American grad students. The student, shielding his mouth, answered too quietly to be heard. Moshe nodded.

"Shelshool is Hebrew word for diarrhea," said Moshe.

The puzzlement on the young volunteer's face didn't flicker.

"What mean die-ree-ahh, sir?"

Moshe feigned his most serious expression. Most of the group were rocking with quiet laughter, trying not to embarrass the student. The Japanese group leader came to Moshe's rescue. He pulled the young man to the side and whispered the explanation to him. The young man's face flushed rising sun red. He pressed his palms flat against his thighs and bowed at a near right angle.

The session ended with names and area assignments. The four who remained in the area were approached by one of Moshe's acolytes, the area B supervisor.

"Hello, hello, my name is Li Moon, Ph.D. You may call me Daktah Moon. I am professor of archaeology from Hebrew University of Jerusalem. I am supervisor of Area B. I not need know you name now; I learn soon in a few days."

Moon pointed to the youngest of the four, a scrawny French undergrad, incessantly adjusting the skull cap he was unaccustomed to. Since Chirac had proposed the symbols ban, kippahs had become all the rage with young French Jews. But so had large crucifix pendants with the teenage Goths.

"You go help Willy; he right there. You understand each other"

A sinewy, middle-aged man raised an index finger; a smile and a nod signaled he was the one. Willy was the sort whose outward mien and manner rendered him impossible to label. Blue-green eyes, straight black hair and cordovan complexion, he could fit well into most of the world's profiles. He wore a black and white checked shmaag, half hitched around his neck, for a sweat rag. So today, he looked Arab.

The young French student started in Willy's direction.

Moon continued the assignments. "You two girls work here

with Tanya; she hot number; my favorite student at University. She teach you what to do."

Li made a sweeping gesture as if presenting an on-stage contestant in some small town, pay-to-enter beauty pageant. The Oriental woman, probably in her early twenties, was obviously embarrassed. She didn't look up from where she knelt, brushing the loose soil from a jumble of pottery shards.

The remaining volunteer, a white haired man of fifty, give or take a few, in evident peak condition, held firm eye contact with Li Moon as he awaited his assignment. Something about the man's posture and demeanor elicited Moon's caution.

"Sir, please assist Miss Michelle there, square number G20; she American too. Here she find what might be terrace or little street. This locus need to be articulated so we can draw and take picture later this morning."

The man nodded that he understood. He picked up his day pack, walked over and stepped down into the square. Then he offered his hand. "Michelle, my name is Kirk Longstreet."

"Hello, Kirk. I'm Michelle Eisner."

Michelle responded with a wide-eyed, friendly smile. She placed her trowel in a pottery bucket, reached out and took his extended hand. She admired his handshake, strong, leathery hands that firmly gripped her own with just the right, gentle strength.

"Where's home, Kirk?"

"Charleston," he answered.

"South Carolina?"

"Yes. Sorry, there is more than one, isn't there. And you, Michelle?"

"Indio, California."

"Then you're used to this dry heat, aren't you?"

"Thought I was but, today, I don't know. So, you know Indio, I'm impressed."

Her first impression was that he might be career military, maybe recently retired. Anyway, Kirk Longstreet seemed to be an okay type. She was glad Moon had put him in her square, especially after the last co-worker she was stuck with.

Until last Friday her partner was an ill tempered, relentlessly complaining, sixty year old from Hamburg. But Hildegard Rentz had left after the first week, apparently not finding the dig to be what she expected. Her only redeeming characteristic had been that she was so damned caustic Li Moon made every attempt to avoid her, which usually kept him away from their square. And that was fine with Michelle.

She did not trust or like the pompous doctor and she wasn't alone. That something which women sense in men to be avoided flamed in Li Moon. He was known for his poorly veiled propositions. Young women, students and volunteers, had complained more than once but, for whatever reason, he was still here. Michelle knew that if Moon had any inkling that she might find a man of Kirk's age attractive, he would have assigned him somewhere else.

"How'd he know you were American; you two know each other?" Michelle asked Kirk with a bit of an impish smile.

"No, never met the guy." Kirk answered, not the least bit defensive at her bantering.

"So, how'd he spot you?" Michelle asked?

Without looking up, Kirk removed a frozen Platypus water bottle from his day pack. He smiled and answered with his own brand of blarney.

"Well, let me think," said Kirk, "Nike Trico Hikers, Cabela Shorts, Marina Del Marr, Key Largo T-shirt and "R.E.I since 1938" on my cap; maybe he's more than just a pompous arse; maybe he's a clairvoyant pompous arse."

Michelle laughed out loud at Kirk's droll answer. She was glad to know he had a sense of humor. Work days were long, hot and mostly uneventful. If you were saddled with a jerk for a partner, the days could seem endless. But, being with someone entertaining and focusing on the reality that a major find may be only a couple of centimeters down made the days slide by and the off time a lot of fun.

"We might just get along okay together... in this dungeon we're digging for ourselves," said Michelle.

"Yeah, we might," he answered.

"Well, you have to be better than who I had in here last week."

"And who was that?" asked Kirk.

"I just don't think I'm ready to talk about it yet. It was a... painful experience."

Michelle spoke in an affected manner but, somehow, Kirk got the message that her words were underpinned by reality.

Nevertheless he would play along with her traumatic experience act.

"Whenever you're ready, you know I'm here for you. Now, show me what we're doing and I'll get at it."

"Okay," said Michelle. "Actually, we're digging this hole with these trowels and brushes. Moshe wants us to try to determine what this layer -we think it's a layer – of stones is. You can see that this edge runs from here, coming out of the west balk, across to... here where they disappear into the south balk."

Michelle stepped sideways. She pointed with her brush to where barely exposed rocks intersected the other earth wall.

"That's why these guys are opening up a new square, G19." She pointed to the workers in the adjacent square. "When they get down to the level of our square, we'll know if this rock, whatever it is, continues on through the balk."

The heavier of the two students, both from NYU attending Hebrew University for the summer, knelt as he hacked at the dry vegetation with a torea hoe. Painfully preoccupied, he didn't realize that Michelle was speaking to him. Every few chops he paused to inspect the bulbous blisters on his tender hands. He was not used to the short handled tool; he was not used to any hand tool.

His roommate and square partner was a thin, scholarly and serious looking young man who wore his yarmulke as comfortably as his old tennis shoes. He peered over the top of his sweat-mud coated wire rim glasses at the narrow path as he struggled to maneuver a barely loaded wheelbarrow toward a dump site on the side of the tel. In a strained voice that confirmed his inexperience at lifting and balancing the weight of an awkward load he acknowledged the introduction with a simple, "Shalom". Kirk and Michelle looked at each other and chuckled at the pitiful suffering pair.

"So, that's where we are," said Michelle. "We need to continue loosening the soil around the stones with our trowels, sweep it up and dump it. When we have all the stones exposed, we can let Dov know we're ready for him."

"Who's Dov?" asked Kirk.

"I'm sorry; Dov is the photographer. He's good; has a professional studio in Tel Aviv."

"Oh, yeah, Doctor Moon did say he wanted to photo the area."

Kirk dropped to one knee and began outlining the stones and

Michelle picked up where she left off when Li pointed her out to him. He was unaware of Michelle's frequent glances as she knelt, silently brushing pan after pan of debris away from the stones, glances not to assess the work but to evaluate the man. She sensed something in between curiosity and a vague sort of attraction to him. She guessed there was fifteen years difference between them. His voice reminded her of Shelby Foote's soft spoken and perfectly enunciated Southern dialect. And she knew there had to be a story behind his appearance at Tel Kefar; there was a story behind every older volunteer at a dig.

"Over here on vacation?" Michelle's question ended a silence of several minutes.

"Yes and no," said Kirk. "I retired a couple of years ago. This is something I've always wanted to do. So, I guess you could say I'm on vacation from a permanent vacation."

"What did you retire from?"

"I was a stock broker with Prudential Securities."

"Well, you don't look old enough to be retired, except from the military, maybe."

"But retirement isn't just a function of age, I'm afraid."

"What do you mean?" Michelle paused from her work and gave Kirk a puzzled look.

"I mean it's hard to retire at any age if you don't have the means."

"Oh yeah, of course," she answered.

"Not to imply I'm a man of means, actually, I just burned out on trying to pile up money and to find some meaning it all."

What Kirk didn't say was that he had been shaken to the core by Corporate America's recent penchant for fraud and deceit. Between Enron, World Com, Tyco and a dozen others, he had helplessly watched lives' savings, college funds and retirement plans dwindle. Many of the clients who trusted him most had been hurt the worst. He had guided them well through the tech stock bubble only to be blindsided by the Wall Street scandals. And that he had been a competent and honest broker didn't change the bottom line; he had trusted the Arthur Andersens and the Henry Blodgets and he paid dearly for that trust. They sang the praises of the corrupt Goliaths even after they had seen the slung stone connect with fatal force. His clients and friends had lost much but so had he, not to mention his good name and a failed marriage, both also casualties of his stint in the financial services industry.

But the last two years had been good, lots of time and not many phones. He had ample resources to live on and he supplemented that income buying, restoring, selling and delivering boats. Trawlers and sloops were his loves

From somewhere down the hill, a loud shout flashed through the quiet squares, "Breakfast, breakfast; Hod boker, hod boker." The summons was repeated by several diggers.

"Well," sighed Michelle, "the morning's half gone." "C'mon. Let's get down there before the food's all gone. Last ones don't get much but cucumbers and bread, usually."

Kirk stood and slapped the dust from his clothes. They started down the side of the tel toward the area where breakfast was set out under a shade tent much smaller than the ones that covered the excavation areas. Like the ones above the squares, the same type of black plastic netting was secured with polypropylene rope and stakes, then elevated like a circus tent with varying lengths of PVC pipe. Beneath the black mesh, the feast was spread on two sheets of dusty plywood supported by saw-horses.

"What else do we get for breakfast out here?" asked Kirk. "I mean, besides cukes and bread, what's the food like?"

Michelle squinted one eye and wrinkled her nose up a bit.

"Hmm… How can I say this? Do you know any great Israeli restaurants?"

"Never heard of any Israeli restaurant," said Kirk.

"No matter, but if you had, I was going to say that the kibbutz food they send out here is probably not going to remind you of it." She said it with that devilish little smile, cutting her eyes to catch Kirk's. "Actually, the food's not that bad. There just aren't enough of the good things, like cheese, fruit, and yogurt. And it's the same exact menu, day after day. Food's better in the dining hall, though; or have you already had the pleasure?"

"No, it was ten thirty when I got to the kibbutz last night. I waited on a bus for two hours, finally gave up and caught one of those ten-passenger taxis. I haven't had a bite since my Biet Shean gyro yesterday afternoon. I'll eat anything they're pushing down here; I'm starving."

"It was a shwarma," said Michelle.

"What are you talking about; what was a shwarma?"

"What you had in Beth Shean, the rotisserie roasted meat in a pita with sauce. What you had is called a shwarma. It was probably turkey. The best are lamb. Delicious, aren't they?"

"Yeah, it really was," Kirk agreed.

"Oh, and that ten passenger taxi? They're called sheruts."

"Thank you, I'll try to remember that."

She caught a trace of irritation in his voice. "Sorry. I didn't mean to sound like a know-it-all. It's the teacher in me coming out."

You're a teacher?"

"Yeah, Western Civ."

"Where?"

"A little place you never heard of, College of the Desert in Palm Desert California."

At the breakfast area they stooped under the netting and took a place at the end of the short line at the plywood serving tables. The sheets were spread with the bland selections of the light dairy kosher breakfast delivered to the site each day by the Kibbutz Massebot kitchen. The menu never varied; cream cheese, small green olives, precracked hard boiled eggs, yogurt, tomatoes, cucumbers and stale bread.

As Michelle had warned, on the table was an empty plastic bag that had held a few peaches. The evidence? Pits remained on the plates of the first, fortunate few. When they had served themselves and found a couple of plastic stools, they sat together and ate.

From beyond the shade of the break area, Abbas Hashim gazed through the rear glass of an abused Subaru truck. Abbas had been obsessed with the young blond teacher since he laid eyes on her the first day of the dig. But a poor Palestinian laborer from Janin could never dare hope for one so beautiful as the rich American; but what a prize she would be.

"Everyone, back to work please."

The order came from one of the area C supervisors who was first through the chow line every morning. The break area was less than twenty-five meters from areas C and D. Willy Dubignon moved close to the grad student who equated his conspicuous authoritarian supervision with a high grade in field methods. Beneath normal volume he spoke in a coarse voice.

"Danny, you worry about your people; don't be barking out your marching orders to us."

Willy Dubignon was from Baton Rouge, Louisiana. He was fond of claiming he was as Cajun as Moses was Jewish. The middle-aged Marine had barely survived some of the worst of the Tet Offensive in 1968 and he was determined not to rehash those times with anyone. After the naval hospitals and medical retirement, he attended college on the GI bill and wound up with a degree in anthropology.

When it dawned on him that American academia didn't need any anthropologists any more than they wanted any Vietnam vets, Willy joined the Peace Corps. The next few years in Zaire he spent trying to promote village water management projects. For the past few years Willy worked as a contract archaeologist along the southern Mississippi.

When they finished breakfast, the Area B crew started up the steep, dusty path back to their squares.

"Willy," Michelle called out, "wait up. Meet my new partner, Kirk."

"Hello, Kirk." Willy extended his calloused left hand. "Pardon the south-paw, but I don't have much grip in this one." He lifted his noticeably smaller right arm and hand.

"Good to meet you Willy." Kirk reached across with his left hand and gripped Willy's.

"First dig?" asked Willy.

"First over here. I worked on a pre-Columbian dig in north Georgia my senior year in college, but that's a long time ago."

"Where you go to college?" asked Willy.

"Emory."

"Emory? You from Georgia?"

"No. Home's Apalachicola, Florida but I've lived in Charleston for the last twenty years."

The little Creole's eyes lit up. "Well, I be dog gone, thought you sounded like home folks. I'm from Baton Rouge!"

"Never would have known by listening to you, Willy." Kirk's wide grin spoke the truth.

Willy grinned back. "Yeah, we can't hardly hide where we from, can we. Where was the dig in Georgia?"

"On the Etowah River, near Canton, it was called Little Egypt."

Why was it called Little Egypt?"

"This ought to be good!" said Michelle.

Kirk's brow wrinkled a bit. "I'm not sure anyone knows for sure. I was told that it was the nickname of the old plantation where the site's located. Maybe because the bottom land and the temple mounds reminded someone of the Nile and the Pyramids."

Kirk cut his eyes toward Michelle. "Sorry I don't have a more intriguing explanation for you."

When they reached the excavation area and returned to work, Willy picked up the conversation. Setting a full bucket of soil behind him and reaching for an empty, he asked. "What all you find up there, Kirk?"

"We found evidence that trade networks among the Indians, 1300 years ago, were much more sophisticated than we thought possible."

"How could you tell?" asked Michelle.

"It was a typical site, significant gaps in the periods of occupation. That's because these were migratory populations of hunter-gatherers. The evidence for long distance trade routes was two important finds, a grizzly bear claw necklace dated to 650 AD and a copper hatchet head from the same period."

Kirk explained that grizzlies had never ranged east of the Mississippi and probably never east of the front range of the Rockies, 1200 miles west of the Georgia site. He said that geologists claim that nugget copper is found in only one location in North America, Michigan's upper peninsula. They were able to date the hatchet head from the remains of the wooden handle—preserved by the copper – using tree ring dating, dendrocronology.

"That's amazing," said Michelle.

"Sure is," said Willy, "when you consider it was all overland and we didn't even have any pack animals."

"What do you mean, we?" asked Michelle. She looked up from her work.

"Just that," said Willy. He grinned and he pointed to his own chest, "French, African, Choctaw, Cherokee and who knows what all else."

Michelle's face expressed her sheepishness. "I didn't mean to be nosy, Willy. Guess I never thought about what your background was."

"Doesn't bother me. Only thing I know, for sure, is what all I don't know. But, like I say, doesn't bother me.

A few minutes later the young French student assigned to work with Willy returned to the square. It was obvious that he was quite shy. Without any conversation, he lifted two buckets of debris and walked over to a sifter just beyond the sandbag parapet.

A pine frame and a sheet of hardware cloth formed a shallow tray with a mesh bottom. The tray was supported by two vertical lengths of flexible steel re-bar. Soil emptied into the tray was shaken, dust and sand falling through leaving the larger material exposed for examination. Except for emptying the wheelbarrows, the young man liked the solitary job. He had already found a small sliver of bronze and a carnelian bead that the excavator had missed.

"Joel, mon amie, laissez les bon temps rouleau! Dump that wheelbar fore you bury it and loose it."

The young guy chuckled at Willy's exotic Acadian French. He had four years of English, was an honor student, but when Kirk's orthodox drawl met Willy's creolized English he may as well have been listening to Arabic poetry.

"Kirk-Michelle," Willy called the names as if he were addressing a single person. "This my new friend, Joel LaRoche. Joel is a pedigreed Frenchman, Michelle."

Willy ignored Michelle's look of protest as he continued the introduction.

"Joel is from Paris and he…"

"No, no; Melun, not Paris," Joel politely protested.

"Joel, who the hell know where Melun is? You just say Paris. That'll keep you from givin every damn American here geography lesson. You think I'm gonna say I from GrosseTete, Louisiana, when Baton Rouge only fifteen miles? Hell no! Most folks don't know where Baton Rouge is; but they know they oughta, so they don't ask. Kirk-Michelle, like I was saying, Joel from Paris but he's student at Oxford."

"Hi Joel." Michelle nodded and smiled.

"Yeah, Joel and I met earlier this morning," said Kirk.

Another hour passed. Michelle stood and grimaced with pain as she gingerly tried to straighten her seized up knees. The fresh air above the pit seemed cool after working in the stuffy confinement. She arched her back into a reaching stretch and then looked to see where Willy had gone. When she caught his eye she motioned for him to come over.

"Willy," said Michelle, "I think we're ready for photos."

"Looks good. Stones stand out clearly; light's good as it's going to get. Go get him."

"Kirk, I'll going down to A to get Dov. Don't let anyone walk through here."

Michelle took a long drink of tepid water from her water bottle. She poured some on a lilac bandanna and guessed at wiping the smudges from her face. When she had tied the wet handkerchief around her neck she started her controlled stumble over the loose stones, down to the base of the tel. A few minutes later she returned with Dov.

From one of the other areas Moshe arrived. For several minutes he stood on a sandbag watching the photographer set up. His eyes rhythmically sectioned the area, square by square. Without rod or level, Moshe correctly estimated the lowest level of square G20. He told Willy that the floor of G19 was still thirty centimeters higher than the stone surface Michelle and Kirk had exposed.

The shape, color and pattern of these stones and the angle at which they descended caught the old veteran's eye. Moshe suspected that they were street pavers and that they ran from the acropolis to the Gates of Kefar. But they could be a terrace, a floor or a dozen other features of lesser importance. The answer would have to wait for a few more days until new squares revealed the size and extent of the structure.

Now close to midday, an immense column of heated air was rising above the great Arabian Desert. Cooler air from the Mediterranean started across the Levant, pulled into the vacuum. Into the Jordan Valley the hot winds rushed, across the tel and under the black netting. The sun shades filled, sailing above the PVC poles which fell into the squares with a hollow, bouncing sound like a dropped tiki drum. The plastic tubes were not heavy enough to do any damage, a direct hit may hurt but wouldn't injure.

As the squares were scraped and brushed lower the last hour of the work day dissolved. The scabrous ground stippled tender knees and salty sweat singed sensitive eyes as the temperature climbed with the sun. No longer was the hope of a trowel clicking across a priceless surface enough to hold the demons of heat and fatigue at bay. It was time for the day to end. Just after noon, the buses were sighted across the quarter mile of black clod furrows separating the tel from the main highway.

Michelle and Willy made Kirk and Joel aware that those on

the second bus would be last in line at the dining hall. Quitting time was a well-rehearsed drill. In the time it took the old Volvos to pitch and roll over the field road to the tel and turn around, an alert team could lock up tools, lower the sun shades and begin the descent to the dust billows which concealed the waiting coaches. The four boarded the lead bus together.

Even though it was like riding in a dusty sauna, the six-mile trip back to the kibbutz was a welcome respite. Within minutes, many of the weary riders had dozed off. And when Michelle's head nodded and then sagged onto Kirk's shoulder, he sat still allowing her to rest—and to enjoy the soft weight of her face on his arm.

4

"MICHELLE, WE'RE HERE." Kirk turned his head and cut his eyes as far as he could toward her, unable to focus on the smudgy face resting on his shoulder.

"Oh wow, I died; god, it's hot!" Michelle sat up and squinted out the bus window. They were at the back entrance of the kibbutz. The driver had jumped off and was entering the security code in the automatic gate's key pad.

The kibbutz name, Massebot, according to the official version was derived from its location. The commune stood only a few kilometers from a ruined city's entrance where massebot (sacred, upright stones) once ensured divine protection. The recovered stones again stood outside the gate into the restored Iron Age city, the Beit Shean National Park. There was irony in the name. Standing stones were despised by the Hebrew prophets of old who cursed them as symbols of idolatry, a certain affront to Yehweh.

From day one, there had been conflict between the mostly nonobservant kibbutznics and the local ultra-orthodox. Whether the name was based on proximity or was a clever moniker in defiance of the theocrat wannabes had been debated for half a century.

Founded in 1936 by Russian Jews, Massebot became a refuge from the scarcity and oppression of Soviet socialism. The exodus was also a product of their prophetic vision into the coming decade. The commune began as one in a defensive network of self-sufficient farms in the fertile inner valleys of northern Palestine. The routine was eternal: long days in the fields, endless nights in steel plate towers standing guard between sleeping families and hostile neighbors. And it would continue for decades.

Following World War II, along with Europe's remnant, surges

of Argentine "aliyahs" joined the Massebot Russians. The cultural concoction was as volatile as the returning Diaspora could spawn. Kibbutz leadership meetings made open debate in the Knesset seem placid. Nevertheless, Massebot had survived into the new millennium prosperity.

The automatic gate where the bus was stopped was a retrofit. It drew attention to the old chain link fence which encircled the compound. Every post was topped with a split "V" of angle iron which cradled a slinky of rusted concertina wire. A thick tangle of crotch-high weeds extending about twenty feet from the fence added another deterrent beyond the perimeter patrol road.

During the few days Kirk had wandered around the country before joining the dig he had noticed there seemed to be no weeds without vicious thorns or toxic spines. Palestine's wild flora fascinated him.

When the frustrated driver finally got the correct sequence of numbers, he turned and got back on the bus. There was a churning hum as the slack bicycle chain was sucked into a garage door type opener. Little by little, the jury-rigged device tugged the heavy steel gate open with jerky surges. The driver was irritated; they all seemed irritated to Michelle. Before the gate was fully open, he ground the gears into low. The bus lurched forward through the open gate which automatically began closing within seconds.

From the back gate to the bus stop was less than a couple of hundred meters. But that didn't matter to the driver with the always-pissed-off look on his face. He accelerated up to the last second, then braked to a annoying, hard stop. Michelle knew the sour-faced jerk relished dumping his passengers into the trailing clouds of powdery dust that engulfed the bus stop.

"I'll meet you in the dining hall as soon as I shower," said Michelle. She squinted defensively against the dust as she stepped off the bus.

"Meet you there."

Kirk started across the ankle deep lawn toward the stucco building which housed twenty of the volunteers. The wide, green blades reminded Kirk of the throw rugs of St. Augustine grass which thrived beneath the Spanish moss swagged limbs of massive live oaks in the Carolina lowcountry. The complex of units which the kibbutz rented to the expedition housed both staff and volunteers. It was part of a package that included meals, laundry service, office and lab space.

Kirk climbed the outside stairway to the second story, turned and walked down the landing toward his door, searched his right pants pocket for his room key. He turned the key three full rounds before the handle would move. The cool, quiet darkness welcomed him in from the hot sunlight and it felt good not to frown against the light and the dust. He set his back pack on the kitchen cabinet, opened it and removed the empty platypus water bottles. As badly as he wanted to jump under a cold shower, he knew he'd better mix tomorrow's canteen and get it into the fridge, or he would be drinking lukewarm Gator-aid. His eyes adjusted to the dark, he looked to see if Bill was in the room. The door to the bath was open. He guessed he had gone straight to lunch.

Father Bill Casey was Kirk's roommate. He was a retired—whatever that meant—Catholic priest who seemed like a nice enough guy. Kirk hadn't had a chance to get to know him. Father Casey was already asleep by the time Kirk got checked in the night before. After a brief introduction and apology for the time, Kirk tried to be as quiet as he could be expected, unpacking for the four-week stay. In the morning, they exchanged a few brief greetings before leaving the room at 4:55 for the bus pickup.

At the sink, Kirk rinsed out the water bottles. He opened an overhead cabinet and removed two packets of "Arctic Ice", a powdered sports drink mix that was rich in potassium and about a million other essential minerals and trace elements. The old-salt back packers on the Appalachian Trail who introduced it to Kirk swore by it to keep the electrolytes balanced. Soon he would know how good it really was. After sweating profusely all morning, if he didn't explode from bed with leg cramps tonight, he'd swear by it too. It had to be better than the daily handful of salt tablets he downed during the hot season in Vietnam; puking them up, which happened a lot, almost guaranteed dehydration and over heating.

When he had filled both bottles he placed them in the freezer compartment of the refrigerator. From past treks he knew that a Platypus water bottle, frozen solid and wrapped in a towel, would remain icy long into the heat of the day. It would still be cool when the others were gulping down the tepid contents of their canteens.

Kirk stripped down and threw his cloths into a five-gallon

plastic bucket. The hours of sweat and dust had dried to a crust that would have to soak in soapy water for hours before washing.

He opened the cold water all the way and stepped under the hard spray. Gasping, to catch his breath, his neurons fired at the welcome shock. The shower head was at least six feet high, the way he liked them, the way women hate them. Leaning against the cool wall tile, breathing slowly enough not to inhale the water that rushed across his nostrils, he almost dozed off. His thoughts floated back to the banks of the Apalachicola, to the secluded sandy bluffs where a young boy escaped his shortcomings, where he inexplicably communed with the sympathetic spirits of ages past. With mystical accuracy they led him to stone tools and flint points and they told him their stories. And Kirk wondered if the spirits of Israel would be as accepting.

Kirk heard the difficult lock clicking. Someone entered the kitchen. He snapped out of his dreams, realizing he better get moving if he wanted any lunch.

"That you Bill?" asked Kirk.

"Yeah. Well, how was the first day?"

"Good. Guess I'm still lagged out from the flight, or this wake-up time. Hope I didn't cause you to lose sleep last night."

"Oh, no. I sleep well through anything."

"What's for lunch," Kirk asked.

"Don't know; I've been down at the office buying script to use at the store. Guess they told you they don't take real money?"

"No, but I read it in the info," said Kirk.

"A damn inconvenience but they have their reasons, I suppose. Guess the help can't carry out as much inventory as they could money." Bill chuckled at his sudden insight into the system. "What's the world coming to? If you can't trust your brother communist comrades on the kibbutz, who the hell can you trust?"

Kirk laughed out loud. He liked the old guy; something about a couple of mild profanities could always break the ice, even make a priest seem like a regular guy.

"You going to lunch?" Father Casey asked.

"Sure am; I'm starved!" said Kirk.

The roommates continued their conversation, maneuvering around the room and each other, as they groomed and dressed. Their deference and orderliness was a recognizable choreography; both were accustomed to sharing confined living spaces. Kirk estimated that the Father must be in his mid-sixties. He liked him, was glad they were roommates.

Kirk threaded his web belt through the last loop of his stone washed canvas trousers and wove the shiny tip through the open brass buckle. "I'm gone. See you at lunch, Father."

"I'll be on in a bit." Bill's voice emerged from the cascade behind the shower curtain.

Kirk fast-walked the few hundred meters to the dining hall and kitchen. He was relieved to see that food was still out and the line was short. The usually patient man hated lines. Often he'd rather do without whatever it was that the herd waited on. Most former enlisted men hate lines, he rationalized.

Midday was always the meat meal of the day from the kosher kitchen. Two women were rationing out today's delicacy from the first of three steam tables, breaded turkey wings. The next two held large stainless pans of lintels, millet, chick peas, soy beans and even some familiar vegetables. The salad bar was an over-choice of Middle Eastern favorites: grape leaves, olives, pickles, herbs, amber sauces and a deep red relish that looked like one of the real salsas of the Southwest.

Willy saw Kirk standing in the serving line. He walked over as the first-timer pondered the selections.

"Try this," said Willy, "one of the specialties of the house, 'skoog'."

"What is it?"

"Closest thang you gonna find to piquante sauce over here," said Willy. "The Yemenites make it; jewelry and hot sauce, that's what they make best. The Israelis think it's hot as fire; I don't have the heart to tell them it taste more like Gerber Baby Tomatoes, to me."

"Yemenites?"

"Yeah, Jews from Yemen. Closest folks Israel has to Coonasses.

"What do you eat it on?" Kirk chuckled.

"Come on over and sit with us; I'll show you."

"Thanks," said Kirk

He spooned out a glob of the thick sauce and tapped it into a soup bowl. He followed Willy toward a table on the farthest wall from the noisy serving area. He stared at his tray: a fried turkey wing, bowl of lintels, olives, radishes, a cucumber and, now, a bowl of kosher Yemenite salsa. What a meal, he thought to himself. Michelle was already seated at the table with Willy and Joel. Kirk was astounded; she had showered, dressed and still beaten him to lunch. He hadn't met many women so expeditious. And she really looked nice.

Her shoulder-length blond hair was clean and silken. There was not a trace of the ashen smudges of tel dirt on her face. Michelle could have just stepped off the page of a Condé Nast travel ad. She was dressed in an Ann Klein royal and ivory sun dress that made her eyes flame blue. Kirk noticed a dozen other pairs of spellbound eyes but Michelle was oblivious to the troop of admirers. This was much of her allure, no suggestive glances, taunting gestures or flirtation. There was none of the body language that draws young men like sand gnats, the same signs that trigger wariness in the older and wiser.

"Well," said Kirk, "I see you beat me here."

"Sure did. I was hungry enough to come straight from the bus, but I was too filthy. Had to be the hottest day so far."

"How's the food?" Kirk asked with a slightly sarcastic tone.

"You're just going to have to decide for yourself." Michelle had one elbow on the table, her hand supporting her face while she stirred at a large serving of steamed eggplant.

"Sometimes this stuff will make you crave C-rations," said Willy.

Still shifting the slime and seed around on her plate, Michelle looked up. "Know what we ought to do after pottery washing this afternoon?"

The others looked over with raised eyebrows.

"We ought to go into town for a cold beer and falafel and maybe a shwarma."

Kirk and Willy were both chewing hard on mouthfuls of something but they nodded positively.

"Let's meet in front of the office as soon as we can get away."

Kirk agreed. Willy, still chewing, continued nodding his okay.

Michelle gave up on finishing the unidentifiable mixture on her plate and dropped her fork and napkin onto it. She and reached into one of the hidden, seam pockets of her sundress and brought out a pack of gum. She offered the pack to the others who both said no-thanks. "You sure? It's the sugar-free kind for when you can't brush. "Have a piece?"

Kirk accepted and placed the stick of gum beside his plate until he finished the last bites of food. He watched Michelle with curiosity as she deftly folded the small piece of gum foil into the shape of a little bird with its wings spread. She noticed his attention.

"Origami," she said.

"Yes, I know. Fascinating art form," said Kirk. "But can you do balloon animals?"

Michelle looked up from her folding, smiled and dropped the little foil dove into the palm of his hand.

"Here," she said. "Now you can't say I never gave you anything."

The four remained at the table enjoying the cool shade and conversation. Frowns of frustration on the faces of the kitchen crew begged the lingerers to leave. Obediently, they cleared the table and carried trays to the scullery and walked out of the dining room, back into the midday heat.

"After pottery washing, in front of the office." Kirk confirmed the commitment before he and Michelle started down the different walkways to their rooms.

"I won't let you forget. See you at pottery washing at 4:30. But right now it's nap time."

5

KIRK WALKED The short distance back to the delicious cool dimness of his room. Father Casey, in only his boxers, was reclined on his bunk with a paperback. He looked up over the rim of his reading glasses.

"Decided I'd rather relax than go to lunch."

"You didn't miss much."

Kirk sat on the edge of his bed and unlaced his shoes. The cold terrazzo floor soothed his bare feet. An aroma rising from Father Casey's cup of tea on the night stand smelled good.

"By the way," said Bill, "help yourself to the refrigerator whenever you want, fruit, feta, pita, and some hummus, I think. Good to have it in here when you want to leave the cave."

"Thanks Bill, I'll add to our supply when I get to town; I'm going in late this afternoon. Anything else we need?"

"Yeah, some dried fruit, dates and almonds, but only if you like them, too. There's a good market behind the Central bus station.

"Sounds good to me, I'll stock up.

"Kirk?" Bill paused for a moment to order his words. "Forgive me if I'm out of line. I'm curious as to your religious background. Promise, I'm not going to try to convert you."

"That's okay," said Kirk. "I'm Episcopalian.

"Really?" Bill voiced his surprise. "Not many Anglicans in the Deep South, I wouldn't think."

"We're in the minority all right."

"Maybe not much longer," said Bill. "I read somewhere that most new Episcopal confirmands were coming from the fundamentalist mainstream churches."

"Yeah, but it's a revolving door," said Kirk.

Bill frowned confusion as he sipped on the cooling cup of green tea.

"I don't think I know what you mean by revolving door."

"Just that," said Kirk. "For every Baptist boozehound and Catholic family-planner we gain, we lose a male chauvinist and a homophobe."

Bill laughed out loud; almost spit his tea.

"Kind of a fortuitous ecumenical equilibrium, I suppose," said Kirk.

Father Casey swung his legs around off the bunk, stood and stretched. He stepped over the vibrating air conditioner and switched the thermostat to a warmer setting. He stood in place for a few pensive seconds waiting for the right words.

"Would you consider yourself a spiritual man, Kirk?"

"I'm not sure how to answer that, Father." Now Kirk paused to gather his thoughts. "I'm not religious, at all. I consider myself spiritually open minded, maybe even a bit spiritual in a personal and private sort of way. I know this: I don't think being religious and being spiritual is the same thing."

Kirk's answer was the best he could come up with on the spur of the moment. He felt a bit awkward about his simplistic answer; he felt awkward about the whole subject.

"I completely agree, Kirk. In fact, I know religion is often the single most powerful obstacle to our spiritual acuity. That's precisely why I'm no longer a parish priest. That's a tale for another time, if you're interested, that is. Another question. Are you familiar with what Saint Paul called the 'gifts of the spirit' from the Book of Corinthians?"

"Uh…No, I'm not," said Kirk. "I know that Corinthians is in the New Testament; that's about it."

Kirk hoped his apathy and irritation wasn't evident. He was apprehensive about where the old priest really was heading with all his questions but, out of courtesy, he didn't ask. He was well aware that for the next four weeks he would be sharing close quarters with the man and he didn't want there to be any friction between them. But he was also determined not to be some off-the-wall Bible beater's summer project.

"Forgive me, Kirk. I'm making you uncomfortable. I don't mean to. I know you're annoyed. You wonder where my questions are leading… and you wonder if you're stuck in a room with some

Catholic version of Jerry Falwell. Go ahead and say it; you won't hurt my feelings."

Kirk hoped that it wasn't too obvious that the remarks startled him. He had nailed down Kirk's true feelings. And he had dealt with them in sequence. But he had done so with the thoughtfulness of a trusted friend. Kirk was not offended but neither did Bill's intuitive apology diminish the apprehension. It did stir his curiosity, which goaded him to continue answering his questions.

"That's okay, Father. You just caught me off guard. I mean asking about my religious beliefs and all that... and, I guess, you being a priest..." Kirk left the phrase hanging. "You're right; I don't like religious conversation. My beliefs are far out; I know that and I don't enjoy defending them. And I'm sure as hell not interested in trying to persuade anyone else to accept them. But now, I've said it. What are the spiritual gifts? I'll even admit I'm curious why you ask."

"You're a tough and honest man, Kirk. But you're a considerate man, too. That can be a tough tightwire to walk. Being a priest, I know all about tightwire walking. I must confess, I envy your sense of balance very much. It would have saved me some painful incidents. Oh my..."

With a sad smile, Bill flashed back into the past and momentarily revisited a few agonizing falls from the wire. Kirk thought he saw the trace of a tear. In another moment, Bill was back in the present.

"Did you know that most scholars believe that Paul's letters to the Corinthians are the oldest books in the New Testament?"

"I don't know too much about the Bible, Father."

"Well, it's true. Mainstream thought is that Mark, the oldest of the four Gospels, was written as much as ten years later. Corinthians is dated to barely twenty years after the crucifixion of Christ, around 54 AD. Mark probably followed in about 65. But, I'm off on a tangent that has little to do with the spiritual gifts, which Paul lists as wisdom, knowledge, faith, healing, miraculous powers, prophesy, distinguishing spirits, speaking in tongues and interpreting tongues."

"Oh my god!" Kirk's alarms went off again. "Father Bill, I've been brow-beaten with that snake-church bullshit all my life. You got any idea how many Pentecostal Holiness Churches there are per acre in the South? Hell, there's no escape!"

"I can only imagine," said Bill. "But, please, don't turn me off quite yet."

Kirk agreed. "Okay, since I'm already in over my head, go ahead; I'm listening."

Father Casey stood and looked out through the shutters into the tangles of ficus that shaded the window. For a second, Kirk thought Father Casey was about to shy away from the conversation. Then he turned, pulled one of the chairs over from the table and sat facing Kirk.

"Tell you what, instead of trying to explain, I'd rather you experience for yourself my specific gift. I understand completely your distrust, after all the false prophets and charlatans we've seen the last few years. Theme parks, prayer towers, political demagogues; Holy Mary, how could you not be a doubter. Even so, Kirk, there are a few ounces of true gold for all the tons of fool's gold. And so it is with spiritual power."

"I'm sure you're right, Father."

"I am right, Kirk." Bill hesitated, then said, "So, how are we to tell, you ask."

Kirk grinned at the sly attribution. Bill smiled even wider and his eyes glistened.

"The answer came to me years ago. I was at Barclay's Bank watching the women shuffle through millions in banknotes, every currency imaginable. Every so often one of the clerks would hold up one of the notes next to another. After the inspection she would either continue counting or rubber stamp the bill in red ink, counterfeit. Then I saw it; at each station, clipped over the desk tops, there was a brand new, genuine note of the currency being counted. The most perfect counterfeit could be detected when examined next to the genuine."

Father Casey spoke with an air of authority. His conviction gained Kirk's respect and seized his attention.

"My friend, it is no accident of time and chance that you're here in this place, at this time. Your entire life has been in preparation for these next few days. And for the rest of your life. You'll understand before you leave here this summer.

"Kirk, I've seen the young guilt-ridden lad, alone, weeping in the forest, convinced he could have saved his father if only he had been there. If only he had accepted the invitation. If only... I know about the secret sand bluff over the black-water river you love. I know the ancient ones who consoled you and raised your spirits. What you never knew was that your high sandy bluff was a holy place; it was the ancient one's winter burial ground. I know that just as you were drawn to that place, you are drawn to this place, at this time, for a very specific purpose. So are the others, as am I.

"Why us? I'm sure I don't know. But I can tell you that there's a grand and wonderful purpose. I don't know what you will find here but I know that my purpose is to show you how and where you will find it when the time comes.

"However, Kirk, I don't know a damn thing about speaking in tongues, so you can rest easy about that."

Kirk was dazed. Who could this be who saw what he had never breathed to a living soul? He sat stunned, in silence as the truth of Bill's words soaked into his psyche. He now realized this old priest knew the structure of his being as a master knew his ship's rigging.

Kirk broke his silence, habitually resorting to expletives, attempting to conceal his trepidation.

"Damn, Bill. What the hell… All I came over here for was to fulfill a dream of working on a dig." He paused, his head turned slightly, starring down into the floor tile, unable to organize his thoughts. "What are you talking about my finding, an important artifact or something like that?"

Father Bill answered softly, thoughtfully. "I really don't know; probably not. The most important things are seldom things. But I really don't know. I suspect that it will be something of spiritual importance. But, again, I don't know.

"I've rattled on too long; forgive me if I've been too forward. Think I'll take a short nap. Have a good trip into Beit Shean."

"Well, you're a lot of help. You remind me of one of my Navy buddies. We'd go into a bar; he'd start a fight and while I was getting my butt kicked, he'd rake all the change off the bar and sneak out the back. Now that you've got the hair on my back standing, you're just going to lie down and take a nap."

Bill was already stretched out on his cot, eyes closed, facing the wall.

"Don't know anything else to tell you now," he mumbled. "When I do, I will."

Then, almost immediately, Bill sat up and looked directly into his roommate's eyes.

"Kirk, there's only one way to recognize the true spirits. Their gifts are for the sole purpose of our edification. I've been given the gifts of knowledge, faith and distinguishing spirits. My words were not to alarm you, quite the opposite. The message was sent to enlighten and guide you so please try to accept it as such.

"And, of course, I know you're still wondering if I'm some psychotic determined to help you to hear the voices, too. Soon you'll know, my friend; soon you will know."

Again Kirk gazed deep into the terrazzo, his eyes opened wide beneath lifted brows. In a hushed, matter-of-fact voice, he said, "I guess we'll both know within the next four weeks, won't we, Father?"

Kirk sat on the edge of his pine frame cot. His weight compressed the scant three inches of foam rubber that padded the spartan bed. Untying his Nikes, he was careful to avoid knotting the laces; the dry dust from the tel could transform ordinary knots into hellish Gordians. He pulled off both shoes and fought to remove his sweaty athletic socks. They were fresh and dry scarcely an hour ago, he thought to himself. He folded his pillow double, placed it between his head and the plaster wall and lay back on the thin foam pad. With a deep breath and a yawn, Kirk closed his eyes and savored the conditioned flow of fresh air that bathed his face. All in all, he thought it had been a good morning. But it seemed strange that, after seven hours on the tel and the main meal, it was only mid-day.

There were televisions in the rooms but the program selection was limited. There were five Hebrew or Arabic stations, CNN and the National Geographic Channel which was regularly preempted by live feeds of various kibbutz committees – it was awful, like watching an Israeli knock-off of the Jerry Springer show.

Kirk liked Michelle's system, watching National Geographic, muted, while listening to lite jazz and new-age selections she had recorded from the DMX channels back home. She had offered to lend him some of the CD's if he could find a compatible player.

Kirk also liked the way the encased window shutters could be lowered to completely darken the room even in the middle of the day. Yet, when opened just slightly, narrow gaps between each slat allowed just enough daylight to enter so that a lamp was not necessary, at least after one's eyes adjusted to the shadows. In Israel the ubiquitous shutters were more common than glass windows.

As he lay there staring at the ceiling, unable to nap, he tried to remember if Father Casey had said where he was from. He couldn't. He thought he detected a trace of brogue but he had a poor ear for geography. It could have as likely been from Maritime Canada as County Cork. His thoughts seemed locked in curiosity about his roommate. Where was he from; where had his parishes been; was this his first time in Israel? There were many questions Kirk wanted to ask but he would have to wait until later when the old man was wide awake—and willing to talk.

Kirk switched on the small wall mounted lamp over the head of his cot and opened his copy of Jerome Murphy – O'Connor's <u>Oxford Archaeological Guide to the Holy Land.</u> He flipped the pages back and forth between the table of contents and the descriptions of the various sites. He marked those that were most interesting to him. He checked the maps to determine locations and distances trying to envision groups to visit over a two-day weekend. He couldn't collect his thoughts away from the conversation with Father Bill.

He thought he should be pissed off at Bill for being so damned presumptuous. It puzzled him why he wasn't. He had a refined disdain for the clergy. He considered the vast majority to be lazy, authoritarian bastards. Most were con men who had rather manipulate the gullible and ignorant than to do honest work. He knew there were a few—damned few—who didn't fit that mold. Without yet even knowing the man, he thought Father Casey might just be one of the few. Kirk realized that he trusted Bill though he didn't know why; Kirk didn't trust many people, let alone preachers.

Unable to concentrate on the book, he laid it down on his chest. He closed his eyes and relaxed to the churning hum of the air conditioner and barely audible music from Bill's shortwave radio/cassette player. The soft flute melody sounded like one of Carlos Nakai's mystical compositions. How appropriate, thought Kirk, considering what the old fart just laid on me. But he smiled at the association.

Kirk dozed off and within moments the boy was again walking along the tupelo flanks of the big river that sliced through the Florida Panhandle. He waded through the black, tannin-stained waters and across the amber sands of the Apalachicola's bars. In this place, neither dreamers nor spirits from the past are dissuaded

by time or distance; their differences become vague and insignificant as the two become one and the same.

6

Kirk awakened to the shuffling sounds of Father Casey pulling on his khakis and cinching the straps of his Tevas. "Time to go clean up pottery?"

"Afraid so," said Bill.

"Ooooooooah," Kirk let out a yawn as he arched his back and stretched. "I'm not used to napping."

"Neither am I. But when you're up at four it'll catch up with you if you don't."

Bill went to the refrigerator, took out a bottle of grapefruit soda and poured a coffee glass half full. "Have you heard what's been turning up at pottery washing?"

"No, I don't think so." Kirk answered without looking up as he laced his boots for the third time since the predawn alarm shook him awake. "What?"

"You do know that pottery shards identify the culture that left them?" Bill asked.

"Yeah, that much I know." said Kirk.

Bill took a sip of the tart soda.

"Last Thursday or...couldn't have been Friday. Oh, you do know there's no pottery washing or lab work on Fridays?"

"Really?" Kirk was listening. "No, no one told me."

"Yes... or no. Because everyone is trying to get away for the weekend before the buses stop running for Shabbat. That's six o'clock. When you leave on Fridays, be sure you have plenty of time to get where you're going. If you miss the last bus—to anywhere— you're stuck until they start running again Saturday after sundown. Of course, you can call a sherut or try to hitch a ride. That reminds me; for goodness sake, don't hitch-hike with your thumb like they do in the America. Over here, that's an obscene gesture. Guess I must have seen a dozen pilgrims dive out of the way of insulted Israelis before I found out what was going on. Why, it's a miracle... My god!"

Father Casey raised his palms as if posing with an imaginary trophy bass. His eyes turned up toward the heavens and then shifted to Kirk.

Bill moaned. "No wonder they said my sermons suck. I never could hold a train of thought. Forgive me again, Kirk. What I meant to tell you was that, last Thursday, we found pieces of both Israelite and Phoenician pottery from the tenth century. Came out of several of the buckets from Area B. That's where they put you, isn't it?"

"Yeah, square G20," answered Kirk.

"I don't remember which square, probably the deepest. What this means is that old Tel Kefar was here, up and running, when King Saul, David and Solomon were on the throne. Sure adds to the mystery of not being mentioned in the Bible, doesn't it?"

"What do you mean, not mentioned?"

"Exactly that. There's no mention of Kefar anywhere in the scriptures, at least not in the ones that are known. That's the mystery; why not.

Kefar was one of the largest walled cities in Israel during the period of the Judges and throughout the time of the united monarchy. It was mentioned by name in both Assyrian and Egyptian records; so why not in the Bible?"

Bill glanced over at his clock radio.

"Hey, we better get moving."

"Yeah, you're right. I'm ready. Don't forget your key; remember, I'll be leaving for Beit Shean as soon as we're done." Kirk pulled one strap of his backpack over his shoulder and started toward the door.

"I remember. Just don't forget our snacks," Bill snapped in good humor.

The two groaned in unison as the afternoon heat enveloped them. They were fortunate that the short walk to the work area was through a shady tunnel of towering sycamores which restrained the heat surprisingly well. Along the way there were reminders of other, more turbulent times.

A veneer of basalt riprap shielded several low mounds of earth.

Reinforced concrete stairwells and screened steel vent stacks descended into the berms. Down the shafts they could see steel entrance doors secured by big, case-hardened padlocks.

"Hope we don't need those." Father Casey nodded toward the locked bomb shelters. "Now, why is it the name of Kefar does not appear in the Bible?"

As the two continued their slow walk, Father Casey explained that there were two possibilities for the omission. The religious held that Kefar was not mentioned because it had been insignificant in the history of the children of Israel. The city was the site of neither notable victory nor defeat for the Israelites – so there was no reason to name it. He told Kirk that the most widely accepted theory, however, was that by the time the scriptures were reduced to written form the writers had no knowledge of Kefar. The city was destroyed by the invading Assyrian Army in 732 BCE and most serious scholars believe that the earliest scriptures were written in the Persian Period and possibly as late as the Hellenistic.

"That's between roughly 550 and 250 BCE," said Bill. "Of course, it could be that it was the central setting of some lost writings. Who knows?

"Really is strange, though, isn't it?" Kirk pondered the enigma.

"By no means the only one either," said Bill. "A few miles up this valley there's the town called Nazareth. When Jesus lived there it was a tiny village. But less than four miles away was the huge Greco-Roman city named Sephoris. Herod Antipas actually used Sephoris as his capital during Jesus' lifetime. But neither is it mentioned by any known name in the scriptures."

"Maybe someone should write a book on what's not in the Bible," said Kirk.

"Maybe one day you will."

Father Casey's words caught Kirk off guard. His remark had more the ring of portent than suggestion.

"And when you do, I hope you'll try to include all the social issues that Jesus never addressed, things he never said, things he never did. Can't quite see your book being well received by The Reverend Falwell, though – or any of the rest who live to put words in God's mouth. But... there I go again and here we are."

Father and Kirk exited the shaded walkway to find several of the team already busy with scrubbing and spreading the wet shards

onto bread tray drying racks. Bill went for two buckets of pottery
which had been labeled and left soaking for three days. He asked
Kirk to pick up a couple of bread trays and brushes and meet him.
He pointed to an unoccupied space on a concrete sitting wall which
encircled the base of a banyan tree.

The old tree was one of six which canopied the area between
two buildings. One building was the expedition laboratory which
included the registrar's office, work stations and supplies. Here the
pottery and artifacts were recorded and packaged to await the next
run into Jerusalem and Hebrew University. The other was an oddly
shaped structure, one of the oldest on the kibbutz. It reflected the
early days when the founders used what they could get or make in
the way of building materials. Not much.

The homemade cinder block walls looked as if they were laid
by white-collar prison labor. They intersected at weird compound
angles and rose to support a sagging superstructure topped with
four-inch waves of corrugated roofing. Inside, the floor plan was an
unlearnable labyrinth of compartments and passages which housed
over twenty student volunteers. And there was a waiting list to
move in, which seemed crazy. But in this dark secure maze no one
ever knew, for sure, who slept, smoked or sniffed what or where.
One of the older kibbutz carpenters claimed that it had been easier
to navigate the ruins and sewers in the Warsaw ghetto.

Bill was already seated on the low wall under the tree when
Kirk returned with brushes and drying racks.

"Found a bucket from your square," said Bill, "let's see what
you've got."

Kirk sat down next to Bill. Several others also sitting on the
low wall were already at work. He leaned back and looked up to
inspect the thick tangle of leaves and limbs. He had no idea what
kind of tree it was, some type of wild ficus he guessed. Whatever
it was, the grackles and doves relished the small currant-like fruit
that littered the ground and walkway beneath the saggy branches.

"First thing," said Bill, "take the tag off the bucket handle
and... hold the rack over here for me, if you will."

Bill took the waterproof tag and tied it to the top rail of the
rack. The dated tags contained vital information about the source of
the tray's contents; expedition, area, square, locus and elevation.

"Now," said Bill, "brush and rinse each shard until the muddy crust is gone. When you're done put the clean pieces on the drying rack; all there is to it.

"I can handle that," said Kirk. "Be sure to show me any of the Tenth Century stuff you were telling me about."

"Sure. They're pretty distinctive styles, not hard to recognize. Another pointer, Kirk, be sure to inspect the handles and rim pieces closely. For seals. You have to clean them really well or the impressions will get by you. You'll think there's just a rough spot on the surface. And be sure to check the body shards for any signs of an inscription."

"Ostraca," Kirk remarked matter-of-factly.

Father Casey glanced up from the fragment he was examining. "You've done some homework."

"Wouldn't exactly call it homework. Just a fascination with this kind of stuff. I've collected Indian artifacts since I was a kid; I took a few archaeology electives in college. And." Kirk accented the word and paused for effect. "I've subscribed to <u>Biblical Archaeology Review</u> magazine for nearly twenty-five years."

"Aha! Suspected all along I was in the presence of a true scholar."

While the small group labored through the routine of cleaning and organizing the racks of wet discoveries, the expedition registrar, a trim and attractive woman of maybe forty-five—Kirk guessed—maneuvered among them. She grumbled loudly about how many of the volunteers were shirking their pottery washing duty. Every few steps she paused briefly to stoop over and examine some object that caught her seasoned eye, but her scolding and complaining didn't cease.

She was Nina Lieberman from Providence, Rhode Island, a museum curator and archivist at Brown University. Beneath her charcoal black hair a flawless, olive complexion enhanced the allure of her ebony eyes. They were alert and penetrating yet soft and hardly threatening, in spite of her daily promises to deal terribly with the no-shows. Kirk quickly concluded that she would have great difficulty being either mean or tough. Nina noticed Kirk's eyes following her and his expression let her know he was not in the least intimidated.

Nina slowly made her way over to where Father Casey and Kirk sat. Still ranting, she leaned over and plucked a cleaned shard from their rack. She held it up to better light, examining the piece from every angle. Then, looking down at her old friend, Father Bill, she started up again.

"I do not understand what keeps so many from coming. It makes it hard on everyone else. This is just as important as digging it out of the ground. It's very irresponsible and inconsiderate conduct."

Bill could contain himself no longer. "Holy Mother of God!" Bill exclaimed. "My dear lady, do you not realize we are the ones who are here, with you." Father Casey and Nina's friendly bickering over anything imaginable had become an almost daily ritual. "When I was a parish priest," he continued, "they told me I was bad to preach to the choir but, Christ me God, I could sit at your feet and take instruction."

The group, even Nina, exploded with laughter. Within moments Michelle and a few others, probably curious about the revelry, emerged from the confusing building with the corrugated roof. Even though the area was well shaded, she stood just outside the entryway squinting, allowing her eyes to adjust to the much brighter light. With her fingers and palm flattened, she formed a visor above her brow and searched the workers. She spotted Bill and Kirk and walked over to where they were seated.

"Good afternoon," said Kirk. "Wondered where you were. We faithful have been catching hell on account of all you no-shows."

"No, she's here every day." Nina, down on one knee still inspecting the contents of the drying rack, jumped to Michelle's defense. "She's not one of the habitual truants."

"See there, I'm a loyal team member." She plopped down hard, bumping Kirk's shoulder with hers. "Scoot over and I'll help you two. Oh!" Michelle read the bucket tag. "This is our bucket from the fourteenth; that was last Thursday."

"Thanks for the help," said Kirk. "This bucket was really full."

"I know," said Michelle. "Hilda saved every tiny piece of everything, no matter how small, every little pebble and rock chip."

"Guess it's better to save too much than not enough," said Kirk.

"Father Casey," Michelle leaned around Kirk to see that he had heard. "Do you want to come to Beth Shean with us?"

"Not this time, darling, but thank you for the invitation," Bill's eyes reflected the pleasure of being asked. "But I would be grateful if you see to it that my friend, Kirk, doesn't forget our groceries.

And remind him that he promised his roommate some kind of surprise, too."

"I certainly will; won't let him on the bus home till he shows me the goods."

Kirk sat quietly, not lifting his eyes from the rim shard he was scrubbing. He pretended to be oblivious to the conversation, but a trace of smile gave him away.

Abruptly, Nina stood and barked toward the office as Willy rounded the corner. "Willy, why aren't you here helping?"

Willy turned and walked toward her. He crossed his forearms with his fingers splayed as if to fend off the imaginary assault. When he was close Nina continued in a quieter voice.

"Willy, we're getting further and further behind with washing and sorting; we really do need everyone's help."

Willy looked to Michelle and Kirk. "Didn't I ask you guys to tell her the dog ate my schedule?" When he saw Nina's stance and expression change to reflect her irritation, he continued with a serious explanation. "Dr. Lieberman, I would have been here but this morning Doctor Benjamin asked me to fix all the wheelbarrows wit flat tires. That's what I been doing ever since lunch time. I'll be here tomorrow."

"Okay, Willy, thanks for telling me." Nina smiled and nodded.

"You welcome, ma'am."

Willy turned and squatted down in front of the other three. "We still going into town?"

"Sure," Michelle answered, "you are too, aren't you?"

"Yeah, I'm ready to relax for a spell; it been a hot today."

"Kirk and I tried to talk Father Casey into joining us," Michelle remarked.

"Thanks again," said Bill, "but I really would rather stay here and read. I'm in the middle of…

Father Casey was cut off by a loud cheer rising from one of the bucket teams on the back side of the big tree. Nina and most of the others moved around to see what had been found.

"Oh my God!" said the student. "I thought it was just another piece of pottery! I almost didn't even brush it! What is it?" asked the co-ed.

She pinched the small artifact between her index finger and thumb and held it out toward Nina. She could hardly contain her excitement. Nina removed a compact leather covered magnifying glass from a pocket of her long sleeved Columbia shirt. The brass framed, convex lens unfolded like a pocket knife; it swung out from its sheath and was hinged so the protective covering served as a handle. She reached out and carefully took the object from the girl and inspected it closely with the naked eye before observing it beneath the glass.

While the circle waited in silence for the appraisal, Kirk noticed how good Nina looked in the gray green fishing shirt. Little did he know sage was the perfect color for her autumn coding.

Nina stooped and dipped her fingers in the water in one of the pottery buckets. In a circular motion, she gently rubbed it on the surface of the mysterious fragment.

"Would someone go to the office and see if Paul is still there?" Nina asked without diverting her eyes from the magnified image. "Well, Miss...?"

"Smith, Sally, please."

"Well, Sally, you've found a very nice scarab; an Egyptian seal. If Paul is here I want him to read the cartouche. He reads hieroglyphics better than most of us read the Sunday Times op-eds."

"What do you think is on it?" she asked.

"Usually the name of a Pharaoh or some high ranking official," Nina stated. "They were used the same way our corporate or official seals are used today, to give legitimacy to documents. But now we won't have to guess."

The group parted to allow Paul Snowden to penetrate to the center of the onlookers. The wiry Egyptologist was one of the perennial team who followed Moshe Benjamin faithfully. He was a PhD candidate at Oxford University and was, already, a recognized authority on The Occupied Territories of the Levant during the New Kingdom, the title of his eight-hundred page—and still growing—doctoral dissertation. Snowden was a soft spoken Kiwi from the South Island who had not been home in over four years. He didn't intend to return until he had earned his coveted Oxford degree.

"Paul," said Nina, "take a look at this."

"What have you got there?" Paul asked, looking at the object in her hand.

"A scarab; that's all we know. Hope you can tell us more." Nina held out the artifact and the magnifying glass to him.

Paul took the scarab and began to trombone the lens back and forth between his eye and the little seal. Within seconds he had an answer.

"Another Ramses," he said. "That's four or five now. This one's in very good shape, very well defined beetle back and cartouche."

"How old do you think it is?" Sally asked.

"Hard to say. There were eleven pharaohs between 1314 and 1090 BCE who called themselves Ramses. Let's see the bucket tag." Paul reached down to lift the waterproof tag. "Area 'C', Square F-8, locus 1174. Whose square?" He looked up.

Sally answered. "Lauren's the supervisor. Jan and I are with her."

"Where is Lauren?" Paul asked.

"In the lab, working on the top plan," said Nina.

"No problem, I can ask her later, unless..." Paul turned to Sally Bergman. "I don't suppose you know what the stratigraphic code for this locus, 1174, is?"

Sally answered, "I don't know the code numbers but we've been in mud brick debris and decayed mud brick for over a week."

"Good for you. That tells me a lot." Paul was pleasantly surprised and smiled with approval.

Paul tweezered the scarab between his thumb and finger and turned it slowly, left and right, so the others could see it. He addressed the whole group, explaining the significance of his question about the stratigraphy.

"Had this little jewel been found in association with a burial or other artifacts, I might be better able to date it more precisely and the scarab could help date the burial or artifacts found in association with it. Unfortunately, that's not the case here. We are not certain about the context. Lauren, Sally and Jan are working in mud brick debris. I suspect that long before it was either lost or discarded. Then, years later, it was inadvertently mixed in with the clay when the brick was made. Of course, if we knew that for certain, we would know that the brick could be no older than this scarab. Likewise, the scarab could be no younger than the brick or the structure that the brick was a component of. The brick, however, could be much older than the wall or building or whatever it was a part of. Am I making sense?" Paul, the teacher, listened for an answer.

"Yes", several assured.

Michelle whispered to Kirk. "Why would a brick be much older than the building it was in?"

Kirk paused a moment, then quietly answered. "My house was built in 1985; it's a brick veneer. The brick came out of a bonded cotton warehouse that was built with slave labor in 1849."

"Oh! Of course," Michelle immediately understood. She sounded embarrassed that the obvious had eluded her.

Nina and Paul spent several more minutes allowing everyone a chance to hold and admire the small treasure. As she passed the ancient piece from hand to hand, she spoke about it in an almost reverent voice. "Our eyes are the first to behold, our fingers the first to touch since it was lost by one of our forebears three thousand years ago."

When Paul had retreated to the lab with the scarab, the teams resumed cleaning the remaining few buckets with a renewed resolve: nothing of value would escape discovery. But there were no more finds for this session. The day's work was finished. They rinsed and stacked the empty buckets and arranged the tagged racks in rows according to area and square.

7

From the Work area at the expedition office to the bus stop outside the main gate was a short walk. An unpaved service road meandered between equipment sheds, turkey houses and a slew of abandoned shacks and nondescript sheds. The route that Michelle, Kirk and Willy walked passed by weeded lots with hodgepodges of farm implements representing as many countries of origin as those who had operated it over the years. The mélange of rust, fence wire and rotting tires created a confusing collage making it was impossible to distinguish the discarded equipment from the shamefully neglected.

Willy ended the silence. "Ever wonder why it is that those who have the least seem to abuse what little they have the most?"

"What do you mean?" asked Michelle.

"Just look around. This damn kibbutz would make a tobacco-road hog farm look like Tara before Sherman. Jeter Lester and his Model A would sure be at home around here. Except when he wanted bacon biscuits for breakfast, I guess."

Kirk and Michelle chuckled as Willy's commentary on the junkscape rattled on.

"Who's Jeter Lester?" Michelle asked Kirk.

Kirk answered while shaking his head in dismay, "Please, don't even ask."

Just past some kind of a large barn, the road turned. And as sudden as a kid's Viewmaster scene change, the three were alongside a small, lush citrus grove. The drooping limbs were loaded with green oranges. After the barn, on the other side, was a flat-topped orchard. The branches were laden with ripe fruit, the little white peaches that so quickly disappeared from the breakfast tables.

Two hundred yards more and they reached the main entrance to Massebot. With its guard towers, this gate was more formidable than the back. The traffic lanes were divided by a formed concrete guard house separating the entrance and exit. On top of the bunker were video cameras, a gang of flood lights and several radio antennas. All this, but no guard was on duty. To the right of the exit lane was the pedestrian gate, a caged turnstile through the chain link fence. Above the fence the same line of angle iron V's cradled the continuous roll of barbed concertina which encircled the kibbutz.

Fifty feet outside the gate was the bus stop. The little shed stood on the shoulder of the Highway 71, the road between Aufula and Beit Shean. The three all crowded into the shaded half of the shelter; it was after 5:00 but the sun was still high.

"What's our bus number?" asked Willy.

"It'll probably be four-twelve." Michelle answered. She leaned forward to look up the road to the west. "All of them are supposed to stop."

Willy, eyes closed, sat on the bench with elbows spread wide; his head was tilted far back resting in his laced fingers. "When you're waiting out here," he said, "all you see are tour buses, flying by."

"One of you answer a question for me," said Kirk. "What's the story on these gates? I mean, how do they decide when to post guards? Last night I thought a smelly old troll with a Beretta and his buddies were going to strip search me. This afternoon, not a soul in sight, you could drive a Syrian tank in the place."

"Who knows?" Michelle snickered.

"I don't have the slightest," said Willy. "Must be the old junkyard dog system they're using."

Willy paused without a word of explanation.

"Okay, I'll bite," said Michelle. What is the junkyard dog system?" She looked to Kirk. He said nothing, but the suppressed smile betrayed him. He knew what was coming.

"There was this junkyard over just outside Bogalusa that had a terrible problem with voleurs climbing in over the fence at night and stealing the junk. So, Maurice LeMeux—he was the owner, good friend of mine—Maurice, he call this private police company cause he wants to hire one of they watch dogs. Well, they got dogs all right, but they want two hundred dollars a month for the dog. And they tell Maurice that he got to buy dog food on top of the two hundred dollars. Well, that a lot of money in Bogalusa, so Maurice call up two more junk yards round there. They was having the same problem and he talk them into going in with him and splitting the two hundred dollars, three way. They can move the dog round from junkyard to junkyard taking turns, don't you see. At first, it might seem like this was a big waste of money cause the crooks might could go in when the dog weren't there. But, Maurice gets these signs, bout the size of a posted property sign, and puts them up all along the fence. Guess what they say?"

Michele, trying to answer in spite of the giggles, finally gets it out. "God, Willy, I don't know. Beware of the dog?"

"Naw. They say, watch dog on duty two nights a week. You guess which two."

Michelle cackled. Blotting her eyes with her bandanna, she looked over to see Kirk's face. He was laughing, too. But more at her reaction than Willy's Cajun fable.

"Seriously." Willy said, "I notice they keep it manned at night and all day on Shabbat. Rest of the time I suspect they keep an eye on the gate with security cameras. There's another one on the phone light pole back there." He turned and pointed to an inconspicuous camera mounted just above the electrical conduit that supported a sodium halide floodlight thirty feet above the ground.

Kirk interrupted, nodding in the direction of an approaching bus still about a quarter of a mile away. "Maybe this is ours."

"Yeah," said Michelle. "Too old and squatty for a tour bus."

"How much to town," Kirk asked.

"Five shekels." Both answered at the same time.

The four-twelve began flashing a right turn signal ensuring the waiting fares that they were seen. The old bus was a grimy white and washed-out red Mercedes, the style which plodded round Europe's inner cities a quarter century earlier. With air-brakes mimicking the progressive jazz screech of a tenor sax, the lumbering box braked to a stop. Pissssshaaaaaahhh-flak. The bifold door's retracted. Willy stepped up first and handed the driver a twenty.

"Shalosh, buhvakashah (three, please)."

The driver took the bill and clicked four coins out of a dash mounted change holder. He dropped three into the fish bowl, tore off three receipts and handed a five shekel coin back to Willy. The doors hissed shut and the new riders stumbled down the aisle to adjacent seats a few rows back.

The bus was less than half full. Absent were the weekend dozens of olive clad youngsters clutching M-16s, Uzis and Berettas and their brightly colored personal back packs. Fridays they slump and sleep away the fatigue of endless marches and watches. Sundays they cast despondent gazes off into the ether, silently lamenting returning to duty, longing to be going anywhere else, for any reason. Today, there was only one, a teenage private returning to his outfit. His shoulder patch and fold-up stock M-16 suggested an armored unit, probably an outfit up on the heights, near the Syrian border.

After a mile or more bouncing toward town, Kirk noticed Willy's pensive stare. His gaze was fixed on the young soldier. Kirk knew the stare. He had seen it before; he had worn it. And instinctively he knew that the kid in uniform was a channel summoning Willy back to another time and place. A place more distant than where he stared, a thousand yards away.

"Hey, you okay?" Kirk asked in a low voice.

Willy sat motionless, unblinking for a few moments more. Then he gave a slight flinch and dragged his thoughts back inside the bus.

"I'm okay," said Willy. "Just daydreaming, I guess."

"Yeah," said Kirk. "I know all about those kind of daydreams… Willy, I know it's none of my business but do you mind if I ask what happened to your arm?"

Willy turned and looked out the window. The pause suggested that he hadn't put the answer in words in a long time. He turned back to face Kirk.

"No… I don't mind. Some gook got lucky with his AK47. Bullet shattered two inches of bone. Severed the radial nerve. I figure it was a mushroomed ricochet, much damage as it did."

"What years were you over?"

"Sixty-seven; sixty-eight," said Willy. "Fifth Marines, Phu Bai. How about you?"

Kirk was taken aback. "How'd you know?" he asked.

Willy shrugged. "I don't know. Same way you guessed right about my arm, I suppose."

Kirk nodded that he understood. Michelle had been listening to a book; she slid the earphones down around her neck and switched off the iPod. She glanced around at the IDF private and leaned closer to Willy.

"How old you think he is? Eighteen?" she asked.

"Looks about right," said Willy. "Strange situation, every kid in this country carries a handgun or automatic rifle but you never hear of an armed robbery, school shooting or drive-by."

"Same in the States, actually," said Kirk. "Highest violent crime rates are in the states and cities with the tightest gun control laws. It's all a matter of getting what you expect. Israel expects eighteen-year-olds to be adults. Back home... we expect fifty-year-old grandmothers in the Guard to report for active duty but we expect our twenty-five year-old little boys to keep on cruising the malls and playing paint-ball war. Highest crime rate of all the developed nations, but we don't need no stinking Selective Service."

"Hey, hey, you two cut it out," Michelle said. "All I asked was how old you thought he was. I don't want to listen to any damned social, political or religious discussions. The whole world is screwed up; it's not going to change. Only thing that makes it bearable is to ignore how screwed up everything is.

"Over here it's car bombs and katusha rockets; back home it's drive-by, workplace and school shootings. And we can thank the rest of the world for ethnic cleansing, terrorism, kiddy porn, child prostitution, sex junkets, and a variety of ecological horrors.

"And let's not forget to thank God for adding Alzheimer's, AIDS, ebola, lasser fever and who knows what else to His old standbys; earthquakes, floods, hurricanes, tornadoes, tidal waves, famine, fire and plague and, oh yes, let's not forget about the goddam comets and asteroids that are headed for us that we haven't even discovered yet.

"What the hell did we all do before Ted Turner and Rupert Murdoch decided that the world needed to hear about all this damn garbage twenty-four freaking hours a day?"

"Okay, okay, we'll shut up and never utter a serious word again; promise." Kirk's wide eyes feigned intimidation. "From now on it's nothing of substance, honest. Swear it, Willy, before she blast our butts again."

Willy was more than a bit amused with this side of Michelle he had not seen. He agreed profusely. "Oh, I swear; I swear it."

Then he lowered his voice and averted his eyes. Restraining a smile, he whispered, "Y'all don't look now but the old feller two rows back looks like someone hit him in the face with a sock full of shit; think Michelle must have scared the hell out of him."

"Touché," said Michelle, "you're right; I'm sorry. No more

ranting, you've got my word. I'll change the subject. What's that growing out there?" She pointed out the window to a large field of pine bark brown plants. "Willy, you've been over here long enough; you ought to know."

Willy turned to look out the window. "Sunflowers. Not very pretty now, but you should see them in May when everything's still green and blooming. The ground's still wet from the winter rains and when you watch the wind and the cloud shadows run through the sunflower fields it makes you feel like you've been sucked up into some wonderful new Monet mural."

"I bet it is beautiful. What do they grow them for, livestock feed?" Kirk asked.

"Livestock and poultry. But they eat them like peanuts over here. See the No Littering sign over the windshield? The Hebrew is an idiom; literally it reads, don't spit zahreem. Zahreem means seed – meaning the shells. Tells you how popular they are, doesn't it?"

"How many times have you been over here, Willy?" asked Kirk.

"I'm not sure. I lived over here for several years, in the seventies, after a stint in the Peace Corps. I was a volunteer on a kibbutz, Kefar Blum. Met my wife up there, she was a new aliyah from the Bronx. We got married in Cyprus, stayed together for four years. Then she met some rich schmuck cowboy from the States while we were digging down near Ashdod. I went back to Louisiana; she stayed. She's still a kibbutznic, designs Roman glass jewelry. We talk every now and then, when I'm over digging."

"Sounds like an interesting life," Kirk said.

"Oh, yeah, it's been interesting. Never made much money, but I always seem to get by. Know something, Kirk? After Nam I decided if you don't enjoy your life, not much else matters."

The answer forced Kirk to reflect back through his own years. How could he sum up his life since returning from Vietnam? And why must Vietnam always be the point of reference. For most who had been there, there was a life before and there was life after. And though the two were coupled, they were not the same existence. The latter life was not a continuation of the earlier; the two didn't fit together. The greatest triumph had been surviving to live it and the greatest shame was having survived at all. That was the paradox above all others. And there were many others. The thought occurred to Kirk that Willy's life got started just about the time his started dying – right after getting home from the war.

In reality, Beth Shean's Central Bus Station was no station at all. The facility was a double lane separated from the main street by a curbed and guttered island. On one side four covered bench shelters, not much larger than the roadside variety, lined the curb. Each position was marked with an elevated sign indicating which bus numbers used each stop. The black letters on yellow were in Hebrew on one side and English on the other. At the end of the row was a ticket office not much larger than the shelter. Behind the bus lane was a cramped parking lot that was more like an obstacle course through double parked cars. Beyond, one of the little city's ubiquitous parks was enclosed like a big courtyard by the main post office, a bank and the old Beth Shean Mall.

The mall was a conglomeration of small retail shops and boutiques and three typical Israeli fast food joints. Two eateries offered almost identical menus: falafel, shwarma, hummus, pickles, olives and sauces. Then there was Palermo Italiano down at the very end of the piazza. Their pizzas reminded Willy of the ones his mother tried to make back in the fifties. The recipe: frozen biscuit dough, tomato catsup, red rind cheese and chipped beef and baked on a cookie sheet. They were god-awful, unless you were a Cajun kid from the back bayous or a Beit Shean Israeli who had never tasted anything else. Today, Willy insisted it would be shwarma and beer in shops on the right, an unnamed place whose sign boasted, "kosher". Apparently, the other was not.

The layout of the place was confusing. There was a dining area with about eight tables for four and a WC with an entry lock that required a one-shekel coin. A long, L-shaped standing counter confined the cooking area behind it and a glass storefront wall parted the diners from the mall corridor. The short leg of the L counter was constructed so that orders could be placed from outside. There was no door between the corner of the counter and the edge of the glass partition's aluminum frame. It was impossible to tell how the place was secured after hours but the large opening and a well-aimed fan ensured that all the grilled onion, peppers and meat aromas wafted out into the big hallway. The place smelled delicious.

Willy, Kirk and Michelle placed their orders from the outside counter and sat at one of the tables scattered up and down the mall. They had just seated themselves when one of the aproned guys behind the counter called Willy back and handed him three cold beers, the caps pried up but not removed. Willy reached into his pocket; the server shook his head, no. He pantomimed writing in his palm to let Willy know that it would be on the check.

"Here we are." Willy sang out as he placed the bottles on the table. "Man, am I ready for this!"

"Yeah, me too," said Kirk. "Thanks."

He looked back down at a business card he was holding and then up at Michelle. "Where did you find this?" he asked her.

"I shouldn't tell you this while we're eating; well, actually we aren't yet. I found it on the floor of one of the Porto-toilets, out at the tel."

"You found what out at the tel?" asked Willy.

"This business card," Kirk answered, "Some antique shop in Jerash."

"Jordan?" Willy sounded intrigued. "May I?" He reached over to take the card.

Kirk glanced over for Michelle's okay.

"Sure," she said. "Sounds like an interesting place. Nina and I are talking about going across either this weekend or the next. Thought we might check it out while we're there. How big a place is Jerash, anyway?"

"Not very big," said Willy. I don't even remember a hotel there. I think most tourists just come in for the day. Claim is; it's the best preserved Greco-Roman city in the world. But it's well worth your time to go see it; even worth the hassle crossing the border."

"Then where is the closest place to stay, if we decide to go, Amman?"

"No. There's one, maybe two, little hotels in Ajlun, only about eight or ten miles away. It's an interesting place, too."

"What's there?"

"Saladin's castle, he answered. "Built to defend against the Crusaders. If you don't plan to go on into Amman it's the only place to stay anywhere near Jerash." Willy was talking as he studied the card. "Where'd you say you found this?"

"Out on the tel, it was in one of the portable toilets. I guess someone dropped it. Sounds like an interesting shop so I thought I'd keep it."

Willy read the card out loud. "Trans-Jordan Antiquities, Shihadeh Jaber, proprietor, Roman Glass, Ancient Pottery, Ancient Coins, Ancient Bronze, 16 Abila St., Jerash. Says they have a shop in Ajlun, too. But what interests me is what's written on the back."

"What's that?" Kirk asked, craning his neck toward the card.

"Not real sure what it means but it lists several pharaohs' names with a price next to it, like 'Ramses D35, Sheshak D50, Merneptah D100'. It's gotta be scarab seals. Can't believe you could buy them for these prices, thirty-five dinars is about fifty dollars. Must be repos; if not, you could triple your money buying there and selling here – Jerusalem, I mean."

"Really?" Michelle's interest perked up.

"Yeah, really. I guarantee it," said Willy.

"Wow, if I buy a thousand dollars worth… I could pay for my trip over here!" said Michelle.

"Sure could. But, if you do, you make sure you get receipts and certificates of authenticity." Willy cautioned her.

"I think our order's up." Michelle stood and walked over to the counter. She accepted the tray from a gentle-eyed bull of a man. "How much?" she asked him. His blank smile and helpless look back toward the other cook told her he didn't speak a word of English.

Willy spoke up from the table. "Ka-mah zeh-oh-leh, buh-va-ka-shah?"

The gentle-eyed bull answered him affably. "Ha-mee-sheem-vuh-shea-va."

"Fifty-seven," Willy told her.

"Oh, no you don't." Kirk protested as Michelle unzipped the outer pocket of her day pack. "This is on me. I appreciate you two letting me tag along."

"Kirk, you don't have to…"

"I know I don't; I want to. You two are good guides."

Michelle thanked him and returned to the plastic table. She held the tray for Willy to arrange the orders. For a few silent moments they were up and down grabbing napkins, sauces, salt and whatever else they realized they needed as soon as they sat back down.

After several meals together Willy had learned that his food commentaries could get Michelle so tickled she could hardly eat. Now, every time they were seated at the same table, he took immense pleasure in doing exactly that.

"Michelle, look a here. What you suppose this is?" He started in on her. "It looks like somebody's old Dr. Scholl's Cushion Sole sautéed in castor oil."

Michelle played along with his pretense. "Why does it matter, Willy? You'll eat it anyway. But I think it's a slice of roasted eggplant in olive oil."

"Well, I don't know if you're right about what it is, but you're right about I'm gonna eat it anyway. Got a tradition to uphold, you know."

"What tradition?" Kirk asked him before taking another sideways bite of his leaking shwarma.

"Tradition about us Coonasses eating anything." Willy amplified his answer by putting on his most serious expression and slowly nodding.

"Oh yeah, of course. Don't know what I was thinking about." Kirk looked to Michelle and winked.

"Michelle?"

"What, Willy?" She managed to mumble through a mouth full of food.

"If Tarzan and Jane was Coonasses, do you know what that would make Cheetah?"

"Wait a minute, Willy, just wait a minute." She raised a flat palm stop sign. "Kirk, do you know what a Coonass is? I know it's got to be a slur but Willy says it isn't."

"It's not!" Willy interrupted. "How it can be a racial slur? We part every race there is, so which one is getting slurred?"

Kirk was now grinning broadly. He answered her. "I've heard it all my life; he's right. More of a term of endearment, in the Deep South, anyway."

"Well I never heard it before, not until I met this nut…"

"Please, I prefer Coonass." He butted in again.

"Okay, I give up. Go on, Willy. If Tarzan and Jane were "raccoon asses" what would that make Cheetah?"

"Okay, I tell you what that would make Cheetah." He looked deep into her eyes. "It would make him 'bout two gallons of gumbo and a nice, big crock of sauce piquant."

Michelle and Kirk chuckled, in spite of themselves.

"Raccoon asses! Gawd-uh-mighty, am I'm never going to teach her the language.

"Now," said Kirk, "back to what you were saying, about getting things through Customs…"

"Right, if she buys anything from this shop and has the receipts, she won't have any problem getting them out of Jordan or into Israel. What you never want to do over there is buy anything like coins or artifacts from somebody on the street, especially near one of the archaeological sites. If you get caught it could take a week and a few hundred dollars to get out of that mess. As long as you got a signed receipt with the shop name on it, I believe you could get out of Jordan with the cornerstone from Zeus' temple."

Willy raised his bottle of Gold Star and took a big slug of the cool, thick beer.

"Well, it would be just my luck to think I was getting a really great deal only to get back here and find out I just bought a bunch of fakes not worth a dime apiece. How can I tell if they're real or not?" asked Michelle.

"You said Nina was going with you? She'll know in a glance. Either way though, real or fake, I expect Mister Shihadeh will catch hell if you take Nina in the shop with you."

"Who?" Michelle and Kirk asked.

"Shihadeh," Willy repeated. "The shop owner's name…here on the card, I just read it out."

"Oh! Yes you did," Michelle said. "But why do you say he's going to catch hell from Nina either way?"

"Cause if they're fake, she'll cuss him out for a crook but if they're real… You know how she feels about private collections of antiquities, don't you? She thinks dealers and collectors are the scum of the earth. She doesn't think much of us contract diggers either, come to think about it."

"I don't know if it holds true over here, with the Biblical stuff, but in the States some of the finest museum collections of North American Pre-Columbian artifacts were donated by private collectors. I'm sure most of it was surface material collected from plowed fields and creek banks, not artifacts from excavation sites."

"Well amigos, I'll tell you one thing. If I find something in some shop with a bargain price on it and I can buy it and make some money, guess what? I have to scrimp and save all year to come over here; three thousand dollars is a lot of money to a teacher."

"I'm sure it is," said Kirk. "And no one should fault you for making a few thousand, either."

"While we're on the subject," said Michelle. She paused to take a sip of Diet Coke before continuing. "Have either of you been reading the current debate over exactly what we're talking about, buying and selling artifacts?"

Willy answered. "I think I might know what you're referring to, but go ahead."

"No, I haven't read anything about it," said Kirk.

"The first I heard of this was in an op-ed piece or an article in BAR magazine.

Apparently, there are a growing number of professionals who are much in favor of museums and universities getting actively involved, selling artifacts."

"Really?" Kirk was surprised.

"Yes." she said. "Some heavy-weight archaeologists have put together a strong argument for the idea, too. Their concern is that their basements and storage rooms are bursting at the seams with tons of artifacts doing little more than collecting dust. They've already been analyzed, catalogued and there are dozens of pieces just alike.

"They argue that properly controlled sales of this surplus could fund every dig and publication project that's on hold for lack of money. A sold artifact would be accompanied by a certificate of authenticity and its history which would detail the date, excavation and location of the find. They insist these controlled sales would literally choke out the black market in antiquities. There would be no incentive to steal or plunder sites. Thousands of square feet of lab and storage space could be freed up for better use, too."

"Sounds like a good idea," said Kirk. "Who's going to buy contraband or from some junk shop when you could buy a genuine piece certified by Hebrew University?"

"One big problem, though," Willy added. "Too damn logical; it'll never fly for the same reason they'll never decriminalize pot or do away with dry counties in Alabama. Makes too much sense— and it makes you wonder who has the most to lose when a logical solution never gets tried."

"Dry counties?" Michelle looked puzzled.

"Counties where it's illegal to sell liquor," Kirk explained.

"There're still quite a few in the deep South." Kirk saw her look of disbelief. "Really, I'm not kidding."

"I thought all that ended in the thirties," she said.

"Not down there," said Kirk. "Every few years it comes to a vote. Talk about politics making strange bedfellows… Some of the most unholy alliances you can imagine during a liquor referendum. A good old Southern liquor fight will line up every moon-shiner, bootlegger and liquor store owner from the next county with every bible beating snake church preacher and reformed drunk from miles around. And on the other side you'll have business owners, tourist industry, Sunday morning golfers, clandestine deacons, the usual drunks and, of course, the Episcopal vestry. Till the day after the election, they're just two big happy families. The most damned ridiculous—but amusing—few weeks you'll ever experience." Kirk concluded.

"You have got to be kidding." Michelle's voice expressed her astonishment.

"No, he's not," said Willy.

"Unfortunately, I'm not kidding. T-total temperance is the essence of fundamental Southern Christianity. When I was a kid, one of my friend's father bought a restaurant that had a beer license… Oh yeah, I should mention that you can buy beer in most dry counties, no matter that beer's the most abused of all alcohol. Anyway, my buddy's dad bought a barbeque place that had a beer license. Within a week or two a delegation of the brothers go to him and ask him to quit selling beer. When he refused he was asked to move his letter from the church.

"Always wondered what would have happened if he had refused to leave. Guess there would have been something like a Protestant excommunication. But… it's a crazy world anywhere you look, I guess."

"It must be like walking a tight-wire, trying to live in a place like that." Michelle's expression revealed that she couldn't quite comprehend such a social system.

"Yeah, it was," admitted Kirk. "But Charleston's far enough removed from all that. And before you start feeling geographically superior, don't forget about your Charlie Manson, Jim Jones and… Wasn't that other nut named Marshall Applewhite? But, you're right, it is hard to live in a place where the percentage of dogmatic idiots is high enough to have political control."

"How the heck did we get off on this stuff again?" Michelle complained.

"We're not off track," said Kirk. "Just more examples of power, greed and hidden agendas being the usual motivators.

"That reminds me," said Willy, "either of you read Ayn Rand's The Virtue of Selfishness? It's not her best known but it's my favorite."

"I haven't," Michelle answered

"Neither have I," said Kirk. "Why?"

"She builds the case that humans are incapable of pure altruism; we are motivated by either fear of suffering or the expectation of reward. Even though there are numerous noble rewards such as peace, love, happiness, joy, satisfaction and so forth, they are personal rewards, nonetheless. Simply put, anytime someone thinks he is doing something out of the goodness of his heart, he is either attempting to deceive or is deceived himself. The most we can do is recognize that we always work for ourselves.

"I remember hearing Mother Teresa tell Barbara Walters that what people didn't understand was that she did what she did for herself. The benefit others received was simply the byproduct. Exactly what Ayn Rand was saying."

"Willy, you amaze me! Does your mind ever rest?"

"I know what you really mean, you sly she-fox. You mean, how can anything that make any sense come out of such a dumb looking package?"

"No I do not. I..."

"Don't you bat those big blue eyes at me like you don't have any idea what I'm talking about."

"Willy!" She was at a loss for words. "Kirk, help me, tell him I think he's wonderful... and beautiful, too."

"You're not getting me into this," Kirk chuckled. "I haven't known either one of you for twenty-four hours yet. But from the way you fuss, I gather that you really love each other and I'm not about to get into some domestic dispute."

"Love! Well, maybe just a little bit." Willy smiled and winked at her.

"Well, I never would have known, the way you pick on me," Michelle said. Then, noticeably more serious, she looked back at Kirk and asked, "You know why I love Willy?"

"No, I can't imagine." Kirk teased. "But by all means tell me because he's dying to know." Kirk pointed with a nod in Willy's direction.

"Because he's real. He reminds me of what I've always thought my dad was probably like." Michelle explained her thoughts with explicit feeling. "I was never lucky enough to know him but I know he was good man."

Michelle pulled out her gum, unwrapped a stick and popped it into her mouth before she continued. She offered the gum pack to Kirk and Willy; both said no, thanks.

"Willy, you owe me one for pulling that out of her."

"Yeah, I guess I do," said Willy. "I've been sitting here too long; my butt's asleep. I'm going to walk around a while before we head back."

"Before I forget, where's that grocery store near here? I want to pick up a few things."

"I'll show him," said Michelle. "Let's try the little market here first; if there's something you can't find, we can walk over to the supermarket."

"You two go ahead," said Willy. "I think I'm going to walk back a ways and enjoy the sights, now that it's cooled off some. Don't wait on me; I'll catch the bus at one of the other stops."

"You sure?" Kirk asked.

"I'm sure. Michelle knows, I've got to have my quiet time," he explained. "I'll see you when you get back."

Willy started off down the long corridor which exited on the street opposite the bus station entrance. Kirk rose and stretched. Before she stood, Michelle held out her hand toward Kirk.

"What's this?" He squinted at her closed fist .

"Take it and see," she answered. He held out his hand, palm up, to accept the surprise. "Another for your collection," she said, dropping another one of the little foil origami birds into his hand.

"Well, thank you very much. I'll soon have enough to decorate my bonsai Christmas tree."

The couple headed down to the small market. Within a few un-hurried minutes Kirk had a bag full of snack food: cookies, Spanish sardines, nuts and the dried fruit Father Casey said he liked. And he bought a surprise gift for the mystical old priest, a bottle of the best wine in the store, Carmel Cabernet Sauvignon Special Reserve. Michelle vouched for it, said it could hold its own with many of the Napa Cabernets. She was sure he would be thrilled with it.

They walked on through the mall and out into the park by the bank and post office. On a bench farther from the noisy walkways than the others, they lingered to watch doves dipping and flapping in a fountain pool. Alone they talked, each becoming more wary of their conversation and the infinity of their shared interests. For each, their own rising sensations and not the other's sensuality put them on guard. Nonetheless, the longer they sat and talked, the more each confided that their presence in this far away land was kind of last-ditch pilgrimage to salvage their own off-track and aimlessly meandering spirits. Neither was yet comfortable enough to admit it, but both Kirk and Michelle began to suspect that the same numina that had called them to the dig had brought them together today.

"How old are you, Kirk?" Michelle asked bluntly after a short lull in their causerie.

"Fifty-one."

She waited; he said nothing else but sat peacefully watching the doves bathe. She opened the door. "Aren't you curious to know how old I am?"

"Yes," he admitted

"You would never have asked, would you?"

"No, at least not anytime soon."

"Well, you won't have to. I'm thirty-eight. I know, you thought I was younger. I hear it all the time."

"Yeah, I did. I would have guessed twenty-seven or twenty-eight but that's a compliment isn't it?"

"I suppose so, but looking much younger than you are can be quite an affliction to a teacher. It's not much of a problem any more but for the first year or two, when I taught high school, it was."

"I bet you did look like an easy mark fresh out of college and in front of a high school class."

"I'm sure I did, must have sounded like it, too. Twenty-four years old. I was going to change the world. But... I'm the one who got changed. Got a real education, too." The memories stung; it was unmistakable in her tone of voice and squinted eyes.

"Tell me what you mean," He sensed her need to talk.

Her eyes searched his face to gauge his sincerity. Satisfied that he was honestly interested, she went on.

"Ever hear the one-liner: a conservative is just a liberal who's been mugged? That about sums it up. I was one of the enlightened few who knew – no question about it – that with enough love and genuine concern and acceptance, I could be the little white chick version of Jaime Escalante. So...against the advice—better judgment, I think they said—of the administration, I chose one of the worst schools in the district. It was a worthy challenge or so I thought.

"Well... after a couple of sets of slashed tires, a stolen hand bag with my driver's license and all my credit cards and a sexual assault with a butterfly knife at my throat..." In ear-ringing silence she numbly gazed off into forever.

Kirk knew her blankness all too well. The grunts in Vietnam called it a thousand yard stare. He knew that to say a word before she did would be to trivialize the gravity of her experience. He would sit there with her, in silence, in empathy, for as damn long as she chose to remain quiet. After a few long minutes, she felt his reticent compassion and she considered it an exquisite gift. And she felt safe and assured with him in the stillness. She cherished his mute attendance, more consoling and cathartic than any conceivable words.

Presently, Michelle turned to Kirk and asked. "You know what hurt the worst of all?" She paused before continuing. "It was the reaction of those I expected to support and defend me the most. My principal, the other teachers, even the damned police, most of them didn't come out and say it, they just gave me that look; what did you expect coming down here in the hood. They acted like all this was just paying my dues, nothing out of the ordinary down here. I could learn to live with it or I could get my preppy little white ass back out to the burbs where it belonged. Remember what you and Willy were saying about kids doing what they are expected to do?"

"Yeah."

"You're right, the kids do exactly what they are expected to do. Why should anyone in the system give a damn if they learn anything or not, they're just going to drop out, sell crack or make a hubba hoe, anyway. That's the attitude. And if you try to make a difference we gonna laugh like hell when you get robbed, raped or shot cause we expected it but you were too damn dumb to.

"Know what, Kirk?"

"What?"

"Ever hear the saying misery loves company?"

"Sure," he answered.

"Not as much as failure, indifference and cynicism do. Love company and demand it.

"So...now you know how I wound up teaching Western Civ at College of the Desert. No more changing the world for this kid."

"Are you happy there?" Kirk asked.

She considered the question briefly. "I know I'm safe and respected, and liked. So, I guess I'm happy; I should be, anyway."

"Yes, I agree. You should be happy." Kirk asserted. "But because you deserve it, not because of your situation. Sounds to me like you tried to do what you thought was right. You did your best; you got your nose rubbed in your good works. And you were even made to feel like a fool because you cared. So you left to go where you would be allowed to teach, to encourage and to make a difference. My God, Michelle, what choice did you have?"

Now she peered down into the depths of the earth. She responded with only a shrug of her shoulders. Moments later she sat up and turned to Kirk with a big smile. "Let's walk over to the post office."

"Why?" Kirk seemed perplexed by the sudden transition.

"You haven't had a chance to see this, but the post offices here have souvenir packages of stamps, even little albums. They make great gifts for kids," she said. "And you can cash traveler's cheques with no commission charge – which means they only abuse you with the exchange rate."

They left the bench and walked slowly toward the post office. Their conversation turned light and cheerful. For no obvious reason, Kirk was reminded of what Father Casey had hit him with just a few hours earlier. He and others were drawn to this place for the mysterious purposes he couldn't predict. He felt that Michelle was here for the same reason, whatever it was. He pondered the various possibilities to himself, all but oblivious to whatever Michelle was telling him about just now. And in spite of her relaxed words, Michelle was baffled. Why had she opened her soul to a man she barely knew, no matter how strongly she felt drawn to him?

8

MOSHE BENJAMIN Turned the Eldan rental van south onto the main road. Route 90 was the longest highway in Israel, stretching the length of the country. From Metula on the Lebanese border in the north, it runs 500 kilometers to the Taba border crossing, eleven miles south of Eilat. The modern highway traces the first great passage known to mankind. Through the Jordan Valley stretch of the great Syro-African rift, Homo habalis left the African continent to inhabit the globe.

Tel Kefar, Kibbutz Massebot and the town of Beit Shean all lay within a five kilometer radius, less than seventy kilometers north of Jericho and just under a hundred from Jerusalem. All were on Route 90.

For years, Moshe and one eternal PhD candidate maintained a debate with the perennial team over the best route between Jerusalem and the Galilee. The team insisted that the straight, well maintained Highway 90 and Route 1 up to Jerusalem was faster and safer. Moshe and Bob refused to give an inch. Tenaciously adamant, they maintained that a meandering maze of regional roads which diverged from Highway 90 at the Mehola Junction saved at least fifteen minutes.

In reality, it was probably a toss-up. Time might be saved by avoiding the Jericho bypass and an endless line of torpid ten-wheel trucks towing eight-wheel trailers up the steep, continuous Route 1 incline. But the advantage was usually offset by loose gravel, rock slides and Bedouin livestock roadblocks on the back roads – unless you drove like Moshe or Bob. Moshe's driving could make a fighter pilot vomit.

Bob Collins had grown up driving the freeways and dirt-biking the unpaved mountain roads of southern California. Even he loathed having to ride with Moshe at the wheel. He swore that if the rental agencies knew Moshe was to be one of the drivers, there would be "no vehicles available" for the expedition.

There was the time when agency employees had to back an abandoned KIA seven kilometers down a wadi. And in another situation, a rental van, wedged under a concrete beam in a Tel Aviv parking garage, had to be dislodged. Last season an overturned van had to be retrieved from a ravine down the slope of a tel. This year, so far, only a minor problem, a steering wheel had broken off of its spokes in Moshe's vice-grip hands. The wheel looked like a B-25 yoke, which was appropriate; Moshe liked it. Everyone loved Moshe Benjamin, but not enough to ride with him or lend him their car.

This afternoon Moshe was alone on the road to Jerusalem in the van with the bomber yoke steering wheel. Actually, he didn't really care if the narrow, regional roads were rougher and took longer. He revered the open desolation which the mountain roads bisected, especially Regional Road 458 from the Shilo valley to the Rimonim Junction. The isolated route penetrated a blinding, bright, phosphorescent emptiness. Bladeless slopes bore countless horizontal traces chiseled by a thousand generations of flock and herd. The lonely road penetrated an immensity which could be upstaged only by the star-sprayed black infinity of the nighttime desert sky.

Since his youth, Moshe had believed that it was this vastness which first compelled man to recognize and to accept his own pitiful insignificance. Out here it was impossible not to concede the incomprehensible magnitude of a supreme creator. And he believed that the simplicity of this vacuous land beneath a boundless sky, unchanging from season to season, year to year, this aloneness, gave man the intellectual capacity to conceive a wonderful idea: One was more knowable, more intimate, more magnificent and, indeed, more powerful than a multitude. Here, an exhilarating solitude allowed man to hear the voice of the one true God; from here His message would permeate the world via one of the three great monotheistic religions.

"Shemah Israel. Adonai Elanahanu; Adonai Akhad! (Hear Israel. The Lord is God; The Lord is One)." Moshe whispered the words in submission and awe.

Every joint and fastener squeaked or rattled as the white van loped over the narrow road. Moshe found the clamor irritating; out here, noise was sacrilege. And it was why he never turned the radio on when passing through the wilderness.

He peered away off at a cave in the side of a rock face, cliff walls cut by the waters of ten thousand winters racing down the wadi below. He wondered if it had sheltered prophets or if yet unknown scrolls were hidden in its niches. But Moshe was intrigued by every cave he saw. He would like to explore them all, an impossible dream; there were thousands.

In just such a cave, high up on a wall of the wadi Qumran another ancient scroll had been found. That scroll was the reason for Dr. Benjamin's midweek trip from Tel Kefar to Jerusalem. The scroll was one of more than eight hundred known as the Dead Sea scrolls. But this scroll was different from all the rest in substance and content. The scroll was of pure copper and the message was an indecipherable code, an enigma—as far as Moshe knew, it was still an enigma.

The legendary account of the discovery and Israel's procurement of the Dead Sea scrolls seemed prophetic. Nonetheless, the account was verifiable. The tale had become as well known as most Bible stories.

A Ta'amireh Bedouin shepherd boy was searching for a lost sheep. He slung a stone into a cave and heard the distinct sound of shattering pottery. After free climbing the rock face and crawling into the cave, he found – instead of the lost sheep – the first of the Dead Sea scrolls.

Less well known was that this was only the first of eleven caves that would be discovered within sight of the ruins of ancient Qumran. The Essene commune had existed on the adjacent plateau. This first cave concealed only seven of the more than eight hundred scrolls that had been found, to date.

Beneath two meters of bat guano and the dust of two millennia, on the floor of cave four, nearly 16,000 fragments of over 500 of the scrolls were found and tediously extracted. It would take ten years to sort and serialize the fragments and even as Moshe drove on toward Jerusalem, over 400 of the scrolls remained secret and unpublished.

In March of 1947 when the Bedouin shepherds discovered the first cave, they were unaware of what they had found. They carried the seven scrolls to Bethlehem where they were all sold, or traded

96   J I M   L E V E R

for staples, to the proprietor of a shoe shop, presumably because they were made of leather.

The shoe shop owner, an Arab named Kando, was an antiquity collector and dealer who ran his hobby business from the back of his small shop. Kando had no idea what the ancient manuscripts were, but he did know that they were, without doubt, more valuable than shoe leather.

He began making contacts and by late summer of 1947, they had been examined by several experts including Professor E.L. Sukenik and scholars at the American School of Oriental Research. Sukenik was the father of Israel's most famous soldier-scholar, Yigael Yadin. There were the usual debates about authenticity, authorship and age of the scrolls but most of the skeptics were silenced by American archaeologist Dr William F. Albright. After examining photographs of portions of the scrolls, he went on record saying he recognized the handwriting as authentic and approximately two thousand years old.

Armed with Albright's recognition, Professor Sukenik urgently sought to raise funds to buy the scrolls for Hebrew University. By late fall political tensions were explosive. Jerusalem was under siege by Palestinian and Arab forces. Sensing that the window of opportunity was about to be slammed shut, the professor mortgaged his own home to supplement the deficient fund. Hopefully he would have an adequate offer for the priceless scriptures. Against dire warnings, Dr. Sukenik applied for and received a pass to cross into the Arab side of Jerusalem and to proceed on to Bethlehem. He set out on the perilous expedition into the Arab town where he negotiated for the treasures.

Late that same day he was on a return bus to Jerusalem with three of the scrolls secreted, literally, in plain brown wrapping paper. The three were over a thousand years older than any known to exist at that time. One of the three was a complete book of Isaiah, the prophet who foretold the destruction of the Israel of old. Isaiah was also the one who prophesied a glorious, messianic age to come. This was the afternoon of 28 November 1947; in less than twenty four hours the United Nations would pass General Assembly Resolution 181 for the partition of Palestine.

As his memory replayed the wonderful story, Moshe thought of his old friend, Khalil Iskander Shahin. Known to his friends as Kando, he was the cobbler to whom the Ta'amireh had sold the scrolls. Before his death, he had become quite a local celebrity. He closed the shoe shop in Bethlehem, moved his antiquities business to Jerusalem and ran it from a shop inside the lobby of the St. George's Hotel on Amar ben Ala' as Street. The shop was less than a block from the Albright Institute.

How long had Kando been dead? Moshe tried to remember. Must be over ten years now, he thought. Moshe smiled widely as he remembered the many tourists who thought they had just met the grandest damned liar in all Israel after hearing Kando tell the story of buying the scrolls. Most never had the slightest idea that they really were hearing a first-person account of a remarkable event.

Several years later, the remaining four of the original seven scrolls were finally bought from an Assyrian cleric. For reasons none too clear, the clergyman, known as the Metropolitan Samuel, brought the scrolls to New York to try to sell them. Apparently, they were not as easy to sell as he had thought so he placed a classified ad in the Wall Street Journal offering them for sale. Yet again, by incredible coincidence, Dr. Yagael Yadin just happened to be in New York when the ad appeared. After locating someone competent to both ensure the authenticity of the documents and to act as a front for the Israelis, the other four scrolls were purchased for $250,000. They were immediately returned to Jerusalem.

Moshe had always been skeptical of this seemingly prodigious acquisition. He thought that a deal had probably been struck before the Metropolitan ever left for New York. He suspected the entire scenario had been an elaborate plan to enable the Assyrian to sell the scrolls to the Jews without having to fear reprisal from the Arab world. Moshe had served under Yadin. He knew him in later years as friend and colleague and it just seemed to fit perfectly, exactly the kind of deal a Haganah commander would have put together. But whoever pulled it off was a mastermind. One of Israel's greatest treasures had been purchased for a trivial sum.

Moshe downshifted the Mitsubishi diesel and braked hard as the secondary road dead-ended into Highway 60. He checked his watch, 3:35. The time never varied by more than a few minutes. Less than ten kilometers to go, there was plenty of time to run by the apartment and freshen up before meeting Thompson at the Albright. He was curious as to who else could be there.

He turned south and shifted through the gears accelerating into the flow of traffic. He remembered that not many years ago this intersection was almost as isolated as Rimonim junction, 15 kilometers back. Now the traffic was always heavy. From out here, new apartment compounds – too many to count – lined the highway all the way into Jerusalem. Less than half a kilometer below the intersection on a hillside to the east Moshe noted the construction progress of a new complex still in the site prep phase. On the barren slopes of these same hills, nearly forty years earlier, Jewish school kids had planted the trees that were now being felled. But fall the trees must as multitudes of the remnant continued to flood in from the Diaspora. No longer did Moshe doubt the demographer's projections; within a decade, Israel would be the most densely populated nation on earth.

Moshe approached his intersection. He darted left into a gap between two cars in the left turn lane as horns behind blasted. But horns always blared in Israeli traffic. He gazed at the street sign wondering how in the hell anyone ever found an address in Jerusalem. The street signs were large and in three languages, but the name of a single street often changed a dozen times in less than two or three kilometers. And the name of the same stretch may have been changed several times over the past few years, even the major connectors. He was turning left at an intersection where there was a different street name on each corner. He was on Derekh Shu' Afat, waiting to turn left onto Ma' ale Adumim. Across the intersection began, or ended, Derekh Ha Shalom and to his right was a large parkway named in honor of his old friend, Yiga'el Yadin. There had been a standing joke in the army; if any invading force attempted to take Jerusalem in a coordinated attack they had better do it with a commando team of old, local sherut drivers.

The light changed; Moshe turned east. The sidewalks were crowded with roughly equal numbers of Hasidim and nonobservant. Tight clusters of each waited at every bus stop. The orthodox, as always, were bundled in their black felts, flannels, furs and wools. They always seemed oblivious to the summer afternoon temperatures never appearing to be more uncomfortable than the miscreants clad in tees, khakis and Tevas. And today was hot, even for Jerusalem.

Like most Jews, Moshe had a love-hate relationship with the ultra-orthodox. He accepted that it was their butt-headed stubbornness, over the millennia, to which Judaism owed its tenure if not its very survival. Nonetheless, Moshe feared this same dogmatic inflexibility now threatened the very fabric of Israel. A distinct minority, they connived to force-feed their agenda of fundamentalist statutes to the nation.

With the solidarity of old-time Southern U.S. senators, the Orthodox wielded inordinate power as the swing vote in the Knesset. They were a force to be reckoned with in nearly every government agency including the Israel Antiquities Authority. And they were a threat to almost every archaeological and construction project in the country. Uncovering of any trace of human bone could jeopardize the continuation of the most important construction work or promising dig if one of the Halakah patrols happened along at the wrong time.

What began in the early years of statehood as fervent differences of opinion over the pertinence of Jewish law in a modern society had deteriorated into a holy feud. Halakah and theocracy on the one side, Western democracy and individual freedom were on the other. The rift had grown so wide Moshe Benjamin feared that civil war was as great a threat to the young nation as that posed by hostile Arab governments.

With fanatics, compromise equals apostasy unless concession is for the benefit of one's own agenda. So, the discovery of any human bones, Christian, Islamic or even prehistoric was just cause to suspend construction of highways and hospitals. On the other hand, large numbers of tombs with Jewish ossuaries could be ignored if they stood in the way of a Haredi housing project or planned community.

And Moshe was one of the moderates who also accepted that much Israeli-Arab and Palestinian hostility had been earned by the ultra-orthodox. More often than not, they incited Arab violence by acts of callous disregard or deliberate provocation. But you had to admit they had balls – Moshe smiled as he pondered his favorite American expression.

Every Friday evening, on their way home after Shabbat prayers at the western wall, more than a few refreshed orthodox zealots would walk an unnecessary detour. Week after week their route through the Moslem Quarter and out the Damascus Gate provoked the predictable reaction. And week after week the blissful entourage marched on, blissfully indifferent to the salvos of garbage and barrage of bottles.

Moshe signaled a right turn and entered the parking area of a cut-faced sandstone apartment complex on French Hill. His was one of the larger ground-floor units in the meticulously landscaped compound. Every time he entered these grounds the garden's ambience lifted his spirits. He was fortunate to live here; there was a long waiting list that took years to ascend.

He pulled up in front of one of the vacant spaces on the far side of the parking area and backed in as close as he could to the stone wall which enclosed the Gan Zeytim apartments. The spaces farthest from the buildings were usually empty. Moshe liked to park here because he could back in close to the wall. That way the back doors or trunk of a vehicle were almost impossible to break into. Besides, he loved the short walk through the plantation to his front door. It took only a minute or two but was always enough to begin dissolving the usual stresses.

Few places in Jerusalem were as beautifully maintained or manicured. Willowy cedars seemed to support the dense canopy of ficus which shaded the ground. The lawn was contained by a meandering border of mulch beds and freeform walkways. The sunny openings were spectacles of frosty green rosemary beneath fiery bracts of bougainvillea.

Professor Benjamin stepped into his entrance alcove. He turned to take a long, affectionate gaze at the gardens. The magnetic tumblers in a state-of-the-art German entry lock yielded imperceptibly as Moshe turned the key and pushed open the heavy solid-stave oak door. After a reflexive glance at the jamb, he pressed his fingers to lips to mezuzah as he entered the foyer. He sat down on a built-in bench seat and removed his boots and socks. A cool, fresh smell, the clean white ceilings and walls and the cold polished marble floor tile under his burning feet all silently welcomed him home. I could sit here for hours, he thought. Not running late but there's no time to waste. He wondered where Ruth was. She did say something about driving over to Rehovot to see her mother, he remembered.

After a few delicious moments Moshe forced himself up. Clutching his dirty socks, he walked back to the master bath. He removed the rest of his clothes and dropped them in a hamper in a corner of the bathroom. He pulled the shower curtain from wall to wall along the quarter circle stainless rod which hung from ceiling supports. He turned on the water and stepped under the downpour. Shower stalls were almost unknown in the Middle East. Instead, bathroom floors were sloped from the walls to a drain beneath the shower head. And water-wasting tubs could only be found in the most extravagant Western hotels.

Moshe took a bar from the soap shelf and lathered himself. American Ivory soap was his favorite; it was shampoo, shaving lather and bathing soap. He had loved it since he was a boy when it came in the Hanukkah gift packages to En Gev from the rich Jews in America. It smelled the way soap should smell, no lilacs, no pine, no spices, no medicine, just clean. He rinsed, tightened off the mixing valves, and dried himself.

Between the lavatory and toilet was a floor squeegee to herd tenacious puddles to the drain. But after the leisurely shower he would make up for time lost by ignoring it. Ruth's most frequent complaint was that he usually ignored it. He finished his grooming on a sopping floor, practically tripping over the invisible squeegee.

Moshe's thoughts raced as he dressed by rote, oblivious to the clash of color and cloth. He couldn't imagine what could have old Thompson so stirred up that he would beg his archrival to come in from the field during the dig. Moshe guessed that he must have something Thompson really needed. Whatever, he knew he'd know soon enough.

In spite of the traffic it was a short, quick ride to the Albright Center. Parking on the street was all but impossible but within the iron and stone fenced compound there was always room for authorized or recognized vehicles. Professor Benjamin was no stranger at the Albright. He turned into the property and drove around behind the main building. He parked in front of one of the garages now used to shelter equipment and supplies rather than motor vehicles. He switched off the van but made no effort to open the door and exit. In relative silence he sat and took in the magnificence of the old building. He barely noticed the muffled horn blasts and filtered clamor from the city outside. He was over ten minutes early. For some reason he didn't want to appear overly anxious to hear whatever it was that Thompson had to say – or ask.

Several people were sitting around the upper courtyard behind the main building center but he didn't see Thompson or anyone he knew. One couple looked familiar, resident fellows of the center he thought. It was just as well; he was perfectly content to sit there and wait for the right moment to make his presence known.

Niles Thompson's talent in the art of international academic politics was only exceeded by his skill as a self-promoter. Bob Collins called him the Doctor Ruth of archaeology. No way the greatest authority or most skilled practitioner, but he was sure as hell the most self-proclaimed and self-aggrandizing expert in the field. He was a master at garnering acclaim for scholarly work completed on foundations laid by others. He expected total credit for discoveries he was led to by trusting peers.

Moshe knew that Thompson must need him badly. But for what, he hadn't the slightest. He was as curious as he was suspicious and on guard and he was going to play this hand for all it was worth. As soon as he knew what in hell the game was, he would. For the moment he would sit awhile longer and continue to calculate just what Professor Thompson may have up his baggy sleeves.

9

FTERNOON TEA At the W. F. Albright Institute for
Archaeological Research was one of life's little pleasures
that Moshe Benjamin most relished. In the backyard of
"The Albright" it was an absolute delight to relax and soak up the
blast of color from myriad desert and tropical flora. The plantings
flourished over the grounds and framed the elevated courtyard of
the old three story building. The garden's always-open smorgasbord
of insects, seeds and nectar summoned dozens of the more than
four hundred species of birds, indigenous and migrants, en route
between Africa, Europe and Asia.

At one time or another, practically every great name in Near
Eastern and biblical archaeology had lounged around one of the
patio tables. There, with a proper cup of tea, scones, strawberry
preserves and clotted cream, they amicably debated the significance
of some recently unearthed artifact or the accuracy of a recent publication. Frequently, it was here, too, that news of a wonderful new
discovery or revelation was first shared with peers and friends. And
so it would be today.

After his shower, shave and change into fresh clothes, Moshe
had driven from French Hill on into downtown Jerusalem with no
delays, a pleasant surprise considering the usual tangle of midweek
afternoon traffic. Just before his turn off Nablus Road onto Salah ed
Din, he passed the old Ottoman Pasha's palace, now the American
Colony Hotel, one of the city's finest. A couple of hundred feet past
the fork to the left he arrived at The Albright.

Moshe hugged the center line as close as he could without nos-
ing into oncoming traffic. The left turn across the always bustling
sidewalk and through a precariously narrow gateway was the final

obstacle. Then, incredibly, an Arab taxi creeping along in the on-coming lane braked to a stop and flippantly, without eye contact, motioned for Moshe to cross and enter the compound. Moshe nodded to the cab driver for the unexpected courtesy as he turned and beeped his way across the sidewalk and through the stacked stone gate. He ignored the irritated stares of the momentarily inconvenienced pedestrians. He followed the driveway to the back and took the only space available, a spot directly in front of one of four garage doors with "DO NOT BLOCK" in the usual three languages painted on each. One of the center's many insider secrets was that the overhead garage doors had not been opened in years. The buildings were now used for storage but "do not block" was more effective than a reserved or staff-only parking sign.

Moshe pulled on the van's door handle two or three times before he remembered that the inside one didn't work. He reached out, pulled up the lift plate and pushed the open the door. The metal creaked and popped protesting the abrasive clog of dust and want of grease.

As soon as he stepped out of the old truck his eyes gravitated toward two newly planted beds of lantana which flanked the steps leading up to the courtyard. He immediately walked over. But it was not the delicate filigree of blues, pinks and gold which caught the old archaeologist's attention; it was the freshly turned and watered earth. His trained eyes searched for a lonely tessera or ostracon or, perhaps, even a long lost coin. The Albright was situated scarcely more than an arrow's flight north of the walls of the Old City and one could only imagine all that might have transpired on this exact site. It had happened many times before; Dr. Benjamin's practiced perspicacity found interesting relics in the ordinary spots ignored by generations of others. But no such luck today.

"Hey, old man, you're wasting your time, I already checked it out." The all too familiar voice boomed down from the elevated courtyard of the main building.

Moshe straightened up peering through the shafts of sunlight attempting to focus on the intrusive form in the cool shadows on the terrace above.

"Thompson! You loud-mouth momser, I should have known. How long you been here?"

"Don't worry, you're not late. I came over a couple of hours ago to try to find some old prelim site reports. Come on up and we'll have a cup of Rida's Ti Kuan Yin."

Niles Thompson, Ph.D., welcoming his longtime rival with an aberrantly cordial air was even more evidence, to Moshe, that he needed his assistance desperately. His curiosity was as intense as Thompson's new persona was amusing. So, for the moment, he would play the part of the convivial colleague, at least until he knew Thompson's true agenda.

"Yes, I've been looking forward to a cup of Rida's tea since I got your invitation to meet here," said Moshe.

Thompson extended his hand in characteristic American fashion. When Moshe took it, Thompson clasped it between both of his in the affected manner of a gushy life insurance salesman. Still gripping with his right, he cupped his other hand behind Moshe's triceps as if assisting a feeble convalescent. He led Moshe to a vacant table shaded by one of two huge podocarpus which flanked the main porte-cochere.

When they were seated Rida Dijani, the concierge of the Albright, appeared with a stainless samovar of piping hot tea. He poured the exotic, aromatic liquid into traditional clear glasses which he then garnished with fresh, green sprigs of nahnah (mint).

Ti Kuan Yin, the most prized of the Oolongs, once known only to emperors and sultans, was reserved for the center's most venerable guests. However, Bob Collins and a few other graduate fellows—those with a taste for the best in tea, single malt, or grande reserve—had discovered that a well-timed pack of American cigarettes worked wonders with Rida.

"I appreciate your taking the trouble to meet me here, Moshe." Thompson continued with the syrupy charm. "I really do."

Moshe avoided eye contact. Pensively, he stared deep into the table top. He raised the glass to his lips and quietly blew steam from the surface before he wisped in a sip of the scalding tea. He set it back down, tonged in another sugar cube and stirred it in with slow strokes. Then he looked up with his characteristic, dissecting stare.

"Niles, I learned a new expression from my American students this summer, 'sucking up'. I like it better than the old 'ass kissing'. So, now I am asking myself, why would my old nemesis, the esteemed Dr. Niles Thompson, with his ego that would make Saddam Hussein's seem like Gandhi's, be sucking up (it came out, sooking oop) to me? Could it be that I am in a unique position to do him some favor... or could I have something that he needs so badly?"

Moshe's stare morphed into an amused smile. Thompson, sheepishly grinning, dropped his head to the side and peered off into the distance. He slowly rubbed his eyebrows between his thumb and finger tips. Then he slid back in his chair and leaned forward with both arms resting on the table top. For the seconds he sat without answering, it was apparent to Moshe that he was gathering his thoughts

Then he picked up his tea glass and held it lightly between the fingers and thumbs of both hands. He looked directly back into Moshe's waiting expression.

"You're right, on both accounts," said Thompson. "I'm completely out of character trying to be courteous or gracious; I'm sure I must appear foolish even trying. You're also right about having something, or at least access to something, I need. That something is Tel Kefar."

Thompson paused to read the first clues of Moshe's reaction. There were none, only the same poker face. Moshe encouraged him to continue.

"I must admit I am surprised," said Moshe. "I thought you rated Kefar way down on your list of important excavations—at least that's what I've been led to believe."

"That's true. Up until quite recently I personally would have ranked probably ten sites as a higher priority than Kefar. But now I'm sure I 'm wrong. This is what I want to discuss with you. And I want to try and work out an agreement with you. You see, a few weeks..."

"An agreement?" Moshe forced in the question.

"Yes, an agreement. Please bear with me and you'll understand shortly,"

Without an utterance Moshe crossed his arms. It was the universal body language that conveyed to Thompson that the success of his sales pitch was in the balance. The next few minutes of his presentation would be decisive. And Thompson knew that Benjamin would never trust his motives unless he could readily explain the necessity of his role in the plan he was trying to sell.

Moshe had good reason to doubt the good faith of any overture from Thompson. He had long been a most malicious critic of

Professor Benjamin's scholarship. He fired off unsolicited, abusive rebuttals to many of Moshe's publications. He challenged the accuracy of Moshe's typing of pottery specimens and disputed the assigned dates in every excavation. The vast majority of the archaeological community sided with Moshe on most major points; nevertheless, Thompson's harassment never ceased. It was as if he had a hatred, or vendetta of unknown origin—unknown to Moshe and his associates.

Thompson had not seen Moshe since they were both at an annual meeting of the American School of Oriental Research in Orlando, Florida, two or three years before. At that meeting he acrimoniously condemned a paper being presented by Dr. Benjamin. Moshe, forced to address Thompson's rude interruption, had immediately eased the tension in the room by responding that yapping little dogs don't chase parked cars. The quick come-back embarrassed and humiliated Thompson, who promptly stormed out of the session.

Later, the main points of Thompson's harangue were discredited, line item at a time, in publications by other respected scholars over the following several months. Thompson had pretty much been quiet and out of sight since then. Now that Niles Thompson, Ph.D. had resurfaced—and with his new sugar coating—he knew that Moshe had to suspect that he was laying the mother of all academic snares. The kinder and gentler Niles Thompson had to convince Moshe that he was not. He had to make the case that he wanted a truce, a new beginning that could lead to the most important accomplishment of a lifetime—both their lifetimes.

"As I was saying," Thompson continued. "A few weeks ago one of my grad students came to me with a remarkable theory involving the copper scroll from cave three."

"Ah, the treasure list!" Moshe injected the eureka-like comment into the conversation.

"Uh...yes." Thompson affirmed with a slightly guarded tone. "If I may ask, how familiar are you with the latest translations and theories about the scroll?"

"Well, let me think," said Moshe. "I remember that Kyle McCarter was working on reediting Malik's work, but I haven't heard anything about it being completed."

"No, it hasn't been completed or, I guess I should say, it has yet to be published," said Thompson.

"Then I only know what Dr. Malik has written about it. I know that John Allegro published an earlier, unofficial report on the scroll. But I don't think his work was very well received, or respected. Am I correct?"

"Perfectly. In fact, Allegro's book got trashed by the critics. One of the reviews may have been the most scathing I've ever read, but that's neither here nor there. So, if you'll bear with me, I'll recap what I believe to be generally accepted about the scroll to date."

"By all means, please do." Moshe consented as he raised the glass of hot tea which was finally cool enough to swig.

"I guess the best place to start is the beginning. In 1952 The École Biblique, ASOR (American School for Oriental Research) and the Jordanian Ministry of Antiquities hired the Ta'amirehs to help them try to find more caves around Qumran where one of their tribesmen had found the two which contained the first of our fabled Dead Sea Scrolls. I'm sure you remember all of this.

"The Bedouin found nine more that contained scrolls or scroll fragments. In the back of cave three, in an obscure crevice, they found the copper scroll in two pieces. First reports indicated there were two scrolls but there was only one, in two pieces. As you would expect, the first, erroneous report of two scrolls gave the conspiracy theorists all the fuel they needed to charge that one of the scrolls was secretly purchased by... hell, I've heard everything from the Israeli Government to the Saudi royal family and even the Mormons!"

"I can believe that." said Moshe.

"It's incredible, seems that for every major event there are a dozen conspiracy theories these days. But in this..."

"Yes it does, Niles. In fact, I have suspected you of being the source of several that targeted me." Moshe was blunt; his stare piercing. Then the stare faded to a relaxed glint. "Why, Niles, your face is red as a baboon's ass. Sorry I interrupted you, please continue."

Niles forced an awkward smile as if to convince Moshe that he thought he was teasing. But he knew that Moshe wasn't teasing and he knew that Moshe was dead on the money. Indeed, it had been Thompson who started rumors about Moshe's professional integrity and conflicts of interest. In the past he had justified his antagonism as opposition to the archaeological "old boy" network rather than a personal attack against the man. But down deep, inside, he knew that it was his own feelings of mediocrity, feelings amplified by the excellence of Moshe's work that fostered his resentment.

Now, after the years of effrontery, Thompson needed the very man he had most resented for so long. He dared to hope that this man, Moshe Benjamin, would realize the importance of what he had to offer. He had to take the risk that this realization alone would persuade Moshe to accept a truce and collaborate on a remarkable new quest. And, above all, he had to trust that Moshe Benjamin was a less vindictive man than he, himself, had ever been.

"Moshe, I should have said this before now. But I apologize for anything in the past that I might have done or said that could have been misinterpreted or misunderstood... And I apologize for Orlando, too. I still sincerely believe that the wrong dates are assigned to several pottery types, but I should have gone about things differently; I admit that. I'm sorry."

As if touched by the apology, Moshe stared into the mahogany liquid in his glass. Actually, he was trying to remember if he had ever heard a more goddamn glibly worded cop-out in his entire life. Even so, for old Niles to have conceded this much... I've got something the son-of-a-bitch wants bad enough to piss on a border fence for, he thought to himself. Now his curiosity was aflame.

"Okay, okay, Niles, I apologize for the interruption. Go on, please."

"Fine...As I was saying, there is only one copper scroll, only one found in the Qumran caves anyway. Shortly after it was recovered, it was taken from Jordan to the University of Manchester. There it was determined that the scroll could not be unrolled so it was sawed into slices and it is the photographs of these slices which have been available for study. The scroll itself is back in Amman."

Finally Thompson took the first sip of his tea.

"Even from the preliminary examination it was obvious that the scroll contained a list of locations – sixty-four to be exact—and the descriptions of a treasure or other objects that are buried or hidden in each location. From the beginning, what made the scroll so unbelievable was the staggering amount of treasure it claims is hidden in so many different locations. We're talking in terms of metric tons of precious metal."

"Correct me if I'm wrong," said Moshe. "But I seem to recall that a great number of these treasure sites are supposed to be in the

Jerusalem area or along the Wadi Kelt and down around Jericho. Am I right?"

"Yes, you are. And the operative phrase is, supposed to be. The large majority fall within a triangle that runs roughly from Jerusalem, down the wadis to Qumran, north to Jericho and then west, up the Wadi Kelt, back to Jerusalem. This, of course, includes the areas you mention. But," Niles paused for emphasis, "now we are focused on a site that is not in this area."

Niles paused further to allow Moshe time to consider his last statement.

"Accepting the authenticity of the scroll," said Moshe. "And I haven't heard of any serious challenge to that. Why do you accept its credibility? I know there are some serious scholars who do not."

"Indeed, and I was among them until Sarah Bergman, the graduate student, broke the code of the Greek letters. Sarah is one of our most brilliant Ph.D. candidates, ever, I think. I tried desperately to get her into the Iron Age with me but her passion is the Hasmonean, Herodian and Roman periods. You do know about the Greek letters?" asked Thompson.

"Only that they are another one of the mysteries. Are you saying that you've discovered their meaning?"

"Yes, that's exactly what I'm saying; Sarah discovered their meaning. Furthermore, as a result of her discovery we have a good general idea where two, possibly three, of the sixty-four sites are located. That's where you and Tel Kefar enter the picture. Sarah is convinced that Kefar contains the key piece of the puzzle."

Thompson searched Moshe's face for a clue to his first impression.

"Are you saying that you think as many as three of the listed locations are on my site?" Moshe's skepticism was apparent. "And am I to..."

"No, that's..."

"And... Even if you, or should I say Sarah, is right, aren't we talking about needles and haystacks?"

"Please, just hear me out." Thompson pleaded.

"Niles, you know how big Kefar is, over 12 hectares, one of the largest unexcavated sites in the Levant. And I sure as hell don't want you and a hundred other Indiana Jones wannabes turning my excavation into some damned idiotic treasure hunt!"

"Are you through? Goddamit, Moshe... Are you through?"

Glaring, Niles rebuked Moshe's implications. His open indignation caught him off guard. Moshe was used to the old snipe-and-run Niles, not this man who stood his ground, face to face and defended his position. It was refreshing and it was this new persona, more than any discovery, theory, or proposition that enticed the old stalwart to continue with the meeting. Moshe was impressed; who's easier to believe in than one who believes in himself, he thought.

Niles noticed that his raised voice had attracted a few oblique stares of curiosity from adjacent tables. He lowered his voice and continued.

"Moshe, you know I'm no treasure hunter. I know I'm not on par with you. I admit that. But I'm no treasure hunter. What I'm bringing to the table is real. It's good science. And I'll stake my future that it'll stand up to the toughest criticism you can muster."

Niles hesitated, obviously searching for the right words.

"Moshe, I well understand why you would be suspicious of any proposal that I come to you with. I really do. But this time, much more than for myself—if you can believe that—I'm asking you to give serious consideration to Sarah's theory. She's already a better scholar than I'll ever be. With any luck, one day she'll be one of the best. Please... I'm asking you; just give her a chance. She deserves that much. She doesn't deserve to suffer because of my past mistakes.

"Even if you can't forgive me – and there's no reason you should; I know that—I'm asking you not to let her association with me or Brigham Young prejudice your opinion against her or her work."

Moshe was amazed with Niles' new-found strength of character. His humility and a concern for someone other than himself almost made the old jack-ass agreeable. He sat steeping in all that Thompson had said and in how he had said it, the changed bent of the man. Could it be possible that old Niles Thompson, Ph.D. had actually mellowed with age and that the old leopard had really rearranged his spots?

Moshe couldn't explain it but his time-tested perceptivity nudged him toward giving Niles the benefit of the doubt, at least with everything he had said and claimed up to now. He had trusted this same intuition – maybe it was a divine sixth sense – before. This was the same sort of feeling that had alerted him to the ambushes on the Golan. And it had also led him to dig where the squares of now famous excavations were staked off.

"Okay, Niles, I'll hear you out, no more interruptions." Moshe slouched back, rested both elbows on the chair arms and laced his fingers. He looked relaxed and at ease for the first time since sitting at the table.

"Tell me what it is that your Miss... Bergman is it? What has she found that has escaped all the others for nearly fifty years?

"Thank you, Moshe." Again Thompson paused to gather his thoughts. "I can give you the essence of what she has discovered. But I want the specifics to come from her. Even if I knew the exact details, I'd rather not divulge the results of her research. I think you understand."

"I do. I'll respect her right to unveil her own work."

"Yes, it is her work. So, as I was saying, essentially, she has discovered what the Greek letters on the scroll mean and exactly why they are there. They are abbreviations or, more precisely, acronyms that represent specific places. They are not a code, per se, but they are the key to locating the legitimate locations listed on the scroll. I'm not trying to be vague, but for obvious reasons, she hasn't even explained to me how these acronyms are used to locate a certain site, or to legitimize it."

"Legitimize?" Moshe asked for further explanation with his expression.

"Yes. She is convinced that the majority of the locations, maybe fifty-five or more, are red herrings. Are you familiar with the term?"

"With the term, I am, but I haven't the slightest idea how it came to mean what it does."

"An interesting bit of trivia. I'll have to share it with you over a couple of cold Carlsbergs one afternoon soon." Niles smiled. "For now, I'll just say that Sarah can make the case for most of the listed locations being bogus – probably to throw off and discourage would-be plunderers. The plan has worked for fifty years, as you just noted."

"True," said Moshe. "Question is, has it worked for two thousand years? Let me ask another question."

"Of course."

"Tell me more about the Greek letters. I remember reading that they appear in the text and that they are probably some kind of code but that's all I know. So, tell me more about them, if you will."

"Okay, here's what I know. A scholar by the name of Al Wolters has shown that the scroll can be diagramed in spread-sheet format with seven columns and sixty-four lines. On each of the sixty-four lines down there is entered information but there is not a data entry in every column of every line. The columns can be labeled with headings something like: (1) designated hiding place (2) additional details (3) dig or measure from here (4) the distance or depth in cubits (5) description of the treasure (6) notes or comments. It's column seven which contains the mysterious Greek letters. An interesting point, not one single line of the sixty-four has entries in all seven columns and only seven of the lines have entries in column seven, two or three Greek letters."

Niles cleared his throat, drank the last inch of tea in his glass and refilled it from the samovar.

"You know," said Moshe, "the thing sounds more like some kind of accountant's ledger than anything else."

"That's how Kyle McCarter and Al Wolters both describe it, an accountant's or bookkeeper's journal. But the way this one is written, it reads like some Mafia bookie's records. I say that jokingly, but that's probably an accurate comparison. Both are written in a manner not readily understood, in case they fall into the wrong hands."

"Yeah, the wrong hands; the Romans, the police and now ours," Moshe remarked.

"Exactly. But neither the Romans nor the police would have to wait two thousand years before trying to break the code. Moshe, that's the most amazing thing about Sarah's theory; she did it. She broke the damn code after two thousand years. At least, I'm sure she's broken it."

"Well… I have to say all of this is fascinating," Moshe admitted. "So tell me, how do I and Tel Kefar fit into all of this? And then, Niles, tell me exactly what it is that you are proposing."

"First of all, I want to stress that no one, to my knowledge, believes that Tel Kefar itself is one of the big treasure sites. I know that Sarah doesn't. What she believes is that Tel Kefar contains the key to identifying the legitimate sites, which is also the key to finding them. So, what I'm asking you to consider is allowing Sarah and me to work under your permit, under your supervision, of course, to attempt to locate this key piece of the puzzle."

Niles hesitated for a moment. Moshe said nothing. Niles continued.

"I also know that the Greek letters are acronyms. They're most likely of Seleucid origin. They're slang names or nicknames for specific places, kind of like our calling Los Angeles LA or the Marines calling Parris Island, PI. Maybe a better example is an airport abbreviation, like TLV for Tel Aviv or GTW for Gatwick at London.

"While doing some completely unrelated research, Sarah noticed that the Macedonians used a lot of abbreviations, contractions and acronyms in their informal writing, like letters to family. On a hunch, she spent the next few days with a collection of these writings on microfiche. She was searching for any acronym that matched any of the seven in the scroll.

"Well, she found three that were obvious referrals to places that are well known, Jerusalem, Jericho and Pella. Their nickname—or airport code, if you will—was the same as one of the Greek acronyms in the copper scroll. Now, three out of seven wasn't bad, but it doesn't get you to first base as far as breaking the code.

"What she noticed next was that there were other identifiable acronyms for places like Tyre, Hazor and Achzib, which do not appear in the scroll, but which were used as reference points to clarify other information in the letters. Then came the break. There was a reference to some ruins, a place named Kochlit. The letter located it as being twenty-five stades south of the acronym nickname for Beth Shean."

"Help me out here, Niles. Isn't twenty-five Greek stades is about… five kilometers?" Moshe asked.

"Yes, very close, and it's about three Roman miles."

"Well, that only seems to fit one place, doesn't it?"

"Yes, only one," said Niles. "The Kochlit in the scroll is Tel Kefar."

"Incredible, but maybe understandable," said Moshe. "Two thousand years ago, when the scroll was written, Kefar had already been in ruins for seven hundred years—unbelievable but true. Neither the Greeks nor the Romans knew it as the Kefar of Egyptian and Assyrian records. This is amazing.

"But for now, here's one of my main concerns. The tel covers a huge area; where do you start? I can't possibly justify sinking a large number of random test probes. Where would you start?"

This time, Moshe's question reflected the enormity of the challenge rather than opposition.

"Moshe, what we're looking for may be a lot easier to locate than we could even dare to hope. Don't I remember you stating during some lecture that it's been your experience that the main, modern-day road which approaches a tel usually leads to precisely where the city gates were placed in the wall?"

"It wasn't a lecture, it was an article in *Biblical Archaeology Review* but, yes, your memory's correct. It's the same principle at work which results in most modern highways following pretty much the same route as an ancient trail or caravan road. The article was based on a survey of numerous sites throughout the Middle East. I had suspected that this was the case but our research confirmed it."

Moshe seemed to take pride in Thompson's recollection of one of his earliest publications. Niles slid his chair back from the table.

"Moshe, before I go any further... I think I told you that we've been over here looking at some records but I don't think I said who was with me. It's Sarah. She's still in the basement looking through some files. Now that we're getting into the details, she can do a much better job explaining her theories than I can. Do you mind if I call her out?"

"No, not at all. I already decided that I want to meet her before reaching any final agreement on any of this."

"Good, good. I'll just be a moment if you'll excuse me to go invite her out."

Niles stood and walked quickly into the Albright. He seemed unconcerned that his tone of voice and lively step revealed his excitement at Moshe's receptiveness. He knew that if anyone could bring the meeting to a successful conclusion, Sarah could. Who else on the planet could have convinced him to swallow twenty years of pride by going to Dr. Moshe Benjamin to beg for his cooperation? If she could make that sale, she could close this one.

Within a couple of minutes Niles and Sarah Bergman emerged from the old building and walked over to the table. Moshe stood awaiting an introduction. Sarah was tall and wiry and she reminded Moshe of Ruth thirty years earlier, when she was a young officer in the IDF. And though Niles was not aware of Moshe's first impression, that Sarah Bergman so resembled the young Ruth, the wife

Moshe adored, he could not have been accompanied by a more effectual advocate.

"Doctor Benjamin, I want you to meet Sarah Bergman."

As soon as they were all seated, Rida appeared from a shaded recess with another glass and sprig of mint on a silver plate serving tray. He raised the samovar from the table and poured the glass barely half full and extended the tray to Sarah. It was the first time she had ever been served by Rida even though she had often enjoyed afternoon tea in the Albright's courtyard. It was also her first taste of Ti KuanYin.

For the next few minutes Moshe and Sarah exchanged the usual questions about home and acquaintances. Niles sat silently, impatiently listening. He couldn't help but marvel at Moshe's down-to-earth and unassuming manner as he talked with the young grad student. Niles had never seen this side of the man; Moshe was charmed. And Sarah navigated her side of the conversation with a savvy beyond her twenty-six years. She judiciously waited for the famous professor to steer the conversation back to the issue at hand, the secret of Tel Kefar.

"So, Sarah, why don't you pick up where Dr. Thompson left off. He was telling me about your theory which places the location of one of the copper scroll sites at Tel Kefar. Sounds like some first-class research and scholarship you've been doing."

"Thank you." Sarah's smile reflected that his compliment pleased her.

"However," said Moshe, "what I'm concerned about is how one would even begin to search for a specific artifact or point of reference within an area so large. So, if you will, please let me know what you have in mind. Are you aware of the size of Tel Kefar?"

"Yes, I am very well aware of its size, Dr. Benjamin. But, at the risk of sounding like a smart-aleck, the size of the tel is irrelevant because of the particular reference to it in the copper scroll."

To Niles, Sarah's self-assurance almost came across as a voice of inexperience but Moshe didn't seem to take it that way. Instead of immediately following up her assertion, she sat quietly awaiting Moshe's next question. When it was apparent that he expected her to continue, she did.

"This is what I mean. The instruction in the scroll is to dig down four cubits at a point under the black stone in its, Kochlit's, opening on the west. I believe the word opening refers to what was a breach in the wall where the city gate had been. Dr. Thompson and I pulled up the Kefar web site. We saw that the field road from Highway 90 leads directly to the western edge of the tel. That fits the description."

Moshe glanced at Thompson. "Now I see why you asked about my theory of modern roads leading up to the position of the ancient gate. Niles and I were discussing this relationship just before you joined us," he explained to Sarah. "Now I think I understand. If I'm following you two, what you've concluded is that if you can locate the city gate of Tel Kefar, you'll know where to dig for one of the treasures listed in the copper scroll."

Moshe's expression projected his fascination with the Sarah Bergman's incredible hypothesis.

"Yes sir, but I should qualify my answer. As far as it goes, you've got it right."

"What do you mean, as far as it goes?" asked Moshe.

"Okay," said Sarah. "Let's assume we find the gate, no unexpected problems, and after it's exposed and cleaned up, there is no black stone. Let's even assume that the street pavers are intact and uninterrupted. Still, no black stone. That doesn't necessarily mean we've got the wrong place or that our search is over because we didn't find the reference point. The black stone could be a reference to a standing stone which, as you know, was always at the city's entrance. This is what was found in the excavations of the city gate at Bethsaida, black basalt massebot. Even if there are no paver stones left in the gateway there's no reason not to continue down in those squares, at least for another four cubits which would be two meters at the most."

Moshe nodded his head. "I agree," he said. "Those stones could have been scavenged or put into secondary usage any time in the last couple of thousand years."

"That's certainly a possibility," said Sarah. "I also want to stress that I see this as a very limited excavation area. Either it's there or it isn't. And I can't imagine our excavation area disturbing any of the work in progress."

Sarah paused to await Moshe's decision. She felt good. She could sense his fascination with the prospect of actually locating one of the mysterious caches. But Sarah was oblivious to the years of discord between the two professors who sat innocuously at the table with her. It was this pattern of friction that Moshe contemplated. He decided to monitor that concern with silent vigilance and he decided to give Sarah Bergman her big chance.

Moshe's mind snapped back from racing through the pitfalls and logistics of expanding the expedition to include the search for Sarah's black stone.

"Well then, I know you want my decision as soon as possible. But... before I make up my mind I would like to know exactly what 'it' is."

"Sir?" Sarah had a puzzled frown.

"It," Moshe smiled. "You said, either it is there or it isn't. What is it? What does the scroll say is buried there?"

"Oh my god," Sarah whined. "I can't believe I left out the most important thing. I was so careful to explain details of the search that I didn't even say what the copper scroll says is there. I can't believe it! I'm so sorry, Doctor Benjamin. I can be so dumb some times."

Moshe chuckled. "Don't worry about it. Remind me to tell you about a similar slip-up I once made. But I was in front of a large group, not at a table with two others. But, yes, I would like to know what it is that we are going to find."

Niles couldn't believe his ears. Moshe had given the strongest possible signal that he was going to accept their proposal. He had said "what we are going to find". He already envisions himself working with us, thought Niles. And Sarah hasn't even told him what is reported to be there. Niles couldn't wait to gauge Moshe's reaction when she told him that the Kochlit, Tel Kefar, location was the key piece to the entire scroll puzzle.

Sarah took in a deep breath. She exhaled with a sigh of disbelief and proceeded to disclose the primary detail she had forgotten to mention.

"There are four specific referrals to the site which I believe to be Tel Kefar and there are probably three other veiled references to it, too. However, of all sixty four, the only 'treasure site' that is said to be in Tel Kefar is the reference to the gate, actually the opening in the Kochlit ruins.

"This reference alleges that a duplicate of the scroll, its interpretation and the protokollon of each will be found here. As you may know, in the Greek language, a protokollon was a leaf of paper attached to the outside of a scroll describing the scroll's contents. Kind of like a label on a file folder, you could say. So, Doctor

Benjamin, if these items exist at all, they are, quite literally, the key to understanding the entire scroll – or perhaps both scrolls if we should find the duplicate."

For a few long seconds, none of the three uttered a sound. Then Moshe broke the silence. "Absolutely amazing! he said. "Miss Bergman, You have an absolutely intriguing premise. Frankly… I see no reason to hinder you from proving your theory."

"That's wonderful." Sarah was gleeful.

"In fact," said Moshe. "My new friend, you may be closer than you think to having your answer." Moshe's facial expression told Sarah she was about to be surprised. "As of this season, we started excavating the area where I believe we will find the city gate of Tel Kefar."

"Are you serious?" asked Niles.

"Yes, quite serious," said Moshe. "We opened three new squares in Area B. In fact, I think we may have already hit paver stones, probably just inside the gateway. There are a number of typical gate designs that could have been employed. It was rather common for the defensive design to be changed several times over a span of years to make them more tenable. I suspect that we shall find that the last gate was a six-chambered, Solomonic style. The same styles have been found nearby at Hazor and Megiddo and as far down as Lachish. I assume that our black stone, if it's either a paver or curb, could be in any of the chambers as well as anywhere in the street."

"Yes, I would think so, too," said Sarah.

"I guess I should make it official. So, you have my permission to join the Tel Kefar expedition for the stated objective of excavating an area, as yet to be determined, where the city gates are found."

Moshe's smile validated his enthusiasm. He rose to accept Sarah's extended hand.

"Thank you so much, Doctor Benjamin." She was almost giggling with excitement.

Moshe was pleased by her elation. Then, with focused eye contact, he extended his hand to Thompson, "Niles, to a brand new beginning, I look forward to our working together."

Thompson dropped his gaze and looked off across the grounds. There was a bit of moisture in his eyes, or so it appeared to Moshe.

"Moshe," he said. "I appreciate this… much more than you know."

"So, when shall I expect you to join us?" asked Moshe. Before either Niles or Sarah could answer, he continued. "Why don't I plan to look for you Sunday afternoon at the kibbutz B&B office? We can go over the final details we think of between now and then. Oh, and I do need to know how many others you want to include so I can make so reassignments."

"How many do you think we need?" asked Thompson. "I mean if your people are already working in the general area..."

"Including yourselves, maybe four but we can adjust as we need to. I'll let you decide on a day to day basis. Now, I hate to cut a delightful visit short but I promised Ruth I would take her to our favorite restaurant this evening. I have to pick her up in Rehovot and get back here in time to keep our reservation."

"I can understand that," said Sarah. "What's your favorite restaurant here, Dr. Benjamin?"

"Come on, walk with me to the van and I'll tell you about it. And please call me Moshe."

Niles spoke up. "Think I'll get back inside before they lock up the library, so if you'll excuse me..."

"Of course," said Moshe. "Look forward to seeing you Sunday, Niles."

Sarah and the professor walked slowly across the courtyard and down the steps.

"My favorite restaurant is a little French place named Eldad Vesehoo, just off Jaffa Street. It's not kosher!" he whispered with exaggerated excitement. Best calamari and langostino in Jerusalem. It's a little hard to find, though, down a little pedestrian alleyway that connects Jaffa and Hillel Street. I think it's Hillel; anyway, it's the street that runs along the north side of Independence Park."

"Oh yes, I know the general area," said Sarah. "There are a lot of little restaurants and shops; they're on a steps and terrace walkway instead of a street. I'll have to give it a try sometime soon, maybe even before Sunday."

Moshe pulled open the screeching door to the van and got in. As he cranked up he bid Sarah farewell and told her that he looked forward with pleasure to having her join the team.

"See you Sunday afternoon, Sarah."

"Yes sir, I can't wait."

10

S CARCELY TWENTY Kilometers stood between Tel Kefar and the impoverished Arab town of Jenin to the west. But the Gilboa range stood in the way so there was no direct road over the mountains. An ageless road connects Beer Shiva, Hebron, Bethlehem, and Jerusalem with Shekem and the heart of Samaria. Near its northern terminus in Nazareth, it winds through the midst of Jenin's meager, stacked stone and salvaged material hovels. The ancient highway passes a stone's throw below the home of Ahmed Hashim, a converted storefront where commuters meet outside every workday morning.

For Abbas Hashim and usually nine others, the commute to the day jobs and produce fields of the Kharod Valley was forty-two kilometers each way. Each passenger paid fifteen shekels for the round trip, almost a fifth of a day's wages. The daily jaunt carried them across some of Palestine's most historic ground and surely some of the most fought for.

In the Jezreel Valley, at the intersection with the ancient Via Maris (The Way of the Sea) they turned right, to the southeast. For twenty-five kilometers more, the nearly-junk Mercedes panel truck traced the foot of Mount Gilboa's north face. At the end of the run the Palestinian laborers were delivered to their fields and job sites around Beth Shean. Most were farm laborers; one was a tire changer. Abbas was a day laborer at the Tel Kefar excavations.

Each morning the workers dozed across the lurching miles of predawn darkness. Ten hours later, silenced by heat, fatigue and air blasting through every window and vent, they napped away the evening return. Day on day, mile after mile the laborers slept, indifferent to the history, prophecy and awesome beauty that flanked their daily trek—men as desensitized as galley slaves chained beneath the deck, oblivious to wondrous seascapes and sunset skies. But not Abbas.

Islamic poetry asserts that nothing obscures splendor as completely as squalor. Neither ignorance, nor poverty, nor hatred alone is sufficient to conceal Allah's wonders and to bind one's faith. The Holy Koran warns that in the absence of Allah's grace the three will merge into a devilish trinity. The merger is called squalor.

Squalor is different. With an ominous power far greater than the sum of its parts, squalor is a satanic synergy with the capability to recruit and muster the armies of Armageddon. Squalor sucks the very marrow from the bone and blinds the eye to truth and hope. Like a demonic cancer, it causes dreams to fester and die and to rot within the spirit.

And Abbas accepted what the imam taught: that Islam enables man to overcome ignorance, poverty and hate and to even use them as scimitars of salvation. Take them as challenges, he taught, as dares to rise above through knowledge, productivity and reconciliation. And each day, despite denunciation from the defeated, Abbas wedged himself aboard the nearly-junk truck, subjected himself to dominance of Jew and infidel alike and obediently suffered long hours under the Arabah sun ever believing that Allah would reward his faithfulness.

His duties were menial: lifting, loading, filling water tanks, cleaning the portable toilets, sandbagging the balks and most of the other routine chores. At the age of twenty six, he had already been doing manual labor long enough to have learned to endure the hours of drudgery by retreating to other times and places deep within the abyss of his subconscious. He withdrew into the scenes of leisure and possessions and pleasures which compose all dreams but there were more. His dreams were plans of escape, visions of success, respect and of fathering many sons in a new land of peace and promise.

A much-loved uncle for whom he was named had moved to Philadelphia (Pennsylvania, not Jordan) within months after the failed Jihad of 1973. The Jews called it the Yom Kippur War. His faith had been shattered with the lost cause. Distraught and bitter at Allah's indifference, he conceded the inevitable, the unthinkable; the Jews had won. Conceding all, he forsook the faith and departed his ancient homeland.

Twenty five years in the States had been good to Uncle Abbas. He now owned a small chain of Middle Eastern markets spread around the greater Philly area. In addition to the first, still operating on Locust Street, just west of Rittenhouse Square, he had new stores in Cherry Hill and Camden. He planned to open others down at the shore, Wildwood and probably Cape May. Abbas dreamed of all these wonderful places, where they were and what they must be like.

During a return visit in a recent year and in his occasional letters since, he consistently offered to sponsor his young namesake if he would save enough to come to America. It was almost impossible to believe that a "green-card" Palestinian could find work that paid enough to live on and even have enough time and money left over to go to an American college. But that's what Uncle promised and Abbas took him at his word.

All of Jenin had heard quite enough of his going-to-America-to-make-it-big dreams. Now that his younger brother was old enough to work, he was almost ready to make the move. And with extra money from America, surely, together, they could better their elderly, frail father's last years.

As best he could, Abbas ignored the sarcasm and contempt meted out by his ever conspicuously oppressed Muslim kin. They resented his dreams as much as his failure to embrace the requisite, traditional hatreds. Abbas detested their blind devotion to ridiculous myths of past glory. And he despised their arrogant presumption of exclusive righteousness and unconditional divine sanction. It was the same perverted pride which ensured the destruction of both future Islamic generations and the children of Zionist Jews.

No! Bismallah! (In the name of God) His allegiance would be to his sons, not to this pestilent nostalgia. He refused to nurture the coming genocidal conflict that would be caused by striving to recreate a fabled past that never was. So he would live for the future, for change and for all things new. He would live to go to America. But until that time he had to endure and he had to survive.

It was late afternoon. Several hours ago the Kefar team had completed the day's excavations and departed on the big Volvos. By early afternoon, Arabia's torrid sands had sucked the last westerly from the cool surface of the great sea. It had gusted across the Arabah as if racing to catch the day's last heated thermal already billowing up into the ethereal blue. The faithful replacements, heat, stillness, and silence, had arrived. They fused into a sensory over-load that engulfed the entire valley and forced all life into a slow-motion that conserves moisture and subdues heat.

Now only a fresh, cinnamon-tinged veneer of loess remained as evidence of the rushing wind and ensuing calm. Finally the heat was breaking. But it would be well after dark and Salat-ul-Isha be-fore the tepid surface waters of the Mediterranean would summon the wind to return from the cold desert night beyond the Jordanian mountains.

Near the top of the northern rampart of the tel, Abbas sat qui-etly on a small ledge of tunnel tailings in front of an old porcupine den—he hoped it was old. Soon the sun would begin burrowing into the higher of two ridge lines that descended south from Mount Gilboa's summit.

His attention was distracted from reverently awaiting the im-pending sunset. With morbid fascination he watched two large, black scorpions apparently fighting to the death. On and on the struggle continued as the swollen sun sank closer to the horizon that would soon extinguish it. Already it was more a bright glow than a blinding glare. Abbas wondered what was here that could possibly be worth such protracted pain and death.

This old tel was large enough for two little scorpions—even little scorpions as big as these. Surely there must be enough dark recesses for all to retreat from the searing, midday heat. There was never enough water, but in the first fleeting moments of daylight there were never so many scorpions as to drink every drop of dew. He supposed that there must be something here that he could not sense, something worth dying for. Surely it could not be that it was just their nature to fight and kill and die.

Abbas glanced across his shoulder down at one of the black pottery buckets with an insulating cushion of light blue terry cloth. One of the towels from the kibbutz was neatly tucked around the bucket's contents, pita and hummus he had brought from home. He remembered that there were also a few green olives, an apple and hard roll. He had saved them from the morning's breakfast plate that the beautiful American had brought to him. He had been too self-conscious to do much of anything but nibble on a cucumber after she defiantly walked over and handed the paper plate to him.

Her classic American good intentions had done little more than push him center stage and into the focused stares of the hard-shell Zionists who already resented his presence. He needed work more than he needed any one meal. He prayed to Allah that her kind ignorance wouldn't cost him his job and kill his chances to earn enough to get to the America.

Since the first day of the dig, Doctor Benjamin had been criticized for hiring the Palestinian. The kibbutz power structure had forbidden Abbas to enter the compound. So each morning when the nearly-junk truck dropped him off across the road from Massebot's back gate, he patiently waited in the dark for Moshe to pick him up and carry him on to the site. Moshe was his staunch defender and the old lion effectively kept the hyenas at bay. He wouldn't tolerate any abuse directed toward Abbas—or any other team member for that matter. But Moshe wasn't always close by and it was then that Abbas was most vulnerable to Rosen and the other bigots from the kibbutz.

Willy Dubignon had befriended Abbas two seasons before. Willy had met the youngster in Jenin waiting tables at an Arab restaurant. The kid had begged Willy to find him a job on the other side of the green line where he could earn wages instead of leftovers. It had been Willy who brought Abbas to Moshe seeking work. Within his trial week he proved to be a hard and obedient worker. And he confirmed the day laborers from the park benches of Beth Shean as a disgraceful, lazy lot.

Abbas loved Willy as a wise, older brother and Willy saw Abbas as the kid brother who had drowned in the Atchafalaya many years ago. For hours on end Abbas would quiz Willy about the States. And Willy never tired of painting the pictures that the young Palestinian yearned to behold.

Abbas was hungry, but the sun was almost touching the ridge line. There would not be time before Salat-ul-Maghrib which must be prayed precisely at the beginning of dusk, in less than five minutes, he guessed. He found it perplexing that the blazing star's movement was imperceptible during the day's long hours of toil but, for the brief stirring moments of its fresh arising and peaceful descending, one could actually see the heaven's eternal movement. So it was this evening as it slipped beneath the great waves of earth called the Gilboa range. Then, at the moment of its vanishing, there was a flash and instantly, a backlit amber canopy relieved the tired blue sky.

Early dusk is the time for evening prayer. From the bucket,

Abbas removed a clear plastic bottle of drinking water. The bottle was labeled Eden Springs but this one had been refilled from a convenient spigot many times. He stood and made the few long steps up to the tel's flat top. His eyes searched the distant Transjordan-Jordan skyline for a familiar pattern of dips and knolls which would align him slightly east of due south, facing Mekkah.

Before the prayer, he must be purified by the Wudu', the partial ablution. He removed his black braided head cord, lowered his shmaag around his shoulders like a shawl and knelt. He twisted off the cap and placed the open water bottle in the dust at his side. In a low voice he began the ritual.

"Bismillah." (In the Name of God)

He professed that his bathing was for the purpose of worship and prayer. He poured a small amount of water into his palm and returned the bottle to the ground. The hands were washed, three times, up to the wrist. Again, three times, he poured a small pool into his cupped palm, raised it to his lips, and sipped in to cleanse the mouth; then the nostrils, by sniffing in water three times. In repetitions of three, with water in cupped palms he continued; forehead, chin, ears. First the right then the left arm up to the elbow. More water. Now with only one hand, the whole head was wet, once. With wet forefingers he wiped the inner sides of both ears; with his thumbs he wiped the outer.

More water. First the right then the left, each foot was washed, three times up to the ankle. The sequence never varied. At last the Wudu' was complete; the Salat could begin.

There are five pillars of Islam: Shahada, Salat, Zakat, Ramadan, and The Hajj. Abbas faithfully observed them all except the Hajj which was not required of those too poor or physically unable. But he would make the great pilgrimage one day, as soon as he could, with the wealth he would earn in America. And he would make the Hajj possible for his father and his brother, too – "Bismillah!"

The pillars are revered by Muslims as are the great elements, principles, seasons and shrines by Jews and Christians;

Shahada as much as the Profession of Faith or The Shema,

Salat as much as Communion or Prayer,

Zakat as much as Offerings and Tithes,

Ramadan as much as Easter or Passover

And The Ka' Ba as much as The Holy Sepulcher or The Western Wall.

Salat is second only to the Shahada, the great declaration of faith.

"La ilaha illa A'llah; Muhammadun rasalu A'llah." (There is no true god but A'llah; Mohammed is the messenger of A'llah)

It is the obligation of believers to pray five times daily in a prescribed manner. When there is precious little or no water – a rather common problem for the Bedouin – a believer may use clean sand to perform the ritual. The prophet has assured that this is acceptable in the sight of Allah.

The Salat-ul-Maghrib (evening prayer) requires three rakas (repetitions). Each is a bit different but takes about the same time to pray, just over a minute when prayed by a practiced believer. Morning salat consists of two rakas; the noon, four; mid afternoon, four; and the night, four.

Abbas stood assuming Qiyam, the first of the three postures of prayer. Raising his arms with the palms opened and forward, he touched his finger tips to the upper back of the ears and proclaimed aloud the most familiar words in Islam, "Allah-o-Akbar," (God is Great). Lowering his arms and with hands clasped, the right on top held waist high, he began reciting words committed to memory since childhood; the Thana, the Ta'awaz, the Tasmia, Al-Fatiha and many shorter suras from the Holy Quran.

Though burned into his subconscious by thousands of recitations, the ancient praises and invocations flowed from the depths of his spirit with a melodious fire.

"Praise and glory be to You O Allah. Blessed be Your Name. Exalted be your Majesty and Glory. There is no God but You. I seek Allah's shelter from Satan, the condemned. In the Name of Allah, the Beneficent, the Merciful. Praise be to Allah, The Cherisher and Sustainer of the Worlds; Most Gracious, Most Merciful, Master of the Day of Judgment, Thee do we worship and Thine aid we seek. Show us the straight way, the way of those on whom Thou hast bestowed Thy Grace, those whose portion is not wrath and who go not astray. Allah-o-Akbar."

Now Abbas entered the second position, Ruku', a low bow at the waist from which he voices the praise.

"Glorified is my Lord, the Great."

Standing erect he affirmed.

"Allah listens to him who praises Him."

Still erect, he again assumed the Qiyam.

"Our Lord, praise be for You only. Allah-o-Akbar."

Abbas kneeled and leaned forward until his forehead and palms touched and rested in the dust. From this prostrate position called Sajda', he spoke.

"Glorified is my Lord the Exalted."

Rising, but still on his knees, he continued.

"Oh my Lord forgive me and have Mercy on me."

Once again in the Sajda, the first raka concluded.

"Glorified is my Lord, the Exalted."

Abbas completed the final verses of his worship. Still on his knees he lingered, slowly turning his head, allowing the loveliness of the dusk to soak in. There were never two sunsets exactly alike, he thought.

At last he stood and started back down the slope to the porcupine's incidental front stoop. As soon as he sat down he dug into the bucket for something to eat. Out came the pita and hummus. The meal was packed in a plastic container that had originally held moutabel', an eggplant dip he relished as much as hummus topped with sunflower seed and olive oil. He tore off a piece of pita and sopped it through the hummus. He was starved and the simple meal was delicious.

It would be a long night but Arabah nights were never too dark in the summer and Abbas never tired of gazing into the great spray of stars. Surely no one would come to disturb the site. There was nothing of value here. The hand tools were locked away in the heavy steel trailers; the wheel barrows and ladders were all chained together.

Who would steal cheap, used tools anyway, Abbas wondered. And if someone wished to steal the partially exposed artifacts, he would have to know exactly where to look. All the sunshades were lowered over the open squares and they were secured with full buckets of soil around the edge of the huge tarp. If there was a whole pot or jar partially buried in the floor of a square, it would be secured, hidden, with loose soil until it could be removed in tact. Unless one knew where to look, it was not likely that anything worth having or selling would be found.

But if Doctor Benjamin was willing to pay him to stay out here, he was thrilled by the thoughts of the extra money and the fifteen shekels carfare he would not have to pay—for one day, at least.

Abbas was proud that the great professor trusted him to watch over his property, even if he could see nothing worth stealing. He knew that there must be untold treasures beneath the soil upon which he was seated, but it would take a thief as long to find it as it would the archaeologists and the diggers.

He remembered asking Bob Collins if there might be any troves of gold and silver coins such as had been found in the nearby excavations at Beit Shean. Bob said there would not, unless they had been buried by others after the final destruction of the city. Rehov was destroyed in the eighth century BCE, which was well before coins were first minted in this part of the world.

Bob explained that no evidence of anything other than a few isolated residences had been found above the eighth century destruction level. He told Abbas it would be hard to believe that anyone living here during the Persian, Greek or Roman period would own anything worth burying to hide—certainly not coins or jewels. And under the Umayyads, the Abbasids, the Mamluks or the Ottomans, no poor farmer or herdsman living here, on this dry mound, would have owned valuables worth burying.

The first few centimeters of mixed topsoil and the Islamic stratum were almost always ignored by the biblical archaeologist. Even so, only a pitiful number of pottery shards and artifacts from the entire Islamic range had been found on the tel. And what had been recovered bore mute testimony of fourteen centuries of sparse living conditions.

But the fragments of pottery which had been collected from these periods, though scant in number, were beautiful. They were decorated with rich colors and delicate designs and they cried out across the years that art and form and beauty are not the exclusive product or property of affluence. Abbas well remembered Willy's prediction that one day the biblical archaeologists and the Israelis would be condemned for their reckless destruction of the archaeological record of all these centuries.

As the evening's first bright stars were joined by the usual crowd of the other millions, isolated drops of light gradually puddled at the base of the mountains across the Jordan. As far as he could see from north to south the pools merged forming a twinkling rivulet that marked the thickly populated flanks of the highway which follows the Hashemite Kingdom's side of the rift river south to Aqaba.

From Gilboa, lights appeared from a military outpost on one of the high knolls. Great banks of floodlights illuminated a stone quarry cut into one of the steep slopes where the work continued all night. Now there were the lights from cars and trucks out on the highway to the west. And, occasionally, a slow moving set of headlights revealed the location of a lonely farm road farther down in the valley between the tel and the river. All was silent except for the winding out of a distant diesel. The overloaded truck and trailer combo downshifted to ascend the upgrade, then decrescendo and, again, silence.

Abbas contentedly munched on the last bite of apple. He reflected on how strangely peaceful he had felt all day. And now it was a perfect night. In some queer new way he had never experienced, his evening prayers had left him spiritually enthralled. He felt an almost euphoric sense of security and well being. Never had he felt such calm or so connected to all creation. He didn't understand but mystically sensed that the significance of this night was beyond his human comprehension.

He could sense the eternal filament of energy pulsing through his own being, down into the guts of the earth then out again through the peaks of the surrounding mountains. Arcing up and out across the galaxies, it shot through the outermost light years and on into the eternity beyond. Then back again, the circuit closed within the very depths of his soul. Abbas knew he should be terrified, but he had never known such peace. He was as an infant in his mother's arms, ignorant of everything, fearing nothing.

Abbas sat up with a start. He was not sure if he had dozed off or if the present had snatched him back from the cloistered sanctity of deep meditation. It was much cooler but he sensed something out of the ordinary. The night was still and quiet and bright but even so, something was out there.

There was no road or footpath to the top of the tel that was not within his view. He could see for miles in every direction except south. The crest of the tel rose behind him and obscured his field of vision except for the first few yards. An approach from the south was not likely. But if a trespasser was willing to suffer through the razor edged and ice-pick tipped weeds which still defended the southern escarpment, scaling the ancient rampart was not impossible. Besides Abbas could clearly see the field road that ran east and west behind the southern elevation, all except the section obscured by the piece of tel behind him. Unless an intruder walked in the dark for a mile or more before reaching the tel, his approach would most likely not go unnoticed by any observer near the summit. Vigilance and tenability were, after all, the primary objectives of the millions of man hours spent moving and mounding earth on this exact site.

But there was movement below. Abbas couldn't see it; he could feel it. His thoughts flashed back to his early years, guarding the family's goats as they scoured lonely cliffs for rough herbage on bright summer nights. More than once the shepherd's gut feeling perceived a predator before the senses. The intuition allowed him to greet the unsuspecting intruder with a perfectly slung stone. But tonight, instead of a sling, he had only a pick handle and the cellular phone that Dr. Benjamin had given him before he left for Jerusalem.

He recalled how it had been, alone at night with the small flock, when he realized that something was out there. He could still smell the numbing fear and feel his knotted guts as he struggled to remain secluded, silent and safe. He remembered the terrible night he had actually slithered behind a small boulder and as slowly and quietly as possible tried to cover and conceal himself with dusty clay soil. Neither daring a silent scratch when ants stung nor a reticent slap at a nuzzling gerbil, he lay there frozen for hours. He remembered how desperately he had craved for daybreak.

Finally the day broke and Abbas recalled that the light brought with it the humiliating, disgusting truth. The terror of the endless night before was a large black piece of snagged plastic film that rustled in the slightest breeze. So perfectly it had mimicked feral dogs panting or wild boars rooting.

In that steamy morning mist as the first light of day finished off the worst night of his young life, the ten-year-old Abbas vowed that no menace would ever again reduce him to the pitiful, fear-stricken weakling who suffered through those last, endless hours. After that night's passage, he developed the mettle which only follows complete failure or shameful defeat. Abbas had learned this; cowardice is immeasurably more agonizing than confrontation.

Still seated on the tailings pile, his movements were barely perceptible. His eyes searched along every radial for the source of his uneasiness. For long minutes he sat there, focusing close and far, dissecting every square meter within his sight. He knew he was not wrong; something was out there.

As if to mock the unseen threat, a faint smile creased the

corners of his alert eyes. The tension of the moment brought back his father's words. The day after the night of horror with the black plastic shabah (ghost), his father had gently gripped his drooping shoulders to lift his spirits.

"Boy, when you're alone in the dark and looking for djin sharreer (demons), you will always find them."

It had been one of the few times the ever stoic Muslim had shown compassion or understanding. Abbas had always suspected that his confessing the embarrassing ordeal had summoned the weathered old man's own repressed memories of flock-watching horrors from his own remote past.

Rrroun ... eeeow ...eeeow ... rrounnn ...

As soon as Abbas heard the sounds, he recognized the unmistakable groans of a four-wheel-drive surging up a steep grade. The monotone churning of its power train in the lowest range all but drowned out the engine's revved up whirr. The truck, jeep, Land Rover or whatever it was approached the tel from the row crop fields to the east. No lights. Abbas knew that the only reason for such an approach was to avoid detection.

Through the darkness he could now see the movement of rising dust barely a hundred meters from his dirt-ledge seat. It obscured the night sky above the crest of the tel. He crouched and slid backward behind the small rise of tailings on which he reclined a moment before. The dust rode the night wind across the top of the tel until the cloud of powder engulfed Abbas. Still, he could make out the dark form of an ATV topping the berm. It paused.

He heard the clacking and grinding of mismeshed gears. The unseen driver shifted the transfer case into high range now that the steep climb was made. Just above idle speed it moved in and backed behind a large container trailer which held excavation tools. The truck parked close enough not to be seen from the usual approach route. Now there was no movement, no sound from the intruder vehicle. Abbas lay on his belly absolutely still and silent. His blinks and the movement of his eyes were intentionally sluggish.

He heard two soft clicks. Rustling sounds and blurs of movement in the darkness told Abbas the occupants were getting out. He could hear the muffled words of men talking in low voices. He couldn't understand them; he couldn't even determine the language. There were two of them, unless someone was still in the ATV.

He could make out their forms as the pair started in the direction of the excavation squares. Even in the darkness the lowered sunshade was visible. Its black form contrasted the surrounding grays and raw umber. They reached the edge of the massive black net and paused. One of the two stooped, lifted something and set it aside. He moved down the slope a few feet farther. Again he stooped, lifted and moved away from the black sheeting. Abbas realized he was removing buckets of soil used to weight down the netting so the night winds would not damage the excavation.

Abbas saw the edge of the sheet rise and then drop back, flat. Only one figure was now visible on the surface. The other was under the netting, in the squares. Then he saw the dim glow from a flashlight beneath the covering. It silhouetted the figure still on the outside. He was holding a folding digging spade, the type used by the military.

Abbas could hear their hoarse whispers but he couldn't understand any of their conversation. His mind raced. The mysterious intruders had ended the quiet peace he enjoyed only a few minutes earlier. He had to call Dr. Benjamin. What had he said? How to make a call? In Israel cellular phones were as common as Lakers' t-shirts, but not to poor Palestinians. Abbas had only used one once before. Amir, the owner of the nearly-junk commuter truck, let him call the Bezek pay phone in the mini market near his parents' home. The little store served as a message center for several of the neighborhood customers.

He remembered Moshe said, only three buttons to push. But which three? It wasn't dark when Moshe showed him the sequence. Slowly, with his eyes locked onto the silhouette less than a hundred feet away, his hand searched for the bucket of food. The cell phone was in it. Inside the bucket he felt the rough softness of the terry towel. Just beneath it his fingers distinguished the shape of the phone.

With the stealth of a pick-pocket he lifted it out and slid as low behind the little mound as he could and still see the dark figure. His fingers traced the pattern of buttons on the touch pad. The top left was the largest. Shielding it as best he could, he held his breath and pressed the large button. He heard the power-on tone in the receiver; instantly, the LCD lit up.

Abbas winced. He knew the piercing tone had surely alerted the intruders to his presence now lit up by the blinding light of the LCD. He hugged the phone into the folds of the shmaag down around his shoulders like a shawl. He waited for the challenge. Nothing, the muffled conversation between the trespassers continued. They had neither heard the tone nor noticed the faint green glow.

Abbas realized that the metallic cracking of the ATV's exhaust system cooling down and the wind weaving through the dry weeds could effectively mask a few more decibels than the little cell phone had just emitted. He relaxed a bit and allowed his pounding heart beat to soften and slow. Again he peeped at the shielded LCD and luminescent buttons. The remainder of Moshe's instructions came back to him, the result of the adrenaline rush, he thought. Press the "RCL" (recall) button and the number "1" to speed dial Dr. Benjamin's personal cellular.

This time he muffled the speaker with the palm of his hand before pressing the two buttons. One ring... two... three rings, connection.

"The cellular customer you are calling is not available. Please leave a message after the tone."

He whispered as loud as he dared. "Doctor, Abbas here. The thieves are here now. Please come right away. Come quickly or send the police."

Again, with the speaker muffled, he shielded the LCD he pressed the "END" button. Carefully, he raised himself to make certain that the pair were still at work. The glow and the silhouette were still there. Abbas rolled over, flat on his back, and stared into the heavens. He tried to organize his thoughts. Should he risk another phone call? To Whom? Maybe he could get the license number of the truck. Too risky. He would surely be seen or heard crossing the open space on top of the tel.

But the swishing rustle of the wind through the waving weeds might cover the sound of his movement through the dry stalks. He could ease around the side of the tel until the curvature of the slope and the extra distance were to his advantage. Then, with the vehicle between them, he could slip up close enough to get its description and tag number.

Abbas rose up on his forearm to make sure the two had not moved. With every measure of care he could muster he began the flanking maneuver around the slope. Before each movement he paused and with every sound that he thought might be heard, he would lie even lower, motionless, his face pressing the sharp weeds into the soil. After an endless few minutes he was far enough around the mound to have to crane his neck to even see the head of the silhouette. In a crouch, he moved swiftly on around for another fifty or sixty yards. Now he was sure that the container trailer and the trespassers' truck stood directly between his position and where the two thieves worked.

He knew he didn't have time to enjoy the relative safety of his new hiding place. He couldn't risk reaching the parked ATV at the same time as the intruders. If they found what they were looking for, they would immediately return to the truck. And, if they were done and beat him to the truck he would be caught in the open. That was the chance he had to take. If he was going to do anything, he had to do it now.

It was not difficult to move silently across the barren top of the tel; it was devoid of the dry, crackling weeds which wrapped up the slopes. In less than a minute he covered two hundred feet in a crouching kind of double-time tiptoe.

He reached the back of the truck. It was an old Toyota Land Cruiser. Through the dusty windows he could still see the faint glow of light from beneath the black net. But from this position the excavation area was no longer backlit by the star-bright sky and he could not make out the outline of a human silhouette.

Carefully, he wiped away a small area of the dust veneered on the tailgate glass. He peered inside but could see nothing. His hands searched the pockets of his tattered trousers for the ball-point he knew was there somewhere in the cluster of five and ten agarot coins. He found it. He dropped low on both knees and tried to read the black numbers on the yellow license plate. Even after wiping off the layers of grime they were not readable in the deep darkness beneath the tail gate mounted spare tire.

As would a novice student of Braille, he slowly traced the raised numerals with his finger tips. He was surprised that they were legible to his touch. He clicked out the ball-point, wiped his dusty palm on the shmaag and tested the pen. He flattened and tilted his palm to catch the most favorable angle of star light. It worked; he could see the ink line in his hand. As slowly as he dared, he recorded each digit and dash onto the dry inside skin of his left arm. "72-228-90 got it. Bismillah." He whispered the words just under his breath. At the same time he began the silent retreat toward the steep slope.

When he was back over the edge of the denuded top and into the safety of the weeds he lay back and allowed his pounding heart to calm. Only now was he aware of the salty sweat burning his eyes and the stinging, itch of the wounds that the thistle and thorns had inflicted. He was pleased with his performance. Courage had again proven to be less painful than cowardice. Doctor Benjamin and his friend Willy would be proud of him.

Emboldened by his own stealth and daring, the security of concealment couldn't contain his curiosity. Still fueled by the adrenaline surging through his veins, he would ease back around through the gauntlet of weeds to see what treasures the two thieves were taking. Now he was more confident of moving undetected through the waist high growth. He quickly returned to the little ledge and the food bucket which held the cellular phone. He must try again to inform Dr. Benjamin about the intruder's presence.

He could see nothing but the glow from beneath the black netting but he could still hear the muffled mumbling that came out of the pit. Again he searched the bucket and found the phone. He pressed the key sequence that would call the professor's cellular. Once more the rings were answered by voice instructions to leave voice-mail. This time Abbas didn't bother; he immediately pressed the "END" key. Some premonition told Abbas there would be no answer, yet he was mysteriously assured that all was as it was meant to be on this mystically peaceful night.

A bit over half the distance to the lower corner of the excavation area and slightly down the slope was a huge mound of loose earth. All of the excavated soil and debris from the Area B were piled there. Abbas knew that the smart thing to do would be to remain quiet and concealed until Dr. Benjamin got the message and sent the police or to wait until the thieves were gone. But it was as if the decision to stay put was out of his hands. He started a slow crawl toward the pile, closer to where the trespassers lurked.

Within moments he cleared the short distance and sank into the mound of loose soil. He knew that he would present less of a silhouette peering around the side than over the top of the mound. In a low crawl he eased around the doubly steep downhill edge of the tailings. With each progression he sank to his elbows and knees. Then he could see it, the flashlight shown from beneath the lowered sun shade. He was barely fifty feet from the spaced line of dirt buckets that weighted down the edge of the netting against the winds. A bulging border of sandbags marked the edge of the excavation pits beneath the black shroud.

From this close their words were almost intelligible, but both persons remained out of sight down in the squares. Still clutching the cell phone in his right hand, he began scooping out a niche in the soft powdery embankment with his left. In the depression he could better conceal himself. Now he had a good vantage point, albeit a filthy one. A coating of ashy dust was plastered on his sweaty skin like a gray fresco. But Abbas hoped the grunge would further camouflage him.

Now, all he could do was watch and wait. Abbas knew that danger distorts one's sense of time; nevertheless, he guessed that he had been in the hiding place no more than ten minutes when one of the pair emerged from the excavation squares. He knelt on the edge of the balk and carefully surveyed the surrounding area. When he was apparently satisfied that all was clear, he stood and held up the netting for his accomplice. The second man climbed out of the pits. Abbas strained his eyes to see if either was holding some valuable artifact. He could see nothing but the distinctive spade shape of a trowel. The two scanned the horizon, slapped dust from their clothing and started up the tel toward the Toyota.

The men had not taken more than three of four steps when.

Tweeeeeeeeeeed......tweeeeeeeeeeeeeed.........
tweeeeeeeeeeeed......

The normally soft ring of the cellular phone pierced the stillness. Abbas frantically searched the key pad for the on-off button. Instantly he switched off the phone but now it didn't matter. Both of the intruders froze in place. Then, as if on queue, both sprinted in the direction of the waiting Land Cruiser. Abbas lay back into the soft mound, his heart again pounding. His mind raced searching for the dilemma's solution. But the default response had been programmed into the young shepherd's psyche those long years ago. He must confront the thieves, face to face, and he must do it now. He had promised Doctor Benjamin that he would look after things; what else could he do?

Abbas was already off the excavation tailings and moving up the side of the tel when he heard the metallic bass-drum sound. The doors slammed shut on the solid built Toyota. As his line of sight grazed the top of the tel he saw the Land Cruiser at the same time he heard the engine start. Then the headlights came on. The high beams doused him with a blinding stab. Abbas shielded his eyes with his palms raised perpendicular to the intense rays. The Toyota didn't move. Abbas walked on, directly into the painful brightness. He approached the vehicle prepared to leap to the side if it should lurch toward him at the last moment. It didn't. Abbas moved toward the driver's side. He tried to determine who sat behind the wheel. No way, the head lights had destroyed his night vision.

"Abbas, erev tov!" The greeting came from inside the Land Cruiser.

With instant release, Abbas breathed out. He took in a deep breath and returned the greeting. "Salaam."

He recognized the voice with a strange, unfamiliar accent, but still he did not know who spoke. The faceless form continued speaking but Abbas could only pick up a few of the mixed Hebrew and English words.

Abbas was not alarmed when the passenger, who had said nothing, opened his door, got out and walked behind the vehicle. The driver continued talking, explaining their presence there after dark. The second man had stopped behind the Toyota. Abbas assumed he was urinating. Now the driver, still talking, opened his door and stepped outside. Abbas stepped back to allow him to exit. Now he recognized him. He did not know his name, only that he had seen him at the site. From the inflexion in his voice Abbas understood that he was asking a question but he had no idea what it was.

In his limited Hebrew, Abbas responded. "Ah nee lo mi veen," (I don't understand).

The driver forced a smile and acknowledged, "Sleekah, (excuse me), sleekah; boi, (come) Abbas, boi," he urged. He pointed toward area B as if he was attempting to explain his presence on the site at this time of night.

Still apprehensive, Abbas made no effort to move toward the suspicious man or in the direction he pointed.

"Ma kareh, (what's the matter) Abbas?" The driver asked.

He stepped toward Abbas with his arms opened. Again he beckoned him toward the excavation pits. Abbas took another step backward, not taking his eyes off the insistent intruder. Suddenly, he was aware of the other man walking up from behind the truck. He turned in the direction of the alarming footsteps. Immediately he flinched reflexively; his peripheral sight caught the blur of an imminent impact. It connected with instant, fatal force. The young Palestinian dropped limp into the dusty debris of the centuries, his skull crushed by the blow.

"What are you doing?" The driver screamed at his accomplice who still held the meter long piece of steel fence post. "What do you think you're…"

"Shut the fuck up. Why didn't you know there was a night watchman out here? You think this is some game?" The killer spoke in a calm, loathing tone.

"No, I know it's not." The unnerved driver regained his self-control. "What are we going to do with him?"

"You're the one who loves to dig; you're going to bury him. Who's going to notice another pile of dirt around this damn place?"

The terrified driver leaned over the Toyota's hood. Propped on his elbows, he held his forehead in the palms of both hands. For the next few moments he remained motionless except for his frequent deep breaths of anxiety.

The killer stooped down and pressed three fingers against the side of Abbas' neck until he was satisfied that the carotid was stone-still. He carefully wiped off the metal post with a corner of Abbas' checked kaffeyeh. With a handkerchief from his own pocket he held the cleaned weapon and walked over to a scattered pile of identical posts. He inserted the one he held into the heap and placed the handkerchief back into his pocket. He looked back at his partner still slumped over the Land Cruiser's hood.

"Well, where are you going to dig the grave?"

Without looking up from the truck hood he answered. "I think I know a better way than digging a new pit." The driver sounded somewhat more composed than he had the few moments before.

"Let's hear it."

"A few days ago the professor had a construction tractor dig a deep ditch at the bottom of the tel, right down there." He pointed down the slope toward the very bottom of the step trench. "I think it's the best place to put him."

"Why"

"Because no one will be digging in the bottom of it for years… maybe never. They dug it to determine how far down there's any evidence of occupation. Anyway, now we use the ditch to rebury bones from the excavations. And, it's very deep."

The killer held his pensive silence for several seconds longer as he considered the driver's information. "Ok," he agreed. "But I don't want the body to touch the truck. So you can either drag it or put it in a wheelbarrow and roll it down there."

"All the wheelbarrows are chained and locked," answered the driver.

"Well, by god, then it looks like you'll drag him! Tie the ankles together and drag him feet first. Cut me a piece of that rope." The killer pointed to one of the closest stakes where a length of rope secured the massive tarp. "And stay away from the head so you don't get blood on you."

The driver walked over to the near corner of the sun screen. There were about eight feet of slack below the clove hitch around the tent stake. It would not be missed when the netting was raised the next morning . He had no knife. He began sawing the polypropylene rope against the sharp braded edge of the iron stake.

"Idiot!" The killer scathed. Then walked over and handed the driver an open Vitrinox Swiss army knife.

The two returned to the lifeless form with the length of rope. They lashed his ankles together with several figure-eight wraps. They both stood at the same time; their eyes searched the skirting fields below. No one approached; they were still alone.

"I'll drive behind you," said the killer. "The tire tracks will cover the drag trail."

The driver grasped the rope lashing like a handle and began the three hundred meter ordeal dragging the corpse to the waiting grave. He quickly realized he was fortunate that most of the distance was downhill. But he still had to make the next seventy-five meters across the flat top before he reached the escarpment.

Behind the sordid cortege the killer followed in the Toyota. He guided the driver side wheels over the drag marks in the loose soil. They reached the edge of the rampart adjacent to another excavation area. The grade here was too steep and the soil too loose for even a four wheel drive. The killer stopped the Land Cruiser at the edge of the slope and watched his accomplice continue to drag the corpse over the side.

Now the trick was to continue downward to the waiting ditch without losing control of the body on the steep grade. But it happened. The driver slipped on loose gravel and lost his grip on the rope lashing. The body first slid and then tumbled randomly into a thorny fringe of weeds at the bottom of the mound a few yard from the trench.

At last the driver reached the edge of the deep ditch with the remains. He released the rope handle. Following closely, the killer came down the same path carefully trying to erase all signs of the evil passage. He kicked at the tracks and shuffled his feet across some of the deeper signs. When he reached the edge of the deep ditch he was holding a military issue type entrenching tool. The driver was still sucking in deep gasps, trying to catch his breath after the long haul.

Unmercifully, the killer thrust the e-tool at him. "We don't have time to slow down; get down there and scoop out a hole."

With a tone of defiance, the exhausted driver snapped back. "On this, you listen to me. If this isn't done right, he'll be found. You be quiet and listen to me, now."

The driver readied himself for the caustic reaction; it never came. Instead, the killer stared at the driver for a few long moments of brooding. Then, incredibly, in a respectful tone he replied. "What you think we should do?"

"If we simply dig down, drop him in and cover him, there's a good chance he'll either be uncovered accidentally or dug up by an animal. We should dig down, tunnel into the side of the trench and place the body into the niche. Then, if we cover it up to the same level down there now, there's little chance it'll ever be found, even if the backhoe returns and digs even deeper in the trench. It'll take longer but I don't think we can afford not to. If we take turns digging and watching and we should be done in thirty or forty five minutes."

"You're right," the killer agreed. "You take the first watch: I'll start down. How deep before we start tunneling?"

"Probably half a meter. It won't hurt if the tunnel slants downward; it'll just hold the backfill in better."

"Okay," said the killer. He started down into the ditch from the end where the excavator had operated. Scooping out the quarter-yard buckets had left an incidental ramp of earth which could be used to enter and exit the trench. The other end, which cut into the steep rise of the tel, was over five meters from the highest point to the bottom of the ten meter long trench. The killer reached the deepest end. Immediately he began shoveling the loose soil into a pile against the leading edge of the cut. Every few shovels full the blade hit something hard, a human skull or other large bone. They had been moved from one of the excavation areas and reinterred here. But the killer didn't have time to contemplate the haunting scenario now.

After a furious few minutes of digging he hit the bottom of the ditch. He could feel the four inch wide lands and grooves left on the trench floor by the teeth of the back hoe bucket. He spoke in a loud whisper to his partner watching above him.

"I'm down about three feet; how about taking over?"

"Yeah, come on out," answered the voice from the surface.

Once they switched places, the driver saw that the pit was deep enough to begin the lateral dig. He loosened the collar nut on the e-tool and folded the blade down into a pick-ax position. He retightened the nut and began hoeing into the wall of the ditch. It took a grueling thirty minutes to chop out the niche and rake aside the loose debris but finally the task was done. He rose, stepped out of the pit and leaned against the rough, sloughing side of the ditch.

"It's ready."

"Okay," answered the killer. "Get out of the way; I'll drop it down."

The killer intended to maneuver the body over the edge and slowly lower it onto the mound of fresh earth at the bottom. But the combination of dead weight, treacherous footing and fatigue caused him loose control and drop the body over the ledge.

As soon as it hit, the driver stepped across the pit and moved closer. "Damn!" he blurted under his breath.

The bloody head was closest to him and the edge of the pit. He would have to somersault the body in order to pull it into the burial niche. He reached across with the e-tool, worked it under the rope binding and pulled as hard as he could. He had to be careful not to get bloodied but at length, he got the body into the pit. With his feet he pushed it into the recess until, on its side, the body was in a kind of final fetal position.

He began shoveling and tamping the soil into the niche and pit. Back filling took only a fraction of the time it had taken to dig it out. The last act was to make sure that none of the uncovered bones was visible. That could be a give-away that something was amiss in the trench. For the first time since leaving the squares, the two risked switching on the flashlight for a final inspection. It was done.

As quickly as possible the exhausted pair returned to the waiting Toyota. They departed Tel Kefar by the same route they had arrived.

11

KIRK BOLTED In the darkness of the cool room. It was 3:45 in the morning. The same little Grundig short-wave that had lulled him to sleep with Andrew Lloyd Webber just five hours ago now blasted him awake with blaring, raucous static. He was tired and would have relished another couple of hours sleep but he knew better than to yield and take another five minutes with the alarm on "snooze".

The work week was nearly over, only nine hours to noon and a whole weekend of free time. The exertion, heat and dehydration—not to mention seven time zones and a radically altered sleep schedule—had all joined forces and were taking their toll.

Kirk was a seasoned trekker and backpacker; he knew all the symptoms of cumulative fatigue. He smiled as that thought brought to mind what Grandma Gatewood once said about the physical demands of hiking the Appalachian Trail.

"Only way I know to get in shape for it is the first two weeks on it."
How right she was. Kirk had learned that the secret to surviving anything is to suffer through the first few days of it. He wished he could lie there and reminisce but quickly reminded himself that one thing he hated worse than forcing stiff muscles into motion was starting off a new day running late. Early mornings at a frantic pace always seemed to screw up the rest of the day.

By four o'clock Kirk had groomed and dressed. He waited impatiently as coffee barely trickled through an antique Krup in desperate need of a quart of white vinegar to purge its clogged tubing. The decanter was not half full but Kirk pulled the pot back and slipped his mug under the stream. He filled his cup and quickly slid the pot back under the trickle with only a slight sizzle tattling that the juggling act was less than perfect.

"Water must have as much damn lime in it as Florida's." He mumbled to himself.

"Bill, you ready for coffee?"

Kirk hoped that he wasn't; he didn't want to have to repeat the shell game with the pot and mug.

"Thanks, I'll get some in a minute. Bill looked around the corner with shaving cream on his face.

Kirk walked outside into the predawn coolness and sat on the steps. It didn't seem as steamy as it had every morning for the past week. He hoped this was a sign that the khamsin had finally broken. The putrid smell from the poultry houses which usually fogged the still morning air didn't seem as insulting today. Of course, it could be that he was getting used to it.

Kirk looked down. One of the kibbutz cats—the size his grandmother used to call a mostacat—was yowing and rubbing against his bare legs. Young as it was, it already wore the scars of its struggle to survive the myriad cat hazards of kibbutz life. As suddenly as it had appeared, it tore off back down the stairway and across the St. Augustine lawn in a crouching series of quicksteps and freezes toward some unseen, juicy critter meal just inside a dense bed of calla lilies. With a gush of speed worthy of the Serengeti the little survivor disappeared into the thicket.

Kirk heard the heavy stave door to the room creak open. Father Casey walked out to join him. He was balancing a saucer with a slice of lemon cake on top of his coffee mug. He pulled one of their plastic patio chairs around closer to where Kirk sat on the top step. When he was seated he remarked to Kirk that it seemed cooler out this morning. In an easy silence the two relaxed with their own thoughts for a time before Bill broke the quiet.

"What you got planned this weekend?" asked Father Casey.

"Nothing really; I may do some hiking. Thought about going up to the summit of Gilboa and maybe camping tomorrow night. What about you?" Kirk blew a long slow puff into his still steaming coffee.

Bill, chewing a bite of cake, paused to take a cooling slurp and swallow. "I'll be hanging around here… Unless I can talk you into going camping with me… up to my favorite place in the Holy Land."

Kirk thought for a moment before he answered. "And where is that?"

"A place called Arbel, the Cliffs of Arbel, actually." Father Casey offered no additional information.

"Never heard it," said Kirk. "Is it a national park or historical site?"

"I would have been surprised if you had heard of the place," said Bill. "It's neither a park nor a major historical site. Only reference to it that I'm aware of is in that guide book of yours."

"My Holy Land Guide?"

"Yes. Best travel guide out, as far as I'm concerned, written by a friend of mine, Jerome Murphy-O'Connor."

"It was highly recommended on Amazon," said Kirk. "I should have read it through twice before I came over. But back to your favorite place, where is it in relation to somewhere I might know?"

"Right in the center of quite a few places you might know, probably."

"Well, where is it?" Kirk's tone expressed his frustration.

"Not too far from here." Father Casey was evasive. He acted preoccupied with his cake and coffee to whet Kirk's curiosity.

"Darn it, Bill, if you're serious about inviting me then tell me something about the place. How far is it; how do we get there; what's it near?"

"Oh, sorry. I wasn't being deliberately vague. I just had no idea you would be remotely interested in the place."

The cagey old priest affected his finest portrayal of innocence. He paused to take a breath and organize his thoughts.

"The cliffs are on the Western side of the Sea of Galilee. They're about five miles to the North of Tiberias and we can get there by bus. We can get to Tiberias by bus, I should say, then we can either hike the last five miles or take a taxi to Moshav Arbel. Do you know what a moshav is?"

"No, I don't. Are you going to tell me or do you want me to have to dig it out of you? What is a moshav?"

Unable not to crack a smile, Bill continued. "A moshav is sort of a hybrid between a kibbutz and a privately owned farm. I think it may be accurate to compare it to a farm cooperative in the States. The land is privately owned but marketing and purchasing is a joint business arrangement."

"Oh, okay... something like a farm co-op, huh? Now, tell me

exactly what is it that you like so much about the place?" Kirk assumed that Bill was probably not going volunteer any explanation.

"Many things," said Father Casey.

Bill caught Kirk's annoyed look. He rushed to elaborate on the meaningless answer.

"The panorama is the most spectacular in the entire Galilee. It's very much off the beaten path; you'll almost never see a tourist or pilgrim up there, a few weekend campers and hikers, but that's about it. The nights are beautiful and cool and there's always a breeze. I really do think it's the best backpack camping place in the Holy Land."

Kirk pressed the night mode button on his Timex Indiglo. "Bus should be here in about ten minutes. When do you need my answer, about going to Arbel?"

"I'm going to be right here. Just give me five minutes notice and we can be headed out the gate. You know something, it just occurred to me, we could borrow Jaclyn's car and drive up to the top of Gilboa late this afternoon. You can decide if you want to hike back up in the morning."

"I don't think I've met Jaclyn," said Kirk.

"You'll like her. Guess you know you'll have to stick to the roads if you do decide to hike back up there?"

"Why's that?" Kirk looked puzzled.

"Lot of the land on the slope is restricted military area. And the stone quarries are off limits, too. There just aren't any good trails to the top, unless you start up from the other side, that is. But they're more suited for rock climbers than backpackers or day hikers." Father Casey tried his best not to sound like he was trying to influence Kirk's decision, which he, indeed, was.

Kirk collected the granola bar wrappers and his coffee mug and stood up. "Sounds like a good idea, if we can get the car. You don't think she'll mind?"

"No, I know she won't. She rents a car for the whole time she's here, every year; I've used them many times before and still she offers. Jaclyn's a very generous lady. She might even like to ride up with us. I'll make sure I introduce you two this morning at breakfast. I think you two will become great friends right away."

"I look forward to meeting her." Kirk noticed that Bill already had his usual gear beside him. "Hand me your mug and I'll take it in."

Soon, the two old buses arrived with the same drivers that picked up the team each afternoon. But in the mornings they seemed cataleptic and pissed off instead of impatient and pissed off. This morning they were about five minutes early so the team members straggled aboard a few at the time.

Kirk and Father Casey were among the first to climb on. The morning peace was over. God-awful, loud Moroccan music rattled the speakers of the driver's beat-up boom box. Twice before the scheduled time to leave, the lead driver started to pull off. Twice he was confronted by one of the Israeli staff pointing at her watch and barking orders for him to wait until the right time. And each time a screaming match ensued with all the hand waving, gesturing and pointing typical of the Mediterranean. But eventually, presumably at five by the Israeli staffer's watch, the buses left for the tel.

The morning's work was uneventful with no exciting finds. As Bill promised, he introduced Kirk to Jaclyn Kruger, a wealthy New Yorker in her sixties and a veteran volunteer. And Bill was right, on all three counts. Kirk and Jaclyn liked each other right off the bat, she insisted that they use her Avis rental and she did want to come along on the trip to the summit of Mount Gilboa.

For all practical purposes, work on Fridays ended with breakfast on the tel. Each week, after breakfast, Moshe led a tour to each excavation area where he explained the week's revelations, square by square. It was the only chance that the volunteers got to keep up with the big picture of Tel Kefar's layered centuries.

The rest of the morning passed quickly. It seemed like only minutes after the tour concluded when the old, dirty buses came greyhounding across the field road to retrieve the tired workers. Kirk and Michelle rushed to lock up the last of the tools in the container trailer before tripping down the slope to the buses idling at the base of the tel. They stepped up into the lead bus and took one of the last vacant seats.

"Decided what you're doing for the weekend?" asked Michelle.

Kirk had mentioned taking Jaclyn's car up to the Mount Gilboa summit park after work. He had also told her about Bill's description of the cliffs overlooking the Sea of Galilee and the invitation to go backpacking.

"I'm definitely going up on Gilboa with them... But I haven't decided about going with Bill up to Arbel. You and Nina are going over to Jordan, huh?"

Michelle had detailed her plans earlier that morning while they were working in the square.

"Yeah," she answered. "But now you've got me dying to see those cliffs. I'll bet Father Casey knows more secret places over here than anyone on the dig, more than most Israelis, probably. You know he's been over here for years, with the Franciscans at the Mount Tabor Monastery."

Kirk's head turned with surprise. "Are you serious?" he asked.

Michelle looked puzzled. "About what, Father Bill being a Franciscan?"

"Yeah, and about him being over here for so long."

"Why...yes. Why do you act so surprised?" Michelle answered.

"I had no idea. All he's told me is that he's a retired priest. Can't believe we've been in the same room for a week and I didn't know he lived over here."

"Well, I didn't hear it from him," she said. "Bob and some of the others were talking about him at dinner one night. Nothing negative; more like what a mysterious and private person he is—always by himself. Bob says he works like a horse, empties buckets and wheel barrows for half of Area D. Almost never says a word. They found it amusing that he's a guide at the basilica on Mount Tabor, the way you have to pry everything out of him. I'm impressed that he asked you to join him camping."

"Yeah, I know. But, he sure talked a lot when I first checked in. I take it he's quite a scholar, too. He's an okay guy; easy enough to room with, anyway. He's been good about explaining things and showing me the ropes around here.

"We had this really strange conversation... Since then he hardly says a word. I like him but he is hard as hell to talk to—answers questions but that's about it. I was afraid that I hurt his feelings, the way I reacted to his bizarre conversation. But then he invites me to go backpacking, so I guess not."

"What do you mean by bizarre conversation, if you don't mind my asking?" Michelle's curiosity was obvious.

"I probably shouldn't have worded it like that. He was just talking about religious beliefs. That always spooks me; puts me on the defensive, I guess."

Kirk downplayed the account and his reaction. And he didn't

want to reveal Bill's prophecy or prediction or whatever it was to Michelle. But he remembered it with perfect clarity.

"That would have probably spooked me too," said Michelle. I don't do religious conversations, not any more. But I do envy you your invitation; I think you should go. If you like the place maybe you can show it to me before the season's over."

Instantly, Kirk liked the idea and said so. "Yeah, that might be fun. And if I don't like the cliffs we'll just have to think up somewhere else to go."

The bus approached the B&B area at the kibbutz. Michelle told Kirk that she and Nina were skipping lunch. She said they wanted to get through the Jordan River border crossing and on to Ajlun early enough to get a room and still do some shopping.

When the bus had stopped, she wished Kirk a good weekend and got off. As it pulled off, she kissed her fingertips and blew the kiss toward the window beside Kirk's seat and gave him a broad grin. He smiled back through the dirty window and waved again as the bus continued on to the dining hall where he had promised to meet Father Casey.

Kirk walked from the bus to the unisex water closet. He stood in line for one of the three lavatories. When he had rinsed off the gray powder coating he entered the dining room and maneuvered through the bedlam surrounding the steam tables and salad bars. After he had filled his tray with the culinary mysteries of the day, he spotted Father Casey sitting alone at one of the small tables lined along a back wall of the dining area.

Kirk placed his tray across from Bill. "How'd you get here so soon?" he asked.

"In the van with Avi," said Father Casey, "with the breakfast coolers. Brought them straight here."

"Aren't you eating?" Kirk noticed that the old priest had only a cup of juice in front of him.

"In a few minutes," he replied. "Don't have much of an appetite till I cool down a bit."

Kirk nodded his agreement as he cut his leaf salad into more manageable pieces. When he had doused the lettuce with oil and vinegar he looked up at Bill.

"I'm going to take you up on the trip to the cliffs.

"That's good; you'll be glad you did, I think." Father Casey spoke as if he already knew Kirk would be going.

"I appreciate the invitation, Bill."

"And I'll appreciate the company, my friend."

"What time should we plan to leave?"

"For Gilboa? 4:30. I told Jaclyn we'd meet her outside the office. And tomorrow, no buses are running so we should leave by mid-morning. Shouldn't be any problem catching a ride up to Tiberias once we get over to the main highway. We can look around there a bit before we head on up to Arbel, if you like."

"Sure," said Kirk. "I'm with you."

The afternoon passed quickly with most of the team departing to spend the weekend in either Tel Aviv or Jerusalem. As planned, the three met at 4:30. Jaclyn drove the succession of switch-backs and inclines up to the summit of Mount Gilboa, a distance of nineteen kilometers. The steep road passed above the stone quarry and then beneath the military communications complex. On up it wound though a handsome forest of pines with almost as many memorial plaques and markers as trees. And as Bill had depicted, the summit was marked by another monument dedicated to an IDF unit and an abandoned observation tower was visible. The scape at the top was an expanse of rounded, weather-worn stone faces with wrinkles of loose rock and gravel crevices partitioned by scraggly beards of naturally bonsaied shrub and pine.

Jaclyn turned off the road on to a small leveled patch of crushed rock with room for only six or eight cars. They were alone in the parking area. They locked the car and walked up to the base of the tower, Gilboa's highest point. The old military structure was neglected and rusty. No warnings were posted but it looked entirely too decrepit to be climbed in the thirty-knot winds gusting over the mountain.

From the crest they could look down into the tiny Arab village of Faqu'a snuggled on one of the range's Western knolls. A lone minaret seemed to cast the rusty old tower in a surreal contrast. Scattered around the top were a dozen or more concrete picnic tables with benches. But only one, on the leeward side of a prominent crag, offered some protection from the wind. Kirk suggested they sit there.

Bill had to almost shout against the blow. "You two go on down and have a seat; I'll join you in a minute."

Kirk assumed that Bill needed to find some hidden place to relieve himself.

Kirk and Jaclyn walked the short distance down to the shielded table. The niche was even more protected from the wind than they had expected. They seated themselves and silently watched as the wind raged across the ridge line. The blast bullied its way through the docile pines forcing them to bow in submission. They did with the pliancy and tedium of having endured the arrogant passage a thousand times before.

"Peace; be still!" Bill spoke out as he stepped out of the gusts and into the torpid air behind the rock protrusion. He carried his knapsack by the hanger loop on top. "What a great spot! We don't even have to shout at each other."

He plopped the pack down on the table top, reached inside it and removed the gift bottle of Cabernet. "Seems like a perfect time to open this up." He smiled at Jaclyn. "Kirk brought it to me from town earlier this week, may heaven bless him."

"What a nice surprise," said Jaclyn."

"I thought you'd like this idea." Bill winked at Kirk as he continued to rummage through his pack. He carefully removed a terry cloth towel with three glasses carefully rolled inside. He unwrapped them and placed them on the table.

"Surely he didn't forget to pack a corkscrew?" Kirk cut his eyes toward Jaclyn.

"Heavens, no." Jaclyn picked up the tease. "A priest without a corkscrew... inconceivable."

Father Casey, completely ignoring them both, reached into one of the outside pockets on the backpack and instantly retrieved an engraved Zyliss wine tool. The sommelier at The 21 Club would have coveted it. Bill uncorked the bottle as deftly as a wine steward and served each glass. He poured his own so full he had to handle it like a vile of nitroglycerin. Kirk couldn't keep from grinning broadly. No cork smelling, bottle breathing, glass swirling and bouquet sniffing for old Bill Casey. No sir, it didn't matter. He was going to drink it anyway, and enjoy it, every last drop, so why bother?

After a toast to the new friendships and a few sips, the glasses were scarcely back on the table top before Father Bill reached for the bottle and topped his off. Now he caught Kirk watching, still grinning.

"I know, I know, me manners are atrocious. I just hope it gives you immense pleasure to see how much I appreciate your gift."

"It does and I'm glad you like it," said Kirk. "Michelle did well."

"Michelle?" Bill looked blank.

"Yeah, she picked it out when we were in town, in the grocery store. I didn't recognize any of these wines. She said this one could hold its own with some pretty good Californias. She thought you'd like it... And I'm thrilled to see that you do."

"Well I completely agree; Michelle did well. I want to remember what it is... probably can't afford a bottle very often. You know something else?" Bill looked up from reading the wine bottle. "She's a very special young woman, Michelle. And it's by no accident that she's here on this dig either... same as you, me boy." The old priest peered into Kirk's eyes with certainty.

"Oh hell." Kirk uttered the here-we-go-again alarm just under his breath.

He glanced over at Jaclyn. She seemed to be preoccupied with some distant curiosity further down the slope. She acted as if she hadn't been listening but Kirk suspected that she had heard every word.

Now, again, they sat silently watching the wind have its way with the trees. It must have only been a minute or two when Bill spoke, calling Kirk back from his daydreams.

"Why don't you two sit a while longer and get better acquainted," he said. "I'm going to walk around to the other side and find a spot to wait for the sunset. Not that I don't enjoy the company, you understand, I just prefer to be alone during my meditation and prayers. Sundown's less than an hour."

"You just go right ahead, dear." Jaclyn assured him. "Kirk and I will get along marvelously. Why, I hadn't even realized that it was getting so late."

"Neither did I," said Kirk. "Peaceful time flies, doesn't it."

"Yes it does," Bill answered. "Hope this darned wind will die down some. Why don't we plan to meet back at the car shortly after sunset, before it gets dark?"

"We'll meet you there." Jaclyn nodded her agreement. "And you be careful."

Bill was barely out of sight around the first curve on the trace when Kirk turned to Jaclyn. "How long have you two known each other?"

"Well, now, let me see." Jaclyn removed her Vuarnets. She

began cleaning the lenses with the tail of her coral SPF shirt. "I met Father Bill Casey in the winter of 1983. I was... Do you want the entire story or an abbreviated version?"

"We've got an hour, why not the whole story?"

"Well, it won't take an hour. I certainly hope I'm not that long-winded. But it is an extraordinary story."

Jaclyn paused, trying to decide just where to start.

"In June of 1982 I lost my husband. We would have been married twenty five years; he died six days before our anniversary. It would be untrue to say that we had a perfect marriage. Certainly we didn't; but we had a wonderful marriage. We were all each other had, no other family on my side or his. Harold – that was my husband's name—was abandoned by his mother. He grew up in a hellish sequence of foster homes before he joined the Navy at the tail end of the Second World War. He was seventeen."

"I was a late-in-life child, an only child. I think my father was nearly fifty when I was born. He passed away my freshman year at Brooklyn College. My mother died less than three years later; it was my senior year. Nevertheless, I graduated and my first job out of school was with Bonwit Teller in the merchandising and display department. I went from store to store doing special displays, usually the windows.

"Once, when I was down in Philadelphia at the Bonwit's on Walnut—or was it Chestnut? I never could keep all those tree streets straight. Anyway, we were doing the finishing touches on an absolutely gorgeous window display. I was spreading some beautiful, jumbo glitter – huge inch and a half squares in every color imaginable – on the teak parquet floor. It was an absolutely fabulous window, maybe my best, ever.

"Well... do you know the feeling that you get when someone is watching you; I don't mean watching what you're doing, but watching you?"

Kirk nodded.

"Well, there was this strange man outside on the street, just standing there, watching every move I made. Now when you're twenty three and reasonably attractive, standing in a display window with nude mannequins... believe me, you get used to every look, stare and gesture one could possibly imagine. One learns very quickly to completely tune out the street. So, to this very day, I have no idea how he caught me so completely off guard. It's quite impossible to put into words. I found myself utterly distracted by this unfamiliar man. I couldn't seem to keep myself from looking back at this stranger. But it was as if I was looking into the eyes and upon a face that I had known forever. He had the strongest face and the softest eyes I've ever seen."

Jaclyn became hushed. She reached for her big shoulder bag on the bench beside her and took out of it a small, lavender bandanna. She folded it so that she could blot away the tears that welled in the corners of her eyes. Out of habit, she barely touched the fold of the little cloth to the edge of her eyes. Carefully, she avoided smudging the eyeliner and mascara she wasn't even wearing. Again, she gazed off across the Kharod Valley, her mind's eye locked upon sweet scenes from the past known only to her.

Then she was back. "Forgive me, Kirk. I'm supposed to be a tougher old bird than the sentimental old lady you see sitting here."

"Perfectly understandable," Kirk assured her. "Nothing needs to be forgiven."

"Well, where was I?" She continued. "Of course, you've figured out that it was Harold standing outside my display. I think he must have relished my finding his attention distracting. Oh, distracting my foot, it was downright unnerving.

"Then out of the corner of my eye I saw him writing something in his appointment book. He held it up to the glass for me to read. It said: 'Sorry for the gawking. Lunch is on me. The deli across the street.' And it was signed, Harold Kruger of Girard Bank and Trust. The moment I looked up from the note he smiled and waved and then proceeded directly to the crosswalk toward Stern's Delicatessen. He didn't even wait to see if I nodded or shook my head no, or just went back to ignoring him. Or, perhaps I should say, trying to ignore him.

"Never had I accepted an invitation from someone to whom I had not been properly introduced. But this time it was as if some queer sort of energy was overruling my judgment, actually controlling my thoughts and actions. So, not only did I walk over to Stern's to meet him for lunch, I took off fifteen minutes early to do it, and it was to be the very first of many wonderful lunches we would enjoy together over the next twenty five years."

Jaclyn fell silent. Her eyes sparkled through the moisture and a peaceful fraction of a smile appeared on her face. Kirk felt that to say anything would diminish the afterglow that she savored. After the last sip of wine in her glass she sighed aloud and looked into Kirk's eyes.

"Do you believe in loving someone from the very first moment you see them, Kirk?"

"Love at first sight? Yeah, I probably do."

"Actually, I don't think it matters a hill of beans whether we believe in it or not... like God," she said.

Kirk wrinkled his brow. "What do you mean, like God?" he asked.

"Just this: I mean that either love at first sight, as you put it, or Divine Power is completely capable of shaking our lives to the very core. Doesn't matter one whit whether we believe in it, or Him, or not. Both have the power to sweep us away in an instant and to do with us as they will; we're as helpless as if caught in a rip tide down at the shore. In fact, I suspect that They may be one and the same, God and an overpowering love. Maybe that's what Saint John meant; wasn't it he who said, God is Love?"

"Somebody said it; one of the disciples, I guess." Kirk answered uneasily.

"Whoever it was, I think he was right. But now I'm rambling."

"Harold was working in Philadelphia as an investment banker. We began seeing lots of each other on the weekends and whenever I was in town or he was in New York. Can you believe it; from that first lunch at Stern's to the altar was scarcely six months? A whirlwind? Oh, yes it was, but a magical one at that. I think we both recognized so much that was familiar in each other's psyche; same loves, hates, hopes and fears. We both knew there could never be another match so close, for either of us.

"We never had children, probably one of those same matching fears from our childhood. It's quite strange; the most important things, like having children, were the things we almost never talked about. We both just seemed to know how the other felt – instinctively, I suppose.

"We had twenty five good years together, Kirk. Not perfect, we had our spats but we were all each other ever needed or wanted. Harold died of a massive heart attack. I knew he was working too hard, not taking care of himself as well as he should have but it was the only way of life he knew. Oh, we had all the money we could have spent in five lifetimes. I really think that when you grow up as poor, as powerless and as alone as he did... you can never quite convince yourself that your balloon is not going to burst, that it's not going to happen to you all over again. I know all too well that I should have been more forceful about his health. But it always seemed like that same force that welded our souls together already had our lives, and our fate, all charted out.

"After he died I felt more helpless and useless than I ever remembered. But I never felt horribly alone, not the way I remember feeling after my mother's death. I suppose I was still young enough to have considered another involvement but that would have been so terribly inconsiderate of me."

"Why do you say that?" Kirk asked. "My mother remarried after my dad was killed at sea."

"Oh, don't misunderstand me. Of course there's nothing wrong about remarriage. It's just that I recognized that I would always be comparing someone else to perfection, an unrealistic standard a new love could never reach and that would be a cruelty. Can you understand my reasoning, Kirk?"

"Yes, perfectly." He answered with obvious remorse. "That's exactly the standard I held my stepfather to, something I regret terribly. So, yes, I do understand."

"Somehow, I thought you would. Well... it's time to bring this story to a close."

"Late that fall I received a call from an old friend who had just been through a horrible divorce. She asked me to join her on a cruise through the Eastern Mediterranean. I really wasn't up to it yet, but once again, some force or something compelled me to accept her invitation. One of our ports of call was Haifa where we were offered our choice of several day tours. Sue and I chose to tour around the Sea of Galilee. One of our stops was at the foot of Mount Tabor. We all had to get off the bus and pile into several taxis that rushed us up to the top of the mountain. This was the site of the Transfiguration of Christ, so they say. I don't think I've asked you; is this your first visit to the Holy Land?"

"Yes, it is," Kirk replied.

"Then trust me on this, you simply have to go up to the Basilica of Tabor. The mosaics are beyond description and it's just a very special place, but I'm getting ahead of myself.

"So, after we reached the top Sue and I walked all over the

grounds before we went into the church. When we finally did, I walked over into the south nave and took a seat behind one of the columns. I could just see into the apse well enough to catch a corner of the transfiguration mosaic – the most beautiful blue and gold tessera. It was so peaceful and quiet, and utterly still. Then, for the first time since Harold died, I wept. Oh did I weep; loud gasping sobs of grief. I felt as if my heart had fallen out of my chest and onto that cold stone floor.

"I haven't the slightest how long I sat there before I regained my composure. But when I looked to my side, Sue was gone. To this day I'm not sure if she thought I needed to be alone or if I was embarrassing her with my blubbering. But, where she had been sitting on the pew beside me, there sat Father Casey in dark brown Franciscan habit. He was watching me with a concerned gaze and that placid smile of his.

"I apologized for my emotional display. I told him that I certainly hoped I had not been too much of a disruption and that I must leave as I was surely delaying my group's departure. He attempted to put me at ease. He assured me that no one else had been in the church so I had caused no disturbance. Then he told me not to worry about my group. They had already left to go back down to the bus, all but Sue. She was having a cup of tea with one of the other brothers.

"He told me that our tour group would be having an early dinner at an Arab restaurant in Daburiyeh at the base of the mountain and he promised that one of the taxis would be back shortly, in plenty of time to get us to dinner.

"Then he asked me to walk outside with him. He guided our way to a stone bench beneath an ancient Holm oak. We sat silently for a few unrushed minutes before he turned to me and spoke."

"Dear child," he said. "These fleeting moments you've spent here in this holy place are by no means an accident. This was the whole reason for your journey. And you should know that the one who loves you so is the one who called you here. He wants so very much to wipe the tears from your eyes and to ease the aching in your heart. But, darling, more than anything he wants you to know without a tinge of doubt that you both are and shall ever be together."

"I'm sure that I must have looked dumbfounded because I certainly was. So, once again, he reassured me that I was perfectly safe, and quite sane, and that I should be exceedingly joyful because this divine insight I had been given was a heavenly gift. He said that it was a gift that was available to all, but delivered and presented to only a very few.

"Our exchange continued for a while longer. More than a conversation, it was mostly of a barrage of my questions followed by his cryptic answers about our spiritual encounter and what was to come. Just then Sue and Brother Alimayu walked out into the garden to meet us. Before they joined us Father Bill told me not to be anxious about what I should do next. He assured me that I would know perfectly well when the time arrived to go somewhere or to do whatever. But, he said, often I would not even know why before hand. And that's exactly the way it has been for the past nineteen years." Jaclyn finished her wine and waited for Kirk's reaction.

"That's an incredible story," said Kirk. "But you know what? He nailed me, too, first day I was here. When he first started up with all the religious stuff, I really thought I was stuck in a room with some fanatical nut. But then he explained some particulars from my past that really shook me up. He sounded a lot like what you just told me... This is crazy, Jaclyn. I don't believe in messages from beyond or spiritual messengers... I just don't."

"And I don't believe you mean that." Jaclyn disputed him bluntly. "I think you believe very much in messages from beyond; I think it's the messengers that you doubt."

Even before she had spoken, the duplicity of his last statement flared up in his mind. If little flint tools could speak from over the centuries, why couldn't our own loved ones bridge the gap of a few years? He knew she was right; it was the messengers he doubted. But why couldn't there be those few who could give spirits a voice... or even teach us how to hear them?

Kirk conceded. "You're right, but what makes you think that?"

Jaclyn smiled as she peered through his eyes. "Could I possibly have been acquainted with Father Casey all these years and not have learned anything from him?"

"Are you suggesting that his... gift, I think that's what he called it, can be passed on to others?"

"And learned." she asserted emphatically. "I'm not merely suggesting it; I'm stating it as fact."

Kirk's elbow was on the table top. His jaw rested in the palm of his hand supporting the weight of his head, his eyes were fixed in thought.

"Why do I have the feeling that our ride up here isn't a sight-seeing trip?"

"Of course it is," she said. "But important experiences always have more than a single purpose just as great literature has several levels of meaning."

Jaclyn removed a little carabineer fobbed watch from her belt loop and looked at the time. "We should probably start toward the car in a minute. But, before we do, I want you to know something, Kirk. In the nineteen years I've known Bill Casey, I can count on ten fingers the times he's invited someone to join him when he goes up to the cliffs. So, what does that mean? I'm quite sure I don't know what it means for you. But I do know this. Every one of us who has gone with him has come back a different person."

"Different in what way?" Kirk asked.

Jaclyn searched for the precise words. "I'm not able to speak for anyone but myself. And I don't think my experience is something I could possibly explain, at least not until you've been there. But you may rest assured that it was a wonderfully positive encounter so, please, don't be apprehensive about going. There's nothing to worry about or to be on guard about. Come, we should start to the car."

They collected the glasses and started up toward the parking area. As they walked the muezzin's sunset hymn arrived from Faqu'a. It reverberated across the rocky heights like a eulogy for the fallen sun whose memorial was the amber horizon and legacy the night's first stars in the eastern sky. And, now, the wind could scarcely call itself a balmy breeze.

"What time do you two plan to get away tomorrow?" Jaclyn asked Kirk as they neared the car.

"Bill said he wanted to leave by mid morning; guess that means around nine or ten. He doesn't think we'll have any trouble hitching a ride up to Tiberias once we get over to the main highway. Then we'll either hike on up or take a cab."

"Hitch a ride my foot!" said Jaclyn. "You'll do no such thing."

She was protesting their plans as they walked up to the rental Mazda. Bill was already there, leaning against the quarter panel.

"Father Casey, I had no idea that you planned to walk and hitchhike up to Moshav Arbel. I insist on driving you at least as far as Tiberias and I'm aggravated that you didn't let me know that you were without transportation."

Bill smiled and nodded, accepting her offer. "Thank you, my dear. I just didn't want to impose on your invariable generosity yet again."

Jaclyn rebuffed the explanation. "Whatever do you mean? I'm quite sure I don't know."

She turned to Kirk and handed him the car keys. "Here, Kirk, I'm sure you can see to drive at night better than either of us."

12

KIRK AND Father Casey returned to their room at the kibbutz just after one o'clock Sunday. Hardly a word had passed between them on the trip back from the cliffs. Kirk was lost in a labyrinth of bewildering recollections. The events of the past twenty four hours were unlike anything he had ever experienced. And Bill was resolved to let him steep, without interruption, reflecting on the experience.

This early on a Sunday afternoon, only a few of the team had returned from their weekend jaunts. The usual gathering spot, the cluster of plastic patio tables and chairs in front of the rooms, was vacant except for the little cat.

He had adopted the Kefar volunteers as extended family. College girls were always good for a handout from the dining hall. But little did they realize his new-found trust was a threat to his survival. The kitchen gang conducted poisoning campaigns whenever they decided the little creatures were a nuisance.

Kirk had stripped down and stepped into a pair of loose FILA gym shorts while Bill vacationed in the shower. He sat on his bunk with his bare back against the cool plastered wall as his mind continued its wandering through the jumble of emotions. His thoughts were trapped in all that had happened last night at the top of the cliffs. He was sure that he had not slept over of thirty minutes all totaled. Now he was zonked but not exhausted, completely relaxed but not really sleepy. He was unable to draw a line between what he had actually seen and heard and what he had dreamed, not that it much mattered, the emotional impact was undeniable.

Doom, doom, doom, dum, dum.

"Kirk, you in dare?" Willy blared through the door as he pounded it with the heel of his fist.

"Damn!" The ruckus jerked Kirk out of his shallow trance. He countered the cacophony coming from the door. "Hold your horses!"

Bill's wet and lathered head slithered out from behind the shower curtain. "What in heaven's name is all that?" he demanded.

"We're fixing to find out." Kirk twisted the bolt to unlock the door and swung it open. Willy and Nina were standing there. Before Kirk could speak Willy blurted out.

"I think we got a problem, Kirk! Can we come in?"

"Sure. What's going on? Hold it just a second... Bill, I'm going to pull the bathroom door shut; Nina's coming in with Willy."

"Thanks," said Father Casey.

"Okay, come on in." Kirk moved to turn two chairs toward the bunk where he sat down.

"Excuse my appearance, Nina; I was waiting for Father Casey to get done in the shower."

Before Nina could respond, Willy spoke up. "Kirk, Nina thinks something bad might have happened to Michelle. Sure sounds like it to me, too."

"What's happened?" Kirk's voice was somber.

Willy turned his head, holding Kirk's eye long enough to convey his concern, and nodded to Nina. "Why don't you start from the beginning?"

Just then, Bill came out of the bath in flip-flops, a threadbare, white v-neck tee and a faded pair of carpenter style blue jeans, hammer loop, rule pocket and all. He quietly hung his wet towel over one of the wardrobe doors and sat down on his bunk. His silence evidenced his attention.

Nina began. "You knew that Michelle and I went over to Jordan for the weekend?"

"Yes," said Kirk.

"Well, Michelle is missing. I've looked everywhere. I notified the Jordanian police. They couldn't care less, acted as if I was worried over nothing. They told me that she had probably gone back without me. I can't believe their arrogance. They wouldn't even question the owner of the gift shop where she was going. So I went to his shop; he acted as if he didn't speak English. How can he run a tourist..."

Kirk interrupted. "When did all this happen?"

"Late yesterday afternoon; let me back up. We spent most of the day in Jerash, at the ruins. I think it was just before six when I took a cab back to our hotel in Ajlun. Michelle wanted to go to some gift shop she'd heard about in Jerash, somewhere right near the site, I think. I was really tired—and something I ate for lunch didn't agree with me—so I told her I just didn't feel up to going with her. She said she wouldn't be much more than an hour behind me. We planned to have dinner together after she got back, if I felt better. Well, she never got back."

"Did you check with the desk to see if she tried to call or left a message?" Willy's question ended the pause.

"Of course I did; so did the Jordanian police. It's a very small hotel and the manager, owner, whoever he was, was adamant that there had been no calls for me. And, by the way, I also had them check with the hospital... and emergency medical services, too."

Nina sounded a bit pissed that Willy considered such a stupid oversight a possibility.

Willy sensed her irritation and tried to smooth it over. "Please don't take me wrong, Nina. It's just that I'm the world's worst at forgetting the obvious things when I'm all upset about something."

"I didn't mean to be snappy," she said. "Honestly, though, I don't know of anything else I could have done. I waited all night. It's obvious that the Jordanians don't consider a missing person to be a priority. So I came back this morning to see if, for some reason, she had returned without me. I even wondered if I might have made her mad by not staying with her in Jerash. Could she have met someone and taken off for Amman or had she had just gotten tired of me? I didn't know what to think.

"As you know, this place is almost deserted on weekends, I mean as far as our people being here. Thank God I found Willy. What in heaven's name can we do?"

Nina's voice begged for understanding, and for help.

Bill broke in above the hum of the air conditioner behind him. "I'm certain of one thing; we have to get her out of there. Immediately."

"Do you mean Jordan or Jerash? How you even know she's still there?" Willy asked.

"No time to explain now," answered Father Casey. "Both of you have to trust me on this, I'm afraid. You and Willy must leave for Jordan immediately. You know where she was going. You can find her but you have to hurry. Please believe me." Bill's voice quivered with urgency.

Willy protested. "Wait a minute, let's just wait a…"

Kirk cut him off. He put his hand on Willy's shoulder and spoke in a low voice. "Willy, please don't ask me to explain right now either, but I know Father Casey is right and I need you with me."

Without waiting for Willy's response he turned to Nina. "Are you sure she said she was going to a gift shop and not an antiquities shop?"

Nina began nodding even before Kirk concluded the question. "Yes, I'm positive. It was some place called Shahadeh's; I think that's what she said. She had one of their business cards. I've already told all this to the police. They didn't seem to think she had the name right; at any rate they had never heard of it."

Kirk turned to see Willy's expression. His eyes were waiting ; something had clicked for them both.

"What was the name on that card?" Kirk asked.

"Trans Jordan Antiquities," said Willy. "Shahadeh… something or other was the owner."

"Bingo! I remember you said Nina would give him hell if he was selling either fakes or genuine artifacts—sorry Nina. That's probably why she didn't say she was going to an antiquities shop."

Bill spoke up again. "You'll find her; you'll find her, but you have to get going. Listen to me carefully."

Bill had written something on a piece of note paper which he folded and handed to Kirk.

"Do not lose this. It's a telephone number of a Franciscan monastery in France; you can relay messages to me. Someone will answer within two or three rings. Then they'll patch you through to my cellular through their phone system. We have to do it this way. Usually it takes an hour or more to place a call from Jordan directly to Israel, if it ever gets through at all. And since we don't know who we're up against over there, this is the only safe way. Now, you have to be on your way. I'll meet you at Jaclyn's car as soon as I get the keys."

Within five minutes Bill was driving the two from Kibbutz Massebot to the Jordan River border crossing in the rented Mazda 626. Father Casey and Willy went through an extemporaneous check list as Kirk listened intently. Neither remembered what time the border closed but they knew it was not before five. There was still plenty of time to get across.

They stopped only long enough to swing through the Bank Leumi ATM in Beit Shean. Kirk and Willy each withdrew the maximum 1,200 shekels on their Visa cards, about three hundred U.S. dollars, a little over two hundred Jordanian dinars apiece. That would be enough for two or three days. If they had to stay longer they would deal with that problem then.

Just over a kilometer north of town they turned off on Highway 71 East, which ran eight more kilometers down to the Naharha Yarden border crossing. Kirk and Willy used the time to rehearse their travel plans; if questioned, they would sound the same. Every answer would be the truth except for their reasons for entering The Hashamite Kingdom of Jordan. Bill was insistent that they should not say they were looking for a lost friend, especially to any official. They agreed on an itinerary of the usual tour sites; Jerash, Ajlun and Pella. And possibly Amman, they would say, but only if time permitted.

When they reached a parking area marked, "Vehicles Not Crossing Into Jordan" Bill turned in and found a space close to the walkway they would take to the first checkpoint. A large sign answered two of their questions: the hours of operation were from 0630 to 2000 and the departure tax was 60 NIS (New Israeli Shekels).

Before they opened the doors Bill turned sideways in the driver's seat so he could see both men.

"Willy, you know as much about the customs in Jordan as I do, so I don't want to sound like a damn know-it-all. But I'm quite concerned about who or what we're up against."

Willy's eyes narrowed. "I don't think I'm following you, Father."

"Can't put my finger on it, exactly. But when Nina was recounting the situation, the first thought that flashed through my mind was that she's been abducted. But I think it's a much more complicated situation than just a kidnapping for ransom or slavery. I'm certain that…"

"Ransom!" Kirk blurted out his interruption. "She's a school teacher forchristsake! She doesn't have any money to pay a damn ransom. Or slavery? You can't be serious."

"Oh yeah, he can be serious," said Willy. "You're in the Middle East, you know."

"My God." Kirk slowly shook his head from side to side in disbelief.

"I'm very serious, Kirk, deadly serious," Bill continued. "If she isn't from a wealthy family, who could pay a ransom, then it's entirely likely she'll be sold as a slave."

"Damn, I can't believe this." said Kirk. Bewilderment was written all over Kirk's face. Wide eyed, he gazed out the window and into infinity.

Father Casey glanced down at his watch. He had to take the time to make clear the threat. He stated again that these were real possibilities. He told that throughout North Africa and the Middle East kidnapping was rampant and a slave trade thrived. He explained that most often it involved poor people in poor countries. They were offered good-paying jobs in Saudi Arabia, Kuwait, Yemen or any one of a dozen other Islamic states. Only lately there had been accounts of young women, especially from the old Soviet Bloc countries, being sold, literally, to wealthy Arabs by the Russian Mafia.

"And from what I've been told," said Father Casey, "it seems that young blondes are in particularly high demand."

"Don't those people have anything like a State Department?" asked Kirk.

"I suppose they do, but that doesn't mean they give a damn about some little girl without a passport or any papers claiming she's being mistreated by the locals. Even if she's smart enough to escape, then she has to elude her captor. He probably owns or controls everything for a few hundred square miles around. If by some miracle she does make her way to a consulate or embassy and is able to convince them who she is, and if those diplomats aren't in league with the very ones who sold her in the first place... then she may be one out of a thousand who eventually gets home.

"Lads, time's a wasting. We can discuss all these horrors and more when you get back with Michelle. But right now, you've got to get moving."

"You're right." Kirk opened the door and stepped out. He bent down so he could see Father Casey. "Father Bill, if this is what we're dealing with, what makes you think Michelle is still anywhere around Jerash?"

Willy interrupted before the priest had a chance to answer.

"Because they weren't expecting her. She just happened along, a target of opportunity, too good to pass up. They couldn't have had any prepared plan. So she's probably still there, somewhere, and they're probably working right now trying to figure out how to turn a profit with her."

"A logical deduction; I certainly can't disagree," said Bill. "But my assurance that she's still there and that you'll bring her back safely isn't just wishful thinking; it's my foresight insight. Something else I feel in me bones... there's more to this situation than a simple abduction. I can almost see her; I know she's still there... I just know it.

Come on, I'll walk you to the gate building; we can talk on the way. Oh! Christ me God, I almost forgot."

Bill reached into his pocket and came out with a photograph.

"Jaclyn got this out of the office when I went to get the keys. Dov just got a batch of photos back from the developer Friday. This was one of them. Great picture of Michelle, don't you think?"

Bill's eyes watered as he took a last look at the picture of the beautiful young woman smiling up from one of the work squares. She was down on one knee with her trowel in one hand and a soft brush in the other.

"Dear Jesus, we should be sending it in for the cover of Biblical Archaeology Review, not trying to save her life with it," said Bill.

Kirk remembered Dov taking the picture, the same morning Li Moon had assigned him to Michelle's square. Bill was right. It should be on the cover of an upcoming issue of BAR.

For the first time since Willy and Nina had burst into the room with the news of her disappearance, Kirk was overwhelmed by all the possibilities. The magnitude of their endeavor was chilling, a pitiful rescue attempt by two ill-equipped, ill-prepared, would-be deliverers.

They started walking toward the first gate.

"Bill, why are you so certain that she hasn't been harmed?" Kirk asked. "I want to be positive; I feel like she's okay, for now. But I'm scared my feelings are just wishful thinking, as you put it. There has to be some danger that she'll be murdered or assaulted, if she hasn't been already?"

"Yes, those are real dangers. But I'm certain we still have some time." Father Casey emphasized the word certain.

"Then may I ask just what it is that makes you so certain?" Kirk's question had a slightly sarcastic lilt.

Father Bill slowed his gate to let Willy get a little farther ahead. He turned to Kirk and spoke in a lowered voice.

"Yesterday afternoon, up on the cliffs, I didn't elaborate on this and I surely don't have time now. But let me just say, that when we learn how to fine tune our spiritual acuity, we begin to receive direction and guidance from the specters that love us. But... very often, what they do not impart to us is as pertinent and as enlightening as what they do. Are you with me, Kirk?"

"I don't know; I guess so, Bill. All of this is new territory. I'm still reeling from everything that happened last night."

"I know you are; and well you should be. You had quite a long night of reunions, didn't you my friend? Point I want to make is this, Kirk. You just said that you have the same feeling, referring to my being certain that she's still alive. It's not a mere feeling, my son; it's faith-knowledge, a spiritual gift. And just like our beliefs and loves, it's beyond our control, no matter how long or how hard we try.

"We cannot make ourselves believe what we don't; neither can we make ourselves not love what we really do. There's many a poor, mentally ill soul a'struggling against that truth, don't you know.

"So, Kirk, what I'm saying to you is this: trust your spiritual gifts, not your feelings. And don't you dare ask me how to tell the difference. Seems to me that your latest gift of knowledge is knowing that you'll bring her back, safe and well."

Willy was standing at one of the visa windows with passport in hand when Bill and Kirk caught up. There were a dozen of the windows in the side of the building, all sheltered by a cantilevered roof. Only one of the windows was open but, fortunately, there were only a few in line. Bill stood beside Kirk as he waited his turn.

Father Casey resumed the conversation in his muted voice. "I know that my talking about the Holy Scriptures irritates you. But you can not separate the two, Kirk."

"Separate the two what?" Kirk looked straight ahead to avoid Bill's eyes.

"What you experienced last night and the written record of so many others who have shared the same experiences. It's the same universal energy, the divine string that connects us all. This same thread spoke to man his first metaphysical ideas, his thoughts of God and immortality. It's all the same truth.

"So don't dump your corned beef trying to pour off the salty renderings. As I told you the first day in the room, Kirk, I didn't know why you were called over here, only that you were. I trust you remember our little talk, the one when you told me I was scaring the urine out of ya?"

"Oh, yeah, I remember all right," said Kirk.

"I think I understand your contempt for the spiritual. You're conditioned to associate the Holy Word with those who would use it to berate you into conforming to their ignorant superstitions and deranged agendas. You have to read and learn for yourself if you want to know what the Scriptures have to say to you. You cannot listen to what some self-serving empiric tells you they say."

"What's holding up this line?" Kirk's question was more of a moan.

"Line will move when it is supposed to. And I'll tell you this, what is not written in the Gospels is as powerful as what is. There is immeasurable spiritual significance in the issues that Our Lord never addressed…"

"Your Lord," said Kirk.

"and…" Bill ignored Kirk's remark, "the things He, apparently, never did." "These absences are incredibly powerful messages. But, like the spiritual gifts, it takes discipline and practice to become attuned to these intentional omissions."

Father Casey nodded toward the service window. "You're next in line so I'll cut it off for now."

"For now, huh? Bet you said that right." Kirk knew there would be more preaching to come.

"Count on it, my son. And I'll bet you're a bit more receptive when you all are back safe and sound."

Willy stepped back from the counter and Kirk took his turn at the window. He paid the sixty shekels and got the visa rubber stamped on one of the departure pages in his passport. They walked on toward a bus waiting to shuttle them two hundred yards, across the shallow trickle of a river and into the Jordanian side. The required bus ride, a one tenth mile trip, cost ten shekels, one way.

After some quick extrapolation, Willy remarked. "On a per mile basis it cost seven times as much to ride this damn junk bus as it does to fly the Concorde, back when the Concorde was flying, I guess I should say."

Their laughter eased the tension of knowing the treacherous legs of their mission were about to begin. Father Casey stood with his back to the bus. He scanned the area for curious eyes and then, very subtly, signed the cross and whispered his benediction on the two men. In slow motion, just as discreetly, Willy crossed himself to receive the blessing.

Bill's voice remained a whisper. "Kirk, give me a call between eight and nine tonight. I'll let you know if there have been any developments from this side. And it would probably be a good idea to try to touch base every few hours if it's practical."

"Then I'll try to call every six hours or so, as long as my MCI card holds out," Kirk agreed.

"Good," said Bill. "Better get on; driver's giving us the look."

"Yeah... here we go." Kirk stepped aboard.

The remainder of the crossing took little more than half an hour. Before five they had purchased entrance visas, changed a thousand shekels into dinars, cleared customs and negotiated cab fare to the hotel in Ajlun. Their driver spoke almost no English, or so he preferred them to believe. He sat silently paying no noticeable attention to the brief exchanges in the back seat.

On this side of the Ha-'arava, the mountains of Jordan began a two-thousand-foot ascent. From almost the edge of the little river's shore line they climbed on toward the high Jordanian plateau. No rails guarded the shoulders of the tar and gravel inclines and switchback curves. The lack of other vehicles on the winding road seemed strange. But their absence was a relief as the taxi straddled the faded centerline around blind curves. Even after they reached the four-lane section that connected Jerash to Irbid, the traffic was still light.

Across the rolling plateau, a Western eye could distinguish little else in the countryside but the stacked stone pens of Hejazi goats and Awassi sheep and the pervasive clusters of black, goat-hair tents. As the hillsides slid by, only now and then could anyone attached to a foraging herd or flock be spotted. But they were there, crouching among the shadows of the sporadic acacia or carob. Occasionally, in the vicinity of an encampment, a red and white checked shamakh atop a white thobe alerted the passing motorists to the presence of the resident Bedouin.

Kirk and Willy passed the last few miles without conversation. Then Willy ended the silence.

"I think we should check in, leave our stuff in the room and then go straight on to Jerash, in time to shop for some souvenirs. What do you think?"

Willy gave a hidden wink and carefully cut his eyes toward the back of the driver's head cautioning Kirk to be careful what he said.

"I think so, too," said Kirk. "But I don't want to be rushed. How late do the shops stay open in Jerash; you have any idea?"

"Pretty much the same, I think. Most of them should stay open till nine or ten. We'll know soon enough; we coming into Ajlun. That's Saladin's castle, up there."

Al-Rabadh Castle stood on the site of an early Christian Monastery. The old fortress was embedded on the crest of the highest knoll above the village of Ajlun. Built in the twelfth century by Islamic defenders against the Crusaders, the castle fell to the Mongols in 1260 and was later rebuilt by the Mamluks. One of the inhabitants of the early monastery was a monk named Ajlun, the one for whom the town below the castle was named.

The little hotel that Nina had directed them to was situated prominently on the main street of the town. As Kirk settled the fare with the cab, Willy entered through a wide open lobby door. Behind the desk was a middle aged man in Western dress. Willy guessed he was the same person Nina had asked about messages from Michelle.

The clerk politely welcomed his arriving guest with the formal 'Asilaam alechem'.

"Good evening, sir. Do you have reservations?" he asked.

Willy answered that he did not and asked the rate for a double. A quick glance at the numerous pairs of keys in the numbered pigeon holes assured that at least ten of the fifteen rooms were vacant. The manager answered that the rate was fifty-five dinars and that breakfast was served from six until nine.

Willy filled out the registration card. He deliberately transposed three of the nine digits of his passport number and listing his address in the States rather than the address of the Israeli kibbutz. Beneath his name, on the second guest line, he printed in Kirk's name but he left the passport number field blank. He expected that it would not be required; it wasn't, or either the omission wasn't noticed. They had resolved to leave as confusing a trail as possible in the dreaded event that they had to quickly escape and evade their way back across the border.

Willy paid for the room with a Visa card. The clerk directed him to room nine, up the stairs on the second floor. The desk clerk passed the key to an elderly bellman who insisted on carrying their small backpacks up to the room. He climbed the stairs, agilely for his age, Kirk noticed.

After unlocking the room door, he placed a backpack on each twin bed and drew the curtains. The old bellman assumed a parade rest position. His eyes meandered around the room without making contact with either guest's. His fluency in bellman body language conveyed the message perfectly; it was tip time. Kirk reached into his pocket and produced three one-dinar coins.

"Shukran; shukran. Asilaam alechem wa barakatuhu." (Thank you, thank you. peace and blessings be upon you) As the old minion raved and bowed, he backed out and locked the door behind him.

"Damn," Kirk muttered. "Did you see that smile? I must have tipped him twice the going rate."

Willy was grinning wide. "Yeah, you made a friend, all right. After a tip like that, for you, mon ami, I bet he could come up with a ham sandwich and a cold beer during the Ramadan fast."

Kirk walked over to the window and looked out over the surrounding area. He could see the upper escarpment and the walls of the old castle. He pondered how many rivulets of blood had trickled down those inclines, how many gallons had leached into the soil beneath the walls, all in the cause of religious dogmas. He wondered if the old monk named Ajlun had died on those very slopes. Incredibly, the Crusaders, the ones sworn to redeem the Holy Land from the Saracens, were the very ones who all but wiped out indigenous Middle Eastern Christianity. If they looked Semitic, wore local garb and spoke Aramaic or Arabic, they had to be Muslims. But in fact the arrows flew and the swords fell on countless Christian villages throughout the Levant.

Kirk looked back at Willy who had stretched out on one of the short beds. "How long you think we should wait up here so we don't seem to be in too much of a hurry?"

"I don't think it matters too much, as long as we don't look preoccupied or in a rush. Tell you what else I think. I think we ought to unpack most of this stuff so it looks like we're coming back, whether we do or not."

"Good idea," said Kirk.

"I'll leave everything except what I can get in this fanny paquet if you can make room for a thing a two in yours."

"Sure," Kirk answered. "What you got?"

"Couple of cheap shamakhs with egals, a khaki shirt... compass, cigarette lighter, a few nylon cable ties... Hell, Kirk, I just threw a lotta shit together; I don't know what we're going to need. I hope we don't need a thing but cab fare to get the hell out of here in about two hours. Cab fare for three, I mean."

"Yeah, I know. Like an idiot, I packed a little first aid kit with a suturing set and forceps. Even brought a little candle lantern and a mini Maglite but I left my damn tooth brush. Okay, we've been here long enough. Let's do something, even if it's wrong."

Willy nodded agreement. "I'm ready when you are," he said.

Before leaving they placed various articles around the room to indicate they would return, toiletries on the back of the lavatory, and a couple of travel guides from the border on the dresser. After the quick shower he missed at the kibbutz, Kirk tossed his dirty socks, undershorts and a tee shirt in a corner of the room. And Willy left his backpack in clear view on one of the beds. Both men looked around the room then, without any more talk, Kirk opened the door and they walked down to the lobby.

At the desk they turned in the room key and asked a few tourist questions, good restaurants, closing time at the castle, how far to Jerash. Of their dozens of recent guests, these two were just as predictable as the rest; that was evident in the desk clerk's vacuous eyes and arduous smile. After their calculated delay at the desk they left through the main entrance. No following eyes, not even a curious glance, they were as boring as they wanted to be.

In front of the hotel, within seconds the first taxi in a short line pulled into the drive-through.

"Jerash," Willy instructed the driver. "Take us to the ruins."

"Yes, Jer-r-rash, yes, yes." The driver repeated the order to confirm that, at least, he understood that much."

Willy looked over at Kirk. "They probably take everybody to the site entrance. There's a gift shop and restaurant at the site office there. We can look round and get our bearings and then plan what we want to do."

"How many times you been over here?" Kirk asked.

"Not enough to know the name of any streets... or anything else for that matter. There's not a lot to the place except the ruins and the shit shops."

Ten minutes later the taxi pulled over to the curb. Willy was right; they were at the main entrance. Within seconds the taxi was besieged by an army of hawkers. Their ages were as varied as the variety of trinkets they pushed: chewing gum by the stick; genuine Bedouin jewelry; real Roman coins; post cards; olive wood crosses and the ubiquitous red and white checked shumaghs and Iggals, the black cord head band which holds the checkered cloth in place.

Willy tried to fend off the entrepreneurial assault and pay the fare to the cab driver at the same time.

"I wait, I wait." The driver insisted.

"La, la, la (no, no, no)." Willy continued to repeat the rejection trying to answer all parties to the barrage.

Once the cab drove off, the street vendors conceded defeat. Kirk and Willy were no longer the most promising prospects. Now the tour groups emerging from the park's exit down the street were the new marks. The little regiment of retailers rushed off to intercept their new target before too many could escape into the sanctity of their waiting tour buses.

Kirk and Willy took advantage of the diversion and quickly walked through the entrance into the Jerash Archaeological Park. The most complete Roman city remaining in the world, or so the Jordanian travel literature claimed. It was probably true; one of the legendary cities of the Decapolis, the site was immense. This remote location, in a rather obscure valley of the mountains of Gilead, had precluded it as a good site from which to pillage building stone.

They followed directional arrows directing them along a gradually curving stone walkway. They continued on past the ticket offices and through stiles leading into the ruined city. The walkway led up to the souvenir and gift shop. Willy pointed out the restaurant he had mentioned earlier, also located in the visitor's center. Just inside the building was an information desk with a number of displays of characteristic memorabilia. And there was a bar area with several tables.

Beyond the bar was the entrance to the restaurant. The reservations lectern held a sign printed in English only: please wait to be seated. As Kirk and Willy neared his station, the maitre d' arose from the table where he was seated, placed his cigarette in an ashtray, and walked up to greet them.

"Good evening, two for dinner?"

"No, drinks only, out in the garden please." Willy answered with a folded banknote in his extended hand.

"Certainly. This way please, gentlemen."

They passed through one of the front dining areas and through a wide opening with no doors, only an accordion iron gate to secure the dining room after hours. The patio was three times the size of the inside dining space. It was covered by an arbor on which an ancient tangle of climbing foliage had entwined itself. The vines reminded Kirk of Florida's tenacious wisteria thickets. But without the drooping clusters of purple flowers to distinguish them, he couldn't be sure if that's what it was.

They were seated at a four-place table next to an outside retaining wall. Behind the stone barrier, red verbena thrived in the fertile back-fill. Several resident cats raced beneath the tables competing for abandoned snacks or a dropped morsel. Across the terrace in a niche near a gated area that closed off the back of the kitchen, three older men in white gutrahs sipped on tiny cups of Arabic coffee. They puffed away on the hose stems of a house shisha. Willy ordered the local beer, Philadelphia lager; Kirk asked for a bottle of lemonade and within minutes the waiter returned with the order.

"Kirk, how you think we should check out this antique shop? I've been doing all the talking so far. But now… I don't know where to start. So if you have any ideas, for godsake, don't hold back."

For the first time since they left the kibbutz Willy seemed overwhelmed by what they had set out to do and dismayed by the possibility that they would find no trace of Michelle.

"Well, all we can do is try," said Kirk. "Even if Bill is wrong about this being a shoo-in… maybe we'll get lucky. As for ideas, I only have a couple. I think we should look around for anything obvious, especially in this antique shop. If split up we can cover more ground. And, separately, we can spend twice as much time looking around this shop without raising suspicion, hopefully. Second, I don't think we should ask anyone if they've seen her or show this picture around until we've first checked out things as best we can on the sly. Still, all we can do is try."

"Okay." Willy nodded in agreement. "While we work our way around looking for this shop, if I run into you I'll just ignore you and go on to the next place. If we get completely separated from each other, let's meet back at the entrance to this place in two hours. That should be at nine fifteen, just after dark. Oh, I mean the park entrance out on the street, not here at the restaurant."

Kirk stood and dropped a five-dinar note on the table top. "Let's do it," he said.

For the next thirty minutes they drifted in and out of a dozen or more of various shops and stores that lined Abila Street. They browsed through souvenir shops and flipped through folds of cloth in clothing stores. Kirk paused to examine menus posted in front of restaurants and he stuck his head in and glanced around each small bistro.

Willy exited a shop that specialized in brass ware. He glanced up and down the street to catch sight of Kirk. He didn't before he started into the adjacent shop. Then it registered with him; this was it. Trans-Jordan Antiquities, the number 16 was painted over the entrance, the first number he had seen on any of the fronts. He paused for a few moments inspecting the artifacts in the show window. He took a deep breath and entered the shop.

The shop was the most neat and orderly place he had walked into. The floor was arranged like a jewelry store with several large displays of inexpensive items, mostly reproduction pottery and glassware. Gangs of track lights were aimed at the wall shelves where individual prized pieces from centuries past were flaunted. The objects were grouped by age and period; Bronze, Iron, Persian, Roman, Byzantine and the various Islamic eras. These exhibits were protectively sequestered from careless tourists and mendacious shoppers by a perimeter of glass display cases. Inside the lighted cases were groupings of countless small treasures; coins, scarabs, seals, bullae, rings, armor scales, arrow points, buttons, beads. They were all priced in euros, dollars and dinars.

As soon as Willy entered the shop a dumpy, overweight man of about forty emerged from behind a beaded curtain which screened off the back of the shop. Furiously he wiped the traces of greasy food from his mouth and hands with a paper towel. Following the fat man through the bead strands came the annoying sounds of an Arabic orchestra. At an ungodly decibel level the squalling ouds rattled the glass doors on the display cases.

Before speaking, the sweaty man tapped out a cigarette from a pack on the counter and lit it. He held it in typical Arab fashion, palm up between the thumb and index finger of his right hand. He took a long draw, inhaled deeply and let out a billow of diesel looking, acrid smoke. Finally, he looked over at Willy.

"Ahlan wa sahlan, welcome." He greeted his shopper and then started in with his questioning. "American; English?"

"Willy wasn't sure what prompted him to lie, but he answered. "Canada; Francais et English aussi."

He gambled that the fat man couldn't recognize the difference between Francais Canadienne and Francais Acadian. No matter, the proprietor opted for whatever English Willy knew.

"YOU SEE SOMETHING YOU LIKE, YOU CALL ME, OKAY?" He pointed first at Willy, then his own eyes and then all around the store.

Willy forced himself to repress a smile, realizing that the shopkeeper was resorting to the time-honored American quirk, talking loudly and gesturing wildly when attempting to communicate with foreigners.

Playing along, he answered. "Merci, merci, I will let you know, monsieur."

For the next few minutes Willy looked around the shop. He was anxious to let Kirk know he had found the place but, now that he had, he hadn't the slightest idea what to look for or what to do next. He didn't want to appear nosy or nervous.

As he browsed, he was amazed at the variety and quality of the artifacts, especially the Late Bronze and Iron Age pieces on the spot-lit shelves. Many were in better condition than anything he had seen in the Israel Museum or at Hebrew University. Willy suspected that Shahadeh's suppliers were much more covinous than the usual Bedouin pot hunters. One thing he noticed was that the prices marked on the scarab seals were four and five times the amounts that were penned in on the back of the business card Michelle had found.

Then it hit him: the amounts written on the back of the card were not selling prices; they were offering prices. The suddenness of his realization started the implications racing through his mind, a dizzying overload of possibilities. He had to get out and get to Kirk with this news. As soon as he thought he had spent enough time browsing through the shop, he started to the doorway.

"Adieu, merci beaucoup." Willy called out as he exited the shop.

His parting words were acknowledged but barely. The fat man raised his eyes and tossed up his hand in a manner that expressed his frustration at having been disturbed for no sale.

Out on the street Willy tried to catch sight of Kirk. He last saw him about half a block back in an olive wood shop. He started back in that direction but three shops back, there he was. Willy saw him through the open doorway. Kirk was looking back at him but remained expressionless as if he were any other stranger. Willy entered and worked his way toward him, pretending to inspect several items as he approached. They stood on opposite sides of a table brimming with little stuffed dolls in Bedouin dress. When Willy was sure that no one was within earshot, he spoke to Kirk while examining one of the shoddy little dolls.

"Found it, but I need to tell you what I just figured out; where can we talk?" Willy whispered hoarsely.

Without looking up, Kirk answered. "This place is probably good as anywhere else... if we're careful."

"Okay, well I found the place, about three or four doors on down. While I was inside looking round something dawned on me. This is a real nice shop, too nice, if you know what I mean."

"No, I don't." Kirk frowned. "What do you mean?"

"Hey, mon ami, they got pieces in that shop that the British Museum would love to have. They ain't buying that kinda stuff from Bedouin looters. My guess, they got some regular suppliers getting it directly from dig sites, maybe even from some university storage rooms. But that's not the important thing. Remember the card Michelle had?"

Kirk nodded without shifting his attention from the wood carvings he held.

"The prices on the back of the card, that's what they're paying, not what he'll sell for. I just saw the prices on some in his shop, four times as much. And Michelle finding that card out at the site... Pretty good evidence one of our folks is selling him stuff."

Kirk looked up directly at Willy. "Oh, lord! You don't suppose she walked in flashing that card and they thought she was some investigator?"

"That's exactly what I think. Shahadeh must have thought he'd been busted. Cause you can bet your eyeteeth he knows who he gave that card to. And it's a damn fact that Michelle's missing."

Kirk frowned; he was not so sure the linkage was that simple.

"There's got to be more to it than that," he said. "Why would he give a damn if someone knew he was buying artifacts stolen from some Israeli dig? I can't believe there are any laws here against buying anything smuggled out of Israel. Just the accusation would probably be pretty good advertising for him and would sure help to validate the authenticity of his pieces. Seems to me the only thing he stood to lose was a supplier. Whoever is selling the stuff to him has a lot more to lose than Shahadeh Jaber."

Willy was nodding. "Yeah, and she could have run into whoever that is. She probably knows him from the site; could even be a woman. And Michelle would probably have trusted them enough to be vulnerable. You know what's strange?"

"What?"

"You usually don't have problems like this on the digs that use volunteers. Paid laborers are the most likely ones to pocket the finds. Damn, Kirk, I think we're back at square one."

"Oh no we're not," said Kirk. "We might not know the details but you can bet our buddy Shahadeh does. We just have to get it out of him." After a few seconds of thought, Kirk continued. "Was anyone else in the shop, not customers, I mean employees, locals or whoever?"

"No one I saw. He came out of a back room; looked like I interrupted his supper the way he was wiping down. Greasy bastard was probably in the middle of scoffing down a platter of pork chops. Anyway, I didn't see anyone else. I couldn't hear shit for the raghead music on his boom box."

"Good. Then I've got an idea. But first we've got to call Father Casey to make sure nothing's changed. You seen a pay phone?"

The two walked out of the shop. There was a bank of four pay phones on the other side of Abila. Kirk crossed the street retrieving the note with the number Bill had given him from his shirt pocket. At the phone he tapped in the access number and when he heard the second dial tone he entered the second 800 number on Bill's note. Before the third ring, someone answered; a male voice repeated the last seven digits he had just dialed.

"Hello, can you patch me through to Father Bill Casey; this is...

The voice on the other end politely broke in. "Please hold, I'll put you straight through. He's expecting your call."

Kirk could hear the faint sound of a sequence of numbers being pushed in. There was a ring, a second, a third. "Hello?"

"Bill?" Kirk spoke louder than he meant to. "Can you hear me?"

"I can hear you fine. Have you got any news?"

"Nothing definite. How about you?"

"Got some useful information for you. So far, we can pretty well rule out a kidnapping for ransom. No one's been contacted and there haven't been any credit reports or account balance inquiries initiated. Her family appears to be going about their normal routine. Her credit cards haven't been used since Friday; that was at one of the ATM's here. Her phone card hasn't been used since early yesterday morning and it was used from the hotel in Ajlun. That's about it. Oh, and her passport number isn't on any Embassy reports and it hasn't been logged back into Israel, either. So, we still don't know what's happened, but we know what hasn't."

Kirk was astounded. "When I get back you gotta tell me how you got all this information inside of three hours. This is amazing!"

"Not much to tell, my boy. Just never underestimate the abilities of fifty Franciscans all working on the same project. Now, listen to me well. When you have her with you, you have to call and let me know you're on the way. We'll have the green police – the border patrol—on the lookout for you just in case. And don't forget that the Allenby Bridge crossing stays open till midnight but it'll take at least an hour to get there from Jerash. Now, tell me what you know."

"We still don't know anything definite but we sure think we know who does. We're on the way to have a little talk with him."

"Well, you two just remember… As soon as you have that little talk, the cat's out of the bag," Bill warned.

"I'm aware of that. I'm scared, but what choice do we have?"

"I know you are, son. Just use your head. Listen to me, Kirk. Are you listening?"

"Yeah, yeah, I'm listening but we have to hurry."

"Kirk, don't you get in too much of a hurry to use what I've been teaching you. Do you understand me?"

"Yes."

"You take the time to do it and everything will be all right. I know what I'm saying." The priest spoke with a convincing vehemence that left Kirk perplexed.

"You mean over here, right now?" Kirk couldn't believe that's what he meant.

"You're damn right I mean right now. Either your spiritual wits have a place in the real world or they don't. This is the perfect time for you to find out if this gift of yours is only for your private amusement in your spare time or, if by some remarkable chance, it's actually meant to be used to save and change lives." Father Casey's scolding voice stung.

"Okay, Bill, okay, I'll try." Kirk promised, his reservations were obvious.

"You'll be fine; you can do it. Bye." Father Casey hung up.

Slowly, Kirk placed the phone back into its cradle. Willy caught the bewildered look in his eyes.

"Something wrong?"

"I suppose not." Kirk answered feebly, trying to avoid explaining Bill's instructions in any detail.

"Look, I need to find somewhere quiet to collect my thoughts, just for a few minutes."

"What the hell did he say?" Willy didn't try to conceal his irritation.

"There's still no word from her. I'll tell you everything in detail later, Willy; I swear. Bill just wants us to take the time to carefully consider our actions before we do anything and I want to think through this plan."

"Okay, whatever you say. But while you... do whatever the hell it is you doing, I'm going to stroll over behind the antique shop just to get the lay of the land. Then I'll get a table, right over there" – he pointed to a sidewalk café back across Abila Street – "and I'll wait for you. Then, maybe, we can discuss this plan of yours. Who knows, maybe I'll see something round back of the shop."

Willy's tone made it known that he didn't understand. Even so, he honored Kirk's request to be alone and began walking toward a cross street just beyond the antique shop.

Earlier Kirk had noticed an isolated area across an adjacent, vacant lot. The ground sloped gradually toward several large poplars and walnuts. The trees gripped the banks of the little stream which ran all the way through the old Roman city.

The perennial waters of the little stream accounted for the location of Gerasa and the settlements which had followed over the past two thousand years. Under one of the poplars at the edge of the creek, Kirk spotted a small natural terrace. A partially exposed root which retained the soil behind it had formed the secluded little area and created a perfect sitting place. And the old poplar's trunk was curved just right to serve as a comfortable back rest.

Kirk sat down. He fixed his attention into the timeless solace of water burbling along a rocky stream bed. As he gazed into the creek, the clamor of the town and street were quietly sealed away inside another dimension. He felt alone in the pristine solitude of some faraway time and place where logic and reason yielded to the ancient senses of intuition and feeling. Within this absolute focus, some new authority seized his psyche; its power bonding the levels of his mind into a single harmonious, receptive equilibrium.

A multitude of scenes arced across his mind's eye flashing through at the speed of light, bursts of insight registering images, places, objects, events and smells, some familiar, some obscure. The extrasensory download programmed his consciousness with the awareness Father Casey had promised. And it confirmed to him the urgency of the situation. Jolted, Kirk leapt to his feet. He started back toward the street almost forgetting his backpack. He forced himself not to sprint to the restaurant.

Willy had expected to be the one waiting at the café. He was not. Kirk took a sidewalk table. He was beside himself with anxiety. He strained to act detached, pretending to be engrossed with the menu. When the waiter greeted him he ordered only a Diet Coke to stake his claim to the table. He resisted glancing at his watch every few seconds. He had to maintain the complacent persona of the traveler.

The waiter returned with a Diet Pepsi. He didn't bother to explain the political necessity of the substitution. He poured a token amount of the barely cool soda into a glass, set it and the bottle on the table and withdrew back inside the cafe. When the foam dissipated Kirk took a sip just as Willy approached from behind. He came from opposite the direction Kirk had been watching. Willy unclipped his fanny pack and dropped it on the table. He looked directly at Kirk clearly waiting for him to speak first.

Kirk obliged. "You find out anything?"

"Found out that the shop is bigger than it looks from the front; it's L shaped. The back's the width of three of the shop fronts on the street. There's a loading dock and a garage back there, roll up steel door on the garage. No windows but I could see enough through a crack between slats to tell there's a car inside, backed in. Look like a big Mercedes. Didn't see any security cameras or anything like that, nothing that sticks out." With a hint of sarcasm he added. "You all done with your cogitating?"

"Yeah, all done," said Kirk. "She's still here." Kirk raised his eyes to meet Willy's; his fixed gaze defending his statement. "I know that she's still here."

"Where?"

"As soon as I get a look around that shop, I think we'll know."

The wide-eyed look on Willy's face expressed his doubts. But he had nothing to offer in rebuttal. Willy conceded to himself that, maybe, Kirk might hear or see something that he missed in Shahadeh's. Maybe. And this is what we agreed on earlier, to split up and look around independently.

What he found unsettling was Kirk's sudden conviction or faith or whatever it was. Kirk's conviction reminded him of someone or some situation that bothered him but he couldn't quite recall the experience. Yet, for some reason he didn't understand, he felt compelled to follow Kirk's lead.

"Like I said a while ago, Kirk, I'm fresh out of ideas so I'll just have to run with whatever you got in mind?"

Kirk pursed his lips and gave a quick nod. "Okay, here's what I think we have to do. Will you attract any attention if you stand around behind the shop for a few minutes?"

"I doubt it. It's not like a deserted alley; it's another little street. There's a small grocery market back there... and a shoe shop. I can probably hang around for five or ten minutes with no problem. Matter of fact, I'll just wait and get a soda back there."

"Good, then if you'll watch the back for five minutes, that will probably give me enough time to take a look around inside. Then you come on around to the front. I'll meet you out on the sidewalk between the shop and the next cross street down. But if I'm still inside, then you start window shopping until I come out. Either way, we'll decide what to do next then. Okay, why don't we get this over with?"

After he walked the few yards down the street from the cafe, Kirk stepped into Trans-Jordan Antiquities. He noticed an infrared sensor monitoring the door but he heard no alarm as he broke the invisible beam. Perhaps it was connected to a strobe light in the back or possibly it buzzed in a closed-off back room.

His eyes scanned the ceiling and high corners for video surveillance cameras. He saw none but the mirrored paneling behind the glass shelves on the back wall caught his attention; he wondered if some or all of it was one-way glass.

Willy was right; the posh showroom was out of place in the midst of all the other cheap, cluttered tee shirt shops that festered along Bail's sidewalk. Trans-Jordan Antiquities could fit in well among the Duval Street treasure shops in Key West or with the other exclusive places on Dizengoff in Tel Aviv. It was hard to believe that a typical visitor to Jerash would be a likely prospect for such expensive pieces. And there was only a smattering of inexpensive reproductions.

"Marhaba." The hello came from behind the bead curtain.

"Hello," Kirk answered.

"Oh, English," said the voice. "I come right out, just a minute please."

"Take your time, I'm just looking." Kirk slowly paced along the glass counters inspecting the contents.

Most of the tags were face down but the few that weren't had penned-in numbers written in fractional form. Kirk noticed that on each tag the lower number was about two thirds the top; he assumed that the greater number was the price in U.S. dollars and the lesser was the object's cost in euros. The whole numbers, he thought, were dinars. Again Willy was right. Of the few scarabs with their tags visible, the prices were four to five times the amounts noted on the reverse side of Michelle's business card.

Kirk squinted. An annoying flash of bright light from the overhead tracks kept reflecting off of something. The beam continued to hit his eyes regardless of where he moved. He was reminded of the irritating flashes bouncing off of a spot-lit mirror ball on the ceiling of some sleazy motel lounge.

Then it registered with him. The reflected flashes were coming from a mound of dirty tea glasses on a brass pendulum tray on the floor. From beside the opening with the beaded curtain the stacked glasses intercepted the last rays from the late afternoon sun.

Kirk moved as close as he could get to the tray of glasses. One of the display cases stood between him and the area behind it where the glasses were stacked next to the back wall. In some of the glasses, cigarettes had been extinguished in the last few drops of tea, in others a wadded paper napkin. Several held the dark, limp sprigs of mint or a small teaspoon. Then it caught his eye, in the bottom of one of the glasses, the one from which the beam of light now glanced. Kirk flinched, he blinked his eyes tightly shut and immediately opened them. Intensely, he focused in on a small object in one of the glasses at the bottom of the pile. He strained to lean over the top of the display counter to see inside the container without the distortion of looking through the curved surface. It was not his imagination; folded perfectly, as if perching in the concealment of the wilted mint leaves, one of the little gum wrapper origami birds sparkled from the bottom of the glass.

Immediately, Kirk turned and started toward the door. Noticing the apparent departure, the voice again boomed from behind the veil of beads.

"Okay, okay, I coming right now."

Still a few paces from the entrance, Kirk paused long enough to answer the voice. "I'll be right back. I want my friend to see one of your pieces. Can you ship to the United States?" Kirk hoped to sound as normal as possible, trying to give the impression of an unrushed exit.

"Yes, yes, we ship anything."

"Good. Then I'll be back shortly," Kirk promised.

Out on the sidewalk Kirk peered toward the corner. No Willy, but then it had hardly been five minutes since they parted. The adrenalin took every ounce of control he could muster to act the part of a leisurely tourist shopper. He strolled by the adjacent shops pretending to be interested in the amalgamation of cheap trinkets on the outside tables. After an agonizing minute or two, Willy rounded the corner and walked up to the trinket pile where Kirk was waiting.

"Well?"

"Time to start asking questions," said Kirk. "I know she's been there so let's see what he has to say."

"You got the picture?" Willy asked.

"Right here on top." Kirk answered pointing to the outside pocket on his day pack.

"What are we going to do if he says he hasn't seen her?"

"I don't know. I'll show him how I know she's been there. But if he won't tell us anything... I don't know. We'll have to figure it out as we go."

Willy looked puzzled. "What you mean, show him how you know she's been there?"

"You'll know soon enough; come on, let's get back in there."

13

Kirk and Willy entered the antique shop together. The fat man had just come out from the backroom; the beaded strands were still swinging in the passage way. His face stretched into a wide salesman's smile as he looked toward the pair who must be returning to buy something. With the corner of an embroidered shamakh draped over his shoulders he blotted away beads of oily sweat from his neck and face.

"Welcome again my friends," he said. "Now tell me what it is that you like. I can ship anything in the shop anywhere, anywhere in the world."

Kirk carried his backpack by the loop on top. He walked over to the counter where Shahadeh was standing fumbling with the double zipper to the section of the pack that held the Michelle's picture. Willy, acting enamored with a display of oil lamps, positioned himself to keep an eye on the front doorway and sidewalk out front. Kirk removed the four-by-six glossy and held it up by a corner in front of Shahadeh.

"I'm looking for my sister. She was shopping around here and never came back to the hotel last night." He didn't know why he lied about the relationship – just one of those sixth sense, snap decisions.

Kirk locked his eyes on Shahadeh, searching for any trace of revelation in his expression. No acuity was needed; the fat man was obviously startled by the image. He snatched his eyes away from the photo. Nervously, he began polishing away some unseen blemish on the glass counter top, refusing to meet Kirk's gaze.

"She is not known to me."

"Is there anyone else in the shop who might have seen her?"

"No; no. I am only one here. Shop is closed when I am gone away."

"And you were here yesterday... all day?"

"Yes, all day, she not come in here. I will remember pretty girl like her."

Kirk lowered his eyes. He turned toward Willy who stood poker faced, perfectly still, waiting to see what card he would play now. The fat man continued polishing the glass top. Kirk moved around behind the counter to the dirty glasses stacked on the brass pendulum tray. He rearranged several to get to the one he wanted. He removed it from the tray and paused with it in his hands. His back was toward the fat man. Shahadeh curiously turned his head slightly in Kirk's direction but didn't protest him being behind the counter.

"Then, if you will be so kind, Mr. Shahadeh... You are Shahadeh, aren't you?" Kirk asked.

"Yes, Ali Shahadeh Jaber. I am the owner."

"Good. Then, as I started to say, maybe you can explain something to me, Mr. Shahadeh?"

Kirk turned and took the few steps to where the fat man stood slumped with both arms on the display case. Again he faced him squarely. Without eye contact, Shahadeh watched his every move. Kirk turned up the tea glass and poured out the saturated contents onto the display case. A few drops of tea, the wilted sprig of *nana* and the tiny bit of gum wrapper all puddled together on the spotless glass top. Kirk reached down and picked out the small scrap. He blew off the drips of tea, placed it in the flat palm of his hand and held it out for the fat man to inspect.

"This is what I want you to explain to me, Mr. Jaber. Who do you know who makes these little origami birds out of chewing gum wrappers?"

Shahadeh's eyes danced around the shop. He tried to pat away a new surge of sweat with the soiled shamakh. Kirk's penetrating stare into the fat man's evasive eyes demanded an answer. Shahadeh straightened and moved toward the other opening between the display cases. He walking on toward the entry door that Willy blocked. His posture and gate indicated that he was attempting to take control of the situation or, at least, put an end to it.

"If you have nothing to buy I have much work. You must leave so I can close shop. I never see the lady in picture so I can not help you. Now you have to..."

At the doorway Shahadeh reached out and cupped his hand behind Willy's bicep to escort the pair out of the shop. Without out so much as a glance at Kirk, Willy's powerful left fist exploded into the fat man's solar plexus. Shahadeh looked as if he had stepped into the path of a truck. With a kind of wheezing scream he crashed backwards onto the shiny tile floor, paralyzed, unable even to gasp. Within a second Willy straddled the helpless hulk. He reached down and twisted the shamakh into a makeshift grip and began dragging the amorphous mass toward the beaded curtain. He glanced back over his shoulder, grinned and then winked at Kirk.

"Big sonabitch sounds like a gut-shot bagpiper, don't he? But I'm gonna have him talking like a pet shop parrot real soon now. Close the door, Kirk; and turn that closed sign around while I help Mister Jaber into the back room."

Kirk could feel his heart pounding as he followed Willy's instructions. He looked out on the sidewalk. No one in sight seemed to be aware of anything out of the ordinary. Kirk tried to calm himself with the assumption that it was not unusual for Shahadeh to lock up when he used the toilet or even when he needed uninterrupted time to close a large sale. But he knew that now the clock was ticking. They were committed; the course of their lives rested precariously on the events of the next few minutes.

In the back room, amid a clutter of boxes, papers and unkempt shelves of supplies, Willy forced Shahadeh over onto his belly. Still using the twisted shamakh like a choker collar, Willy knelt on the fat man's back to control his movement as Kirk entered through the beaded curtain.

"Door's locked," Kirk said. "Everything seems to be okay outside."

"Good. Look in your pack and hand me some of those cable ties. I going to try and make Mister Jaber more comfortable."

Kirk retrieved the pack from the counter. He found the ties and held them out to Willy.

"Just one at a time," Willy said.

Willy took the tie and gripped it with his teeth. He pulled one of Shahadeh's arms behind his back and secured the nylon strap around his wrist. He repeated the sequence on the other arm, run-

ning the second band through the first to form an indestructible
pair of interlocking bracelets, the kind of plastic cuffs used to secure
paddy wagon passengers departing a civil disturbance.

Shahadeh regained control of his bruised diaphragm and began
protesting his predicament. With his leathery left hand, open this
time, Willy slapped the side of Shahadeh's face and ear so hard that
Kirk even winced before the fat man groaned with shock and pain.
Willy looked up at Kirk, no grin this time.

"Help me sit him on his big ass."

Kirk stepped over to the Shahadeh's side. Together they
twisted and lifted the cumbersome hulk up into a crossed ankle
sitting position with his back against two stacked boxes of fan-fold
computer paper. His face no longer projected contempt or deceit,
only discomfort and fear. Willy squatted down directly in front of
Shahadeh; he peered straight into his eyes.

"Kirk, keep an eye out front; this may take a few minutes."

Kirk positioned himself so that he could see through the beads
to the locked front door.

"Now that we've got Mister Jaber's attention... Least I hope
we've got your attention, Mister Jaber, because your life depends on
it. So, you listen carefully to what..."

"Please, don't..."

Willy drew back his open left hand. Shahadeh flinched and
tucked his head. Both held their positions.

"Shut your mouth," said Willy. "I'll tell you when to talk. For
now, you listen to me. You understand?"

Shahadeh nodded, yes.

"Mister Jaber, I think you should know that I'm not going to
play some kinda game of wits with you. Cause, you see, I ain't too
bright; I know that. I have to keep things simple, so I can understand them. And once my mind is made up, nothing change it.
Most us Cajuns are like that, ya know. Now, I suppose you might
be thinking, what in the hell do all this bullshit have to do with my
predicament. I can understand that; so I'm gonna explain it to you
real simple, so we both understand each other.

"You see, Mister Jaber, my mind is made up about two things.
First thing, I think you know all about what happened to Miss
Michelle, that's her name just in case you was wondering. Second
thing, if we don't get her back real quick... I intend to make you
suffer a lot and then I'm gonna kill you. Now, I know you got to be

wondering just how committed I am. And I can understand that, too. So, I'm gonna show you.

"Damn, I almost forgot! Mister Jaber, me and my friend here, we don't give a rat's ass what all you're mixed up in. It don't matter to us if you dealing stolen artifacts or smuggling hash. We don't even care if you sleeping with the sheep. So you got nothing to lose by helping us. But if you don't help us... You're gonna die in a bad way, I guarantee."

Shahadeh's eyes gaped with panic. Rivulets of sweat raced down his face and neck but he remained quiet and still. Willy knew the fat man's silence could signal his continuing resistance as well as his submission. He would wait for Shahadeh to speak first. It was a proven technique he had witnessed many times, years ago. He despised the memories and the flashbacks into those demonic times but now, after thirty years, those same, terrible recollections might well be Michelle's last chance.

Willy had served with the First Marine Division, First Recon Battalion in Vietnam. The objectives of every long-range reconnaissance patrol always included the capture of prisoners for intelligence. If a VC or NVA was taken, a member of the capturing recon team was required to sit in on the G-2 (Naval Intelligence) interrogation to validate the prisoner's information. The experience was never pleasant.

Effective interrogation is a morbid art with proven methodology. Volunteered information is much more reliable, and revealing, than answers to questions. Never start off with questions to which you don't know the answer. The fear of pain is a more powerful motivation than pain itself.

"Kirk, you're going to have to give me a hand here," said Willy.

Through the hanging beads Kirk took a look out front before moving to where Willy knelt next to Shahadeh. When he was positioned at their side, Willy stood up. He leaned over and gripped the obese man's ankles.

"You gonna have to help me with this, Kirk. You know I don't have much strength in this right hand."

"Okay, what you want me to do?"

"Let's pull him back and roll him over."

With Shahadeh again lying on his belly, Willy took his knife out of his pocket, a Camillus with a locking three-inch blade, sharp enough to shave paper. Willy reached down and forced his hand inside the waistband of the fat man's pants. He raised the fabric just below the belt and sliced through the seam. Then he lifted the knife and clamped it in his teeth to free both of his hands. With two quick jerks he ripped the fat man's trousers open all the way down the seat and through the crotch to the base of the zipper.

Shahadeh started kicking as if he was trying to crawl away on his knees and forehead. Willy caught a glimpse of Kirk's face. He could hardly suppress a grin; Kirk's eyes were almost as wide as Shahadeh's. Again, he slapped the fat man's ear hard with his open left hand.

"*Bismallah*! *Bismallah*! I know nothing. I know nothing."

Willy held his silence, ignoring the pitiful denials. Kirk turned, trying to see out front if Shahadeh's cries were attracting any attention. Nothing. The noxious Arabic music still repeating itself through the CD changer was good cover; the vocalist's god-awful falsetto warbling could mask the moaning on a burn ward, Kirk thought.

Again Willy used the knife. This time he severed the elastic band of Shahadeh's under shorts. He ripped them open to the base of the fly exposing the fat man's bare buttocks. They were dimpled with cellulite and covered with black body hair.

"Damn," Willy said. "You ever see such an ugly ass? Old Paul Rodriguez is right; these guys got hair on em in places where monkeys don't. Hand me a couple more cable ties. And, Kirk, unplug that telephone from the wall and bring it over here, too"

"Here," said Kirk, "these are the last two."

"That's all I need. You can take the phone off; all I need is the cord."

Willy held one of the sixteen-inch nylon cable ties and inserted the pointed tip back through the lock-clasp end. He pulled it far enough through to form a four or five inch loop. He slipped the loop over his own right wrist and then ran about two feet of the phone cord through the same loop and secured it with a loose overhand knot.

"Okay, come on, I'm gonna need your help," said Willy. "Hold him down as flat as you can cause he's gonna start bucking."

Kirk looked puzzled but agreed with a grunt. He knelt at the fat man's head, facing Willy. He rested his hands on Shahadeh's trapeziums and then nodded at Willy. Willy crawled over one of the fat legs and placed himself just below and inside Shahadeh's knees. He used his own knees to spread the fat man's legs apart. Shahadeh lurched and squalled, convinced that he knew what was coming next. Kirk glared at Willy but continued to push down hard on the convulsing captive's shoulders. Willy answered Kirk's threatening stare with another grin.

"Just trust me, *mon ami.*"

Skeptical but silent, Kirk continued to force the fat man's chest into the wet tile floor.

With a lightning quick motion, Willy seized Shahadeh's sweaty scrotum, slid the nylon loop down over his fist and cinched it tight trapping the testicles below the loop. Willy was delighted, the technique worked as well on a fat man's balls as it did on alligator snouts in the bayous. Kirk was astounded, damn well relieved and astounded. He fought to hold the porpoising Arab on the piss-slickened floor.

"Okay; okay; okay," Shahadeh bellowed. "Don' do this thing; I help you; I tell you everything. She here, she here; I show you now."

Kirk leaned back in amazement. He relaxed his control of Shahadeh's shoulders. Willy, now holding the phone cord, tied an overhand knot into the line so the end would not slip back through the cable tie. It would be one hell of an effective leash.

"Why, thank you, Mister Jaber," said Willy. "Please go ahead; we're listening."

"Down there, she down there."

Shahadeh tried to nod in the direction of a cheap copy Persian rug hung on the wall like a tapestry. Kirk sprang to his feet and darted over to the wall. Behind the rug he found a closed door. He pressed down on the handle and pushed; it was not locked. With his back against the wall and hinges, he eased the door open with his fully extended left arm. It swung over a passage way landing not quite wide enough to accept the full width of the door.

From the right side of the landing, a ship-ladder style stairway descended into the darkness. Kirk started down the steep steps sideways holding onto each treadle behind him for balance. Ten or twelve feet down the wooden steps ended on a bare stone landing. Another series of steps, cut into the soft sandstone, continued down. Kirk's eyes were beginning to adjust to the darkness. By the light from the doorway above he could see further down the stone steps. Now he could see a dim light coming from below. A few more steps down he stepped into a large cavern of a room. He recognized it as an old—probably ancient—cistern. The pit was now used as a basement, to store junk. And, perhaps, it held stolen artifacts too risky to display openly.

One naked light bulb hung from high above, it barely lit the big room. He could smell the musky odor of bat guano and mildew. Something moved. Kirk jumped. He turned toward the corner to his left; the movement came from behind several bales of packing straw. He eased around the bales.

"I've got her!" he shouted.

Again Kirk yelled at the top of his voice, unsure if Willy could hear him so far above. Michelle was lying on a thin cot mattress on the floor. Sleeping? He gripped her shoulders and shook her gently. Repeatedly he spoke her name. She responded only with incoherent, tonal sounds.

In the dim light Kirk strained to see if she was hurt. No injuries were visible. He pressed his wrist against her forehead. No fever. He opened her eyelids; they moved but neither fixed nor focused. Her slacks and blouse were on her day pack at her feet. She was dressed in a typical, light gray Arab dress, ankle length with long sleeves. And a white *shayla,* which had fallen down around her shoulders, exposed her short blonde hair.

Again he shook her and called her name. Still her only response was muddled mumbling. Kirk reminded himself that there was no time to waste. Already it was doubtful that they could get back in time to cross at the Hussein Bridge. Still kneeling beside her, Kirk slipped his arms under her legs and back and stood with her in his arms. She wasn't very heavy, at least not until he reached the top of the steep wooden ladder way and stepped out into the backroom.

"Got her," Kirk said between puffs.

"How is she?" Willy asked.

"Okay, I guess, but I think she's been drugged."

Kirk dropped down on one knee and tried to sit Michelle up with her back to another stack of boxes. Her head slumped forward. Again he searched for visible injuries. There were no bruises or cuts. She didn't even appear too unkempt.

"Hold this cord a minute," said Willy. "I wanna see something. If he make a move, just jerk it a little."

Kirk moved over and took the phone cord leash attached to

the little collar. Willy slid on his butt over to Michelle's side. He searched her face and visually inspected every inch of her body. He raised the hem of the dress and examined her ankles and feet. He unbuttoned the sleeves and slid them up above her elbows. She was beginning to flex, slightly.

"Just what I thought," Willy said. "He got her doped up, all right. See these tracks? Musta knocked her out with a Mickey and been shooting her up since then."

Kirk strained to see the punctures. He winced. Then his eyes flashed fire and focused on Shahadeh's face like lasers. With two short steps, like a place-kicker, his boot connected with the fat man's gut. He jerked the phone cord hard. Shahadeh howled with pain.

"Kirk, no! We gonna need him. We gotta get back out of here, ya know, and he's gonna take us in that big Mercedes. Matter fact we need to leave right now."

Kirk hurried back down into the cistern basement to get Michelle's backpack and clothes. Not taking his eyes off Shahadeh for more than a couple of seconds, Willy found a hand towel and soaked it with cold water from a demijohn cooler. He patted the cold, wet terrycloth on Michelle's face and then draped it around the back of her neck. She responded, struggling to emerge from her deep sleep.

After Kirk stepped out of the stairwell with Michelle's things he and Willy spent the next few minutes whispering through alternate escape scenarios. They decided it had to be down to the Allenby bridge; the Hussein Crossing would be closing at eight, only fifteen minutes away. Willy was sure they could make the Allenby by the 10 p.m. deadline; they had to.

Shahadeh offered no resistance as the men lifted him to his feet and directed him through the garage door to the driver's side of the big Mercedes. When Kirk had opened the door, Willy again restrained the fat man with the shamakh. Facing him forward, pressed against the inside of the open car door, Willy stooped low and slid the leash cord between the seat cushion and back rest. Kirk opened the back door and took hold of the tag end as it emerged into the back seat area. Willy opened the knife and started to cut through the plastic handcuffs but then leaned around to face Shahadeh.

"I'm gonna untie your hands but don't forget about your little mooring line here."

Shahadeh remained silent nodding his head in understanding. Willy inserted the point of his knife into the clasp on one of the wrist bindings and pried it up enough to slide the lead end back out freeing his hands to drive. Gripping the shamakh, he told Shahadeh to sit. His face contorted with trepidation, the fat man lowered himself behind the steering wheel of the big 450SEL, his every movement as calculated as an old explosive ordinance disposal expert. And as he settled into the soft leather, Kirk reeled in the slack in the phone cord, ready to set the hook in an instant.

"Oh," said Willy, "better fasten your seat belt."

"Oh, god, yes!" agreed Shahadeh.

He stretched the seat and chest belt across himself, snapped it shut and gave the straps a couple of good test tugs. Willy maneuvered his way around the front of the car just making the tight squeeze between the bumper and the garage door. Once on the other side he climbed into the front passenger seat. Inside, he ran the lead end of the spare cable tie through the stitched in loops on both ends of Shahadeh's seat belt and cinched them together. The ties were never as strong when they were reused; nevertheless, the fat man was effectively secured in the driver's seat.

"Soon as you get Michelle we can haul ass," Willy said.

They were back in a trice. This time he supported her using her arm around his neck and his arm around her waist. He lowered her into the back seat behind Willy. He snapped the seat belt around her hoping it would help to keep her sitting up. It did but still her head hung limp, her chin resting between the clavicles. Kirk returned to collect the packs and was back within seconds. He leaned down into the door and looked at Willy.

"We ready?"

"Yeah," said Willy. "Key's in the car. Go ahead and open the door."

Again Willy made certain that the fat man was completely aware of the consequences of not following instructions. Shahadeh swore an oath to Allah; he would be obedient and helpful. When Kirk had the door open he shifted into drive and eased out of the garage. He swung the door shut and climbed into the back seat carefully avoiding tangling his feet in the coils of phone cord on the floorboard. Before he buckled himself in he leaned over, raised the shayla from Michelle's shoulders and fixed it over her head with a loose knot under her chin.

"Good thinking," said Willy. "While you're at it, pull those two shamaghs out of your pack."

Kirk and Willy wrapped the checked shawls loosely around their necks, and over the shoulders. From the outside, the car and passengers appeared quite ordinary as it negotiated the streets of Jerash. Willy knew enough about the area to question each turn as Shahadeh worked his way out of town and into the countryside heading south toward the Allenby Bridge border crossing.

On the straight stretches Willy continued to quiz Shahadeh about his reasons for abducting her. What he had planned to do with her? Why Michelle? Shahadeh never once mentioned the business card. Instead, he gave a vague explanation of being forced to participate. More than once he claimed the limited English excuse to evade an answer.

Twice within the first few kilometers they passed Royal Jordanian Police, once checking the papers of another driver and once stopped on the side of the highway as one of the two observed salat. They were easy to spot in their British green Land Rovers, starched khakis and red checked *shamaghs* with big black e*gals*.

"Here," said Kirk. "This ought to help. It was in the pocket behind your seat."

Across the seat back he handed Willy a road map of Jordan. Willy opened and refolded it so that the right sections were now the top panels. For several minutes he studied various routes. Holding the map so that Shahadeh could see it too, he used his finger to point out a bypass route around both Suweileh and Salt, the only large towns between them and the border. On the map his finger continued south along the road that skirted the east side of the Dead Sea, on toward Aqaba, an attempt to keep Shahadeh unaware of their real destination. Shahadeh nodded that he understood.

In just under an hour the big white German car began the descent from the Jordanian Plateau and down into the river valley. Shahadeh shifted the transmission back into third to assist the brakes with the steep grade. The lamps of Jericho were already visible in spite of the backlighting of the dusk sky.

Michelle was beginning to awaken from the drug induced sleep. She sat stoned limp with her head resting against the padded quarter-panel. Her groggy stare was interrupted by extended blinks.

But she was waking and that would solve one hell of a problem, how to get an unconscious woman across an international border.

Willy noticed that Shahadeh was visibly more nervous – maybe even on the edge of panic – the closer they came to the Israeli border. He was afraid that his finger tracing the route on the map hadn't convinced him that they were actually going to Aqaba. Willy was sure that Shahadeh was no fool. The fact that only a quarter tank of fuel didn't seem to matter may well have been a tip off that they were on their way to Israel, a destination much closer than the Gulf of Aqaba, over 400 kilometers to the south. Regardless of the cause, Willy thought that Shahadeh's growing uneasiness was the most immediate threat.

"Pull off down there," said Willy.

Shahadeh obeyed and turned off the highway onto a two-path trail which most likely led to some Bedouin's camp a few miles up the wadi. When they were out of sight of the main road Willy ordered Shahadeh to stop the car. Then he rolled down the window and listened. Silence.

"What's up?" Kirk asked.

"We gonna leave him here."

Willy turned to Shahadeh. His eyes revealed his apprehension at having stopped in so remote a place. Willy knew he had to reassure the fat man that he would not be harmed if he continued to cooperate.

"Mister Jaber, listen to me. The safest thing we could do would be to kill you. And you deserve it for what you did. But we not going to. What we gonna do is leave you here and drive away. In about two hours we're gonna have somebody call and tell the police where they can find you. When they do, what you tell them is your business because, like I say, we don't care what you mixed up in. But, if they should catch us and start asking questions, we gonna tell exactly how it was. And you're the only one who knows what all else they might find out about you if they start looking.

"So... seems to me the best thing for us all is for you just to wait till somebody come and get you. By then we'll be home. We sure as hell ain't gonna say nothing bout what happened. All this mess will be over for everybody. So now we gonna help you out of the car and, like I said, nobody gonna hurt you if you do what we say. Okay?"

Shahadeh nodded big as if what Willy had said made perfect

sense to him, too. While he was still secured by the cable-tied seat belt, Willy told Shahadeh to reach down, find the leash cord and to pull it back into the front seat. With the first glint of relief in his eyes, he quickly followed the instructions. Willy and Kirk got out of the car at the same time.

"Wait a minute, Kirk, I gotta get the tie off the seat belt so he can get out."

Willy removed the knife from his pocket and stooped back into the front seat.

"There, Mister Jaber, now let's go find you somewhere comfortable you can wait till they come to get you."

The sun had been down for over fifteen minutes but there was still enough light to see by. Down the slope to the right of the trail Willy saw a small grove of tamarisk and one larger tree. On the slope just above the lone algarroba was a jutting rock level enough to sit on in relative comfort. Slipping on loose gravel and soil all the way, the three made their way down to the rock. Kirk held onto the phone cord as Willy tried to steady Shahadeh. When they reached the flat rock Willy told Shahadeh to sit. Then with the last cable tie he again locked his wrists together, behind his back.

Willy had Kirk slide the few feet on down to the carob tree. He climbed up and tied the end of the phone cord out on a limb that grew back toward Shahadeh's rock perch. The knot was too high to be reached from the ground, the cord too short for Shahadeh to slide down to the base of the tree. Willy made sure that Shahadeh was aware of these restrictions to his travel.

Willy placed an open bottle of water at Shahadeh's side. He made sure he could maneuver well enough to grip the neck in his teeth, turn it up and drink. Willy and Kirk paused before starting back up, both trying to think of any detail they may have overlooked that could endanger their escape.

For the first time since his ordeal began, Shahadeh looked into their faces. Both knew what he was thinking: are they leaving me here to die? Kirk reached over to the man and loosened the twisted shamakh. He folded it tricorner and placed it properly on Shahadeh's shoulders.

"We will send someone for you."

They left him sitting on the rock, sweating, wheezing, watching their every step as they climbed away. After tread-milling up the incline, they paused to catch their breath.

"Why do I feel like a damn criminal?" Kirk's were the first words spoken as they reached the car. Willy didn't answer.

Both climbed into the front seat. Kirk leaned over the back of the seat to check on Michelle. She was a bit more responsive but still groggy. He poured more water on the damp towel and again sponged her face and neck. Willy started the car. For a heart pounding moment, the tires spun on the loose gravel but then caught traction. They backed up onto the main road and were away, on down into the valley and to the bridge.

At the base of the mountain face the secondary road dead-ended into the river valley highway. Like Israel's Highway 90, it spanned the length of the country, from north to south, through the great rift valley. They passed the first road sign directing the way to the border crossing. Now the darkness protected them as again they drove through the more populated areas.

Nine twenty, forty minutes to spare, they were at the border. Willy turned into the parking lot. He was relieved; the lot was over half filled, enough cars to make this one more difficult to spot. Signs were everywhere. He didn't care what they said as long as they could abandon Shahadeh's car and get across before any time limits expired or authorization was questioned. There was a vacant space surrounded by other cars near the center of the lot. Willy took it.

"Let's get these scarves off," said Willy. "Stuff them up under the seat. Damn! Did you check to see if her passport's with her stuff?"

"Turn on the dome light," said Kirk.

He leaned over into the back seat and pulled the backpack back over with him. He unzipped the front flap, shuffled through the loose articles and ripped open the Velcro security pocket.

"Yeah, it's right here."

"Hell of a time to be thinking about that." Willy softly pounded the palm of his hand on the rim of the steering wheel. Godahmity! What else ain't we thought of?"

Michelle began mumbling a moan. Kirk leaned back and held the back of his hand to her cheek. She leaned onto it trapping it between her face and shoulder. He felt her warm tears and he knew her ordeal would not automatically end after her first few steps across the border. The thoughts of her torment rekindled his rage. Now he wished that he could give the fat man a few more kicks

in his repulsive gut. And he longed to maim his spirit the way he
feared Michelle's had been, yet again. But now he had to get her
out; out of the long dress, out of the car and out of Jordan.

Willy stood outside the car and kept watch while Kirk wrestled
with getting Michelle back into her khaki slacks and stone washed,
denim shirt. With every button, snap and hook he reassured her
that she was safe and that now everything was all right.

When he first felt them he was stunned. Tears were pooling in
his own eyes; it had been years. Must be the stress of the situation
he thought, couldn't be anything more. I've only known her for a
couple of weeks, he told himself again.

"Michelle, listen to me," Kirk said. "You have to try and
walk."

She gave a weak nod and a mumbled okay. Willy walked around
the car and together they pulled her up and out. She leaned back
against the quarter panel, swaying, her equilibrium still impaired.
She offered no resistance, the way sleeping drunks always seem to.
Kirk thought to himself, how strong she is, to feel so bad and yet
fight so hard.

All together, they started the walk to the first of three
Jordanian stations. Kirk knew they must look like fiesta goers staggering home after a hard night in some Mexican border town. For
sure, they weren't the typical tourists returning from the ruins of an
ancient civilization in a conservative Islamic nation.

But the incredible happened; neither the Jordanian Border
Police nor Customs raised any protest when Kirk stepped forward
with Michelle to take her turn at each checkpoint. When she was
asked the purpose for her visit to Jordan Kirk answered for her.
Even then, he did not detect any misgivings and there were no follow-up questions. Then it occurred to him that Jordan's finest may
well have respected him all the more for exhibiting such dominance
over his woman, an honored Oriental tradition.

They exited Jordan with no problem.

At the first Israeli checkpoint, Passport Control, Willy crossed
the yellow line when he was summoned to the window by a young
woman in a familiar blue uniform. After a few moments he turned
to Kirk. He and the girl in the blue uniform were beckoning for
them to come to the same window. As soon as they reached it a
young man emerged from the area beyond the passport booth.

"Would you please come with me, all three of you," he said.

Willy looked at Kirk with an oh-shit expression on his face. The young man led them into a small, bare room with only four vinyl on metal tubing chairs and a partition curtain. The fabric screen was the kind that slides in a track on the ceiling to give the illusion of privacy. He politely asked them to have a seat and said he would be back with them in a few minutes. Then he left the room through another door and closed it behind him. Michelle drooped over on Kirk and let her head drop onto his shoulder. Even in such a precarious situation, he enjoyed the sensation of her weight pressing against him and of her hair on his neck. After all these hours, it still had a hint of the fragrance of her shampoo, or so he imagined.

"What you think?" Kirk asked.

"Don't know," Willy answered. "Could be anything from a strip search to a drug test. They may give us the works cause we the only ones here and they just bored. I don't know."

"You don't think that…"

Willy read his thoughts. "Not hardly. They would have had to find him, find the car, make a lotta calls and then alert the Israelis through official channels. I don't see how, not in the ten, fifteen minutes since we left the car."

"Hope you're right."

A long thirty minutes later, the door opened. Two men entered the stark room, one in uniform and one in street clothes who identified himself as the Internal Security Commander of the Border Passage Unit. He assured them there was no problem with their credentials and that he was there at the request of his superiors to provide whatever assistance that they might need. He told them that one of his men would be driving them to another location just a few miles away. He all but ignored Michelle's stupor, except to ask if she needed medical attention. They tried to explain that they were all just dog tired. They thanked him for his help but assured him that all they needed was to get back to the kibbutz to get some rest. The seasoned Shin Bet operative wore a perceptive smile but said nothing to indicate how well he recognized the difference between travel fatigue and an adrenalin drain exhaustion. He told them that Sergeant Major Mor would return shortly to show them to the car.

They had been in the new Toyota Land Cruiser less than ten minutes when it turned off of Highway 90 into the Monastery of Saint Gerasimos. The mute driver stopped at a side door to one

204 ᥑ JIM LEVER

of the few buildings which flanked the main church. One of the brothers met them with a soft-spoken greeting. As he escorted the three into what appeared to be the living area of a small dormitory the Toyota drove off. The monk introduced himself as Brother Spyridon. He offered tea and insisted that they make themselves comfortable and he started his retreat to prepare it.

"Oh, is there a telephone here?" Kirk asked.

Willy gave him an are-you-serious glance.

"No, I'm sorry," the monk answered. "We don't have one. Someone will be here to assist you shortly. I'm sure he can get you to a telephone. I'll be right back with your tea."

Kirk opened his eyes wide; he had dozed off. He was still unrested since the exhausting night on the cliffs of Arbel, He wasn't even aware that Brother Spyridon had returned with the pot of tea. Now it stood tepid in his glass. Michelle was slouching sideways in one of the cushioned chairs, also sleeping. He heard a car's engine idling. Willy was talking to someone just outside the cracked door. Before he could sort through his clouded thoughts, Willy entered the room followed by Father Casey.

The old priest walked straight to where Michelle was slumped in the chair and knelt in front of her. He took her hand, clasped it inside both of his and fixed his eyes on her face. Within moments she blinked into focus and shifted her eyes to his. Immediately the tears puddled up but she kept silent. They both remained still; neither spoke for long, precious seconds.

"Well now," Father Bill spoke just above a whisper. "Why don't we get you home?"

14

MOSHE HEARD Someone outside asking one of the volunteers where they could find him. He opened the office door; two men were approaching.

"I'm Moshe Benjamin. What may I do for you?"

"Shalom, Doctor Benjamin, it's Avi Landau from the IAA."

"Well of course it is, Avi. Didn't recognize you till my eyes adjusted to the sunlight. Thank you for coming up so promptly."

"Certainly. Moshe, this is Inspector Efi Shimon from the Galilee Police Sub-District. We're in his jurisdiction here, and down at the site."

The men spent almost no time with typical introduction small talk.

"Professor," said Inspector Shimon, "Mr. Landau filled me in briefly but why don't you start over and bring me up to date and… let me know how you think we can be of assistance."

"Fine," Moshe said, "Why don't we have a seat?"

Landau walked over to the sink in the kitchen nook of the efficiency apartment in use as the expedition office. He took down a coffee glass from the cabinet, filled it with water from the tap and gulped it down without lowering the glass. He refilled it and walked back to the table where Moshe and the inspector were sitting. He stood and continued sipping the water as Moshe recounted his reasons for calling the Israel Antiquities Authority.

He related the account—at least the parts that Willy decided to tell him about—of Michelle's trip into Jordan and of her abduction and rescue from the Trans-Jordan Antiquities shop. He described the business card with the offering price for the various scarabs penned in on the back. He told the inspector that many of the pieces of pottery Willy had seen for sale in Shahadeh's shop could have only come from Israeli coastal sites and that they were probably missing from some university's lab or storage room if not from one of the museums.

Inspector Shimon cautioned Moshe that regardless of where Shahadeh's inventory had come from, it would be next to impossible to ever get any of it back. Landau entered the conversation and assured the inspector that they, both Professor Benjamin and the IAA, were more concerned with how the artifacts were winding up in a Jordanian retail shop in the first place. They had to know who was stealing them and who was taking them out of the country.

Moshe informed the inspector that, this year alone, several artifacts had been stolen right out of the squares and two scarabs were missing from the field lab. Shimon asked if he had any suspicions about anyone in particular. Moshe told him that he did not but that now he was concerned because the business card from Shahadeh's had been found in a portable toilet on the site. He said that before he heard about the card, he thought locals or resident kibbutznics the most likely culprits.

"It must have been dropped by someone connected with us," said Moshe. "I think it highly unlikely that a thief in the night would make the effort to use a Port-a-pot."

"Do you still have this card?" Shimon asked.

"I don't; I haven't seen it," Moshe answered. "The girl might still have it."

Inspector Shimon told Moshe that his account of the situation was pretty much what Avi had written in his IAA "Request for Investigation" form. He promised to do what he could but explained that his hands would be tied as far as pursuing the matter on the Jordanian side or expecting any help from them. He added that, depending on who was involved over there, it might actually hurt their chances of solving the case if the Jordanian authorities became aware the investigation. Both Moshe and Avi understood, and agreed.

"I do need to talk with your people, the ones who were in Jordan," said Shimon. "But you can tell them not to be alarmed. The girl is back, unhurt. That's the important thing. Other than that, I could care less what happened over there."

Moshe sensed that Shimon suspected there was more to the

story of the girl's rescue than Willy had related. He thought so, too. But he was resolved not to know any more than he did.

"I'm sure they'll be willing to help in any way they can. The young woman is still quite shaken over the whole event, as you can imagine. Most young women – men too for that matter – would already be packed up and trying to get home. She's determined to stay, if you can believe it; she's a tough one."

"Sounds like it. May I use this room? I'd like to interview them this afternoon, while everything is still fresh in their memory?"

"If you don't mind, I'll let you use my room," said Moshe. "It's private and there won't be any interruptions. All of our area supervisors will be showing up here shortly to do the day's paperwork and this is the only place our photographer is set up to do his sorting and cataloging."

"Of course," said Shimon. "By the way, there's something else I need to ask about. Probably nothing to it but last week we got a call from the Palestinian Authority Police in Jenin about a missing person... Give me a minute."

The inspector flipped through the leaves of his note pad then back through them again muttering to himself "what was his name, what was it." Asking for another minute, he unfolded a Nokia and tapped in a two-digit speed dial. He held the tiny cellular with one hand and continued thumbing through the note pad now on the table top.

"Leor, what's that missing Arab kid's name? ... The one the PA called about last week. ... I don't know; check the phone records on my desk. ... Thursday, I think. ... That's it; got it, thanks."

Shimon scribbled the name into his pad along with some other information he thought was related before he looked back up at Moshe.

"Name's Abbas Hashim. Supposed to be working around Beit Shean at one of the archaeological excavations. Anyway, he hadn't been heard from in two days after working all night. Probably been home since Friday and they just forgot to let us know, like they usually do. Damn PA, most incompetent bast..."

Moshe interrupted. "I know him. He works for me. He is missing. At least, I haven't seen him for a week and he's always been dependable."

Moshe told Shimon about the vandalism and thefts out at the site. He said that when a five hundred liter plastic water tank was stolen over the weekend, he offered Abbas overtime pay to stay out on the tel and keep an eye on things. Abbas seemed excited about the opportunity to earn the extra money but he hadn't been seen since that first night, last Tuesday. But neither had there been any more problems at the site. Moshe explained that he had thought Abbas might have misunderstood and thought that he was to work nights instead of days.

"I guessed he would show up pretty soon for his pay envelope. Oh, he still has one of our cellular telephones," said Moshe. "I left it with him and gave him specific instructions not to confront anyone. He was to call me if he saw anything out of the ordinary. Now that I think about it, I tried to call him but got no answer."

"Do you remember the time," Shimon asked?

"Not exactly; probably between eleven and twelve, just before I went to bed. I was in Jerusalem. I had just checked my voice mail, from my home phone. I'm bad about forgetting to recharge my cellular. The battery was down for... I don't know how long. I don't check my voice mail as often as I should either so there were quite a few messages waiting. The last one was one really garbled, impossible to understand, but I remember thinking that it might have been Abbas."

"Do you have the number for that cellular?"

"Yes, I've got it right here."

Moshe opened a dirty, green canvass brief case. The support straps that should hold the case open at ninety degrees had torn away long ago; dust flew as the strapless top flopped all the way back onto the table top. Shimon noticed that the contents were rather well organized in spite of the condition of the case. Moshe located a typed list of names and numbers. He held it up and pointed to a number for Shimon to copy.

"This is it," Moshe said. "This phone was to be used by the local who runs our errands but he wanted to use his own."

Shimon copied the number into his notes. Then he made another call and asked someone on the other end to run a printout on the usage. He switched off and told Moshe he'd let him know when he found out anything. He asked if Abbas had a battery charger with the phone. Moshe replied, no. He pointed to a plugged in charger on a table against the wall and told him that was it.

"Well, in my experience," Shimon said, "we're probably wasting time to even bother with this. You know how those people are; don't think they ever owe anyone an explanation for anything. Just part of their culture, you know. They all think they should be treated like some damn Bedouin sheik. Damned if I know how you can work with them."

Neither Moshe nor Avi made any comment; neither did they make eye contact with the inspector though his pause asked for their concurrence.

"Okay... then why don't I go ahead and get a statement from your people about their adventure in Jordan?"

"I'll show you to my room," said Moshe. "Do you want to talk to them one at the time?"

"Yeah, but I don't think this will take too long."

The interviews took longer than Shimon expected. Michelle was still foggy from the drugs and could do little more than give vague answers to most of Shimon's direct questions. Her account of the events from the time she left Nina until she began to feel Shahadeh's cushioned chair bobsledding her into unconsciousness was unremarkable.

It had been as Willy and Kirk suspected; she had gone into the shop and shown the card hoping to buy a few pieces at the prices written on the back. There had been another man in the shop, just a tourist Michelle thought.

He was wearing a turquoise bolo tie, with a shiny, maybe sterling, buffalo skull she thought. He was using the telephone but she couldn't hear what he was saying, not even enough to know if he was speaking English. With Shimon guiding her memory, she seemed to recall the feeling that the man acted rather at home in the shop, like a frequent customer or a business associate.

He and Shahadeh had retreated to a corner of the shop where the tourist appeared to be chiding Shahadeh with a scathing whisper. Michelle could remember nothing else but that he was tall and thin with a gaunt expression. As soon as he left the shop Shahadeh insisted on the tea-before-business courtesy. After she drank it the walls began to warp in and out of focus. She remembered thinking she must be sick from food poisoning. It was the last detail she could recall.

But she did still have the card. The inspector had her drop it into a plastic envelope. He would take it back to the lab not expecting it to be of much help. Shimon concluded that if the young woman had any more useful information, he would have to get it from her at a later time. He knew that the recurring thoughts must now be torturing her. The uncertainty of what might have happened while she was out had begun tallying its emotional toll. Shimon agreed with Moshe; she was a tough young woman. And he sensed that she was no newcomer to traumatic abuse.

Willy was a different story. Without much hesitation he gave an accurate account of the rescue with blunt, candid answers. Shimon seemed to relish the intriguing story which rang true to his tempered ear. He liked Willy. He liked his morgue humor and his all-bullshit-on-the-surface-no-bullshit-when-it-counts type personality. He would have made a good cop, he thought... maybe even a good partner.

"One last question. Did you guys leave Shahadeh where he could be found? If you didn't, he's probably on his last legs in this heat."

Shimon's glint and tone suggested more morbid fascination than worry about the fat man dying a terrible death.

"I marked the spot clearly in my mind. It's exactly seven kilometers from the river valley highway and a hundred meters down the dirt trail road. Anyway, Father Casey made a call; he told me someone would cut him loose before sun-up this morning, somebody else in the Franciscan mafia probably."

Willy's comment brought the first grin to Shimon's face when he heard the term applied to the Franciscans. He was well aware of the religious network's worldly powers. In the Middle East, the Greeks and Mormons had the political influence but the Anglicans and Franciscans owned the streets. With Franciscans handling his rescue, the fat man was in better hands than the Jordanian authority's.

The time spent with Kirk and Father Casey added almost nothing to the inspector's notes. Willy had pretty much covered it. One remark that Father Bill did make, however, was center target, or so Shimon thought. There had to be more to Michelle being held captive than her stumbling into some illicit antique business. The ready market for beautiful blondes in the clandestine world of Arab wealth? Maybe. But there were easier, safer and younger targets than an American school teacher in her thirties.

Things just didn't quite fit. Both the inspector and Landau could feel what they couldn't quite piece together. And Moshe could sense that Shimon was intrigued by the illogic. Moshe, who had remained silent throughout the questioning, now realized that this stick-carrot curiosity was the best chance for this case not to become sediment on the bottom of the inspector's prioritized stack of open files.

On parting, Shimon and Landau gave Moshe the assurance that they would do their best. Together, all three men walked to the IAA Citroen. Before they got into the old car, Shimon's cell phone rang. He answered and stood in the open car door with one foot on the rocker panel, listening to his call.

"Thanks, Na'ama. Yes, I'm on the way."

"That was my office calling back," Shimon said. "The last record of any call on the number you gave me was at 23:11 last Tuesday night to 05-369060, a one-minute call."

"That's my cell number," Moshe said. "He must have called just a few minutes before I tried him."

"Well... I still doubt there's anything to this missing person stuff. But I'll keep you up to date. And speaking of missing, I don't know if it'll help – we're spread pretty thin – but I'm going to ask the Rural Crime Unit to keep a watch on your work site. Actually, I think I'll bring Gavia out there myself.

"He just spent a couple of weeks on a law enforcement exchange tour in Georgia learning how to deal with farm-type crimes. I'm anxious to see if he learned a damn thing besides how to get fifty pairs of Levis in a carry-on bag.

"I want to nose around a bit and maybe Gavia can get an idea of what's been going on out there, too. We have a problem with everything from farm tractors to ag chemicals being stolen in this..."

"Big farm tractors? You must be joking," said Avi.

"I wish I were," said Shimon. "But you never know, it could all be connected."

From his expression, Shimon saw that Moshe couldn't see a likely connection.

"Not the artifact thefts," he explained. "I mean the water tank and tools stolen from your site. There could be a link between your stolen tank and... About a week or so ago over twenty thousand shekels worth of liquid herbicide was stolen from a moshav not far from here. But anyway, I'd love to see what you're digging up out there."

"I'll see that you get a tour of the site," said Moshe.

"Then I'll plan to get out there tomorrow morning, if that doesn't conflict with Gavia's schedule."

When Avi Landau and Inspector Shimon drove away Moshe returned to his office from the parking area. Three more visitors were slumped on the molded plastic furniture out front. Their faces and fanning hands expressed their discontent with the air force of insects, the wafting aromas, the cow sounds and the heat. They were strangers but Moshe recognized them as journalists, a film crew most likely. Writers were usually alone but even if a photographer happened to be along, they didn't huddle together like the video teams.

"Hello, Professor Benjamin, Colin Blair with the BBC. I recognize you from file footage. Our man, Reggie George, shot your dig down at Timnah a year or so ago. Great piece, if I may say so, sir. We came straight up from Ashkelon when we got word that you and Niles Thompson were on the verge of something big up here. Plan to spend a few days on the dig, with your permission, of course, sir. Why you won't even know we're..."

"Something big, you say. And just who told you that?" Moshe asked. "As if I didn't know," he mumbled just under his breath.

"Actually, sir, I don't know. My call, to get up here, came from our office in Amman. We would like to shoot some interviews this afternoon, you and Doctor Thompson for sure, and prob..."

Moshe interrupted, telling Colin Blair with the BBC that he was quite busy for the rest of the afternoon but he could find Niles Thompson in room twenty one.

"Niles is probably there now, taking a nap, but do go ahead and wake him. I'm quite sure he'll be thrilled at the opportunity to tell you everything that's going on up here, especially about his next major discovery. I'll have to get with you later, maybe tomorrow. By the way, where will you be staying? I think we're full up here on the kibbutz."

Blair said they were booked at a hotel in Tiberias, the closest they could find with fax and internet access. Even as Moshe attempted to withdraw back into the office, Blair followed, still quizzing him about the copper scroll. Just when would they get down to the treasure, he wanted to know.

Standing in the doorway, hands on his hips blocking the entrance, Moshe paused long enough to explain that he only learned of Sarah Bergman's theory the week before. He told Blair that she and Thompson had arrived yesterday, today had been their first day on the dig and the search for the scroll was their project, an adjunct to the Tel Kefar Expedition.

"Mister Blair," Moshe continued, "you and your crew are welcome on the site... And you're welcome to stay as long as you need. But I want you to give your viewers an accurate picture of the project in its entirety. Archaeology is about gaining knowledge and sharing it; it is not about searches for sensational treasures. I should hope that is what you think journalism should be about, too. I'll get with you later; now, good afternoon."

The door thudded shut.

15

"Good morning, Niles, Miss Bergman." Moshe greeted the pair as they walked toward the parking lot and the waiting buses.

"Oh, good morning to you Moshe," answered Dr. Thompson.

Sarah smiled and also returned Moshe's greeting. Niles and Sarah stopped on the pathway, waiting for Dr. Benjamin to lock his room and join them. It was 5:55 Tuesday morning, the fourth week of the Tel Kefar expedition. The days were getting shorter; it was still dark. The first shades of amber were not yet visible over the mountains of Jordan. There would not be enough light to work by for another thirty minutes.

Moshe had intended to make the announcement – and to call and instruct the bus company – that the schedule would be moved back fifteen minutes. But yesterday afternoon's interruptions and unexpected guests had taken his mind off his list of things to do. He made a mental note to make the announcement at breakfast on the tel.

"Well, Niles," Moshe said, "so how did it go with Colin Blair of the BBC? I guess he found you?"

"Uh...yes, yes he did. I was rather surprised that you sent him down, actually."

"Why so? I assume it was you who called him to cover the story."

Both Niles and Sarah responded with a surprised look.

"No, I didn't." Niles was emphatic. "In fact I'm rather uneasy about them being here. We've got a lot of work to do just to locate where to begin to search. And if... God, I don't even want to think about this. But if we don't locate the city gates—or even if we do but we don't find the codex this season—every damn treasure hunter in the country will be trying to sneak up here for a shot at finding it. So, no, I didn't call him or anyone else.

"Sarah? I'm sure you…"

"No sir," she answered. "I'm concerned about this much exposure, too. I mean, I'm sure of my theory but… Well, I've got a lot at stake. I was alarmed at the amount of talk going around the university. Guess you heard that our search for the, quote, Temple Treasure, was announced at an alumni banquet?"

"Yes, I knew that," Thompson answered.

"I guess I shouldn't be surprised," Moshe said. "I can't remember a secret ever being kept in this business for very long. What is it you say… that's water over the bridge? I suppose that all we can do now is to make certain that our expedition isn't turned into a damn baligon."

"A what?" Sarah asked.

Thompson grinned before he explained.

"A baligon," he said, "it's Russian for circus. The word was brought in by Russian Aliyahs; now it's pure Israeli vernacular."

"Yes, circus," Moshe said. "What I think I must do is tell all the area supervisors that every visitor must check in with me first. I will explain my rules to them."

"What rules?" asked Thompson.

"Don't know yet, I must make them up as we need them."

Moshe was right; it was still dark well after the teams reached the work areas. And after they had stretched the black mesh canopy aloft on the palisade of PVC poles, it was even darker in the squares below. He used the down time to introduce Niles Thompson and Sarah Bergman to the rest of the staff and volunteers.

Moshe also informed the team that, based on Ms. Bergman's brilliant research, the expedition mission now included the search for specific articles dating from the Roman period. The search, he told them, would presently be limited to a six-square area within Area B.

Moshe answered the team's barrage of questions by announcing that there would be a lecture that evening after dinner. The program would detail the particulars of Sarah's research and her theory having to do with the copper scroll from Qumran.

"So," concluded Moshe, "save all your questions for Ms. Sarah Bergman's lecture tonight." Moshe turned and gestured toward

Sarah. He laughed to himself when he saw the look of shock on her face.

As the audience started toward their work areas, Sarah made her way through the group to where Moshe stood, expecting her arrival. Before she had a chance to protest the sudden assignment, he addressed her.

"Ms. Bergman, I apologize for not giving you more notice but the idea only occurred to me as I was speaking. And, besides, I expect you to be a speaker in great demand very soon and this will be excellent preparation for you."

"But Professor Benjamin…"

"Don't worry about it; you're among friends and admirers. The time will be more like a question and answer session than a formal lecture. We'll all have lots of fun. Now, come on, I'll show you up to Area B."

Both Moshe and Nina had insisted that Michelle stay back for the day and Kirk had insisted on staying with her. Sarah Bergman had met Willy when she and Niles first checked in at the office. He was the only one of the volunteers that she had met. When Sarah offered to jump in and work with him, Willy immediately accepted her offer, not waiting to get it approved since it probably appeared to him that Moshe had brought her.

This morning Li Moon was not his usual contemptuous self. Even he realized that more could be lost than gained by attempting to work in the darkness so he didn't push the diggers to get to work.

In fact, Willy had noticed that Moon had seemed quite pre-occupied for the past few days. He was still just as arrogant and rude but he was not as out front with it. Instead of the old egotistical extrovert, he now seemed more of an irritable introvert who just didn't want to be bothered. Willy had also noticed that he was cautiously attentive to any unfamiliar vehicle approaching the site. And strangers seemed to really make him nervous.

Li's behavior was amusing. It reminded Willy of a guy he had worked with back home in the oil fields; poor jerk was always on the lookout for bill collectors, girlfriends' husbands or the law. Willy couldn't help but grin as he mused about who old Li was trying to keep off his ass.

Over the past weeks of excavation, the balks had been removed between four of the squares where Willy and Sarah now worked.

The floors had been excavated down to the same level as the paver stones Michelle first uncovered in G19. And last week two new squares had been opened. As quickly as was prudent, these adjacent squares were being excavated down to the level of the pavers in the adjoining four. Within one of these two, Moshe believed his team would find the first remains of the ancient city's gateway. He knew much better than to get his hopes up. But, just possibly, here they may find the copper scroll's black stone.

Sarah rose and looked around. Still on her knees she wiped the perspiration from her eyes with her shirt sleeve. She hadn't noticed Moshe and Niles standing on the far balk across the squares. From their gestures and the angle of their outstretched arms, she thought they were discussing the significance of the paver stones; plaza, courtyard, street or whatever it was that they were a part.

"Hey, Sarah, look at this." Willy held a small object in his cupped hand.

Sarah reached out and he dropped a small, smooth teardrop shaped stone into her open palm.

"What it this?" Sarah asked. "Looks like it's been polished."

"It's a fidget stone; and it has been polished," Willy answered. "Polished by somebody's thumb and fingers. Down this deep… Bet I'm the first to hold it in twenty-five hundred, maybe three thousand years."

"A new one on me," said Sarah. "Never heard of a fidget stone."

"I've always wondered why some folks always got to have some something to hold on to. Lucky charm, crystal, down my way they carry a buckeye or a silver dollar; no different from playing with rosary beads, I reckon."

"You're probably right but I wouldn't think it wise to say that to someone counting beads on their rosary," said Sarah.

"Oh, hell no," said Willy. "I wouldn't do that. Dumbest thing in the world is belittling somebody's bullshit superstition. And don't think you can reason with 'em either. I think if they had something to reason with… they wouldn't be counting them damn little beads."

Sarah laughed and went back to brushing debris from the stone surface.

"Willy, you'd last about as long in Salt Lake City as I would in Kabul."

"Tell you what, Miss Sarah, I'll just add Salt Lake to an already long list of places I need to stay the hell away from. How is it that you get along there? I mean, from what little I've picked up, you're the bright shining star of BYU's archaeology department."

"I may be the luckiest star in the archaeology department."

"Why lucky?"

"First of all, it was unbelievable luck for a Jewish girl to land a graduate fellowship at BYU. Then it was luck that I ran across this Greek nickname reference to Beth Shean which nailed down Tel Kefar as the place called Kohlit in the copper scroll. And, most of all, it was luck that some anonymous alumnus would come through with the entire funding for me and Dr. Thompson to come over here. I keep pinching myself, wondering when this charmed life bubble is going to burst."

"You lost me. All I heard was that you and Doctor Thompson have a theory about the city gate. I figured it had something to do with Dr. William Dever's theory about six chambered gates being evidence of a Solomonic empire during the tenth century."

"Now you've lost me," said Sarah. "I only have a vague recollection of what Dever's theory is. The tenth century's about nine hundred years before my time."

Sarah looked up from the stones and caught Willy's puzzled expression.

"So, now you want to know, what a nice Greco-Roman period girl is doing in an Iron Age place like this."

"Yeah," Willy said, fanning away a fly with his trowel, "I guess I do."

Over the next half an hour or more Sarah told Willy about an obscure collection of ancient Seleucid letters which had been recently discovered in an Orthodox monastery. With still-fresh excitement, she described in detail her accidental discovery of a slang reference to a place in Palestine, a city which had been under Seleucid rule since the defeat of the Egyptian Ptolemys by Antiochus III in 198 BCE. Sarah said that the author was probably one of the officers in a decisive battle fought at the foot of Mt. Hermon, along the headwaters of the Jordan.

She giggled, telling him how the writer had complained at being stuck in such a hot, uncultured, desolate duty station. She said she wondered if he may have even been the one who gave the place its derogatory nickname. Anyway, she said, the epithet stuck until well into the Roman period, a couple of hundred years later when the copper scroll was written.

"What was it that he called the place?" Willy asked.

"A KEN; Kappa, Epsilon, Nu," she spelled it out. "It's probably a corruption of an Aramaic term for a dung pit or garbage pit, maybe even armpit or crotch. Whatever it meant, you can rest assured it wasn't a term of endearment."

"Well I'll be darned. So that's what they called old Beth Shean, even way back then. Still not exactly what you would call the garden spot of the world, is it?"

"No, not exactly," Sarah answered, still chuckling.

"Go on now, finish the story."

Sarah changed her position, now she sat cross-legged as she brushed at the stones beside her. "One of the other letters in the collection mentions some sort of outpost on the 'ruins of Kohlit' and describes it as being 'twenty-five stades south of KEN'. Well, guess what?"

Sarah paused, waiting for Willy's excited reaction. Instead, all she got was his blank stare but before she could elaborate Willy spoke up.

"There's something I'm not getting here. What's the significance of all these nicknames and references?"

"Willy! Kohlit is named in the copper scroll as being the key to all the other treasure locations. No one has known where it located until now. We may well be sitting directly on top of one of the most important archaeological treasures ever. I mean literally, within a few feet of this exact spot." Sarah tapped the tip of the hand broom on one of the pavers.

Willy sat still allowing the magnitude of her last statements sink in. "Damn!"

He was intrigued, not as much with the possibility of being on the verge of a major find as he was with Sarah and her account of the string of events that brought her here. He sat for a long few moments gazing off into the distance. Within his own thoughts he reminded himself that he knew not to ever get excited about some treasure. And, God forbid, he should ever allow himself to have feelings for another woman. He blinked and then focused his vision on Sarah.

"What are all these, *treasures,* suppose to be?" he asked.

"That's another confusing part. From the way the scroll is written, almost any of the named treasures could be here. But the scroll is pretty clear that there are three specific articles in this location; a duplicate of the scroll, the interpretation and the protokollon of each. It says that it will all be found about six feet below the black stone at the western entrance."

"Hot damn! Well, let's get digging." Willy exaggerated his exhilaration. "Hey," his tone switched to serious. "You don't suppose that 'black stone' is a reference to a standing stone, do you?"

"Definitely one of the possibilities we've considered. But I'm hoping that, right smack in the middle of the gateway, there's one black stone in the middle of all these whites and creams." Again she tapped on one of the pavers at her side.

The call to breakfast came at eight thirty, for once, right on time. Most mornings the diggers would drop tools where they stood and all but race to a front place in line. This morning was different. Almost no one so much as glanced in the direction of the breakfast tent. The teams from the other areas hurried not to the food but to the edge of the balks around Area B, anxious to observe the progress in the city gate squares.

Willy waited, expecting Li to start screaming at the visitors to get off his balks, but it didn't happen. Now he was even more curious about Moon's behavior, his subdued manner as much as his uneasiness with visitors. He was disconnected from the anticipation enveloping the team as word of the copper scroll treasure spread.

Eventually, one of the volunteers ran down to the food coolers and returned with a couple of bags of food. He moved from square to square handing out hard rolls, cheese and jam to whomever would be distracted long enough reach into the bags.

"Here, take a break," said Willy.

Sarah looked up; he was holding out half a bread roll and a little individual serving pack of apricot preserves. She sat back, removed her heavy cotton gloves and reached to take the food.

"Thanks, Willy. I needed to eat something; I get awful headaches when I don't, something to do with blood-sugar levels I guess."

The progress seemed painfully slow. Several times during the morning Moshe admonished Area B that their eagerness was no excuse for sloppy work.

Willy picked up on the words of caution. "Remember your training; excavation is destructive, so do your best not to miss anything. Who was our famous American writer? Thomas Wolfe, I think. Remember what he said, 'You Can't Hoe Loam Again'."

Several of the team winced at the corny corruption. Willy and Sarah both tittered at several others nodding their agreement in serious contemplation. Willy saw through all the orders and admonitions; Moshe was up this morning, not his usual life-with-a-grain-of- salt self. This morning the reserved old stoic could barely contain his own verve. What might lie just below the surface? The possibility was titillating.

Again, Willy's attention was drawn to Moon. He watched him walk over to the edge of the work area, raise the sagging black netting and peer out across the farm field. He had spotted a dust cloud between the tel and the highway, some sort of minivan driving up to the site. It pitched and rolled over the rutted tractor road and disappeared around the base of the tel. Then, in low gear, it reappeared climbing the gravel stabilized incline to the top and stopped at the break area tent.

Willy recognized the emerging company as the BBC film crew but it was apparent that Moon did not. He had not returned from the weekend until late last night, long after Colin Blair and his crew had left the kibbutz for Tiberias. Willy didn't dream of saying anything to ease Moon's anxiety which he found so delightfully entertaining.

His amusement was short lived, however. Within a few minutes of their arrival the crew extracted some equipment from the cargo hatch and followed Moshe up the slope to the Area B registrar's table. There Li Moon and one of the square supervisors were standing. Willy chuckled out loud as Li's body slumped with relief. He could just about hear Moon's sigh of reprieve when Moshe introduced Colin Blair with the BBC and his crew. Then Moshe raised his voice to the entire area.

"Everyone take a break for a moment to listen. We have with us for the next few days a documentary film crew from the BBC. Please assist them in any way we can. They know to ask permission before entering any of the squares." With a formal smile, Moshe gave a nod to Blair which confirmed that he expected him to do so. "These are professional journalists; they will do their job without hindering us or compromising the quality of our work in any way." Another smile and nod which was returned by Colin Blair, the ground rules—which Moshe, too, had just heard for the first time – were agreed to in front of a few dozen witnesses.

Actually, Blair respected the way Moshe handled the situation; the dig team and the film crew were both aware of what was expected of each other.

"Okay, let's get back to it," said Moshe.

Blair started to praise Moshe by telling him that he would make a great TV commentator but, then, thought better of it. He sensed that Professor Moshe Benjamin might not hear it as the compliment he intended. Instead, Blair settled for simply thanking him for the introduction. Then he set about choosing the best-lit location for his first section of background footage. The mid-morning cloud shadows and subtle, undulating colors on Gilboa's slopes would do perfectly, he thought. He turned to find his camera operator.

"I say, Bryce, might you set up the D30 over there. I want both the mountainside and the excavation area in the background."

The next two workdays passed quickly. Michelle and Kirk returned to the dig on Thursday. She insisted that he not stay back with her but he wouldn't consider leaving her at the B & B while the team was in the field, not after the ordeal she had endured. He didn't argue with her; he just stayed back. And from where he could keep an eye on her door, he sat in the shade on the grassy lawn and continued a reread of Wouk's The Hope, for the fourth time, he thought.

Until the team returned each day and he knew that someone would be with her constantly, he only left his spot in the shade long enough to relieve himself . She declined his invitations to the dining hall or to just walk along side the spring-fed stream that ran through Massebot. In spite of the kitchen maven raising hell about food leaving the dining hall, after he had eaten every meal, he returned with an assortment of carry-outs and she would eat something.

Now Kirk's concern was for more than her physical state. He couldn't shake the feeling that there was more to her captivity than he and Willy knew, maybe, more than she knew or remembered. All he knew for sure was that even though she was back safe and reasonably sound, he was not completely convinced that Michelle was out of harm's way. So, he would keep up his guard, high.

Since Monday morning, when first word of Sarah Bergman's

theory began to circulate through the squares, the initial waves of excitement had waned. There had been fewer finds these last days than any since the opening week of the season.

After having been out for the three work days since Friday, the floor of Kirk and Michelle's square was now noticeably higher than the others nearby except for the two squares that had just been opened. Although their floor lagged prominently higher, Willy had been prepared to raise hell if Moon decided to assign replacements to G-20.

To his surprise, the confrontation never came. Li's attention continued to be consumed by whatever it was that had him spooked; he was unconcerned with any lack of progress in the squares. And something else had occurred to Willy; he remembered from past digs, whenever a camera or a reporter showed up on the site, Moon consistently did his best to maneuver himself center stage. But not this week and not today.

"Kirk?" Willy stood looking over the balk that separated them.

"Yeah, Willy?" Kirk answered.

"Keep an eye on ole Li."

"Okay," Kirk answered, "but why?"

Willy smiled as he folded a red bandanna into a sweat band and cut his eyes in the direction of the registrar table where Moon was sitting.

"Something got the old boy nervous as a blind queer at a church weenie roast."

Kirk grimaced. Sarah's eyes opened wide but she pretended she hadn't heard. And she tried not to laugh.

"Okay, Willy, I'll watch him," said Kirk. "By the way, how's that sensitivity training going?"

"What are you…?"

Willy turned to catch Kirk nodding toward Sarah, alerting him that she heard what he said.

"Excuse me, Sarah. Some of my expressions, I know, are a mite… off color. Didn't mean a thing by it, just a bad habit. Comes from too much working the oil rigs with men only, I reckon. I wouldn't hurt anybody's feelings on purpose."

"I'm sure you wouldn't, Willy," said Sarah. "Don't worry about offending me. I was raised with three brothers so I never hear anything I shouldn't."

All three chuckled, realizing the endearing power of disregarded indiscretions. Michelle was silent. Her detachment was no act; not a word of the conversation was registering with her. Kirk hoped that she could remain engrossed with her work, at least to the point of giving her a break from the surges of recall. He knew all about flashbacks. And he knew the worthlessness of well-meaning words, nothing to be said, nothing to be done that can insulate or mend. What he could do was to be there, to stay near, a silent presence more healing than insight and eloquence.

Kirk moved over to where the Styrofoam thermos was wedged between sandbags. He lifted it and poured a cup full of pink Kool-Aid. He knelt down on one knee, beside Michelle, and held out the cool drink to her. She dropped the trowel, wiped her brow with her tee shirt sleeve and sat back on one of the big stones. She took the cup from Kirk and looked directly into his eyes. He thought it was the first time he had held her gaze since her nightmare. He could see the tears trying to pool before she turned away to wipe her eyes. Then she turned back and looked into his eyes again.

"Thank you, Kirk," she whispered.

His response was an expression of understanding. Her tears welled again. He leaned over and placed his rough hand on the back of hers. His hand was rough and dirty and covered with the scars of a hundreds of nicks and cuts. But at that moment Michelle thought it was the most wonderful hand she had ever felt. She leaned into him and rested her cheek on the thick muscles beneath his collar. He raised his other hand and softly pressed her face to his chest.

Willy saw the puzzled expression that washed over Sarah's face. He responded to her with a nod of reassurance and a silencing index finger over his lips. Then he leaned over to Sarah and whispered that he would explain later. She nodded, okay.

At the same moment, Willy caught a glimpse of Li, who had just picked up on the sight of Kirk holding Michelle. His face stretched into a wide, suggestive smile and he started to walk in their direction. The old, repulsive Li Moon was back.

Willy sprang up on the balk closest to Li. Without a word he stretched out his arm and aimed his finger straight between Li's eyes. He didn't say a word; he didn't need to. The blowtorch stare could have killed kudzu. His look explained all Li needed to know about the situation. Just in time to catch the final seconds of the face-down, Kirk loosened his embrace and stood. He looked first at

Willy, then Moon who pirouetted to return to the registrar table. Willy relaxed, mumbling under his breath to Kirk.

"Son of a bitch! First time he pay any attention to anything going on round here all week."

"Don't be too hard on him," said Kirk. "He might not even realize what happened... I mean, unless some has told him about last weekend."

"Yeah, maybe so. All I told him – Monday, I guess it was – was that Michelle was sick and you had some personal business to tend to. He just nodded his head. I don't know if it registered with him. Like I was telling you, he's been acting mighty strange for the last week."

Michelle went back to work articulating another one of the large stones protruding from the balk. During the first days of the season this section of stones was thought to have been part of a street or courtyard. After another week of excavation, the stone grouping was recognized as one of a number of levels, a section of a terraced walkway which probably connected the main street with one of Kefar's structures on the city's citadel. Moshe claimed that it could be something like a walkway up to the palace area.

Each unearthed terrace would take them down, that much closer to where the terraced walkway intersected the main street. That intersection would most likely be just inside a six-chambered city gate.

The morning wore on. Scattered patches of muffled conversations and the metallic sounds of excavation drifted between the squares of Area B. Already after 11:30, it was hot and the regular winds from the Mediterranean were late. Another opposing Arabian khamsin palled the valley with heavy, stagnant air.

After three weeks, Joel LaRoche still hadn't gotten used to the rigors of the dig. The tender young grad student's heart just wasn't in it, not in this heat, not after weeks of this food, not with this case of shelshool. With lethargic repetition he sat slumping, dragging a bouncing trowel over the crust at his side. Then he felt it, the edge of the blade hit something hard. There was something symmetrical just under the surface, still encrusted and gripped by the soil that had surrounded it through the ages. It lay in a wide space between two of the large terrace pavers at the base of a stone wall.

At first Joel thought it must be just another large pottery shard. But it was different. The clay was thick, maybe thirty millimeters, like a piece of taboun but there was no curvature. As he brushed away the dust he could see a beautiful reddish orange finish. An enthusiastic digger, Joel was not, but neither was he reckless. He pushed the trowel back out of the way, from now on it would be a chopstick and brush extraction.

Now he could see a corner, a perfect right angle. He had no idea what he had but he knew that it wasn't just another potsherd. Joel stood. In his usual, subdued voice he spoke into the adjacent square.

"Willy, when you are free, please tell me what you think I have here."

"No problem, mon ami, be right there. Nothing happening over here."

Willy rose, dusted himself off and climbed out. From the balk above he could see the shape and the contrasting color where Joel pointed. He turned and backed down the nailed board ladder into the pit. He squatted down beside where Joel knelt on a cushion strip of closed cell foam.

"What on earth you got here?"

"We don't know; is why I call you," Joel answered.

"Well, let's take a look. Gimme that chopstick."

Willy held the strong sliver of sharpened bamboo as he would a pencil. He picked and pried into the debris encasing the strange red form. He carefully avoided contacting the piece itself as the probe broke the soil into tiny clods. When Willy lifted the chopstick out of the way after loosening a small area, Joel whisked the spall away. After ten minutes of pick and brush, three corners of the piece and most of the surface were visible. It was rectangular, approximately fifteen by twenty centimeters and twenty-five millimeters thick.

"Whatever it is, it's gonna be labeled a special find," said Willy. "They'll want to take measurements and photos before we take it out, so why don't you call Moon on over here."

Joel climbed out of the square and walked around to the table where Li was still sitting. He stood there waiting for Doctor Moon to look up. Li was either too engrossed in his worries or too devilish to acknowledge the young man's presence. After Joel had waited patiently for a couple of minutes more, Willy stood and looked over toward the table to see what the delay was. He could see that Moon was neither busy with some task nor in another conversation. The thought of his inconsiderate arrogance angered him to the point that he barked across the squares.

"Doctor Moon," Willy bellowed, "the kid has been standing there trying to tell you we have something over here. If you're too busy, I'll be glad to call Doctor Ben."

Without changing his slouching posture, Moon turned his head and looked over the frames of his glasses. Still, he didn't bother to speak to Joel or answer Willy. He just sat there showing no inclination to get out of his chair, an obvious calculation to save face after Willy's railing at him. Some of the others who heard Willy began moving toward the square to get a look for themselves. When Moshe and Niles Thompson noticed the gathering from where they stood at a far corner of the area, they also walked over to take a look.

Over the next few minutes precise measurements were taken of the artifact's position within the locus and the exact elevation was referenced to the area's master benchmark. Someone alerted Dov that photos were needed of a special find in-situ. When all the shots were taken Moshe told Willy to finish removing the piece.

"Doctor Ben, if you don't mind, I'll let Joel do the honors since he found it."

Joel's head jerked up. He wide-eyed Willy, scanned the group standing around the balks and then looked to see Doctor Benjamin's reaction. Moshe shrugged and gave his permission. "Yes, of course," he said with an understanding trace of a smile. Willy stepped to the side. Joel repositioned his foam knee pad to a better working spot. Just as he started to flake away some more of the crust, he was interrupted by Colin Blair's irritating Cockney whine.

"I say there, give us a minute more to get set up, if you don't mind. I want to get this on tape. May I join you down there?"

Joel straightened up. Although Blair had asked Joel, he looked at Moshe to ensure he had no objection. Then he climbed down into the square and knelt on the other side of the locus, facing Joel, as he prepared to remove the artifact. When Blair was satisfied with the field of view one of the crew attached their top of the line Sony DXC digital to an opened tripod and made the adjustments. Blair then turned to Joel and Willy.

"Oh, forgive me. I'm Colin Blair, BBC."

Joel and Willy answered with their names.

"Good show," said Blair. "Now we can get started; I see Bryce is nearly done with the setup."

A moment later the DXC was sighted in; the cameraman gave a three, two, one and point signal. Joel began the tedious extraction as Blair narrated, whispering into a well-concealed collar mic while Joel continued picking around the object. When Joel paused, Willy brushed away the loosened soil. Within five minutes the articulation was done; the red-orange rectangular object rested on a pedestal of remaining soil.

Whatever it was, it appeared to be in nearly perfect condition. Joel looked over his shoulder to Moshe for final confirmation that it was to be removed. Before Moshe could respond, Blair stood up and stepped toward him asking a question as the Sony rolled.

"Doctor Benjamin, you've been doing this for a long time. You are one of the most respected authorities in Near-Eastern archaeology. Before we awaken this mystery piece from its rest of, perhaps, thousands of years, just for the fun of it, tell us what you think we have here, professor. I suppose what I'm asking is: do you already know what this piece is by its shape and size or maybe even the color?"

"I suspect that it may be some sort of ornamental or official plaque. The size is right and its location is right."

"What do you mean the 'location is right'."

"It's here just inside the city's gate. Or, perhaps I should say, where I am convinced we will find the city's gate. This is a customary location for such things."

Blair turned and peered directly into the DXC lens. "Then let's lift it out and give it a good going over, why don't we?"

Moshe told Joel to remove the piece and give it to him first. Bryce held the boom mic low enough to pick up the final scrapes of the chopstick. The cameraman scrambled to release the Sony from the tripod and reposition himself. Through the view finder he focused in close as Joel tenderly lifted the fragile piece and passed it up into Moshe's hands. Now he zoomed in to frame the professor's initial examination.

The underside of it was still caked with dirt. Moshe asked for one of the small, four-inch paint brushes. One of the observers who had gathered around the square passed one forward to him. The onlookers were silent as he lightly brushed and then blew away the centuries of accumulated dross. He gave it one last brushing and a strong puff of compressed breath. Moshe's eyes widened and his stare fixed on the piece he cradled with both hands. After a long pause he spoke in a quiet, almost reverent, tone.

"This is wonderful find."

The BBC camera that had panned the artifact up from the pit floor now zoomed in on Moshe's captivated face and then on the piece itself. Moshe positioned the piece so that Niles Thompson could get a good look.

"Oh my!" said Thompson.

Both of the men traced their fingers across the surface but neither spoke a word. They were clearly fascinated with the find. Blair could stand the silence no longer.

"Gentlemen," he said, "what's the verdict?"

Moshe answered. "Of course, it must be studied in depth. But at first glance, I think I can say that we have a complete inscription. It is written in Phoenician script—Paleo-Hebrew, same thing. The red slipped and burnished finish is indicative Iron Age and… What more can I say at this point…? The piece is in near perfect condition."

"Do you have an idea as to its age?" Blair asked

"Yes, Iron Age." Moshe cut his eyes at having to repeat himself ; he caught Blair's clueless look. "The stratum is tenth century BCE, which means before current era… The red burnish fits this time period. So, that would be about three thousand years."

"Can you read it, Doctor Benjamin?"

"Yes, I can read it clearly."

Moshe left Blair hanging with another dumb look on his face. Niles Thompson repressed a smile, knowing what was coming next. Moshe's eyes were fixed on the inscription; he seemed oblivious to Blair's impatience for the translation.

"Well, by all means, sir, please tell us what it says."

"Mr. Blair, you asked if I could read it. I can. The inscription is in excellent condition; there are no gaps in the text and no damaged areas. But clear letters do not automatically mean a clear message. I am not an authority on Phoenician script Hebrew. I have already noticed two letter forms that I do not recognize. I think I recognize one, maybe two biblical names. But I'm going to hold my tongue until it is inspected by experts from…"

"So then, are you say…"

"Let me finish," said Moshe. "You must realize that often the experts disagree on the meaning of an inscription, even a specific word. I remind you of the so-called 'David inscription' found up at Tel Dan. For years now, they have argued about one word. Is it 'David' or is it a word for bread? And we may never know.

"But I will tell you this, a complete inscription — and that's what I believe we have here—is much better to work with than just a few words from a larger text, most of which is missing. I can also tell you that I think our clay tablet is promising enough to justify my calling in the most respected experts in the field.

"As soon as we get back to the office I plan to email several photos to Hebrew University, to Ada Yardeni, personally. I believe it is fair to say that most scholars consider her the greatest living authority on Paleo-Hebrew script. But we should all know her interpretation soon enough."

"How soon, do you think, sir?" Blair asked.

"Maybe tomorrow, maybe Monday," Moshe answered. "And I'll work on it along with two or three other colleagues. If we generally agree on the text, I will make the announcement at breakfast."

Moshe broke away from the flood of questions by reminding the team that the buses would be there within minutes. They still had to gather up tools and drop the sun shades. Areas A and C had already knocked off and they were walking to the pickup point on the lower tel.

Kirk mentioned to Willy that he could see what he meant about Li; he hadn't even walked over from the registrar table to get a look at the tablet.

"Isn't that unbelievable!" said Kirk. "If a find like this can't light his fire, what the heck is he working here for? He's got to be sick."

"Sick, my foot!" said Willy. "Mean shit-ass may be worried sick; but he ain't 'sick', sick. With everything that's going on over here in B, wouldn't you expect he'd be on his best behavior, especially with Niles Thompson and Doctor Ben both hanging around? Gotta be something else. He's not even trying to put on a show for them or the damn TV folks. Don't know what I'm the most curious about, what's up with ole Li Moon or what's written on our little clay tablet."

16

"HELLO, HELLO Already!"

"Moshe?"

"Yes, who's calling?"

"Moshe, it's Avi…Avi Landau."

"Avi Landau, where is your watch; don't you know what time it is?"

"Yes, Moshe, it's just after ten. Are you sitting down?"

"No, no I'm not sitting down; I'm lying down, trying to sleep."

In his thoughts Laudau muttered to himself that most Israelis weren't even finished with supper, let alone already in the bed asleep. He started to mention that to Moshe in jest but thought better of it. He wasn't sure he knew the distinguished Professor Benjamin well enough for that. But he was sure enough about the importance of the call which would explain the ungodly hour.

"Forgive me for interrupting your rest, Moshe, but I need to talk to you about your find."

"The clay tablet we found today?" Moshe's voice sounded groggy.

"Yes. Have you begun work on it?"

"Yes and no. We spent so much time with the photos and the scale drawings… and then we had a hard time uploading the images from a new digital camera into the PC. We didn't get them off to the university until late in the afternoon. I didn't get started on the inscription. I hope the images we uploaded are clear enough for Ada to use."

"Oh, they're clear enough all right. She's working on the thing as we speak. Moshe, since my call woke you, I take it you haven't seen the ten o'clock news on Israel 10?"

"No, we haven't seen any TV all week." said Moshe. "Damn kibbutz satellite is down again. Why?"

"Ya'akov Eilon is reporting 'a major find at Tel Kefar which justifies reclaiming of all of Eretz – Israel'..."

"Ma?" Moshe sat straight up on his cot. "You aren't serious?"

"Wait, let me finish." Landau insisted. "He reported – I'm quoting him—'a ninth century BCE clay tablet in near perfect condition was unearthed today and first reports indicate that the inscription contains several prominent biblical names in their proper historical context'."

"What in the... On television news? Incredible! How in the name of heaven could..."

"I was hoping that you could enlighten me. I just got a call from Dormann himself. You can imagine the hell he's raising about not being informed. Moshe, you gotta help me out here."

"Avi, right now it seems that I know less about what's going on than most everyone else in the country. Where did Eilon get the story?"

"We don't know. I was hoping you may have some idea. But we can work on that later. Right now I need to know where the tablet is."

"It's locked up in the lab with everything else. Where else would..."

"Moshe, I think you should get it and not let the thing out of your sight until I get up there in the morning. I'm not sure what the hell's going on but everything needs to be by the book on this one. I can smell an ambush waiting."

"Yes, so it would seem. Okay, I'll walk next door and get it and keep it here with me. And now that I'm wide awake, thank you, maybe I'll work on the translation some. How's Ada doing with it?"

"She's moving right along. Amazing thing is, it's turning out pretty much like channel 10 reported. She's got three variant letter forms that we haven't seen before. Several of the names may be real prizes; two or three others that aren't recognized. Moshe, who else do you have up there who's reasonably competent with Phoenician script?"

"Only Niles that I know of; can't think of anyone else."

"Niles Thompson, there with you?" Landau seemed dumbfounded.

"Yes, I know," said Moshe. "Tell you all about it tomorrow."

"Well I can't wait to hear this. Anyway, were any other photos emailed out besides these, I mean the ones here at the university?"

"Not that I know of, I doubt it. But some of the kids did take pictures. And we have a BBC film crew up here. But it's a safe bet they didn't give up a story to Israel 10."

Moshe felt a glint of amusement as he envisioned the expression on Colin Blair's face when he got wind of the TV report. He recalled of one of Willy's Cajun expressions and broke out with a wide grin. When Mister Colin Blair of the BBC heard about this he would, indeed, look like someone hit him in the face with a sock full of shit.

Moshe caught himself. "I tell you, Avi, I'm at a loss to explain it from this end. There's only one computer here. No one could have sent out the images until after we sent them to Jerusalem. But, even then, who could have come up with a translation before Ada and her people? Had to be someone down there. Do you think Eilon will reveal his source?"

"I don't know. But if anyone can get it out of him I suppose the director general can. God, is he pissed. I pity the poor shmuck if Dormann does find out who let this out; hope he never needs an IAA permit."

"And you can pity the poor shmuck if it was one of our faculty or staff...or a student. This tabloid jiffa does nothing but hurt, even if their report turns out to be fundamentally accurate. Nothing should ever be released before official publication; a wonderful discovery and it could wind up as problematic as the James Ossuary, all because of this debacle."

"Yes, Moshe, how well I know. And, of course, you know the political implications. A discovery like this will make it instantly suspect to a great number of people.

"Well, we're not going to settle anything tonight. I'll be up there first thing in the morning. Where will I find you, Massebot or out at the site?"

"I'll be out on the tel at 5:15. I'll have the tablet with me."

"Beseder. Laylah tov, Moshe."

"Good night to you, Avi."

Moshe switched off the cell phone and retuned it to the charger cradle on his night stand. He switched on a lamp, grabbed his key ring and walked outside. Wearing only gym shorts and a tee shirt, he walked on the knife edges of his bare feet trying to miss the sharp little landscaping rocks out of place on the walkway. Muttering to himself, Moshe gingerly made the few steps to the field office next door. Inside, two of the square supervisors were entering data from their field notes into the PC's.

"Paul, Erik, erev tov," said Moshe. "I didn't expect to find anyone still working."

Aware of the professor's usual bedtime, both men looked up with wide grins.

"Moshe, what's got you up in the wee hours?" Paul asked.

Moshe answered the affable sarcasm with only nodding and a smile. He searched through his ring for the storage room key. When he was in, he then unlocked a metal cabinet which held the most important artifacts that had been found over the past few days. On the center shelf he spotted the cardboard box he was after. It was rubber stamped with the distinctive green ink; Tel Kefar, Area B, Square E-21, Locus 20141, date and elevation. The description was listed as, Tablet/Clay/with Inscription; the top and each side of the box were red stamped, Special Find.

Moshe removed the box, locked the cabinet and sat down at a table with his two supervisors. He opened the box and removed the tablet from a double layer of bubble wrap. Erik and Paul watched as Moshe began copying the letters onto a fresh sheet of quarter-scale graph paper. He studied each tiny shape beneath the light of a swivel arm mounted magnifier before reproducing its form on the paper.

Just after midnight the young men departed, trying not to disturb the professor as they left. Moshe worked on for another two hours frequently referring to his lab-worn Hebrew Bible. At last, the translation was complete. He held the graph paper up to better light as he sorted through every word of the text, probing his memory for every possible variation or corruption. Now, in the late night quiet, he sat still, deep within his own thoughts.

After a few minutes Moshe caught himself nodding off. He replaced the tablet into the folds of packing, returned it to its box and took it back to his room. Inside he lay back on the cot and stared into the scuffed ceiling. Musing on the incredible message, he finally dozed off, the box and its priceless contents cradled on his lap.

Three hours later, groggy from the lack of sleep, Moshe was back out on the tel. He remembered that not too many years ago he could go for weeks at a stretch on only a couple of hours a night. Not any more, now it hurt, clouded his mind and made him feel like hell. He felt the cellular vibrating on his belt. He fumbled with the clasp and had it free by the third buzz. It was Avi Landau; he was on a helicopter flying up to meet him.

"Yes, I understand," said Moshe. "Yes I, have it here."

Moshe stood silent with a strained frown on his face.

"Ma...? Ma? I can hardly hear you."

Avi bellowed into the mouth piece as he tried to shield it from the chopper noise.

"Okay, Moshe. We ... there ...... thirty min ..."

Moshe, assuming that if he couldn't hear he couldn't be heard, bellowed back to Landau.

"Okay, okay thirty minutes. Make sure you watch your rotor wash. I don't want that thing anywhere near the tents or work areas. Better yet, I'll drive down the field road closer to the highway; make them land it there. Ma...? Lo, I can't. We'll talk when you get here. Shalom."

Moshe heard the helicopter well before he saw it. It had not been thirty minutes, fifteen at the most he guessed, glancing out at his watch. He ducked under the outer edge of the black netting which was lowered to block out the blinding morning sun and drove off toward the main road.

At the base of the tel, he could now see the old Huey popping its way in from the south. Moshe stopped the van in the middle of the field road. The chopper's nose pitched up as the pilot sticked back to brake and with a little right rudder, he crabbed them on in. When they were perpendicular to the road, he reduced collective until they touched down and then released it completely and cut the throttle.

Moshe remained in the truck with the windows up until the blast of dust and thatch died down. When he saw the door slide back and Avi hop down, Moshe got out of the truck to greet him.

"Tell the pilots to come on." Moshe shouted the invitation in Avi's ear. "We'll give them a ride to the top."

Avi turned and ran back to the UH-1N in the customary

crouch, an unnecessary exertion on the level ground as the blades rotated over fourteen feet above. In a moment Avi returned to the truck.

"They say, todah rabah, but someone has to be with the aircraft at all times. They'll take turns and walk up if there's time."

On the short drive back to the top of the tel, Moshe ran out of the ruts and nearly stuck in the freshly harrowed field. And on the incline to the top, the van bottomed out and almost turned over trying to get back on track when Moshe failed to straddle a rivulet gully. Silently, Avi cursed himself for forgetting; no one in his right mind ever rode with this driver from hell. Back at the top, Avi's white knuckles flushed pink with relief as Moshe parked along side the breakfast tent. He switched off the truck and grabbed a brushed aluminum protective case before getting out.

"Come, Avi, we can talk here without interruption."

After he ushered Avi to the tent and they stooped in under the shading, Moshe lifted two plastic stools from a stack and placed them at the serving table. He opened the aluminum case and removed the box with the green and red ink stamps. When he had unwrapped the tablet and placed it on the bed of bubble wrap, Landau removed the lens cap from a Sony Mavica and began filling a 32 meg memory stick with the highest resolution images of the tablet.

"So," Avi said, "how far did you get with it?"

"Far enough to know that we probably have the most important inscription since the Merneptah Stele," Moshe answered.

"Ada said, 'since the Dead Sea Scrolls'. One thing for sure, it's the best evidence for Biblical Israel so far, not to mention the other names. Do you think this could actually be the site of biblical Ophrah?"

"I'm so damn sleepy I don't know what I think, Avi. I know better than to get my hopes up; you know how these things can turn around."

"Yeah… and bite you in the ass." Avi paused to find the right words. "Moshe… Dormann lined up this helicopter so I could take the tablet back to Jerusalem. He thinks this is important enough to rate extra security, especially after last night's news. I hope you'll forgive me for being the one he sent to pick it up."

"Avi… the minute I heard you were coming up by helicopter I suspected the IAA was going to seize it. And when I saw you scrambling off it with your own little heavy duty, aircraft aluminum, armored briefcase, I knew it. Tell me, can you handcuff that thing to your wrist? This one doesn't." Moshe made a glance to where his case lay on the ground.

"Don't say, seize it, Moshe. It's your find. You'll have access to it any time you wish."

"Okay, Avi, then let's say, taken into protective custody. And, furthermore, I understand your position so there's no need for any forgiveness on my part." Moshe smiled at and griped Avi's shoulder to seal his statement. But, I tell you this, Doctor Avi Landau, my friend with the Israeli Antiquities Authority, you are my friend; nothing changes that. But you better hope you can write me an official receipt for our little tablet here." Moshe patted his hand lightly on the cardboard box. "Or we wait for another helicopter to fly some IAA stationery up here."

Landau repressed his smile. He opened his protective case and removed an official Antiquities Authority receipt which he held out to Moshe. Moshe took it, looked it over and broke out in a wide grin. The receipt was in order, signed by the director general himself and only lacking Moshe's and signature and Landau's witness.

"Come on, Avi, I want to show you what's going on up in Area B."

"Thanks, Moshe, but I really need to get back as…"

"Not for five minutes, you don't. I want you to meet Sarah Bergman, Niles Thompson's grad student."

"Oh, yeah, tell me what's up with you and Thompson on the same dig. Thought I was hearing things last night."

"That's what I'm trying to explain to you, why he's here. If Sarah's theory pans out, you just might be on your helicopter on your way right back up here in a day or two."

Before Moshe and Avi Landau walked back down to the waiting Huey – Landau insisted on walking a cramp out of his leg – Sarah gave him a detailed account of the serendipitous discovery of the Greek acronyms, which led her to Tel Kefar as the possible site of one of the copper scroll treasures . When she related what might lie just beneath their feet Landau was enthralled, so much so that Moshe had to remind him that he was in a hurry to get back to Jerusalem with the priceless tablet. At the helicopter Avi slid the aluminum case in on the floor, turned and held out his hand to Moshe.

"I appreciate your understanding, Moshe…and your hospitality. I'm happy for you, my friend. After all the years of grunt work… Looks like you've finally wound up on that glamour dig. And if Hershel Shanks gets so much as a glimpse of young Miss Bergman up there, you've got yourself a *Biblical Archaeology Review* cover for sure."

Moshe chuckled at the allusion to the old editor's affinity for salting the magazine with glamour.

"Seriously, Moshe, you know you're going to have a lot of press up here now that this news is out?" Avi glanced inside the chopper and patted the side of the aluminum case.

"That's what I would expect" said Moshe. "Locals and tourists, too."

"Tell you what," said Landau. "Why don't I convince Dormann to get a team of green police out here to help you keep things under control? There's just too much going on around here. The thefts from the site—can you believe they can't find a damn stolen water tank? – the looting, now this tablet, can you imagine this place if that copper scroll does turn up in a day or two? What a damn baligon."

"You're right. I'll probably need all the help I can get."

"And you'll have it. As soon as I work things out with Dormann I'll call you with the details. I'll try to have some details for you by this afternoon. Shalom, Moshe."

When the helicopter lifted off Moshe walked back to the top to Area B. He had decided to call the team leaders together before the breakfast break to disclose the message of the inscription. And he wanted to prepare them for the likely onslaught of visitors to Israel's newest archaeological hot spot.

17

As HE HAD promised, Avi Landau called Moshe in the early afternoon to let him know that the director general of the Israeli Antiquities Authority had made arrangements for security at the site. A detachment would be arriving within the next two hours and would be on duty 24/7 until further notice. They knew to coordinate their efforts through him. Avi asked Moshe if he would assign someone to meet the security team to brief them on the site.

"Yes, of course, I'll see them personally," said Moshe.

"You're not going to have time. I also called to tell you that we're sending the helicopter back up there to pick you up and bring you down here. Both Dormann and Ministry of Religious Affairs think there has to be some sort of official preliminary report on the tablet. They want you and Ada to do it personally. We'll call the press conference as soon as you're ready."

"Such a rush; what does Ada say about all this?"

"Moshe, Ada agrees that we have to do it as soon as we can put something together. I don't know what it's like up there but phones are ringing off the hook down here. Every reporter I ever heard of is calling with questions. Can't believe you haven't already been besieged."

"No, it's still quiet here. You know these Beit Shean kibutznics; they haven't heard that Arafat died."

"Ha ha!" Avi laughed out loud. "Well, it's just a matter of time before you are swamped, locals, press, tour buses, too, I expect. Okay, the helicopter should be there by three. Where should I tell them to set down?"

"Tell them to look for the big open area just west of the dining hall. It's the only large grassed area in the compound; they can't miss it. I'll be there when I hear them coming in."

Moshe showered and dressed, gathered his field notes on Area B and went to the dining hall to wait for the helicopter. It was empty except for the regular afternoon huddle of elderly men seated around a table beside the hot water urns.

At the counter he rounded off a spoon of coffee from a big can of Elite instant, stirred it into a glass of steaming water and joined the old kibutznics. On the table was an assortment of pickles, olives, moutabel and pita but a greasy smell floated out of the scullery. The steam reeked of chicken feathers soaked in soured milk; it staunched his appetite, except for the coffee, the only redeeming aroma in the place.

Shortly before three the old Huey came in and made a turn to land into the strong winds from the Mediterranean. As it passed over, the rotor blast whipped the ficus trees around the dining hall into a frenzy and the old men rose from the table in a unison of "what- the-fuck." Moshe realized he should have told them to expect it. Too late now, they were lined up at the windows like a cage full of owls.

Outside, on the grassy area, the chopper set down. The copilot released his harness, moved back and slid open the door. He dropped to one knee to assist his passenger. Inside, Moshe buckled himself into one of the drop-down canvas benches hinged to the firewall. Then they were airborne, out across the olive and date groves surrounding the kibbutz and over the stone quarries cut into the flanks of Gilboa.

Upward the Huey climbed, a thousand meters above the mountain ridge, the green line separating Israel and Palestinian territory. Then banked south to a heading of one-ninety-five degrees to Jerusalem. Moshe removed the noise canceling headset from its bulkhead hanger and slipped it on. He puffed and tapped on the mic.

"This thing on?" Moshe asked.

"Yes, Aluf Mishneh (Colonel)," said the pilot. "It's voice activated."

"Where will we be landing?"

"Eldar helipad, sir, at the Knesset. ETA… just over twenty minutes."

"Thank you, Seren (Captain)."

Within minutes the helicopter banked off to the east to give Ramallah a wide berth and in a few more Moshe could see the leading edge of Jerusalem's urban sprawl. Ten degrees right bank, they began the descent over West Jerusalem, over the Central Bus Station and south, the last mile, to Eldar helipad. The chopper circled once before turning on final approach. Moshe could already see Avi Landau at the base of a walkway leading up to the Knesset. On the pad, Moshe slid back the door, hopped out onto the macadam and walked over to Avi.

"Shalom, Moshe. We're set up in Science-Tech committee room on the first floor. Come I'll show you to it."

"Todah," said Moshe, "I need to step into the W.C. first."

"Of course." said Avi as they started up the long walkway to the Knesset.

"When is the press conference?" Moshe asked.

"Tonight at eight, in the new wing auditorium."

"Auditorium! How many are you expecting for this little press conference?"

"I haven't the slightest; not enough to fill a three hundred seat auditorium... Dormann's idea. I've never known him to get this personally involved with anything. Anyway, we'll know what he's thinking soon enough. He's already here waiting on you."

Eight others were inside, at work, when Avi and Moshe entered the room. In standard Israeli procedure, no time was wasted with introductions and niceties. Moshe seated himself beside Ada and across from Dormann who was slouched back with crossed arms listening to the intense whispers from a young Hasid. Ada leaned toward Moshe and patted the back of his hand.

"Quite a find you have here, Doctor Benjamin!" she said.

"Yes, so it would seem." Moshe answered as he inspected the surroundings.

The committee room was a peaceful balance of warm, wood paneled walls rising from a cool, smooth stone floor. The melding fragrances of sandalwood and stone must were pleasing to him. He thought to himself that the simple beauty of such materials shouldn't be obscured by the lofty line of official photos, portraits and maps. And indirect lighting would have been much preferable to the harsh glare beating down from the tracks directly above the massive teak table.

Maybe he should have been an architect instead of an archaeologist. Surely there was more money in creating new structures than there was in unearthing the old ones. He smiled at the absurdity of his thoughts, the idea of not doing what he loved; digging up the past, discovering the truth, shattering myth with science. The amplified voice snatched Moshe from daydream. Dormann addressed the group from his seat.

"Now that we're all here, let's get started.

He began with of a summary of the tablet's discovery and asked for corrections and important additions. Moshe nodded each time Dormann raised his eyes for confirmation. When he was finished, he asked for Moshe's critique.

"I think you have it all." Moshe assured the inspector general. "I didn't hear anything that I think needs to be changed."

"Good," said Dormann, "then let's hear just how close you two are on the translation of this thing."

Moshe and Ada opened their folders. One of Dormann's assistants moved in behind a Dell Latitude connected to a projector and switched it on. From a furler attached to the ceiling a large movie screen descended as if to conceal a large color photo of Menachem Begin. As the track lights dimmed, a perfect image of the terra cotta tablet against a tekhelet background appeared on the screen. It was impressive, imposing; it projected authority even before its message was disclosed.

For the next two hours of round-table the small group volleyed questions and explanations. The pungent scent of cardamom floated over the room with each fresh cup of Arabic coffee. When Avi reminded the team of the approaching hour, Moshe, Ada and the other three scholars of Paleo-Hebrew script were in virtual agreement as to the text itself and in complete agreement on the meaning of the message.

"Beseder (Okay)," said Dormann, "I wouldn't have believed this group could reach agreement on anything so quickly. So, I guess we're ready. Let's take a break and," he took a moment to study his watch and calculate the timing, "get to the auditorium by 19:30."

Dormann turned to Moshe as the others rose and started out. "I'll do the intro, turn it over to you and then open the floor for questions when you're done. Guess you know you're about to be manifest destiny Zionism's greatest hero since Joshua?"

"Yeah, I'm afraid you're probably right. And what a trick of fate it is. As long and hard as I've fought to keep secular and sacred apart... now I'm the rabbi conducting their damned wedding."

At eight sharp the director of the Israeli Antiquities Authority walked out to the podium in the Knesset's New Wing Auditorium. He bent the flexible chrome conduit to position the microphone below his line of sight and scanned the waiting clusters. Sixty to seventy mostly press, he estimated, more than he had expected considering the hour.

This was the time of day that this crowd, at least the ones on expense account, could usually be found in the American Colony's Garden Bar or dining at Fink's. But it had been a slow news week, no suicide bombing or major clashes. There had only been an "occupational accident," the code term used when some terrorist's bomb detonated prematurely. As likely as not, it was the term also used when a bait car, stolen in Israel, was driven across the green line or into Gaza and then mysteriously exploded—when the GPS coordinates looked promising.

Director Dormann tapped the face of the mic. "Please take your seats and we'll get started." He glanced over at Moshe with a here-we-go expression and turned back to the audience.

"My name is Shmuel Dormann; I'm director general of the Israel Antiquities Authority. As most of you are aware, yesterday at the ongoing excavation of Tel Kefar there was a major discovery. For religious scholars it is possibly the most significant find since the Qumran Scrolls; for Israel, it may well prove to be the most important find since the creation of our state. It has already been reported by one of the organizations represented here tonight that—and I'm quoting—'the inscription on a clay tablet unearthed yesterday contains references to Biblical persons and events which provide irrefutable proof of our just claim to all of Eretz Israel'."

A score of reporters blurted out an attempt at the first question. Dormann cut them short.

"Your questions will be addressed after our presentation is completed so hold them until then. Now, I want to call Professor Moshe Benjamin of the Hebrew University of Jerusalem who will present a detailed description of the tablet, its inscription and the translation. Dr. Benjamin..."

Moshe had a lifetime of experience speaking in public; classroom, auditorium and broadcast studio. But he abhorred a press conference. The mumsers didn't come to learn; they came to glean every word and phrase that could be tinted or twisted to promote their organization's agenda, if not their own. And he knew they would have a field day with what he was about to throw out to them.

"Erev tov, my name is Moshe Benjamin. I am director of the Tel Kefar Expedition which is a project of the Hebrew University of Jerusalem's department of archaeology. I won't go into a detailed description of the Tel Kefar excavations since most of what's been published to date is available online at www.telkefar.org/siterep. I will tell you that this clay tablet was unearthed in one of four probe squares on the west elevation, which we believe will soon expose the city's main gate complex.

"After its conquest by the Assyrians in 732 BCE, Kefar was abandoned and not occupied again until well into the Islamic period; our excavations confirm this. The tablet was found at a depth of 2.92 meters below the existing surface elevation, in situ with numerous other artifactual debris consistent with established eighth and/or ninth century BCE prototypes. The stratal evidence, the depth and the artifacts in association give us no reason to believe that the piece is culturally intrusive from any subsequent period recorded by our excavations.

"Furthermore, our preliminary examinations in the lab indicate the piece is authentic. Our opinion is based on the style and usage of the script and characters, the patination and microscopic crystalline growth visible on the surface."

Moshe asked for dimmed lights. As the auditorium darkened, the image of the tablet came into focus on a massive screen to his right. With a laser pointer he underlined the scale marker on the screen. He recited the dimensions of the tablet as he outlined it with the distracting little red dot. He explained that the text was in an ancient form of the Hebrew language which used Phoenician characters. This form, called Paleo Hebrew, was in use until the Persian Period or around the 5th Century BCE when it was superseded by the familiar Aramean block-style characters in use today. Moshe gazed at the image in entranced silence for a long moment.

Dormann stood and pointed to a paper he held up to call Moshe's attention to it.

"Oh yes, thank you, Director. We have prepared copies of the text and a line-by-line translation for you, plenty to go around, no need to try to keep perfect notes."

Moshe paused as the copies of were passed around. Again he gazed at the beautiful image on the screen. The magnitude of the discovery hadn't completely hit him until this very moment but now he was excited. His stoic reserve began to wane as he considered the importance of the clay tablet to his 3,700-year-old culture. This may, indeed, be his finest hour. Could it also be Israel's finest hour, proof and justification of our right to the land; our right to fight for it, our right to win it back, our right to possess it and control it, all of it, fee simple, absolute?

"Moshe?" Dormann's muted voice broke the trance.

"So," Moshe continued, "the next slide shows the message in the original script with the translation beside each line."

Moshe pressed the forward button on the projector's controller. A fresh image of the enhanced script with the translation super-imposed over a fade-out background of the tablet appeared on the screen. He had not yet seen this slide; he was impressed with its professional quality. Again he stood in silence admiring the scene before he continued.

Lehi, servant of YEHWEH
Seed of Machir, seed of Gilead
Tribe of Joseph through Manasseh
Here before the altar of Jerubbaal
Where the mighty man of valor sleeps
Here this day in Ophrah's Gate
Dedicate Nephi my son
to bear the glory of the Lord
to the uttermost corner of Earth
the two ends of East and West

"There you have it, a message from the Iron Age, probably twenty-seven, twenty-eight hundred years ago. A remarkable message on several accounts which I shall now try to explain.

"First," Moshe said, "five of these names are well known. The names Joseph, Manasseh, Machir, Gilead and Jerubbaal are listed in their proper sequence as claimed by all Jewish scriptures. Jerubbaal you may better recognize by the name Gideon.

"Second, the tablet refers to 'Ophrah's Gate'. Ophrah is the place named in the Book of Judges as Gideon's hometown and the place of his burial. Until now, its location was unknown. It had been widely accepted that the most probable location of ancient Ophrah was the present city of Aufula. I should note that Tel Kefar is less than eighteen kilometers from Aufula, still within the lands allotted to the tribe of Manasseh. Gideon was of the tribe of Manasseh.

"Third, the book of Judges states that an angel of the Lord addressed Gideon as 'mighty one of valor' or 'mighty warrior' and Judges also records that Gideon built an altar to the Lord in Ophrah.

"Within these few ancient lines, we have the first outside confirmation of these names, places and events. The other two names, Lehi, the author of the tablet, and Nephi, his son, are not known from biblical texts. And Lehi claims direct lineal descent from the above five.

"In closing, I want to state that we well understand the political and religious implications of this discovery. But the application of this information must rest with the legal and political authorities; we are merely the messengers. I will affirm, however, that we are ready to defend our findings, as presented, within the arenas of peer review and scholarly debate. And now I'll turn the program back over to Director Dormann"

For the next forty-five minutes the team fielded a salvo of questions. When asked for political or religious conjecture, Dormann deflected with the honed skill of a career bureaucrat. Others tried to force an estimate of the tablet's market value.

Moshe, shielding his mouth, leaned and whispered to Ada that he had not heard one insightful question. He added that Dormann was a master of the diplomatic answer; he says nothing but says it in a way that avoids pissing off the one who asked. Ada chuckled softly. She asked Moshe if he had noticed the Lap-blonde young man near the back of the group. He had been standing quietly, his hand raised through several questions. Ada was about to call Dormann's attention to him when Dormann pointed him out for the next question. The young man took the wireless microphone which was passed back to him and held it up to speak.

"My name is Kirby Robertson. I'm a freelance writer and regular contributor to the Salt Lake City Sentinel. I have a question and a follow-up, please. Could this tablet be younger than ninth or eighth century BCE?"

"Dr. Benjamin, Dr. Yardeni," said Dormann, "what about it?"

Moshe nodded to Ada yielding the floor. She smiled at seeing Moshe's expression, knowing exactly what he was thinking: finally, an intelligent question.

"The short answer," said Ada, "is yes. It could be but only by one or two centuries. I base this on the specific style of two or three of the characters, or letters, if you prefer. For example, the letter 'lamed' which is used... maybe three times, much more closely resembles the style we see used in the seventh century Lachish letters than the style used in the ninth century Mesha stele. Or the style we see in the eighth century Siloam inscription. There are at least two more examples but—and this is a big 'but' --the floor date must be before the Aramean Invasion after which we see only the block letter form Hebrew letters with which we are all familiar, the style of letters we most commonly use today. Dr. Benjamin, do you have anything to add?"

"No, not that I haven't already said. But I would remind you that the city of Kefar was abandoned after its conquest by Tiglath-Pileser III in 732 BCE. And we have found no evidence of its occupation as a city between that time and the Islamic period, nearly fifteen hundred years later."

"So, it is possible," Robertson continued, "that this tablet could date to the years just before the Babylonian exile in 586 BCE?"

"Textually and morphologically, yes, it is possible," said Ada.

"In my opinion," said Moshe, "that would be possible only if it had been buried, like a time capsule or something, at that time. Don't forget that it was found along with other debris and pottery consistent with established eighth and ninth century types. I suppose that if the later, resident population was aware, or if it was generally believed, that this was the site of Ophrah, Gideon's altar and burial place, the ruins would have been considered a shrine or a holy place long after the destruction of Kefar. As we know quite well, people are attracted to what they consider 'Holy Land'. So, from this perspective, I would have to say, yes, it is possible."

"And my follow-up question," said Robertson. "You stated that two of the names are not known from Jewish scriptures. But that in this inscription they are listed as direct descendents of Joseph, Manasseh and Gideon."

"Yes, that's correct," said Dormann. "What's your follow-up question? Please make it short."

"Yes sir, I will. I take it that none of you are aware that both of these names, Lehi and Nephi, appear in the Book of Mormon? They are well known; in fact they are accepted as patriarchs of the Church of Jesus Christ of Latter Day Saints."

"No," Dormann said, "I wasn't aware of that." He turned toward Ada and Moshe, his eyes squinted in disbelief and his face was flushed with irritation. "But I want to reiterate what was said at the outset. Our examination of this artifact is only in the preliminary phase. We have a long way to go with many more tests and much more detailed analysis. As new information comes to light we will bring it to your attention. That's all the time we have this evening. Thank you for coming and good night. Todah rabah; lila tov."

Ignoring the detonation of questions, Dormann walked away from the podium. He tried to avoid making eye contact with Moshe's stare as he growled through clinched teeth. "Hold it till we get back to the committee room if you please."

Back on the Knesset's main floor, Landau instructed the guard at the security desk to post someone outside the committee room door to make sure they were not disturbed or overheard. Ada was the last one into the room. Avi closed the heavy solid-core door and stood backed up to it.

Dormann began, barking out the obvious. "What in the hell's going on here? Who knows anything about this Book of Mormon bullshit. And who the hell is this Robertson schmuck? Avi, as soon as we're out of here, you find out who he is, who he's with, every damn detail. And I want a copy of that Book of Mormon, in Hebrew if it's been translated. Moshe, what's happening here?"

"We went public too soon; that's what's happening here, simple as that. I'm not going to say I ..."

"Yeah, don't. I had no choice. But that doesn't matter now, What does matter is that we find out exactly what we're dealing with here. We're either being used or played for fools; hell, probably both! Ada, do those two names appear in any Jewish writings that you know of?"

"Not that I know of, Shmuel."

Dormann turned to the young Hasid. "Mordechi, I want every rabbi, every researcher, every staffer we have on these two names."

"Ken, beseder, Director."

"Damn it! I can see tomorrow's papers already. Well, we have a lot of explaining to do in a short time and we had better get it right.

First thing I want to see is a copy of this Book of Mormon. Moshe, if this thing is a fake, who did it and how did they do it?"

"Either this Robertson is making a hell of a stretch with these names or we probably do have a fake, which means someone salted my site. If that's the case, this someone knew exactly how to do it. And if it is a fake, it's the best I've ever seen. And another thing, if it's a fake we're going to have to go back and take a second and third look at a lot of other finds. How on earth would you even start to duplicate the surface crystallization?"

An echoing silence filled the room as the small group sat staring into different corners of space trying to sort through the devastating possibilities. Moshe interrupted the somber silence with a soft but serious voice.

"The reason we were concentrating our efforts in these four squares was because of a theory one of Niles Thompson's grad students developed. Has to do with a link to one of the copper scroll sites. I'll give you all the details you want later. But, suffice it to say, I have a few questions for my old friend Thompson. I thought it rather coincidental when the BBC team showed up on site the night before we began our probe squares to find the city gate. Niles swore on his mother's soul that he knew nothing about it. That reminds me, if we do have a hoax find, you know we're going to have a mighty hard sell discrediting it. By then the whole world will have seen the 'astounding discovery' in situ, coming out of the ground, even a close-up in my own hands on the BBC tape. Who could be doing this; why?"

Dormann sat turning his head slowly side to side, bewildered. "There has to be a logical explanation. No one goes to this length without having a lot to gain, but what? The settlers, the Orthodox, the whole country had everything to gain if the names of these two schmucks weren't there. Let's just hope our Mr. Robertson's got his facts screwed up. But he doesn't; I know he doesn't.

"Well, we're not going to get anywhere sitting around here. Just keep me informed. I want to be the first to know if we have a great find with a plausible explanation for these two names. And… I have to be the first to know if this is the worst hoax since The Protocols of the Elders of Zion. Damn it!"

In less than an hour the helicopter had Moshe back at Kibbutz Massebot. He walked directly to his room. His first inclination was to confront Dr. Niles Thompson but he wouldn't do that until he himself knew the answer to every question he planned to fire at Niles. Now, alone in the darkness, he stripped to his boxers and lay down on the bed. He gazed through the ceiling fan's slow blades and began watching the parade of likely headlines ticker across the curtains of his mind.

18

MICHELLE LET Her head rest against the sherut's chattering window. The vibration on her temple was relaxing. She gazed out at the barren land sliding by like a river of rock running between the weathered face of a cliff and the highway that traced the contour of the rock wall's base.

She fantasized escaping to a safe hermitage deep within the cool, quiet seclusion of one of the myriad caves far back up one of the many wadis. But she knew that most were already claimed by Bedouin or goats, probably both. No peaceful escape, even out here, she murmured in her thoughts.

"I shouldn't have let you talk me into this, Kirk. All I wanted to do this weekend was sleep." Michelle spoke without shifting her eyes from the rocky flow.

"This'll do you a lot more good than being alone at the kibbutz," said Kirk. "Besides, you can sleep all you want to at the hotel, go for a swim and then sleep some more, by the pool if you want. But I'll bet when you see the place you won't want to sleep away the whole weekend."

Michelle forced a slight smile but didn't respond. She didn't have the energy to disagree. She was frustrated with her inability to control her vacillating emotions, aggravated that she couldn't snap out of it. She remembered the words of the psychologist she had seen for a couple of years after the beating and rape.

"You can't will yourself away from the effects of traumatic stress anymore than you can will yourself cured of any crippling physical disease," he had counseled.

She had told herself that the horrors and the devastating aftermath of those years had made her stronger. But now she was afraid

252 ⁓ J I M L E V E R

she may actually be the weaker for it. And this time, she was tormented by the incubus of not knowing for sure what had happened to her in Shahadeh's dungeon.

After the first assault she had scorned herself for being so naïve and trusting. But this time she had no idea what she could have done differently, short of staying home behind dead-bolted doors. What angered her most was that the sleazy Arab had destroyed the very sense of freedom and adventure it had taken her so many years to regain. She had not even gotten excited about the clay tablet discovered right next to her. And she felt almost indifferent about any other treasures waiting to be found in Area B. Why then was she so determined to stay in Israel and at the dig, she wondered. Most perplexing of all were her confusing feelings for Kirk. All she knew for certain was that he made her feel safe, comfortable and appreciated. And she liked being with him, regardless of the gulf of years between them.

Across the street from the gate of the American Colony Hotel, the sherut pulled up over the curb and onto the sidewalk. Kirk knew it would be useless; nevertheless, he told the driver to pull through the gate to the bellman's station at the main entrance.

"Lo, lo; is good here." The driver scowled and refused to move.

Kirk knew that he wouldn't; he was a Jew driving a sherut from rural Beit Shean. He was tense enough already, just being in downtown Jerusalem. He was not about to drive onto the property of an Arab hotel in East Jerusalem. The nervous driver could not have cared less that the American Colony was the most respected neutral sanctuary in the entire city, even if he had known it.

The American Colony Hotel was just across Nablus Road, the line that divides Arab East from Israeli West Jerusalem. Until the late 1800s, the hotel complex had served as a palace for the Ottoman Pasha of Jerusalem when it was sold to an American couple, the Spaffords. They had moved to Jerusalem after losing their four daughters in a disaster at sea. The grieving couple used the tragedy to redirect the course of their lives. Accompanied by sixteen others from Chicago's Swedish community, The Spaffords came to Jerusalem to serve the poor. The colony soon established a medical clinic and a soup kitchen for Jerusalem's indigent.

Later, during World War I, the American Colony established itself as a respected, apolitical institution in the city. At the height of the fighting, the kitchen was feeding two thousand a day and treating wounded from both sides. This service earned the American Colony both its neutrality and the reputation as an oasis of peace.

Whenever a meeting was needed between Jews, Arabs and their mediators, it was most likely held at the American Colony Hotel. This awareness attracted the international press. It was not unusual to relax in the garden bar near Jerrold Kessel or Christiane Amanpour or to have breakfast a couple of tables away from Peter Jennings or Dianne Sawyer.

Inside the lobby while Kirk checked in Michelle sipped on her complimentary glass of fresh melon-mango nectar with a sprig of nanah, delicious she thought. She drifted around the lobby enamored with the art and furnishings. There were also some of the most beautiful carpets she had ever seen, worth thousands she guessed.

On the wall above a small desk was a plaque with the names of distinguished past guests engraved little brass plates. The roster included politicians, painters, writers, and actors, many of the twentieth century's greatest: T.E. Lawrence, Winston Churchill, Peter Ustinov, Marc Chagall, John Steinbeck, and John Camp among them.

Kirk gave their backpacks to a bellman who asked them to follow him. He led back out the main entrance and across the driveway loop to the Palms building. As they walked the bellman pointed out Barakat's antique shop. He encouraged them to come back down and take a look around, promising that there were many Oriental silk carpets and other priceless pieces for sale at a fraction of their true value.

To the right of Barakat's was the entrance to the garden bar. Kirk nodded toward one of the cafe tables. He remarked to Michelle that he would be happy to while away all the hours she spent napping, right there.

Inside the Palms building they were welcomed by a hand printed sign in front of huge bowl of fresh fruit. It read: For our Guests. Please, Help Yourself. When they were settled in the suite, Kirk tipped Ali and excused him.

"Okay, the place is all yours," said Kirk. "I'm going back down to browse around. If you need me I'll either be in the antique shop or in the garden doing some reading."

"Thanks, Kirk. I'm going to take a long, hot bath, do some primping and … What time do you want to meet?"

"Let's see, it's 4:15; you tell me."

"6:30?"

"Good. I'll be waiting at that table in the garden bar or close to it," said Kirk. "We can have a drink and decide what to do for dinner."

Kirk passed the time exploring the grounds. He found a stone bench in a secluded area between the side of the east building and a verdant wall he thought to be the property line. He sat down to admire a pair of tiny sunbirds nursing a lava red hibiscus.

A few steps later, from a shady concealment of low limbs over the walkway wall, he realized he had stumbled into a chance theater. The kitchen loading dock made a perfect stage as he was entertained by one of the chef's impassioned negotiations with an Arab produce vendor.

In the hotel bookstore he browsed through the shelves and back outside he met George, the American Colony's resident artist. He was sketching the layout of a still life on a still damp gessoed canvas. At last inside the antique shop, Barakat gave Kirk a crash course in Oriental carpets. He contrasted a pattern unique to one obscure Afghani tribe with another from some remote region of Persia. He revealed how to read the knots on the reverse side and fringes which distinguished the thousands of hours of hand-work from a few minutes mechanical repetition. One beautiful, dusty rose-colored Persian Shiraz which Barakat swore was at least sixty years old hooked Kirk. Within minutes it was on its way to Florida; he was sure that his mother would like the way it looked on her refinished oak floor.

Shortly after six Kirk went to claim the solitary table in the garden. Early enough; it was still vacant. From the gazebo bar a waiter spotted Kirk. He filled a serving basket with a rich snack mix of salty cashew halves, toasted pumpkin seeds and the other crunchy stuff and took it to Kirk's table.

"Salaam, good evening, sir. What may I get for you?"

"Salaam, Omar," Kirk noticed the waiter's name badge. "Good evening, to you." "I don't suppose you could make me a jalapeno martini?"

"I'll ask, sir, but I don't believe so."

"No, don't bother; just bring me a gin martini on the rocks, with a twist, please."

Kirk was sipping on the piney tasting drink when Michelle

arrived and took the other chair. "Sorry I'm late; I dozed off," she explained.

"Doesn't matter a bit. We're not on any schedule. I could be content to sit here for hours, the perfect spot on a perfect evening."

Kirk wanted this was to be a perfect weekend for her, too. He hoped it to be her turning point, a time that would obscure her last weekend of horrors. What he didn't want was to allow his own imagination to continue dwelling on what hell she may have gone through in Shahadeh's prison. Envisioning her at his mercy torqued his rage like old flashbacks of Vietnam.

At times, he regretted not having skewered Shahadeh from rectum through mouth, the way he'd seen the ROK's do with their special VC prisoners. With his scrotum still wired to the tree, it would have been the perfect finale for a big greasy hog.

Something within snatched Kirk's thoughts back away from the shadowy animus. He glanced down looking for the wide rubber band around his wrist; it wasn't there. For years he hadn't needed its sting to snap him out of a flashback. And that reminded him of other old sensations from years past, his feelings for Michelle.

The very idea scared him and excited him. Fifteen years age difference almost placed them in different dimensions. But he couldn't help but wonder about her feelings. He knew she had grown close to him.

"An agora for your thoughts." Michelle's voice broke the silence.

"Just an agora? That's only about a fifth of a penny, you know? They're worth more than that. And, besides, we don't have time; here comes our waiter."

Omar returned to the table with another staff member who introduced himself as Ibrahim, the head bartender. He was an erect, perfectly groomed gentleman who spoke fluent British English with a soft, buttery Arabic accent. When Omar had taken Michelle's order Ibrahim inquired about the kind of garnish that Kirk had asked about. He was curious to know what other cocktails it would be served with.

"It's a hot pepper; pretty much a regional favorite," said Kirk. "A lot of the restaurants and bars in the Southwest U.S. and along the Gulf Coast offer them with martinis and Bloody Marys... even beer."

"Oh, I see," said Ibrahim. "Let me see what I can do."

256 ⊘⊘ JIM LEVER

"Please," said Kirk, "don't go to any trouble; my drink's fine the way it is."

"No trouble at all, Sir." He insisted with a genteel dignity. "I need to know these things because you never know who will want the same drink. I'll see that Omar is right back with the lady's Campari."

As Kirk watched Ibrahim return to the gazebo he thought how well Ibrahim's amiable reserve would have served him as a diplomat or top level executive.

"He should be the general manager of the hotel rather than the bartender." Kirk commented to Michelle.

"Well, maybe he is," said Michelle. "Couldn't he be both? Oh, while you were walking around, I don't suppose you noticed a bookstore? I saw on the hotel's info channel that there's one here."

"Yes, I did; it's right over there." Kirk pointed back over Michelle's shoulder to the stairway running up beside the antique shop to a second floor entrance. "I've already had a look around."

"Do they have much in English?"

"Yeah, a few shelves."

"Anything interesting?"

"Actually, they do. I've been looking for a copy of Salman Rushdie's new book and they have it."

"Satanic Verses?"

"No, the new one," said Kirk.

"I wouldn't have thought they'd have any book of his here. What is his new one?"

"You mean the title?"

"Yes, of course, I mean the title."

"It's called <u>Buddha, You Fat Slug</u>."

Michelle burst out with a gleeful, giggling scream. It was the first time Kirk had heard her laugh since the awful weekend. Several other patrons a few vacant tables away turned at the sound of her laughter.

"Would you please try to control yourself?" Kirk's mischievous reprimand only pushed her further out of control, as he expected it to. Showing no mercy, he pressed the attack.

"Really, Michelle, you're making a spectacle of us both. Not all Buddhas are fat, lazy either for that matter. The fat Buddhas are usually found high up in the Himalayas but the skinny ones are all down around the rice paddies. That's quite a paradox, don't you think? It just doesn't..."

"Stop it, darn you. I can't breathe!" Michelle begged.

"Okay, I'll stop it. But you have to promise me something."

Michelle looked curiously as she blotted the corners of her eyes with a cocktail napkin. "And what might that be?" she asked, still snickering.

"That you won't... stop laughing or smiling."

Michelle stared off into the distance. "Is it that obvious?" she asked.

"That you're dealing with a lot of demons? Yeah, it's that obvious... to me."

"I'm sorry, Kirk. I need to learn not to wear my feelings on my shirt sleeves. It's just that..."

"Hey, that's enough of that. There's nothing you should apologize for. No one could expect you to be the jolly old soul after that." Kirk lowered his voice and leaned in close to her. "Look at me," he said. "I know what it's like trying to deal with my own gang of demons. I've been fighting post-traumatic stress for... well over half my life, now. What you've been through was probably worse than anything I had to deal with."

Michelle's eyes fixed on the glass of primrose yellow wine. She wondered if what she had been through, as Kirk had put it, would be forever confounded in her mind. "Well... one thing's for certain," she said, "this time I know better than to waste time asking, 'why'. It's all just so damned unfair. I know a thousand women who have never been a victim of anything. And now it's happened to me for the second time. Wonder who was the fool who said lightning doesn't strike the same place twice? Seems to me that that's exactly what it does do, strikes the same place over and over."

Kirk reached across the small table and slid his fingers beneath hers. His thumb softly caressed her knuckles but he said nothing. He knew what she needed most was simply the presence of someone who really cared. In a minute or two she blotted her eyes with the cocktail napkin and looked up at him.

"They shouldn't have hurt me, Kirk. They had no reason, the kid from the gang or the fat man. I didn't do anything to either of them, nothing."

"No, they shouldn't have, darling. But they did; yes they did. They hurt you and not because of any wrong you did to them. They're both just bad people. You're not to blame in any way. None of this was your fault." Kirk, holding her gaze, raised his eyebrows and squeezed her hand. "You know something else? You're right about the lightning, too; it does strike in the same place, and often.

"I was hiking through the Appalachian Trail through the Smoky Mountains. Up on a stretch of razor back ridge that led up to Clingman's Dome I started noticing all these small circular rings on the rocks along the foot path. They looked like little bull's-eye targets about two inches across.

"That night at the shelter I asked one of the park rangers about them. He told me that they were where lightning bolts had hit the rock. Hundreds of them, all within a few yards of trail. I realized that this was a section you didn't want to do during a storm, no matter how wet and cold you got waiting for it to pass.

"I'd heard the warnings to hikers about lightning on the trail a dozen times. But until I saw the hundreds of hits on the rock, it never sank in. So maybe just knowing, without a doubt, that it does strike over and over again in the same spot, gives both of us an edge from here on out."

"Dear God, I hope so, Kirk." Michelle smiled, squeezed his fingers and held on

"Yeah," said Kirk, "me, too. By the way, didn't you tell me that you didn't know much about my roommate?"

"Father Casey?" What seemed like an abrupt change of subject caught her off guard.

"Yeah, Father Bill."

"No, I barely know him at all, only what I've heard about him being one of the monks who lives up on Mount Tabor."

"And you were right about that," said Kirk.

"He seems like such a private person." Michelle continued her answer. "I see him sitting alone in the dining hall. And during breakfast, out on the tel, he's usually wandering around off by himself, in meditation or praying, I guess. So, no, I really don't know him. You probably know him better than any of us. You like him, don't you?"

"Yes, very much. He's the most unusual person I've ever met. I doubt you know just how much he did to get you back out of Jordan; I should say how much he did to get all of us out. But there's a reason I'm asking. I think you should get to know him. At the very least you'll have one heck of an interesting conversation."

"Kirk! It just dawned on me. I haven't even asked you about your drive up Mt. Gilboa or the backpacking trip with him; where was it that you were going?"

"The Cliffs of Arbel," Kirk answered without elaboration.

"Well?" said Michelle.

"We had a good two days, beautiful panoramas, no pilgrims or tourists. The whole thing was quite... This is really hard to explain; I don't even want to try right now. It would trivialize the whole experience. I'll tell you all about it; I promise."

"Well, now you have my curiosity piqued."

"I want you to hear the whole story in detail, but later."

"That heavy, huh? Well, don't think I'm going to let you forget."

Michelle was puzzled. She believed Kirk, that he did want her to know about the trip, at least something about it. She wondered what were his reasons for feeling this was not a good time. She also sensed that it had not been a bad experience for him, not his time with Father Casey, or he wouldn't be encouraging her to get to know him. She assumed that he really was waiting for a better time and place – and, maybe, for the right words.

"Hungry?" Kirk asked.

"Sure am," she answered, "and I don't want to fill up on this snack mix. But I'm going to hold you to that promise."

Kirk ignored her reminder. "I'm glad you're hungry," he said, "because the Friday night buffet here is something to behold."

When their drinks were finished and Kirk signed the check they left the garden for the dining area in the courtyard of the main building. They were seated, waiting for the buffet to open, when the Halakah siren began screaming its dogmatic demand that the city shut down. Wailing the official commencement of Shabbat all the way from Mea Shearim, it blared in over the usual cacophony of street sounds.

Almost within the same moment the sanctimonious siren was drowned out by a rapid fire burst of tambourines and cymbals. The percussion heralded a writhing blur of blue fabric and cinnamon brown flesh. A beautiful, young belly dancer slithered into the courtyard; the Muslim Sabbath had ended and the celebration had begun.

Michelle noticed that the dancer was the same girl she had

seen on the hotel's info channel. She leaned over toward Kirk and whispered.

"She's an Israeli."

"You're not serious?" he said. "How would you know?"

"I am serious. They said so on room television in the room. There's a video about the hotel on one of the channels. And that's how I know."

"Sorry, said Kirk. "Thought you might be baiting me."

When the dancer left the courtyard Kirk and Michelle went up to the buffet in the main dining room. After a few endless minutes watching Michelle's selection of one grape, one leaf, one slice at a time, Kirk had endured it as long as he could. He asked her to excuse him as he stepped around her and headed straight for the line of covered steamers which held the main entrees. His plate was served before she had moved more than a few inches further along the fruit and salad bar. Again, Kirk stood waiting on her and realizing that this game of hurry up and wait was of his own making.

"Michelle, I love you," Kirk moaned. "But you wouldn't last one meal in a mess hall chow line."

Without looking up from the assortment of cheeses, she smiled. "May be why I never joined." she answered.

Accepting his fate, Kirk stood to the side as Michelle inched her way on through the buffet. He happened to glance out one of the full length windows. Two men in an animated conversation caught his attention. One shook his finger in obvious irritation as the other beckoned for one of the cabs in the waiting line. Suddenly, one of the faces registered with him.

"Michelle, Michelle, come here." Kirk confirmed his beckoning with a hard nod.

Michelle frowned with uncertainty at being called out of her time honored place in the serving line.

"I'm serious; come here a minute," he persisted.

A grin appeared on his face as she stepped over to where he stood peering out the window.

"Look outside. Recognize that butt ugly mug? Li Moon in the flesh. Think we should ask him to join us?"

"No!" Michelle snapped back, frowning at the face on the other side of the window.

"Don't worry," said Kirk. "I'm not a fan either. Wonder what he's…"

Michelle gasped. The other man had turned; his face was now visible to her as he waited for the taxi door to open. Kirk saw the color leave her face; the plate of salad fell from her hand. The hard china wobbled on the tile floor with a reverberating peal that summoned a squad of waiters to the crash site. Before Kirk was able to fathom her reaction Michelle lunged past a foursome of diners, darted back out into the courtyard and ran through the lobby anteroom.

When he caught up with her she was outside standing on the center line of Nablus Road. Her jaws clinched, her eyes wide, she searched the distance in every direction. Car horns blasted and tires scrubbed the curb as drivers swerved to avoid her. In an instant Kirk was at her side. He grasped her arm and in one adrenalin fueled move he had her back across the sidewalk and inside the hotel's entrance drive. He pulled her on toward a spot on the same stone wall where hardly an hour earlier he had watched the loading dock theater.

"What are you doing?" Kirk sucked in a deep breath. "Michelle, look at me. What's going on?"

She was trembling; her eyes were glazed with rancor. "It was him," she said.

"Who was him?"

"The other man," she answered, continuing to stare out the gate and up the street as far as she could see.

"Michelle." Kirk called out. "What other man? I don't know what you're talking about."

She turned her head back to meet Kirk's stare and tried to remember. She was sure she had told him. Her voice dropped to a normal level as she regained control. "The other man at the antique shop in Jerash," she answered. "That was the other man."

"The man with Moon?"

"Yes." Michelle answered matter of factly. "Kirk, surely I told you?"

Kirk slowly shook his head in disagreement.

"You don't know about him, do you?"

Kirk could feel the panic, confusion and anger brewing in her voice.

"Michelle, listen to me. I was not in the office when you talked with the inspector, remember? I haven't asked you the first question about any of it. I figured if you wanted to talk you would when you were ready. Inspector Shimon is the only one you've talked to; surely you must have told him about this guy. What the hell is he doing with Moon?

"I don't know what to do. I have no idea how to get in touch with Shimon. Maybe we should call Doctor Benjamin. What do you want me to do, Michelle?"

"I don't know." she answered.

"Just let me think a moment." Kirk paced in front of the wall. "I heard Shimon say that there was almost no chance of getting the Jordanians to do anything. Of course, you know Willy and I are probably on their damn 'most wanted' list by now."

Michelle managed a subdued chuckle at the thought.

"But," Kirk continued, "if this guy is involved in illegal antiquities over here, that's a different story. One thing for certain, no Jordanian Arab dresses like that. I'd love to know his connection to Li Moon, as if I couldn't guess. You found the business card from Shahadeh's out at the site, right?"

"On the floor of one of the Portolets," Michelle answered.

"Well what do you think the odds are that old Moon didn't drop it there? Do you think either one of them saw you chasing after the taxi."

"No. I never saw the taxi after I got outside. I don't even know which way they turned out the gate."

"Then I think it's safe to assume that they don't know they've been seen." Kirk crossed his arms and pursed his lips trying to decide what they could do.

"Yeah, I suppose so," she said. "Kirk, know what I think we should do?"

"What?"

"I think we should call Dr. Ben and then we should go back to dinner. And we should not to let this ruin our weekend." Michelle eyes searched his. The resolve in her voice had caught him by surprise. Her words were more a plea than a suggestion. And Kirk saw that in her face.

"There's really nothing else we can do," she added, "except call and tell Doctor Benjamin what we saw and where we can be reached."

"You sure?"

"Quite sure," she said.

Kirk reached Moshe on his cell phone. He was also in Jerusalem, home for the weekend. Moshe asked if they were positive that it was Moon they had seen. And he asked if the young woman was sure that this was the same man she had encountered in Jerash. Kirk assured him that they were not mistaken.

Moshe told Kirk that he had Inspector Shimon's card and would get in touch with him as soon as possible. He left it that that they would be called at the American Colony if they were needed before Sunday evening when they were to get back to the kibbutz.

After their dinner, which they were determined to make leisurely, Kirk and Michelle passed the evening walking down Derech Shechem and back up Salah Ed-Din past the Albright to the hotel.

Kirk found it hard to comprehend Michelle's resilience. There was no trace of the angst she suppressed. Their conversation was light and as varied as the scenery by which they strolled. In a numinous moment of illumination, he recognized himself in her. Hers was the same brand of tough softness born to those who have known indescribable horrors and incomparable compassion within the same eternal moments.

In the room a CNN fashion report was running for the third time; the volume was too loud. Kirk had dozed off on the sofa bed in the suite. He didn't hear the door open as Michelle came in from the bedroom. The wispy scent of the hotel's terrycloth robe and Nina Ricci bath soap awakened him as she lay down next to him. His pulled his pillow by the case to share it with her.

She gazed directly into his eyes; her face was mesmerizing. Kirk responded, smiling his acceptance and his pleasure at having her close beside him. Neither spoke; no words would fit. Michelle arched her back and brushed his lips with hers. Soon she was napping snug beneath his arm. Just to have her so close was warm and wonderful.

He could hear her slow, deep, steady breathing above the muted fashion descriptions and runway music loops. He eased back just enough to raise his arm and support his head in his palm. Now his weathered eyes could focus more clearly on her beautiful face. She changed position, lying more on her side and pulling her knees up, out of the robe.

Kirk glanced at the clock. Only 11:15, it seemed more like 2:00 or 3:00. He pressed the remote to search the music channels for smooth jazz. He found it and he thought he could be content to lie there forever, looking at her, soaking in her every curve and feature.

Carefully, Kirk reached over to stroke her hair with the back of his hand. She responded with a slight turn of her head. He traced the outline of her lips, her ears, her chin. Gently Kirk lifted the robe and laid open the folds to see more of her. He ached to touch her, to caress and to taste her lips. He sat up on the edge of the bed, beside her with one foot on the floor.

He could see her breasts slowly rise and fall with her breathing. He craved to touch their softness and to feel her nipples tighten as he moved his flattened palm lightly over them. He could stand the detachment no longer; in slow, gentle circles, barely contacting the very tips he began those caresses. For a moment she tensed… but then her slow breathing continued. He could see her eyes move under the lids and her eyebrows slightly rise as she lingered in her twilight sleep. He wondered if she was dreaming and if he was in them.

Now her nipples were hard and taut. She felt it. And it felt good, even in her dreamy subconscious. He noticed her stomach muscles contract and he heard an almost imperceptible gasp as she inhaled more deeply. But he was sure she was still asleep. She rolled over, all the way, on her back. Her head was turned, the left side of her face resting on the pillow. That's good, Kirk thought, her right side was even more stunning, more expressive; he could read it even better. For a moment he was afraid she would awaken. But then he heard a soft sigh and knew she was still deep and far away. Even so, he sat back to let her retreat deeper.

The hem of her loose top was high up on her thighs. Kirk leaned over, watching her face for any sign that she was disturbed; he raised the hem higher… and higher. She moved with a slow twisting from side to side and then moved her legs a little, apart. Her right heel was over the edge of the mattress. Now Kirk could see all of her; she was beautiful beyond belief. He flinched with excitement, trying not to awaken her with his jerky breaths. He wanted inside her so badly he could barely stand it.

Again he watched her muscles tighten, maybe there was even a quiver of excitement. He thought she may have awakened and was pretending to still sleep to assure that he continued, to see what else he had in store. The uncertainty was thrilling; he waited and watched, almost trembling with anticipation. He didn't think she was that good an actress, not to be asleep.

He longed to know if his touches, the pressure of his palms and fingers and the sweeps of his adoring eyes were moving through her dreams giving her all the pleasure he wanted her to feel. He sensed that she did. He suspected that she was wet with eagerness. Kirk's heart pounded within his chest; he could stand the denial no longer.

He kneeled on the thick Berber loops beneath the sofa and gently pressed her knees farther apart. He could smell the lingering traces of some fragrant bath oil melding and rising with the scent of her dreamy excitement. He positioned himself with his chest pressing into the side of the mattress. Slowly, softly, he brushed her knees, her stomach, her breasts with his lips and traced the firm ridge of her quadriceps with the tip of his tongue. He moved his arms across her silky legs and slid his hands under the small of her back, his face mere millimeters from the pathway to her soul.

He was right; she was swollen and slippery and wonderful and he could feel and taste her eagerness. He hungered to hurl her into a heavenly oblivion where every fiber of her being pulsed with pleasure. Now he could clearly hear an unmistakable gasp; she moaned as she surfaced from the delicious dream into an even more wonderful and electrifying reality. She could no longer contain her frenzied writhing. She pressed her flesh into Kirk's waiting lips and he felt her convulsive arching demanding that he concede to her crescendo of desire.

As quickly as he could he slid up onto her. His strong hands gripped her chest; his thumbs tenderly massaged her still firm nipples. Her eyes were locked onto his face in an ecstatic stare as she reached to guide him into her. Dizzy with excitement he responded, pushing into her as strenuously as he dared. Again, again; on, on; far inside, sealed within her as she gripped down on him even more tightly. It seemed that he could not pull out even if he tried. Some powerful force pinned her body to his, some perfect tightness, some total vacuum.

The rapturous contractions came with flashes of light. Michelle tried to muffle her soprano groans of delirium. Kirk's whole body locked down in seizures of unspeakable pleasure, surges of his soul exploded, bursting into the depths of hers as together they leapt across time and space.

And when, finally, they lay face to face on their sides in the soft music, the precious last drops of his thick liquid surged once again bathing her belly and breasts in the slippery warmth. They hugged each other as closely as their waning strength allowed as the diminishing gushes subsided slowly as a falling tide.

Several soft instrumentals later, Michelle whispered. "Kirk?"

"Umm?"

"Thank you," she said softly.

"What?" The surprise in his voice was obvious.

"I mean thank you for everything; for being my friend, for coming after me, for being as sensitive as you are… for just always being there for me."

"Michelle… You don't…"

"No," she halted him. "Let me finish."

"I know that tonight was all my idea, my call. I know you would have never come on to me. I just want you to know that."

"You're right," said Kirk. No matter how often I dreamed about it and wanted to, I wouldn't have. But I sure am glad that you did. At least now I know I'm not just some old fool fantasizing… Well, I may be, but now it isn't all a pipe dream."

"Then I'm glad I made it happen, too. Just, please, don't let this change things. I mean I… uh, don't want you to think that… Damn it, Kirk, I don't want things to change because we slept together. It would crush me if I wound up being a been-there-done-that girl to you. I don't expect anything more from you – as much as I may wish for it – but, god, Kirk, I don't want anything less, either. I just don't want to lose what we have. Am I making any sense at all?"

"Yes, you're making perfect sense. But you can put your mind at ease; I adore you, Michelle. I realized that I had already fallen in love with you when I found you in Jerash. But I didn't dare to dream that you might ever feel the same way. I mean, this has all happened so darned quickly… and our age difference. I don't know what to say except… Now's the time to bare my throat, I guess. If you're telling me that you would like for us to stay together, I'm telling you that nothing in the world would suit me better. I would be the happiest, and the luckiest, man in the world to take this thing as far as you want it to go."

"Really, Kirk?" Michelle responded, obviously elated. "And by 'this thing', you mean our relationship?"

"Yes, hell yes, relationship. That's just not the kind of word a man ought to be using. Got to be one better."

Through her joyful tears Michelle laughed out loud. She couldn't believe it; there actually had been someone out there for her. Someone wonderful in this unfair, unjust, lonely world she had known for so long. Could she possibly be living this dream?

And Kirk shared the same thoughts, minus the crying, of course. Then again they slept, deep within the strength and tenderness of each others arms. Merged bodies, melded spirits, mated souls.

19

THERE HAD Been a sniper attack near the Mehola Junction and Highway 90 through the Jordan Valley was closed off by the IDF. The ride back to Kibbutz Massebot had taken over three hours. From Jerusalem down to Tel Aviv, up Highway 2 to Hadera then back east to the Beth Shean Valley was twice the distance. To make the trip worse, the air conditioning in the sherut was blowing hot air. But neither Kirk nor Michelle seemed to be bothered by the trivial nuisances. The weekend had been too perfect to be diminished by a couple of hours in a hot sherut. They both slept most of the way, exhausted from their perfect weekend.

Kirk awoke with a start. A crop duster pulled up hard just clearing the eucalyptus trees which divided the highway from a soybean field beyond. The bright yellow AgWagon's tenor scream had crashed his nap and now an acrid smell assaulted his nostrils. He looked out the window and saw the swirling vortices of pungent Malathion trailing off behind the big plane's wings. At any rate, he was awake. Kibbutz Beit Alpha was passing by; they would be back within minutes.

Kirk knocked on the door as he turned the key and pushed it open. "Bill, you dressed? Michelle's with me."

"Yeah, come on in. I'm just reading. Glad you're back and how was the weekend?"

"Quite eventful," said Kirk.

"I trust you two enjoyed yourselves, and each other." Father Casey avoided eye contact as he marked his page with a bookmark. "Oh, before I forget, Dalya came up a little while ago; asked me to give this to you." He removed a folded note from the foot of his cot and held it out to Kirk.

When Kirk had read the message he handed it to Michelle. "Inspector Shimon wants us to call as soon as we return. I guess Dr. Benjamin found him. Why don't I run back down to the office and make the call. You can let Father Bill know what's going on."

"Okay, sure," said Michelle. "Besides, Kirk tells me I should get to know you better, Father Casey. I'm looking forward to that."

Shimon told Kirk that he wanted to drive straight out and talk to them. He arrived in less than an half an hour. Kirk walked out to meet him and to lead him back to the room.

"Good afternoon, inspector," said Kirk. "I guess you've talked with Dr. Benjamin?'

"Yes. Is he back yet?"

"No but Dalya – girl in the office – said he's due any time."

"And how about our Dr. Moon?" Shimon asked.

"Don't know; I haven't seen him," said Kirk.

"Good, I don't want to question him until I've talked with all of you."

Kirk gathered that Michelle and the old priest were already engaged in a deep conversation. He noticed that she hardly looked up as they entered the room. When she did, she smiled up at Kirk from where she sat and nodded to him that she was all right. Kirk glanced over at Bill who winked and nodded his agreement that all was well.

Shimon exchanged greetings and routinely inquired if she was "getting past her bad experience". It was obvious to Michelle that Shimon regarded the courtesy talk as an irritating formality and that irritated her.

"I'll get over it," Michelle answered with a tinge of snap. "But so I won't waste your time, why don't we get started?

"As you wish," said Shimon. "Please…"

"I'll go ahead and tell you what I saw. Kirk, correct me if I miss something, please. First of all, I need to be sure I told you about the other man in the antique shop in Jerash?"

"Yes, you did," said Shimon. "I didn't press you for any particulars because I knew it would be useless to contact the Jordanian police. And, as you know, we have no authority there."

Michelle repeated the details of first noticing the man in an intense conversation with Shahadeh in the antiquities shop. When she asked if he might be from California he seemed caught off guard and evaded her question. But then he had Shahadeh order tea and it was he who had insisted she have a glass, the one that knocked her out. Then when she saw him again, in Jerusalem, with Dr. Moon… She fell silent, unable to put her reaction in words.

Kirk picked up the story. He related the account of her reaction to Shimon, the initial shock turned to rage and then the chase into the street. When Michelle continued, she was emphatic that he was the same man. Shimon asked if he had any distinguishing features which made her absolutely certain it could not have been someone else who happened to look very much like the man in Jerash. Gingerly, he explained how easily one can be confused after a trauma, with faces, features or even an isolated mannerism enough to trigger a flashback.

This time, with a genuine concern for her feelings, or so Michelle thought, Shimon assured her that this kind of confusion is a normal mechanism, the mind's way of protecting us, of keeping us away from the same danger. His explanation worked; Michelle was not offended by his suggestion that she might have been mistaken.

"Inspector Shimon, I know it was the same man, not a look-alike, not even his twin. His height, weight, hair color, even that contemptuous expression, it was all the same. But what first caught my eye was the western shirt and that tacky buffalo skull bolo tie. He was wearing the same bolo tie in Jerash."

"What caught your eye?" asked Shimon.

"His bolo tie and shirt," she answered.

Michelle could see by Shimon's expression that he had no idea what she was talking about. She described a western cut shirt; pointed pocket flaps, yoke and snap studs and she described a bolo tie. She told him that the guy looked like he ought to be dealing high stakes poker in Reno. Michelle enlightened the inspector that his outfit, the Frommer boots, croc belt and all, could easily have cost several thousand dollars.

"If he's mixed up in all this," Kirk asked, "why do you suppose he would want to stick out like a sore thumb?"

"Why did Richthofen paint his airplane red?" Shimon asked. It's been my experience that deluded people often want to make sure others see them as who or what they believe themselves to be."

"Or, maybe, for what one wants others to believe them to be," said Father Casey. "Funny, but I read somewhere that when the

Baron Richthofen slipped away to visit his mistress, he always wore the uniform of a private."

"Your point is well taken, Father," said Shimon. "So, I suppose our answer is: just who or what does our mystery man need to be or who does he want us to believe he is. When we know that, we may well know just how he fits into all of this. In the meantime, let's hope that Dr. Moon has a pretty good explanation for the friends he keeps."

Shimon turned and looked directly at Michelle with his severing stare. "I believe you, Miss Eisner; I think you know what and whom you saw. And I also have reasons to believe that it's quite likely there's much more to your abduction and imprisonment than a case of your accidentally getting caught up in an illegal artifacts deal. I don't think there's much chance that Mr. Shahadeh Jaber or this other shmuck – pardon me, Miss Eisner – had any plans to sell you as a slave to some rich Uday Hussein type. An American woman would just be too risky for them, especially when there are so many beautiful and younger – pardon me again Miss—Russian girls that no one will ever come looking for."

There was a knock on the door. Moshe and Willy Dubignon entered, interrupting the inspector. After brief greetings they arranged the furniture to sit in a circle.

Shimon continued by explaining that that he had been in Haifa, spending Shabbat with his family, and had only gotten Moshe's voice message that morning. He repeated his belief that there was much more to Michelle's capture than he had first thought. It was indeed a case of her stumbling into the wrong place at the wrong time but he asked for everyone's cooperation to help him fill in as many blanks as possible. He said, possibly then he could determine exactly what she had stumbled into.

"I got another call this morning," said Shimon, "shortly after yours, Dr. Benjamin. This call along with a fax I received may tie some of the loose ends together.

"A few weeks ago there was a car bomb explosion in Jerusalem. Nothing too unusual about that except for some of the circumstances. The car was parked off by itself in an empty section of an apartment complex parking area in French Hill, very near Hebrew University and the Hyatt Hotel. The driver was killed in the blast.

"At first it was assumed that the bomb had detonated prematurely but the pieces just wouldn't fit together. Bombs that go off accidentally either explode where they're being built or enroute to a specific target. It's a given that this bomb wasn't built in a nice Jewish neighborhood on French Hill. Furthermore, this parking lot is not on a route to a target or near any logical target.

"The car was registered to a Yoram Perlman. It had not been reported missing or stolen; however, Perlman was missing. No one had seen him since sometime on the afternoon before the bomb exploded, which was around 9:30 that night. When investigators went to Perlman's apartment – from what I'm told it was more like a studio workshop – they found a vault box key Scotch-taped to a piece of note paper and placed in the center of his dining table. On the paper, the words, 'Bank Hapoalim, Zion Square,' were written, nothing more.

"When the safe deposit box was opened, there was a sealed letter addressed to the Commander of Jerusalem Police. The letter was signed by Perlman; the bank verified his signature. The letter was short and to the point, few details, read more like an atonement than a confession or an expose. It opened with a statement saying if the commander was reading his letter then he, Yoram Perlman, was already dead. He went on to state that he had been commissioned by a man named James Adams, an American, to create an Iron Age period clay tablet with an inscription; the wording, he claimed, was provided by Adams. He had enclosed a photograph of both the written inscription provided by Adams and the finished artifact with the inscription baked into the clay.

"Then he revealed that he had perfected a microsurgical technique of implanting microcrystals, which he farmed from authentic pottery shards of an appropriate period, into his fakes – fake is my word, not his – using ceramic polymers developed for aerospace applications and now used in state of the art dental procedures. He said the exact process was explained in technical detail in a journal that could be found in his shop."

Moshe sat in stoic silence. Shimon couldn't read the professor's reaction to the news he was breaking. Then Willy spoke up with what they had already deduced.

"This wouldn't, just by chance, be our clay tablet, would it?"

"Give me a minute to finish," said Shimon. "Perlman goes on to confess that he has been creating counterfeit artifacts for several years and says that a photo portfolio of his creations can also be found with the technical journal. He says that his reproduction business, as he calls it, was not the result of his personal greed. He claims that every shekel he could scrape together had gone to his family, still in Russia, to make aliyah.

"Finally, Perlman explained that when he was given such a lucrative commission to produce the clay tablet, it raised his suspicions. Then, after he translated the inscription he knew that this was much more than a sophisticated scheme to sell a fake artifact. He said he knew that it must be part of an attempt to rewrite sacred history for heretical purposes. Probably some radical Jews like the Kahane or the expelled American cult, Concerned Christians, he assumed. He stated that, if he were alive, he would have exposed the tablet himself, after he had the rest of his family safe in Israel but now it's up to us – the police, I suppose he means.

"His final statements admit his part in the fraud and deception but he denies that he ever intended to be a part of any heresy or blasphemy. And he closes by saying that all the claims made in this document can be proven by x-raying the tablet.

"Well, that's what I have, so far," said Inspector Shimon. "Were you aware of any of this, Dr. Benjamin?"

"No, none of it," said Moshe. "How long has this letter been in police hands? Did you not have it in time to save the IAA from making fools of us all jumping the gun with their damned press conference?"

"Yes, we had it," said Shimon. "But our priority is to find a bomber and solve a murder, not to keep bureaucrats from making fools of themselves. I'm sorry you archaeologists are caught up in the middle of all this. It's unfortunate… the investigation of a serious crime almost always causes some innocent suffering."

"I'm sure of that," said Moshe.

"May I say something?" asked Father Casey.

"Yes, of course," said Shimon.

"I believe most of us have been under the impression that what we found was a sort of dedication message and that the importance of the find was that it contained the first secular references to several biblical names and places. By now, I would suppose, most of the world has had the opportunity to witness the tablet, or one that looks exactly like it, being lifted from the earth, after nearly three thousand years.

"Mr. Perlman must be correct in his assumption that there is some inspiration here much greater than money. Such an object would have the kind of value that would make it as difficult to sell as a stolen Mona Lisa or Hope Diamond, even if the ones who had it made and planted could steal it back. It seems to me that we, or I should say, you, Inspector, have to determine just who has more to gain from the message itself than from possession of the tablet."

"I may have the answer to that," said Moshe. "From the preliminary translation, it seemed that the Ultra-Orthodox and all the other manifest destiny Zionists could rejoice. Finally, there was proof of Israel's just claim to all the land within the scriptural boundaries. As you can imagine, such moral high ground would be beyond any monetary price."

Moshe continued with the story of last week's press conference where it was learned there was another slant to the inscription. He told Shimon about the freelance writer who announced from the crowd that the two names that were not recognized from scripture were both patriarchs of the Church of Jesus Christ of Latter-day Saints.

"I knew next to nothing about the Mormon Church," Moshe admitted, "just that it was another one of the dozens of American Christian sects. Now, here it is, a few days later, and I can assure you I know much more than I did."

Moshe related that over the past few years the Mormons had made some rather remarkable inroads in Israel, especially in Jerusalem. He told how, against all odds, on the slope of Mt. Scopus there was a new facility, The Mormon Center. He asked Shimon if he could even imagine how many building permit requests, submitted by mainstream Christian denominations, had been denied over the years. Shimon shrugged. Moshe told him of the rumors that a world class architect and an internationally connected general contractor – both just happened to be Jewish – were given open checkbooks by the church. "Well," Moshe said with a subdued smile, "let's just say that seas can, indeed, still be parted. And now, after our most providential find, the Mormons may well be on their way to the center of mainstream Christianity and Judaism. So, tell me, Inspector Shimon, where to from here?"

"I'll tell you, where to from here, Professor; I'm ready to interview your Doctor Moon. If I'm right he's the key piece to this whole puzzle. If I can break him we'll have the rest of our answers. Can you see if he's returned?"

Even though it was only a few steps from the room to the office, Moshe called on his cell phone. Dalya answered. She told him she would check and see if Moon had returned. Moshe asked her to tell Moon to come up to the lab office when he got a moment. Then, if she would, call back and let him know if she had found him. Less than five minutes later Dalya called back; Moon was in his room. After promises to let the others know the results of the interview, Shimon and Moshe headed down to the office area. Moon was not there yet.

"Good," said Shimon, let's go get him and bring him to the lab. Oh… Dr. Benjamin, I'm going to lean on him pretty hard. Please don't interrupt or try to correct anything I say. I may feed him some misinformation just to see how he reacts. If I can convince him that he's our main suspect in the car bomb and murder, he might just tell us all he knows. Even so, I'll still have to take him in until we can check out what he tells us, if anything. If he doesn't tell us anything out here I'll continue the interrogation at district headquarters."

"I understand, said Moshe. "Why don't you let me go down to his room, by myself, and bring him back? There's no need to embarrass him with a confrontation in front of his students. I suppose there's still an outside chance that's he's an innocent third party in all of this. So, if you have no objection, please wait for us here in the lab."

Moshe knocked on the door to Moon's room. It was answered by one of his grad- student roommates who called back inside. Moon, without his glasses, came forward tucking in his shirt. His body language and searching eyes betrayed him; he sensed that something was amiss. His voice had a shaky and overly cordial quality as he greeted Dr. Benjamin.

"Dr. Moon," said Moshe, "Can you join me in the lab office, I need to get some information from you before we start back up tomorrow."

"Yes, yes sir, just give me minute, please."

Inside the lab with the door locked, Moshe got right to the point. He told Moon that he didn't need any information about the dig, he had just used that as a courtesy cover. He introduced Inspector Shimon and told Moon that there were some serious problems involving some of the volunteers and even the expedition itself and that he expected his full cooperation. Moon was trembling visibly. He wiped his palms on his trousers and a rapid fire of blinks and swallows confirmed his stress. Nonetheless, he tried to present an agreeable demeanor and he agreed to help in any way he could.

Shimon thanked Moon for his cooperation and began explaining that he was looking into a murder that might be connected to the Tel Kefar expedition. With painful detail he explained every nuance of needing to know where some of the staff and volunteers had been on certain dates and at specific times.

An hour passed. Moshe was growing stir crazy. He knew Moon must be mired in his own private torment. The room was hot as hell; every light in the place was on. Moshe walked over to the thermostat; then he remembered. He paused with his hand on the switch, turned and looked back at Shimon. Shimon's eyes were waiting as he continued feeding the bait information to Moon. With almost imperceptible motion, Shimon turned his head from side to side. Moshe got the message; everything about this session was to be as uncomfortable and miserable as possible for Moon. This was the same technique they had used with Syrian war prisoners so many years ago. Moshe turned around and sat on the sleeper couch.

Another hour passed. Shimon must have heard some signal in Moon's voice or seen some sign in his face. It was time to close in. He shifted into a soft, hypnotic and understanding tone, almost a whisper.

"Doctor Moon, it's time to get this behind you. We know you're behind the kidnapping, the murder and the artifact thefts. It will be so much better for you if you tell us the whole story. Then I can tell the chief magistrate that you cooperated and that without..."

"Noooooooooo," Moon screamed out in terror." I kill no one. I not know what had happened until it was done. It was Mr. Adams. Abbas was at the site when we got there. He try to hide but we hear cell phone ring. I tell Mr. Adams that he probably just miss his ride home and he don't know anything wrong. He probably hide cause he think we Israeli Police or maybe the ali-babas who beat him up if they find him there. We not taking anything away from site so he don't think anything wrong and what can he say? And I tell Mr. Adams not to worry, he don't speak good Hebrew. But Mr. Adams not listen. He the one that kill Abbas. Was not me; was not me."

Moon wailed, burying his face in his hands. Moshe sat in stunned silence. Shimon tried to rethink his strategy, to reindex his bank of questions. Where to from here? Indeed, he had just solved a case but it was a crime he hadn't even known had been committed.

Memories flooded back into Shimon's thoughts. He cursed himself for assuring Moshe that the Arab boy had almost certainly just quit without notice. And Moshe cursed himself for listening to Shimon, for not demanding a real investigation into the case of his missing worker, the loyal boy with the dreams, just a kid.

The inspector continued to question Li Moon on into the night. He feared that if he broke it off, even for the short drive to headquarters, Moon might not continue to be as informative or he might clam up altogether. Shimon was collating Moon's wealth of information on the crime at hand as well as the black market in stolen antiquities.

For several years, Moon had been selling artifacts from the myriad shelves and boxes stored in the basement of the Hebrew University's Archaeology Department. Items that were not likely to be missed, he sold to an antiquities dealer on the Via Dolorosa in the Old City. Those that might be recognized, especially the small ones, he carried into Jordan, to the shopkeeper Shahadeh. These could easily be concealed on his person.

He boasted of carrying twenty thousand shekels worth of scarabs through the Allenby Bridge border crossing in the cuffs of his trousers. He claimed that once he even wore a rare cylinder seal as a pendant on a gold chain. An Israeli Customs girl noticed it and had actually complimented him on it. The seal was a special order; Shahadeh already had a buyer for it, a collector who read published lists of artifacts from past excavations and then placed orders for some of the listed pieces. Moon admitted that he suspected James Adams was the special order buyer but he didn't know that for a fact. What he did know was that Adams was one of Shahadeh's best customers and that Adams knew about the artifacts that he had sold in Jerash, even the special orders.

Moon did know that it was Shahadeh who put Adams in contact with him to plant the tablet at Kefar. Adams had told him that Shahadeh had tape recorded their business transactions. Adams used this veiled threat to coerce Moon to take the job of planting the clay tablet. Moon admitted that he was well compensated for it but he swore that he was threatened with exposure if he refused to cooperate. Moon said that he was paid ten thousand shekels to conceal the tablet in the appropriate stratum where it would be found by one of the Area B volunteers. He had to make sure that the one who found the tablet would not be experienced enough to detect any difference in the recently disturbed soil medium.

Shimon paused with the questioning long enough to openly remark to Moshe that this surveillance video, if it actually existed, might be the only reason Moon hadn't suffered a fate similar to Perlman's. Shimon intended his 'similar fate' remark to bait Moon. Any sign of trepidation could indicate his involvement in the Perlman murder. But Shimon saw only a perplexed mien in Moon's eyes; maybe he didn't know.

"Dr. Moon," said Shimon, "tell me exactly what happened to your friend Yoram Perlman. Did he try to hold out for more money, threaten blackmail? You know, don't you?"

"No, sir. I don't know who you talking about. I tell you everything I know."

"Then please allow me to fill you in, just as if this is all news to you."

Shimon gave Moon an abbreviated version of the car bomb blast that killed Perlman, or so he thought. Moon was convincing in his denial of any knowledge of the bombing. He insisted that he had no idea where Adams had gotten the tablet and he had never known or heard of anyone named Yoram Perlman. Shimon believed him but he continued to badger for every scintilla of information he could provide. Several times he told Moon that the Jerusalem Police had evidence linking him to Perlman and each time Moon swore that they could not.

In the early hours of Monday morning Shimon decided that he had all he was going to get from the one marathon session. Moshe, still on the couch with his eyes shut, was an uncomfortable looking contorted mess. Shimon pressed the two-way function on his cellular and called for a patrol to come out to Kibbutz Massebot. There was time for only a few more comments before the police arrived. Shimon's tone of voice softened with his suspect.

"Dr. Moon?"

Moon glanced up at the inspector and then resumed his coma-like stare into the depths.

"You know we're going to have to take you into custody?"

Moon nodded slowly, now his eyes were shut, squinched tight against the awful message.

"Listen to me, Li," said Shimon. "Your only chance for leniency is your complete cooperation. You do understand that?"

Again, Moon nodded.

"There are two things I want you to do. One, I want you to make a note of anything you think of, anything that may help us find Adams. Nothing's too trivial to jot down. I'll see that you have pen and paper. Two, first thing in the morning I want you out at the dig site. I want you to show us exactly where to find the boy's body... okay? Then I want you to reconstruct everything that happened out there... the entire sequence of events... moment by moment. Are you with me, Li?"

Moon whispered a barely audible, "Yes."

When the armored police jeep had driven away with Doctor Moon, Moshe and Shimon parted with awkward nods, each blaming himself more than the other for the failures. In his room Moshe stretched out on his cot without bothering to undress. He passed the few hours before driving out to the tel lying there trying not to think about a damn thing. When his clock radio did power on at 0430 he immediately switched it off, tied on his boots and left the room. When he turned down the field road to the tel he could see that the authorities were already there.

A soft alpenglow cowl on the crest of Kefar backlit the macabre chore underway at the base of the tel. The floodlit area created a scene of surreal contrast. Before the sun topped the mountains of Jordan the Galilee Crime Scene Unit had recovered the body of Abbas Hashim.

The dry, gray talc soil that had covered the corpse had preserved it well; the ballpoint ink remained in the palm of the left hand; the license number was clear and readable. Within ten minutes Shimon had learned that the tag was registered to Avis and the vehicle had been leased from the King David Street rental office in Jerusalem. Even if the required identification was fake, there would still be security camera footage and a handwriting sample. The hunt for James Adams was on.

20

SOMETHING WAS Wrong; Aldrich sensed it. He got up from the bed and pulled back the musty smelling curtain. The midday light gouged at his eyes. He squinted down into the parking lot below. The blue police were stopped behind his Avis rental.

He had used public parking instead of the hotel's for this very reason. The lot on Shamai Street was within a couple of blocks of seven or eight hotels and about a dozen apartment buildings. His room on the fourth floor of the Olive Tree Hotel had a direct view of the public lot.

One of the police got out of the patrol car and tried the doors of the big Toyota. Aldrich felt his heart leap as he watched her shade her eyes against the glare and peer in through the dark tinted glass. "Damn it," he mouthed the words as his thoughts raced. Maybe he had been caught running a red light by one of the ubiquitous traffic cameras. But for that, they wouldn't do anymore than trace the tag number to Avis and mail the citation.

He moved away from the window, pacing the small room, trying to collect his thoughts. Back to the window. They had moved the blue and white up onto the exit ramp. A plain car turned into the parking lot and backed into one of the reserved spaces. A Sephardic-complexioned, stocky man in jeans and knit shirt struggled to get out of the car. One of the blue police walked over to meet him.

"Boker Tov, Inspector."

"Where is it?"

The uniformed policeman turned and pointed to the Land Cruiser.

"There, sir," he said. "Nothing inside to indicate how long it's been here; nothing visible inside at all."

"Beseder, Aviram. Continue your rounds. I'll take over from here."

"Ken, Sir." said the policeman.

"Oh, and Aviram," said the inspector.

"Ma, sir?"

"Good eye; good job."

"Todah rabah, sir. But… actually, it was Tamar who spotted the tag."

The inspector looked back toward the blue and white patrol car. He nodded his approval to the young woman sitting in the passenger seat. She smiled back, pleased by the recognition.

"Tell her I said good job, Aviram."

"I will, sir."

Through the slit of light between the curtain and wall, Aldrich continued to watch as the police cruiser eased off. The man in plainclothes returned to the white Mazda and got in; it didn't move. His rental car was under surveillance.

This was not about any traffic ticket. How much did they know, the question tortured him. How much could they know? Neither Moon nor Perlman knew his real name. Even so, Perlman wasn't talking; that much was certain. Somehow they must have zeroed in on Moon. He had used the fake Adams passport and driver's license to rent the car and he had paid with a private Cayman debit card. That account was also in Adams' name. They could only be looking for James Adams. And Adams was some American in western wear.

Regardless, it was time to get out of the city. As much as he would dearly love to stay for the next press conference and to bask in the glorious redemption of his beloved church—"the church I just saved," he whispered aloud – he must leave, now. And it was time to become invisible again. But, first, the western garb must help him create one last diversion.

He dressed quickly, wet his hair with a bit of soapy water and combed it back with a high part. He inspected himself in the clouded bathroom mirror. "I look like Cowboy Copas' damn steel guitar player," Aldrich muttered to himself. But this should help the hotel staff to remember what James Adams looked like.

In the lobby he stood at the counter waiting for the clerk to finish some paperwork he frowned into. Aldrich didn't want to seem

282 JIM LEVER

impatient or irritated with the inattentive little man behind the desk. Finally, the clerk spoke without looking up.

"Yes?"

"I want to pay in advance for room 420 for two nights, with cash please," said Aldrich.

The stooped and balding clerk took a long draw from an unfiltered Prima. He exhaled the blue smoke and carefully positioned the cigarette in an overfilled ashtray. He shuffled through the registration cards, licked his index finger and removed one from its celluloid sleeve.

"Very good, sir. Do you want to leave tonight's stay on your Visa and add two nights?"

Aldrich caught a whiff of the clerk's foul cigarette breath; it was nauseating.

"No," said Aldrich, "I'm only staying tonight and tomorrow night. So, tear up my Visa charge slip, please."

"Why, of course, Mr. Adams."

Back up in his room, he went straight to the window and peeped out. The plain car was still there. No time to waste, he had to get moving before they started checking out the whole area. First, he had to get rid of the western clothes.

One good thing about the weird-looking toilets over here, he thought; you could flush a sleeping bag if you had to, and for good reason. For an instant he forgot the stress of the moment and smiled at the recollection of stories he had heard about Bedouin first encounters with modern plumbing.

An oil company's plumbing subcontractor was going crazy over sewer lines jammed with rocks. They thought their work was being sabotaged until they realized that the desert Arabs knew nothing of toilet paper; they used small, smooth stones to clean themselves. You use what you've got, Aldrich thought with amusement. Then, his smile vanished as he wondered if Jesus himself had used rocks to clean himself.

He removed the shirt with pointed pocket flaps and mother of pearl snaps from his duffle bag. He began cutting it into small rags with his pocket knife and flushing a few at a time down the gushing toilet. The sudden surge of water and four stories of fall assured there would be no clogs. The tough khaki twill trousers took longer but still, no problem. He couldn't bear to cut up the $2,500

Frommer boots and decided to leave them in a trash container on another floor.

On the top floor, he decided to leave only one boot concealed in the trash bin here and the other on one of the lower floors. Little chance of them both getting back together on someone's feet before he was well on his way.

Back in the room he began a methodical search of his belongings for anything that could connect him to Avis, Moon, Perlman or, god forbid, the clay tablet. Every receipt, card, tag and note he ripped up and flushed. After he was satisfied he was clean he changed into the dark gabardine trousers, brace, and white band collar shirt from the used clothing store. He clipped on the jacquard yarmulke and positioned his gold rim reading glasses on the bridge of his nose. Even though the lenses above the bifocals were clear glass, he didn't like them on his face. But they enhanced the disguise so he would tolerate them until he was away from the Olive Tower and Jerusalem.

Aldrich moved to the window again. He eased the side hem of the curtain back just enough to see down into the parking lot. The big man's elbow was jutted out the driver's side window of the unmarked Mazda. One last time his eyes searched the room for anything he might have forgotten. He decided to leave some dirty clothes and toiletries in the bathroom and a travel guide on the bed and hoped this would be convincing that he planned to return. Aldrich picked up his duffel bag and opened the door. He removed the hanger sign from the inside grab handle and placed it on the outside with the "Do Not Disturb" showing. He thought to himself that, maybe, he should turn out the side requesting, Please Clean Room. Sure as hell, that would keep them out and assure that his departure was not noticed for another day.

The elevator door jerked opened on the Olive Tower's lobby floor. Aldrich stood there for a moment looking for any reason not to exit. Across the lobby several older men were sitting around the bar in a bank of tobacco smoke coddling glasses of grappa and coffee. On a divan, a tourist family sat in a cluster surrounded by their tumbling stack of baggage, waiting for an airport Neshur, he thought.

No one cast a glance toward the open elevator. Aldrich stepped out clutching his duffel bag. With his head turned away from the desk, he made the brisk walk across the lobby and through the re-

volving door out onto Darom Street. Five minutes later Aldrich
was on Yafo Street boarding a city bus for the short ride to the
central station.

By the time the bus reached his stop Aldrich thought his blad-
der would explode. He knew it was more nerves than urine but
that didn't ease the urgency. As soon as he was off the bus Aldrich
rushed across the street, pushing his way through the crowd in the
crosswalk, and entered the terminal building.

Inside the hasherutim he stood at the urinal trying to produce a
full stream instead of the aggravating trickle that delayed his relief.
Out of the corner of his eye he noticed someone step up to the adjacent fixture. There were eight urinals along the wall, seven in a row,
vacant, yet some jerk takes the one next to his. Then Aldrich felt the
stare and instantly he knew; his perverted admirer was waiting for
any sign of encouragement.

Aldrich shook himself, dressed right and zipped up. Then he
turned and square faced the glass-eyed pathetic remnant of a man
standing next to him. Aldrich inspected him from his disordered
hair to the flip-flop clad feet barely visible beneath his baggy, draw-
string pants. He focused on the frail, needle-bruised arms hanging
limp from a faded red muscle shirt.

"Anglit?" asked Aldrich.

In little more than a pitiful whisper the derelict answered,
"Yes, I speak a little."

With the speed of a steel trap latch, one of Aldrich's strong
hands gripped the stranger's windpipe and pinned the frail wretch
against the wall. His left fist was clinched, cocked, ready to smash
the gaunt, death-camp looking face. The frail creature didn't resist;
he offered no protest.

Aldrich caught himself. He knew he could ill afford to draw
attention to himself, especially the attention of the police. He
couldn't allow himself the satisfaction of breaking up the faggot's
face, no matter how much he would love to. He released his grip
on the throat and stepped back. He scanned the room to be sure
there were no witnesses to the confrontation. There was no one else
there.

"Get out of here you God-damned sodomite. I'd like nothing
better than to knock out your cocksucking teeth. Get the hell out
of here."

Holding his throat, the middle-aged man retreated and disappeared through the entrance way. Aldrich rinsed his hands at a lavatory—no soap, of course, he mumbled in his thoughts – and dried them with his own handkerchief. Outside, he looked up and down the walkway. There was no sign of the lonely derelict.

Aldrich was irritated with himself, not for his treatment of the man but with his own lack of control and for allowing a real possibility for the wrong eyes to notice him. No matter how righteous his indignation, he knew he was stupid to have dropped his guard so completely. All he had to do was to ignore the man for a few seconds. This time he lucked out; there couldn't be a next time.

At the far end of the concourse he spotted a bank of orange Bezek pay phones. It was time to call Shula. She would be pissed at not having heard from him for... however many months it had been. But, in the end, she would welcome him. He had considered calling her to apologize for the silence and smooth things over just in case he needed her, as he did now. But he had then decided that the safer course would be for no one, not even Shula, to know he was in the country this time.

The phone's LCD showed one hundred eighty credits on the prepaid card. He tapped in the number and waited as the phone rang. He wouldn't leave a message. If she didn't answer he would wait and call again from Tel Aviv. He was in luck; he recognized the familiar voice that answered.

"How are you, Shula?"

"Peter?"

"Yes."

"Where are you?"

"Jerusalem. I would have called but this was a spur of the moment business trip, just wrapped it up this morning."

"How long will you be here, Peter?"

"I guess that depends on whether or not you have plans."

Aldrich waited for her to answer but she held her silence."

"Actually," he continued, "I was hoping to come down for a day or two, buy some of your beautiful jewelry and... whatever you want to do. We could go over to that fish restaurant you like in Jaffa."

"No, I don't have plans. I just never know what's going on with you. I never hear from you except when..."

"I know; you're right. We can talk about it when I get to

Revadim. I'll explain everything. Can you pick me up in Tel Aviv?"

"Where? Traffic is horrible in Tel Aviv."

"I can meet you at the Azri'eli Center Mall, by the taxi stand in the parking garage. Better yet, I won't put you in rush hours traffic. The South Tel Aviv Station is right there at the mall. I'll take the train to Ashdod."

"Yes, that would be better. What time should I expect you?"

"I'll call from Tel Aviv, before I catch the train. That should give you thirty to forty minutes. So listen out for me say... 5:30 or 6:00."

"Okay, Peter."

Her acceptance of his self invitation was much less than enthusiastic, about what he expected. It always was. But he knew she would not have plans; she never did.

Shula was overweight, reclusive and in her mid fifties. And, slight by slight, over the past decade and a half, Peter Aldrich had broken her heart. Her tiny apartment on the kibbutz encapsulated her life with her jewelry designs, the latest best-selling thriller and a siege supply of sugar wafers. Her computer carried her creations to the outside world and Amazon.com brought John Sanford's in. The sugar wafers required an occasional short drive to the moshav mini market.

Out on the street Aldrich beckoned to a taxi but before it could switch lanes and pull over to him an old Subaru cab cut in and pulled alongside the curb. The driver leaned across the seat and tossed open the passenger door. Aldrich gave him a scowl and waved him away. Again he motioned for the late model Mercedes. When it was close in behind the paint-bare Subaru, Aldrich opened the back door and crouched in.

"Afo?" asked the driver.

"Azre'li Mall; Tel Aviv," said Aldrich.

"Two hundred twenty-five shekels." The driver quoted the cost in a tone that told his fare he could pay it or find another cab.

"Beseder, beseder." Aldrich agreed with the customary palms-up shrug of indifference.

The driver heeled down hard on the horn and held it demanding that the old Subaru get out of the way. Once they were out and in the traffic flow the driver pressed the two-way button on his cellular and announced his destination to the dispatcher. Aldrich leaned his head back against the headrest and closed his eyes. His stomach was in kinks but it was too much of an effort to dig through his bag for a Zantac: a short nap would probably work just as well. Besides, the cool air wisping from the vents felt too good to move.

"Azre'li Mall."

The querulous voice announcing their arrival startled Aldrich awake. The cab pulled up in front of a glass wall and three sets of doors, the underground entrance into the mall's multifloor atrium from the parking garage. Aldrich had slept the entire forty-minute drive. He handed the driver three one-hundred shekel notes and got out of the car not waiting for his change. Puzzled, the driver shrugged, returned the seventy-five shekels to his shirt pocket. Without a word of todah for the fifteen-dollar tip he barked the tires and sped off.

Groggy, Aldrich stood on the taxi stand curbside for a few moments trying to get his bearings. He would have to pass through security to enter the mall but that was no cause for concern. He was clean of anything self-incriminating. He remembered; he couldn't let himself forget to buy batteries. And he wanted a couple of Rohypnol, if he could find a pharmacist who would sell under the counter for an extra few hundred shekels. He glanced down at his watch, almost two hours to kill in the multistory shopping mall. Aldrich put off calling Shula until the last minute, 6:30. He told her he would be on the next train leaving Tel Aviv South, 18:48, scheduled to reach Ashdod at 19:27.

As he sat on a moulded fiberglass row-seat beside the rails, he mulled over how much he dreaded the next couple of days with Shula. But he realized full well that he had to conceal his true feelings about her – he found her repulsive. He knew her well enough to be sure that if she ever got the faintest inkling of what he really thought of her she would be venomous – and dangerous. And the last thing he needed right now, and until he was safe out of the country, was to have to deal with a scorned woman's wrath.

On the train Aldrich seated himself as far from the other riders as he could. He opened his duffel and inspected his purchases from the mall: six roofies and a four pack of Duracell D's. God, how he hoped he could lace Shula's wine with a small, but sufficient, dose to sidetrack her unavoidable amorous expectations. And, god forbid, if that failed… He didn't want to think about it.

Never again would he be trapped into a repeat, command

performance by dead batteries in her worn out vibrator. Just the memory of that night was frightful, one of the most disgusting experiences of his life. It reminded him of a movie: an inmate crawled and swam through a half mile of sewer line to escape from a prison, unspeakable, but the only way out.

Shula Lutz had not always been so unattractive, quite the contrary. A quarter-century earlier, when Peter first saw the young aliyah from the Bronx, she was striking, a sturdy, bronzed young woman in her twenties. He could still see the blue eyed beauty, her soot black hair held in check by a blue bandanna, made dull by those eyes. A new member of the Revadim community, she worked in the jewelry factory and as a volunteer on the Tel Miqune excavation when she was not on the time clock. It pained Aldrich immensely that they never shared an intimate moment until she was forty years and two hundred seventy pounds.

Aldrich zipped up the duffel and placed it in a seat across from him. He leaned back and rested his head against the metal bulkhead behind his seat and peered out into the vacant fields sliding by.

A few days earlier an improvised bomb exploded in front of the lead car splattering the operator with glass shards. Within minutes the IDF and police were on site. They tracked the Hamas bomber back across the green line and into the squalid village where he was soon captured.

What a league of idiots, Aldrich thought. One long burst of automatic weapon fire into the last couple of cars packed with weekend riders would yield dozens of casualties. The ambush would probably go unreported for several more kilometers more down the line. And the longer it takes to find a sniper's hide, the colder the trail.

So much of their strategy was as flawed as their missions were counterproductive. In a strange sort of way, Aldrich thought, the Israelis were better off fighting the terrorists. Had the Palestinian cause ever produced a Gandhi, a Martin Luther King or a Mandela, the Zionists would have had no viable defense and the present state of affairs may well have been much different. But then again, the Arab-Islamic leadership was only interested in the eradication of the Jewish state, not in the fair treatment and civil equality of the Palestinians.

"And sometimes killing is the only way." Aldrich whispered the words to himself.

He felt the train slowing; Ashdod would be the next stop. Through the big side window he could see Shula standing on the platform, waiting.

"My God!" Aldrich exclaimed, almost out loud. "She must have put on fifty more pounds!"

Even from the distance he could clearly see the darker blue side panels of her denim muumuu. Aldrich guessed she must have just let it out two more sizes off the chart. Despondent, he rose from his seat and clutched the duffel. Again he whispered under his breath. "Blessed are they who suffer for righteousness sake."

The reunion, the ride out to Revadim, the hours of conversation seated on Shula's futon and the inescapable intimacy were, all, every bit as excruciating as Aldrich had envisioned. At least now, the dreaded, endless first night was almost over; Shula was asleep.

With all the stealth in him, Aldrich eased out from under her heavy, limp arm and away from her side. He tipped across the chilly terrazzo to one of her two refrigerators, reached inside and found a can of mango nectar. Maneuvering like a burglar, he opened the side door of the two room residence and stepped out into the garden. He closed the door behind him but it was not thick enough to baffle the bellowing snores ringing out from the futon.

Beneath an arbor loaded with green bunch grapes he pulled back the tab on the can of nectar and took a deep swallow of the thick, syrupy sweet liquid.

Aldrich did not hear the shot. The report didn't arrive until a second after the bullet wake of blood, flesh and bone fragments exploded from the exit wound in the center of his back. His hand contorted, crushing the soft aluminum can, its contents spewing on the still standing body. He was dead before he fell limp on the bare ground. Neither the shot nor Peter Aldrich's collapsing mass interrupted the rhythmic snoring within the adjacent room.

21

FROM A Distance of over six hundred yards and for hours on end the shooter had watched the Lutz residence through a Leupold Mark IV set to 12 power. He had forgotten how onerous the endless hours in a hide always were. The physical discomfort was a constant; cramping muscles, fatigue and carnivorous bugs. But boredom was the real enemy. Within a few fleeting seconds, at best, you could miss a shot op; at worst, you could expose your position and get yourself killed. He had thought he could never forget the constant torment of a hide but he had; the memories had paled over the last – he did the math in his thoughts—close to forty years now.

The exact instant of the shot had caught the shooter by surprise, just as it should to preclude a flinch or buck. He had been in the hide for two days and was over halfway through the third night by the time his kill stood behind the mil-dots of his rifle scope, on Shula's patio.

He had caught several glimpses of Aldrich. When he walked from her car into the apartment Shula was close to his side—too close. Then he caught a glimpse as he passed in front of a window. And for a few moments, around sundown, he watched him gazing out the sliding glass patio doors. But he knew that if he held out he would get the good shot; and he had.

At this range a 168 grain bullet took almost a full second to reach its mark; the shooter recovered from his blink reflex quickly enough to see its force smash through Aldrich's chest. He knew he had a confirmed kill even before he spent the long seconds watching for any twitch of life in the slumped corpse. And he had watched for any reaction to the rifle's report or some response from inside

Shula's dimly lit apartment. Only a light or two came on in units down the street and then only for a few moments each. Still, the shooter knew to lie frozen in place for a short while longer to assess the situation before starting out along his well planned egress.

His eyes scanned every square inch of the area around him. Trying to conceal the hide now, after the kill, would be to waste precious time, time better used to put distance between himself and Revadim's farm fields. The better plan was to let the investigators find the site along with the few clues you want them to have. He had already placed an empty 30-06 casing to the right of his position. He hoped they would not suspect a rifle like the .308 Remington 700 he cradled. And he had emptied a sandwich bag of cigarette butts into a shallow hole he had excavated, all the same Golf brand he had procured from a backgammon parlor ash tray. They would find no matches and should assume that the shooter would carry a lighter.

Except for a kibbutz dog barking in the distance, the night was as placid as before the single shot split the silence. It was time to begin the 10k run back to where he had parked the car in the Nekhei Tsahal Park. The straight line distance, he estimated, was only 6k but it was across open terrain most of the way. He needed the concealment and protection that a careful retreat alongside the fence rows and drainage ditches would offer.

The safe route would take him out to the northeast to the Wadi Timna which he would follow past the old Tel Miqne excavations and on another four kilometers to a regional road. Once through the two meter culvert under road 383 he would run the last 3k through the park's memorial forest to the car.

He had worried about leaving the car in the park for, possibly, four or five days. In an area popular with campers and hikers and lovers parking overnight, the risk was not that a car parked for a day or more would arouse suspicion. The risk was that the parking area was less than forty kilometers from Gaza where chop shops were the number one industry. A car could be reduced to a mélange of marketable parts and panels within a matter of minutes, not that he gave a damn about losing a rental car. But being stranded could be a fatal situation.

As he fell into the familiar pace of four point five minute kilometers, his senses were charged by the sheer pleasure of movement. And the cool dampness of the night with aromatic wisps of the wild rosemary through which he ran was exhilarating. It was a good night to savor the thrill of a fresh kill, a clean, necessary kill; a kill that would save lives and avenge others.

As he focused on the 8/1 rhythm of his steps to each breath, his thoughts drifted to the old gunsmith's shop back home. He remembered a three hundred pound, cow pasture deer hunter's claim that he would have made a damn good sniper in the war. He could outshoot half the rifle team at Ft. Benning or so he had said. He remembered answering the braggart, agreeing that he might have. But, he had told him, he should also consider the four or five days with only a couple of cans of C-Rat peanut butter and the 10 click run after the shot. That was, if you even got a shot.

The thirty-minute run to the regional road seemed more like ten. He approached the right of way with caution; it was quiet, no car lights in either direction. In the undergrowth beside the culvert he concealed the rifle, still in the sock of camouflaging burlap, beneath the dry thatch of dead weeds and grass. He matted the straw down so that there was no recognizable shape to catch an eye. The Remington should be safe here until he could return in the car to recover it. But he couldn't risk carrying it through the park all the way to the car where he might be observed. Satisfied, he crouched and worked his way on through the culvert.

Five hundred meters past the main road he came to the gravel access road into the tiny village of Gefen. There were three culverts under it but they were much smaller and badly silted in. Here he thought it would be safe to slip across. He continued on up the wadi and into the park property. After a short distance through the wooded area he reached one of the nature trails that crossed the wadi, now no more than a small, wet weather stream bed. Minutes later the forest trail ended in an open area of picnic tables and fire rings.

The parking area was just beyond where he stood at the trail head, watching. The car was in sight. He scanned the clearing with care; there was no movement; he heard no voices. A musty smoke veil shrouded the clearing, the only evidence of nearby campers and their dying camp fires.

He walked on toward the parking area with the slow gait of a camper returning from a piss in the dark, quiet but not sneaky, just in case unseen eyes were following. At the car he opened the door, pulled off his small back pack and climbed in. No interior lights to worry about, he had turned the rheostat all the way down when he left the cheap Arad rental here two days earlier. From the backpack he removed a pair of Teva sandals. He unlaced the black Reeboks on his feet and pulled them and his filthy socks off. It felt wonderful to be rid of the hot shoes and free from the irritating pricks of weeds and stickers that penetrated the socks. When he had strapped on the Tevas he took one last look around the perimeter. Then he started the car and drove away.

A few hundred meters down the park road out he found a trash container, a rare convenience in Israel. They were considered bomb drops. When the shooter had pulled alongside the barrel, he threw in the shoes and dirty socks, a tactical variation from his military days.

Scout sniper teams were trained to carry some soles from civilian or even enemy shoes with them on patrol. Then, when crossing mud or soft soil, the last man or two would strap on the footwear and their tracks would not give them away. Now, if he were stopped, the Tevas would not match any tracks he might have left. And no one in their right mind would wear sandals over the distance and terrain he had just covered.

Out on the regional road he pulled over by the culvert where the rifle was hidden. Still, there were no car lights to be seen in either direction. Within seconds he had retrieved the .308 and concealed it in the back seat.

As he drove west he looked out across the fields at a meandering line of bull rushes. They marked the run of the Wadi Timna, the escape route he had just run. When he was within a couple of kilometers of the main road, Highway 3, he could see the sodium vapor lights of Revadim, just over a mile to the north. There was no indication of any activity, no blue lights flashing across the distance, nothing to suggest that the body had even been discovered. Within ten minutes he would reach the Ashdod Interchange and be heading north on 4, back into the Galilee. Barely an hour had passed since the shot dropped the murderer, Peter Aldrich.

The shooter's drive up the freeway and across the green line was uneventful. Before he reached the checkpoint he called Hashim from a card phone in Khedera and let him know he would arrive within the hour. Hungry as he was, he would not stop. He needed to get rid of the rifle more than he needed food. And, besides, once in the Hashim home there would be more than he could eat and drink.

At the checkpoint when his stamped up passport was scanned, it was quickly recognized in the Israeli data base. He was a frequent tourist with no incidents on record. The cheap Arad rental's registration was just as boring to the sleepy young crossing guard and he never gave the rolled and doubled Oriental rug on the back seat a second glance. But inside its folds was the rifle that had fired the HPBT (hollow point boat tail) bullet that transformed Peter Aldrich's torso into an indistinct viscid pulp.

Leaving the Leupold scope attached, the shooter had removed the Remington's floating, bull barrel from the composite stock. The two pieces fit neatly inside the small carpet on the back seat. The borrowed rifle he was returning; the prayer rug which concealed it was a memorial gift to Ahmed Hashim, the father of the shooter's murdered friend, Abbas.

Ahmed was waiting outside when the shooter arrived. Without greeting he was ushered inside the crumbling, store-front home where three other somber figures sat in silence. Ahmed introduced them as his brother and the brother's two sons.

The atmosphere in the meager room was a dreamlike calm. Amid thick tobacco smoke laced with the scent of cooking spices the shooter was greeted with kisses on his cheeks and with small talk and compliments. A young-teen boy entered the room with a pendulum tray of hot drinks. After the first sips the room grew quiet, the men stared into the rising aromatic vapors. Now, Ahmed alone raised his eyes to his guest, listening.

"May I have the honor of addressing you as Abu Abbas, my friend?" asked the shooter.

"Such an honor would be mine alone," answered Hashim. "Yes, my friend, you may call me Abu Abbas."

One of the brother's sons wiped away tears with the corner of a thread-worn black and white shmaag that shawled his shoulders. To the shooter the boy appeared to be about the same age of his dead cousin.

"Thank you, Abu Abbas. I have come to return your property… and to bring you a gift, inadequate though it is to honor one so worthy."

The shooter unfolded the carpet on the floor. He picked up the rifle, replaced the receiver group into the stock and tightened the set screw into the pillar-blocks, marrying the pieces. Hashim nodded to one of the nephews. The young man rose, accepted the rifle and took it out of the room. Now, Hashim's guest spread the beautiful silk prayer rug at the old man's feet.

"Would you do me the great honor of accepting this meager token of my friendship for your son? May it serve as a memorial to this night, Abu Abbas." The shooter looked deep into the old man's black irises. "For, this day, my friend, your son's death has been avenged."

Hashim's eyes flooded. He lifted his palms to heaven. "Allah be praised. You have given me a gift no man could repay, though he live a thousand years." Hashim stood and placed his hands on his guest's shoulders. He placed on the shooter's cheeks three kisses of honor and gazed into his eyes.

"In my house," said Hashim, "from this day on, you shall be called Ben Abu Abbas, son of the father of Abbas. The doors of my poor home shall always be open to you and your house. My food and my possessions are yours... in the name of God. I have nothing more of value with which to honor my debt."

Even though it was nearly four in the morning, Hashim called to the women to bring food. Within minutes trays of fruit, olives, dates, vegetables and kabob were spread before the guest. The shooter had never known the honor and acceptance he now felt, never known the feeling of family. And he had never felt so alive.

By the time the small fete was over and the shooter had driven back to the green line checkpoint it was long after four in the morning. Now he was leaving Palestinian authority territory and entering Israel; this time the Israelis inspected the car closely. Trunk, hood, they even raised the back seat cushion.

He reached the Arad Rental office in Aufula shortly after daylight. The office would not open for several hours. He laid the seat back and closed his eyes; they were dry and stung. He was almost too exhausted to fall asleep, but when he did his dreams carried him back to a distant war.

Once again, as he had a thousand times before, he silently snipped at stalks of thick foliage to excavate a kind of verdant tunnel through which he would watch and wait for a target. The wait may well be for the next five days, a stay that would try the endurance of an old Buddhist monk. He would watch myriad creatures creep and leap and slither and fly by. A hundred species of insects would sting and bite, burrow and suck his flesh. And in spite of tormenting rash, festering pustule, inflamed rectum and fiery feet that burned from being wet for days on end, he would wait.

Then, often when the mind was a world away, something un-seen, something unheard would alert the senses. An eye would search the killing zone and into focus the long awaited image would emerge within the nine power circle of his Redfield scope. The crosshairs would shift from target to target. Which one should the lucky bastard be, The little guy with the heavy RPG or the ar-rogant looking son of a bitch, the one who carried no load, the one he could see barking orders at the suffering line of little men?

He always opted to take out the big shot first. If there was time and opportunity he would take out every one he could cap-ture beneath the crosshairs. And when he could find no one else through the scope, then it was time to begin the long, loping run back along the trail he had memorized on the way in. It might well be a dozen kilometers before he reached a friendly position. Then friendly fire was the danger. Escaping sniper teams on the run were always vulnerable to green, boot units and jumpy, sleep deprived grunts on a perimeter.

Over those last thirty years of recurrent nightmares, he had fallen victim to every conceivable threat, for nights on end. Only the faces of comrades and enemy changed; the ways to die never did. His spectral body counts revealed the faces of family and friend. There were times he dreaded laying his head on a pillow more than he ever remembered dreading the real war. And in his waking hours he recalled seeing the photo of a 1945 New York Times. The headline, "The War is Over" covered the front page. But the shooter knew that wars were never over for those fought and survived them.

A rap on the side window startled him. He peered out at the blue work uniform standing beside the car. For a moment he thought, police. But it was only one of the Arad Rental employees arriving on the job. He wore the kind of smart-ass smile that said if he had to be awake he wanted everyone to be awake. He took great pleasure in disturbing the tired driver, customer or not. As the shooter rolled down the glass the uniformed man began explaining in Hebrew.

"Anglit, Anglit, buhvakashah," said the driver.

"Okay, little," said the Arad man. "Not here, tesha, tesha." He pointed to his watch.

The shooter knew the word, tesha; it meant nine. Apparently, the office wouldn't open until 9:00. He glanced at his watch; it was already 8:30. What was the problem, he wondered. Why did this smiling asshole with bad teeth and camel breath have to wake him? The Arad man now pointed to a sign the driver couldn't read. It was suspended from a chain that roped off the entrance to the rental car service and parking area. He was blocking the entrance. Maybe this gap-tooth grinning moron wasn't deliberately trying to harass him after all.

By ten the shooter had checked the rental back in and made his way the few blocks to Aufula's Central Station. Shekels in hand, he boarded one of the frequent intercity buses to Beit Shean.

As the plains of Jezreel glided by, his mind drifted away to the many ancient battles and wars that defined this valley. At the foot of Tel Megiddo, he waxed reminiscent of Michener's book, The Source. He mused that Christians accept this valley as the site of the world's final battle. But the very word, Armageddon, was one of hundreds of misnomers courtesy of the Crusaders. They heard the locals refer to this place as Har Megiddo (Mount Megiddo); from which the corruption became scripture.

Again the shooter's thoughts reverted to the night before. In his mind's eye, he saw his shot find its mark through the rifle scope. He watched his target flinch, almost off the ground, then wilt and spill onto it, all within the same second. He thought he should feel some kind of guilt, at the least, some lament. But he didn't.

He counseled himself that, of all the hits he had watched convulse in the throes of death, last night's kill may have been the only one who really deserved it. And the one last night would not be one whose personal effects would haunt him. Nothing about his friend's killer could ever infect his spirit like the crucifix that hung from a lifeless old wood cutter's neck, glistening in the jungle shadows. Nothing could sear his soul like the blood-wet photo of a young wife holding a little one.

Hell no! To lament Peter Aldrich would dishonor all the rest.

The sign beside the highway read Kibbutz Massebot—1km. The shooter stood at the back door and pressed the red button on the pole. As the bus pulled off he walked a slow gait toward the steel cage entrance into the kibbutz. On the shaded side of the guard house the weathered old kibbutznic on duty sat in a rickety chair leaned back against the wall. He recognized the man who had exited the bus and walked through gate.

"Boker Tov," said the old man.

"Shalom," answered the shooter. He was glad to be back inside the Massebot fence. He had completed his mission and made it safely back through the perimeter. He wondered if there may still be some food out in the dining hall. He was starved.

22

OUTSIDE HIS ROOM Moshe sat reclined, as far back as he dared, in one of the cheap and prone to shatter plastic chairs, engrossed in Tom Clancy's latest to be published in Hebrew. Even in the building's late afternoon shade, it was still torrid. But the peaceful chesh-chesh-chesh of the lawn sprinklers and the alfresco perfume of cool water falling on hot grass made for an almost ideal reading spot.

"Dr. Benjamin." The kibbutznic began talking before his fatigued golf cart came to a stop.

Moshe looked up without speaking.

"Dr. Benjamin," he continued, "someone from Jerusalem called, said they can't get you on your cell or at the office. You need to call a Mr. Landau. Here's the number."

"Thank you," said Moshe. But he didn't mean it. He should have known that his quiet reading time was too good to last. He held his cell phone out, far away enough to focus on the tiny LCD window. No charge. "Again; damn it." Reluctantly, he stood and went into the expedition office to use the hard wired phone.

When he had Avi on the line Moshe asked, in an unusually dour voice, what he wanted. His curt tone caught Landau off guard. He stammered a sort of apology but then he blurted out that Moshe needed to know what had come to light over the past few hours.

"The IAA committee is calling another press conference to proclaim the tablet a forgery." Landau announced. "This one's going to be hyped more than the James ossuary announcement."

"Well, I wouldn't expect them to call one to affirm the authenticity of anything." Moshe's bothered tone shifted to sardonic. "Hell, Avi, Yuval Goren, alone, must have pronounced over a hundred artifacts as fakes. Problem is, this time, we all know we've got a fake. But now, because every piece he ever examined has been a fake, to hear him tell it, his credibility is suspect. The public will think he's crying wolf for the umpteen dozenth damn time. I almost wish he'd say the thing was genuine; that would cast more doubt on it than another one of his indictments.

"You just make sure that Goren isn't the one behind the podium making the announcement. Wouldn't surprise me if, sooner or later, some cynical bastard at the IAA labels the goddam Rosetta stone a fake."

"Don't worry, Moshe. Goren's not making the announcement; you are. That's why Dormann told me to call you. We're scheduling the conference for day after tomorrow at ten. Old trusty-rusty will fly back up there for you tomorrow afternoon so we can brief you before hand. You'll have all the proof you need that the tablet is an elaborate fraud – probably the most elaborate we've ever exposed – but an absolute fake, nonetheless.

"And something else you should know, we've established motive and opportunity. The forger considered it a sacrilege and heresy. He gave us all the proof he knew we would need to totally discredit the damn thing. I don't have time to explain now; just trust me, old friend, you won't be hung out to dry."

"I trust you, Avi, but there are some things that are out of our control and this may well be one of them."

"You'll feel better about this tomorrow, Moshe, I promise. See you tomorrow evening. Erev tov. Oh—can't believe I almost forgot to tell you this—they think they've found our mystery man, Mr. Adams. He's dead; a sniper got him down on some kibbutz just north of Gaza. Ain't that a hoot?"

"You can't be serious? What happened, a standoff with the police or something?"

"No," said Avi, "not the police. His girlfriend found him dead on her terrace early this morning, shot through the chest. Whole damn kibbutz went nuts; first full alert since Yom Kippur '73. Hell, the door hinges on the guard towers were frozen up with rust."

Moshe and Avi laughed at the thought of the chaos on the kibbutz. All over the country the defensive towers were more historical reminders than functional structures.

"Damned sniper was probably back across the green line sipping tea and sucking the old nargileh before the body was ever even

301 ☙ OPHRAH'S GATE

discovered. And to thicken the plot, Adam's passport is a forgery. Every spook down here is trying to figure this one out. Maybe they'll know more by the time you get down here."

"Yeah, this is crazy all right. Go figure the odds on this co-incidence: a sniper kills the prime suspect before he can be caught and questioned. Zealots, no doubt, but that doesn't narrow it down much. About the only group that wouldn't have anything to gain from the tablet's acceptance are the damn Arabs. Surely they would…"

"Moshe, we're already way ahead of you. We have it narrowed down, way down. But I can't say anymore over the phone. I'll explain tomorrow when you get here."

"As I said, Avi, I trust you. But I hope you realize we better have an ironclad case and some clear, simple proof or millions of Jews, Christians, especially the Mormons, are going to be screaming government conspiracy at the top of their lungs. Regardless of what we do, biblical archaeology's been irreparably damaged this time."

"You're right," said Avi. "But all we can do is to present the truth."

"Yes, it is. Good night, Avi."

23

THE NEW Wing Auditorium at the Knesset was filled to capacity and more, far more than the few dozen who had shown up for the first press conference. Moshe guessed the crowd to be over 450 with many standing and leaning against the back wall. The stuffy air caused him to glance down at his watch every few minutes, anxious for the announced 10:00 am time to arrive. On stage beside Moshe, Avi Landau sat still, reading over some of the supporting documents, while a sound tech made last minute adjustments to the sheaf of temporary mic cables that trailed down from the podium and across the floor.

Avi raised his head. Director Dormann was looking toward him, waiting to catch his eye. With his stare fixed on his subordinate he gave a slow, deliberate nod toward the lectern. Avi tightened the stack of papers, leaned over to Moshe and whispered, "Well, here we go, my friend." He stood and took up his defensive position behind the big lacquered oak stand. He bent into the mic and asked the audience to take their seats or find places to stand along the side aisles or back wall. And he asked them to hold all questions until the prepared statement was concluded.

"A few days ago it was announced from this auditorium that there had been a rather remarkable discovery at the ongoing Tel Kefar excavations under the direction of Professor Moshe Benjamin of the Hebrew University of Jerusalem. This morning, it is our duty to inform you of other significant information and additional facts which have come to light concerning the origins of this artifact which the popular press is now calling the 'Ophrah's Gate Tablet'.

"As you are by now aware, the inscribed tablet is a type of dedication memorial. The inscription states that it was placed in or near the city gates of the ancient city of Ophrah. It was recently unearthed within one of the archaeological squares in the vicinity of the city gates of the site we know as Tel Kefar.

"First, I want to call on Professor Moshe Benjamin of the Hebrew University to give us an abbreviated overview of the Tel Kefar project and the work leading up to the discovery of the Ophrah's Gate Tablet."

Avi turned toward the others seated at a table on his right. He nodded toward Moshe and beckoned for him to come up to the lectern. As Moshe stood and moved his chair back out of the way, Avi turned to the table on his left to make sure that Shmuel Dormann, the director of the IAA, appeared content with the proceedings. Dormann's bland expression and the fact that his eyes didn't shift to meet his own assured Avi that, so far, he was okay with everything. Avi stepped back from the mic. "Dr. Benjamin…"

Moshe began with a brief historical background of Tel Kefar and the archaeological progress that had been made up until the beginning of the current season. He related how he had been contacted by Niles Thompson, who told him of his graduate student's discovery of a Roman slang name which pointed to Tel Kefar as the probable location of one of the sites named in the famous copper scroll of Qumran. He explained that it was this information which led to opening the new squares where the clay tablet was later found. He stated that he did not believe that Sarah Bergman's scholarly discovery was in any way connected to the discovery of the tablet, with a possible exception that would be addressed later in the presentation.

As usual, Moshe's session was short but crisp. He folded his notes and sat down as Avi resumed his place at the lectern.

"Many of us witnessed the BBC film coverage of the discovery of this tablet. We saw it in situ and we watched its removal from what we believed had been its resting place for the past 2,600 years. We now know that we are all the victims of one of the most carefully planned and brilliantly executed deceptions ever perpetrated on the science of archaeology, not to mention the many faiths descended from Jewish scriptural tradition.

"We have, therefore, called this press conference, not as a follow-up of the earlier announcement of the discovery, but rather for the specific purpose of informing the public of our findings.

Those findings are that this clay tablet discovered at Tel Kefar, the Ophrah's Gate Tablet, is a forgery."

The auditorium exploded. Both Dormann and Avi had expected it would. They had prepared for just such an outburst with a contingent of police and Knesset security standing by. Avi turned and gave Moshe a warning glance. Then he turned the sound system volume way up and the squelch back. He snatched the mic from its holder and stuck it in front of one of the large speakers. The feedback scream was deafening. The entire crowd was stunned into a momentary silence which Avi instantly filled.

"People, take your seats and come to order. Anyone who continues this interruption will be immediately expelled from the auditorium. There will be no further warnings. Security," Avi called out as he motioned for the uniformed officers to come forward. "Please remove anyone who causes a disturbance."

About a dozen of the uniformed police lined up in front of the platform. Others in plainclothes began walking up and back, down the aisles, their eyes locked into the flabbergasted audience. Within a few awkward moments order was restored.

Moshe blinked in amazed appreciation of Avi's command presence. He had a thorny situation under complete control. Now squelched back up and with the volume down a bit lower than normal, Avi spoke into the mic in a low voice.

"Now," he said, "please allow me to continue. As stated earlier, we will entertain your questions as soon as the presentation is completed. I expect many of your questions will be answered in our prepared statement.

"Our findings that the inscribed tablet is a forgery are based on not only circumstantial and scientific evidence, evidence which we fully intend to disclose and make available to you this morning. Our findings are also based on the sworn testimony and criminal confession of an accomplice who assisted in concealing the tablet where it was subsequently found at the Tel Kefar excavation site. I now call Colonel Eial Lezek of the Jerusalem Police District. Colonel Lezek..."

"On the evening of June fifth of this year a car bomb exploded in the French Hill section of the city. The car was traced to a Mr. Yoram Perlman. The remains found in the car were identified as those of Yoram Perlman, who resided on Strauss Street here in Jerusalem. Perlman and his male partner, Yitzhak Fink, lived at this Strauss Street address until Fink's death approximately two years ago.

"Both Perlman and Fink were actively involved in the Agudah – the Society for the Protection of Personal Rights for Homosexuals in Israel—but had no other known affiliations of note. Since the death of Fink, Yoram Perlman had lived an almost reclusive existence at this same address. And it was during the initial search of this Strauss Street address, Perlman's residence, that a note addressed only 'To Jerusalem Police' was found, by itself, on top of his kitchen table. I have a certified photocopy of that note in my hand. It will be available for your inspection following this presentation. The note had a key taped to it and the message: 'Vault box 4107, Bank Mizrahi, 12 Ben Yehuda St.' Upon opening the lock box we found a letter, also addressed simply 'To Commander, Jerusalem Police'. I have here a certified photocopy of that letter, which I will now read for the record. It will also be available to you. The letter is dated 25 May of this year."

'My name is Yoram Perlman. I reside at 441 Strauss Street, Jerusalem, Israel. I was trained as a fine art restoration and reproduction specialist at the St. Petersburg Academy of Arts in Leningrad. I was on staff at the Literary and Art Museum Priyutino in Vsevolozhsk until I made aliyah in 1995. I am currently employed as a custodian at the Israel Museum. If you are in possession of this letter then I am most certainly already dead.

'In April of this year I was contacted by a Mr. James Adams who wished to commission a work of art. Mr. Adams supplied me with exact specifications and scale drawings of the object he wished to commission. Copies of those specifications and drawings are enclosed with this letter. I was paid an advance of twenty-five thousand U.S. dollars in cash with the promise of twenty-five thousand more upon delivery and acceptance and payments of fifty thousand a year for the rest of my life. The future installments are to be made to a numbered European bank account which I can drawn down with an ATM card I am to receive within a few days after delivery of my work. These payments are to continue so long as I am silent about the origin of the artwork I have created.

'No sooner than I saw these drawings and specifications and heard the offer proposed by Mr. James Adams, I feared for my safety if I were to refuse the commission. Now that the work is complete I fear that I am in danger after it is delivered. I intend to use the existence of this letter to bargain for my safety should the need arise.

'*During my meeting with Mr. Adams he asked if I could read Paleo-Hebrew text. I told him that I could not. However, I am able to interpret enough of the inscription to recognize it as heresy and to know that I am the heretic. My sin I confess, but mine is not a sin of greed. I have much family still in Russia and my janitor's income is not sufficient to pay the bribes and purchase the airfares to bring them here, to Israel.*

'*As additional support for the claims I now make, I have also included herewith the processes and techniques I have used to give my creations the appearance of age and authenticity. If there is still doubt as to the truth of these claims, the proof you require to discredit this clay tablet I created shall be found if the clay tablet itself is examined by x-ray.*

'*May God have mercy and forgive my transgressions.*

Yoram Perlman'

"As Mr. Landau stated earlier," Lezek continued, "this document as well as the ones Mr. Perlman references in his letter will be available to you at the conclusion of this program.

"I want to emphasize, that although we had this letter in our possession within hours after the car bomb which killed Perlman was detonated, we did not have any leads as to where this inscribed clay tablet might be located. Naturally, we made the assumption that it was making its way into or through the black market for antiquities so – if you'll excuse the expression – we began checking out the usual suspects.

"We hit a brick wall. No one, not even our most reliable informants, had even heard of the existence of the tablet described in Perlman's documents. Realizing that if we pushed too hard we might force whoever had the tablet further underground, we backed off hoping that the tablet would surface into the antiquities market and thus lead us to the bomber and murderer of Yoram Perlman."

Next Lezek revealed the details of Michelle Eisner's kidnapping and imprisonment in Jordan. Moshe thought he detected a slight amused inflection in Lezek's voice. But even if he knew the whole story, he skirted around the fine points of her rescue by Willy Dubignon and Kirk Longstreet. The way he worded his account of an abducted female volunteer, "She was tracked down and brought home by a couple of Professor Benjamin's Vietnam veteran volunteers who obviously remember some of their training from thirty-five years ago,." Something in his voice made Moshe think that the colonel knew most of the story, including the particulars of Shihadeh's hell. And Moshe suspected that the salty old colonel and former Shin Bet operative relished it.

He told the audience about Michelle later seeing Li Moon with a man she remembered from the place of her abduction. When Moon was questioned about his association with the mystery man by Inspector Efi Shimon he fell apart. He confessed his association with a man he also knew by the name of James Adams. He confessed to being on the excavation site and being a witness to the murder of one Abbas Hashim, a Palestinian who was employed as a laborer with the Tel Kefar expedition.

Lezek related that Dr. Moon led Inspector Shimon to the body but that Moon has passionately maintained he had nothing to do with the murder of Abbas Hashim. He had been blackmailed into assisting Adams in planting an artifact in one of the excavation squares. Adams needed him to place the tablet where it would be sure to be found but not for a week or more. Lezek said that Moon's coercion was made possible because Adams was aware that Moon was selling stolen artifacts to an antiquities dealer in Jordan.

"It was to this antiquities shop that the young volunteer Miss Eisner had gone," Lezek explained, "because of a business card, presumably lost by Moon, she had found on the dig site. And it was in the basement of this shop where she was held against her will until her rescue."

Lezek told the group that even as Moon was still being interrogated in the Galilee, a nationwide alert was put out for James Adams.

"The alert was cancelled this past Sunday morning when the body of the man known as James Adams was discovered outside a residence on Kibbutz Revadim. He was killed by a single thirty-caliber bullet fired from a concealed position approximately 550 meters away. We now know that James Adams was an alias used by a Joseph Peter Aldrich of Salt Lake City, Utah, in the United States.

"Aldrich entered the State of Israel using a forged passport in the name of James Hyde Adams. He was identified by fingerprints and his identity was confirmed by the U.S. Federal Bureau of Investigation through dental records. Once we had the deceased suspect's true identity, many other details began to fall into place. In fact, Joseph Peter Aldrich has been a frequent visitor to Israel with visas issued to his valid U.S. passport. We know that Mr.

Aldrich was a key figure in the political and contract negotiations for the new Mormon Center on Mt Scopus—a man of miracles, some might even say."

Lezek continued into a detailed explication of information gathered from round-the-clock interviews with associates of Aldrich over the past two days. He thanked the U.S. Embassy staff in Tel Aviv and the other agencies involved, noting that before the 9/11 changes it may have taken several weeks or more to have just received a positive ID, let alone the information gained from interviews with the suspect's acquaintances in Utah.

"In conclusion," said Lezek, "I will address an issue that Professor Benjamin mentioned a few minutes ago. That's the issue of a possible connection between Brigham Young University and the surfacing of the Ophrah's Gate Tablet. As Dr. Benjamin mentioned, he was first made aware of the possible location of one of the treasures named in the copper scroll by Professor Niles Thompson of Brigham Young. Although this matter will continue to be thoroughly investigated, it is our considered opinion that this connection is entirely circumstantial.

"We are satisfied that no one connected with either Brigham Young University or the Church of Jesus Christ of Latter Day Saints—no one other than Joseph Peter Aldrich – was knowingly involved in this plot. To the contrary, we now believe that when Joseph Peter Aldrich was made aware of the significance of Sarah Bergman's discovery, the seeds of his scheme were sown.

"Although not an alumnus, Aldrich was a wealthy real estate developer, a long time member of the BYU foundation and a major contributor to the university's athletic program. He was also a zealous member of one of the most fundamentalist Mormon cults in the state of Utah. In short, we believe that he saw Miss Bergman's discovery as the means by which he could convince the religious community, if not the world, of the 'truth' as he saw it. We also believe that it was Joseph Peter Aldrich who made an anonymous gift to the BYU Department of Archaeology, a gift that was designated as a travel fund for Miss Bergman and Dr. Thompson to come to Jerusalem to pursue her theory.

"Mr. Aldrich knew that it would take an exceptionally sensational project to attract any major media attention and he had to have international exposure. The whole world had to witness the discovery of his Ophrah Gate Tablet and the search for the lost temple treasure was the perfect project to ensure that coverage.

"As far as his motive, as I stated earlier, we first assumed that this was a case of artifact forgery for profit. Obviously, if an antiquity of this nature surfaced and made its way into the collector's market it would command an incredible price. Of course, if an artifact is discovered in a legally permitted excavation, it is not available to the collector's market, unless it is later stolen. And then, it is doubtful that a collector would want to pay a king's ransom for a piece as 'hot' as a piece of this notoriety would be. So, as you might assume, we were baffled as to motive when we became aware that the tablet for which we had been searching was, on the BBC no less, 'discovered' in the excavations of the Tel Kefar project.

"However, also as a result of our investigation, we believe that Joseph Peter Aldrich was motivated by a force more powerful than monetary gain, especially considering that he was already a very wealthy man. We believe that motivation was some sort of twisted quest of his to redeem the reputation and good standing of his peculiar brand of Mormonism.

"We have learned from interviews with several of his acquaintances that James Peter Aldrich was greatly distressed if not enraged over a series of reports which were widely circulated in the American press. The incident was commonly known as the Mark Hofmann scam of the Mormon Church. For those of you who are not familiar with this account – I readily admit that I was not – I'll be as brief as possible.

"In the mid nineteen eighties, the senior leadership of the Mormon Church in the state of Utah was approached by a local rare documents dealer, Mark Hofmann, who offered for sale an original letter penned by the church's founder and prophet, Joseph Smith. Mr. Hofmann was soon paid in excess of $225,000 for the letter. The document, commonly labeled the White Salamander letter, was a variation of the original story of the revelation Joseph Smith claimed to have received from Heaven. The church obviously considered the letter an embarrassment and wished to suppress the contents if not the document itself from the public, especially those of the Mormon faith.

"Eventually, when it was discovered that Mark Hofmann was a master forger, the plot to acquire and suppress the 'White Salamander Letter' blew up in the faces of the church's top leadership. Now, I told you that I would be brief and, believe me, this is a painfully brief account of a very complex case of forgery, fraud and murder. For those of you interested in the details, I have a list of publications about the Hofmann scam and a web site where the whole story is also available. That site is: http://www.utlm.org/onlinebooks/trackingcontents.htm

"It was this scandal, the shameful and humiliating exposure of his church leaders, men believed by their followers to be infallible, which we believe pushed James Peter Aldrich over the edge. His motive was this: he hoped to restore the church's good name and to, finally, give legitimacy to the Church of Jesus Christ of Latter Day Saints. His motive was as simple as his scheme was complex.

"As of this time we have no leads on any additional accomplices and we have no indication that these were the acts of anyone other than those we have already named. Of course, we have concerns and questions about the killing of Joseph Peter Aldrich. We would very much like to have had the opportunity to question him in detail but that is no longer possible and we now consider these cases closed.

"Don't get me wrong;" said Colonel Lezek, "the case of Aldrich's murder is certainly not closed. We are not ruling out any possibilities; however, at this time we're operating under the assumption that this was a terrorist incident. I'll be available for your questions as soon as we've concluded."

As the colonel moved away from the lectern, an audible murmur surged up from the attendees but it was nothing like the previous outburst. It petered out almost as soon as Avi Landau returned to take the floor.

The lights in the auditorium dimmed. Avi turned to look over his shoulder as the large projector screen unfurled from its roller concealed above the platform. A still of the seal of the Israel Antiquities Authority began to fade in on a tekhelet background.

"Ladies and gentlemen," said Avi, "I suppose that it will be to his enduring credit that Yoram Perlman foresaw the havoc his clay tablet could spawn. And to his greater credit, even knowing the pandemonium he could wreak on the religious community, he attempted to prevent these hostilities. This is rather remarkable in light of the fact that these same groups of fundamentalists usually revile and ostracize men such as Yoram Perlman.

"Perlman knew that normal archaeological analysis of a vitrified clay object would not include x-ray inspection as there is nothing to be gained from such a test. At least, not usually. So we were more than a little perplexed when this last testament of Mr. Perlman implored that the tablet be x-rayed to substantiate his claim that it is indeed a counterfeit of his creation."

The image on the screen split into a scaled photo of the tablet on the left and another photo of a certified copy of the scale drawing which Perlman had referenced in his letter. The screen brought soft whispers from the hushed audience. Again, Landau spoke into the microphone.

"There is one piece of background information that I need to give you before advancing the slides. Several years ago the international press reported that several fundamentalist Christian-based organizations and denominations in the United States were seeking to boycott corporations that recognized either homosexual unions or domestic partnerships among their employees. One of the more highly publicized was the boycott of Walt Disney Incorporated by the Southern Baptists as announced at their convention in Salt Lake City. Although the Mormon Church has not officially joined the boycott, they expressed support for the Baptists' action by publicly affirming their canon that homosexual unions and acts are grounds for excommunication. This having been said," Landau paused. "I call your attention to this photograph of the x-ray image of the clay tablet, the 'Ophrah's Gate Tablet' if you prefer."

Avi turned and faced the screen. In an instant the split-screen photos disappeared; in their place flashed the unmistakable translucent x-ray gray outline of the tablet. Once again the auditorium erupted into a roaring cacophony of exclamations. Through the roar it was impossible to distinguish between the screamed curses of protest and the bellowing laughter. But this time Avi made no move to call the audience to order; he knew better.

There were expressions of rage on the aghast faces of the orthodox Jews. There were wild stares of disbelief and frowns of doubt. The security personnel shifted about in a sort of tense shuffle. They looked about nervously to each other and up to Avi for some sense of direction. Avi nodded in a manner that conveyed an at-ease to the police and guards.

There on the screen, for all the world to either affirm or to try and discredit, was the unmistakable silhouette. Reflecting the projector's brilliant, white, unobstructed, undiluted light back into the crowd, it lit up the wild assortment of facial expressions, every reaction imaginable except indifference. The radiant white shape was as clear and as contrasted as a lead bullet embedded within the shadowy image of a shattered femur.

With all the righteous indignation that the little creature could muster, he stood flatfooted in his unmistakable bubble-toed shoes and spats. His limp left wrist rested on the waist band of his lederhosen and his lunar eclipse ears stuck straight out. His gloved right hand was raised aloft with only the middle digit extended. Mickey was giving them the bird, the finger, flipping them all off. If a picture was worth a thousand words then the x-ray photo of this little belligerent cartoon rodent must be worth ten thousand articles of evidence. Yoram Perlman's claims were proven.

24

THE FRIDAY Morning following the bombshell press conference was unseasonably cool for late July in the Arabah. Kirk and Michelle were back in the excavation square they had shared for the past few weeks. As the dig team's slow descent continued on down through the strata, the hunt for Sarah Bergman's black stone paver was the only encouragement nurturing their wilted morale. Michelle sat on one of the foam rubber kneepads listlessly scraping away the crust from the floor of the square. Kirk shaved the balk with a sharpened square ditching shovel trying to expose whatever detail the section may contain.

"Kirk," said Michelle, "look at Dr. Benjamin."

"Where is he?"

"Sitting at the registrar's table, down the hill."

"What about him," asked Kirk?

"I don't know, he just looks like he's had the wind blocked out of his sails. Usually he would have been up here walking through the area a couple times by now. It's almost time for break and he hasn't moved."

"Well," said Kirk, "with all that's happened, he's gotta be at his wit's end."

"He's been in his own world, ever since we found Abbas. But, my gosh, Kirk, just think about it." Michelle shifted her position and reached for her water bottle. "He's been betrayed by a colleague, lost a kid he really liked, murdered no less, and had the expedition used to promote a fraud... I should think he is down."

"Yeah, I'm down and I'm just a damn volunteer! You know, I've always been fascinated with history and archaeology. But I think the real reason I came over here was to try to escape. I gave up try-

ing to make sense out of things a long time ago but the past couple
of years have been tough. And from what you've told me it sounds
like you wound up over here to get away from a lot of hurt. And,
damn it... here we are right smack in the middle of a whole new
world of shit. There's no getting away from it, I guess."

"Well, you old grouch!" Michelle slung some water at him. "It
hasn't all been bad. I think our weekend at the American Colony
was pretty terrific."

Kirk looked up from his work; Michelle's gaze was waiting.
Kirk's eyes caressed her face reassuring her of the depth of his
feelings.

"Know what else?" she asked. "You told me the trip up to the
Cliffs of Arbel with Father Bill was a good experience, too?"

"You're right; it was... probably the most liberating two days of
my life. I didn't mean to sound so negative. Ought to be ashamed of
myself, I guess. But a word in my own defense... before the experience had a chance to sink in, we were off trying to find out what had
happened to you. So much has happened since; I haven't had a good
time to sort out what it all means." Kirk leaned on the shovel handle
and stared off in the direction of Mt. Tabor and Arbel.

"You remember promising to tell me about it, don't you?"

"Yes," Kirk answered.

"Well... I've got the rest of the morning to listen," she said.

Without saying anything more Kirk resumed shaving the balk's
rough surface with the shovel. Michelle couldn't bring herself to
press him. She well understood how much in her own life was just
too bewildering to grasp, let alone explain to anyone. She knew he
would tell her what happened when he was ready.

"Hat boker; hat boker." A young Israeli shouted the call to
breakfast up the slope of the tel to Area B.

Fridays were more relaxed than the other weekdays and breakfast was followed by the weekly tour of all the excavation areas.
Moshe was faithful to guide the group over the site and give his
interpretation as to what each square was yielding. The big-picture
tour was a great boost to morale; even the most inexperienced volunteer could feel like a member of the team.

But this morning there would be no site tour. Moshe would use
the time to put in plain words all that had happened and how he
thought the project would likely be affected. He was blunt and candid in his review of the impact the fake clay tablet would have on

the public perception of archaeology. But he avoided what pained him the most, the murder of Abbas and the betrayal by Li Moon.

As for Abbas, after a lifetime in the IDF, Moshe knew all too well the agony of losing men and friends. The loss cannot be articulated; neither can the pain be shared. As for Moon, the man's name would never again cross his lips or taint his thoughts. Nor would he allow, ever again, the mention of the name in his presence. In his heart and mind it would be Abbas who lived and Moon who was dead.

"In closing," said Moshe, "I want to ask each of you to focus on what I asked you to do when we were just getting started. I want you to focus on finding the truth. The truth alone is what we dig, sift and search for... not any artifact, not any theology, not any treasure. But, ah ha!" Moshe's voice lilted, he threw on a beaming smile and rose to his feet pointing up to Area B. "We still have treasure here, right here within a scant, few centimeters beneath our feet." His eyes sparkled as he held up his hand and measured off a few centimeters between his thumb and index finger. "Sarah Bergman, where are you, Miss Bergman?"

"Over here, Doctor Benjamin."

"Sarah, is there any reason we should doubt the message in the copper scroll now, even in light of all that has happened? Do we have any reason to believe we are searching in vain, or not searching in the right place?"

"No we don't," answered Sarah, "There's no connection between any of these events and the scroll... or my research."

"Thank you, Miss Bergman. So, there you have it. And she's right you know. There is no connection. Next week is a new week; next week one of you may make one of the great archaeological finds of our time. We only have a couple of hours till buses come so let's get back to the areas and dig up something, already! Until then, as you dig, try to think on this one thing: Truth is the great constant. False faith, capricious creeds and all that comes from them will eventually fail; only the truth endures. This you can call Moshe's Midrash and it is the foundation of Torah and Gospel and science. All of you have a good weekend and be careful. I see you here at sun up Monday morning."

A few minutes after the team returned to the area Kirk realized that no one was working in either of the newly opened quadrangles next to theirs. Two new squares had been strung off, cleaned and sandbagged. A coaming of sacks filled with soil from the tailings dump had been placed around the perimeter that would become the tops of the new balks. He watched a panicked gerbil trying to find its burrow entrance in the new barren landscape. It scampered in and out of the raked line of weed straw and dried grass a few feet beyond the nylon gridline.

Kirk couldn't remember the new area supervisor's name, a nice enough young Israeli grad student. He thought that he had most likely decided not to start excavating the new areas with only a couple of hours left in the work week. There was no one now within earshot of them. Maybe it was the right opportunity to try and put his experience into words, to let Michelle know what had happened that night on the cliffs. He had promised her he would, so he would. Besides, He wanted her to know what he had seen and felt. And she deserved to know since she was now, in a real way, an important part of it all.

"Okay, Michelle..."

"Okay, Kirk." She answered him with a trace of the teasing smile he remembered so well from the first time he laid eyes on her.

"Be serious," he said. "Know what I want us to do?

She held her trowel still and looked up at him. When he saw she was waiting for his answer he sat back on a full bucket of dirt and wiped sweat from his eyes and brow with his shirt sleeve.

"I want you to go with me to the Cliffs... tonight."

He watched the contemplative expression that formed on her face.

"Several times I've started to tell you about what happened up there but I'm not sure I can put it into words. The more I think about it, the more I think that we should go there together. I don't know why; it's just a strong feeling. As a matter of fact, I asked Father Bill if he thought it would wise for us to go together or, for that matter, for me to even go back alone."

"What did he say?" asked Michelle.

"He said that it should not be a question of okay or not. If I felt led to go back, with you or alone, then that's exactly what I should do."

"When are you going to tell me what the hell went on up there, Kirk? All this mystique has me befuddled. What do you mean 'led to'?"

"Darn it, I'm trying to tell you now, as best I know how," said Kirk. "This is really awkward for me so I would appreciate you trying to understand that. I was thinking that what I don't know how to explain… maybe you can find out for yourself. That is if you want to go, of course. It'll be my luck for us to go up there and… not a darn thing, nothing. Even so, it's a beautiful place; I don't suppose that'll be any different.

"Michelle, if I'm not making much sense… don't jump to the conclusion I need to be on a high dose of lithium. Just promise to trust me… Promise?"

"I'm sorry; I promise. Now, go ahead, I'm listening."

"Okay, here goes. You're probably gonna think I need a smaller crack pipe, but here goes. Oh, almost forgot, Father Bill says he would very much like to talk to us – actually to you I think – before we go. If we decide to go, of course."

"Sure, that's fine. You said I should get to know him better."

Kirk took in a deep breath and held it. He let his lungs empty with an audible puff out. Then he cut his eyes at Michelle who had dropped her trowel, crossed her arms and now peered directly at him.

"Okay! Do you remember when I first told you that Father Bill had invited me to go backpacking with him?"

Michelle nodded.

"I didn't tell you that I had pretty much decided not to go. I only changed my mind late that afternoon, after I had a conversation with Jaclyn. . If you remember, we drove her car up to the observation tower park on Mount Gilboa for a picnic supper.

"Bill wandered off by himself and while we sat there at the picnic table we had a long conversation. She convinced me that Father Bill was quite a special person and that I could trust him completely. Did you know that Bill came over here to die?"

"Die?" The surprise was obvious in her voice. "No; what are you talking about?"

"That's what Jaclyn told me. He was a parish priest, somewhere in the Southwest… New Mexico maybe. When he discovered he had advanced cancer and only a few months left, he put in to come over here to live out his last days. That was over twenty years ago, if I'm doing the math right; Jaclyn says he's never had any medical treatments either, not even a checkup. She also told me that he was revered as a mystic by the brothers, quite a few others, too, Jews and

Arabs. I'm telling you all this because I told you he was the most unusual person I've ever met. Remember me telling you that when we at the American Colony?"

"Yes," she answered.

"The next morning, after we all went up to Gilboa, Jaclyn drove Bill and me up to Tiberias. We bummed around there for a few hours and after lunch we hitched a ride on up to the entrance road into Moshav Arbel. We wandered around through the village and then hiked on out to the cliffs, spent most of the afternoon just sitting around talking. It's a beautiful place. You'll see for yourself, I hope.

"Bill pointed out dozens of historic places that you can see from up there. Part of the mystic of the place is that that the Cliffs of Arbel are not mentioned, at least by name, anywhere in the scriptures. He said that after all his years of travel in the Middle East, he had never found another natural wonder more awesome or beautiful. From up there on the ledges you can see Mount Hermon, the entire Sea of Galilee and the Valley of Jezreel. And, at night, the lights of Tiberias, Capernaum and Nazareth are all visible along with a dozen more little towns and villages he could name.

"The face of the cliffs towers fifteen hundred feet above a small valley. Bill pointed to a small road that runs below, connects the Sea of Galilee with the Mediterranean Coast. He said it passes through Nazareth and it's the most direct route between Nazareth and Capernaum, was then and still is. He says there's no doubt Jesus passed below many times and he said it was inconceivable that He never bothered to make His way to the top, just as we had done, if for no other reason than to enjoy the panorama and the cool summer night breezes.

"Do you know the New Testament story of the Transfiguration?" Kirk asked.

"Only vaguely," Michelle answered.

"I'll try to get it right," said Kirk. "Goes something like this: Jesus and three of the disciples – I don't remember which ones – were all up on a high place where they could be alone.

"Three of the four Gospels use the description either a high place or a high mountain apart. The Gospels record that while they were up there Jesus' face shone like the sun and his clothes became as white as the light. All three of the disciples claimed that suddenly both Moses and Elijah appeared and were talking with Jesus.

"I asked Bill how they knew who the other two were and he told me that it was by divine recognition. I guess I must have smirked a bit because he told me that, by morning, I would completely understand... And he was mighty right."

"The interesting thing, according to Bill, was that the exact location where the Transfiguration happened is not named in any of the Gospels even though both of the traditional sites, Mount Tabor and Mount Hermon, were well known by their present names during Jesus' lifetime. To believe that at least one of the three Gospel writers didn't know the names of Tabor and Hermon is hard to believe. Bill explained that he believed the Cliffs were the actual site because he experienced the power of the place every time he went there.

"He told me that there are certain, very special places—he used the term, holy ground – where the power of the cosmos is focused. He was right. I had no idea what he meant but I would soon experience it for myself."

"What do you mean?" asked Michelle.

"I mean he was right! I've never been through a night anything like what I was about to experience," said Kirk. "Just bear with me."

"Late that afternoon we sat down on the flat rock surface right at the very edge of the precipice. We ate a snack supper; pita, moutabel, those big red olives that come from... What's the name of that kibbutz just up the road from Massebot that sells all the gourmet olives?"

"Beit Hashita," said Michelle.

"Yeah, that's it. And we had another bottle of that Gamla Cabernet that you picked out for me in Beit Shean. Bill tracked one down in Tiberias so he must have liked your choice.

"Anyway, down below us was that road from Nazareth to Capernaum and in the distance you could see the lights start to come on around the Sea of Galilee. While we were eating Bill came right out and asked me if I often prayed all night when I was out under the stars on my boat. I told him I didn't remember ever praying all night, except maybe in the bush in Vietnam. He explained that what he meant was spending all night in prayer, praise, meditation, just silent worship. I admitted to him that I never had.

"By then the sounds of the evening call to prayer were wafting up from this little Arab town far below us. Bill told me he knew I

320 JIM LEVER

was uncomfortable with the conversation and I was. I think most men are reluctant as hell to discuss spiritual beliefs or experiences, especially with each other.

"Once again he assured me that he was not out to try and save my lost soul. He explained that we were in one of those special places of power where spending time, or an entire night, in meditation and prayer was a powerful way to spiritual truth. I remember asking him if he had found spiritual truth here. He said he always did; he said that anyone could, if they only would. I asked him how. He suggested that I do exactly what he was just asking about, for the first time in my life, simply try to spend a night listening and paying attention – the whole night, right there, in meditation and prayer.

"He said that's exactly what he intended to do that night, because this was one of those special places, maybe the most special, where all the energy of creation is available to us. He stood up, said he was going to walk around to the second best seat in the house; he told me I had the best. Then he smiled and said he hoped I didn't sleep a wink.

"As he started away he stopped and turned around and told me he should warn me that whatever I learned that night, I should be very wary who I share it with. He said I should keep it to myself until I know the time is right.

"'The spiritual truth that sets you free is your truth, meant for you alone. You'll know when and what to share when the time comes.' I think those were his exact words," said Kirk. "So... I suppose the time has come."

He paused to search Michelle's eyes for whatever her reaction may be. All he could detect was her complete attention to his story. He continued, confessing to her that he expected nothing more than to spend a few uninterrupted hours gazing into the infinity of a wondrous Middle Eastern night sky. But that was not to be. Sometime during that night, he had inexplicable encounters straight out of the deepest essence of his past. He explained that it was difficult to adequately relate many of the details of the personal significance of these encounters.

The first encounter was with the father who had been lost at sea when Kirk was a small boy. He told her he could sense his father's love permeating his very soul. His father had admonished that his memories of him as an almost mythical hero were false. Fixing him as a role model of perfection could do nothing but doom the son to a lifetime of failure. He told Kirk that his worship of the myth had also blinded his eyes to what a good and loving man his stepfather had been. He revealed to Kirk that this man, the stepfather whom he had held to an impossibly high standard, had been a more complete father to him than he himself would have been had he lived.

"He told me that the most important of all spiritual freedom is the freedom to fail," said Kirk. "We must give it to others and we must give it to ourselves. Finally, Michelle, he told me that I must go to the graveside of my stepfather and tell him what I have learned."

"You're going to do it, aren't you?" she asked.

"Oh yes. I had almost decided to check out of the dig and go straight home. But then you went missing in Jordan. But I'll go, as soon as I get back.

"Good," said Michelle, "I really think you should. Now, go ahead."

"My next encounter was with a young Vietnamese, hardly more than a teenager. He was a NVA soldier. He was killed during Tet in 1968... I'm the one who killed him."

Kirk recounted listening to the young man's gurgling moans for hours on into the night after he was shot. He described stripping the body the morning after and finding a French Crucifix, matted with his gelled blood, still chained around his neck. He told Michelle that the young man taught him that what had happened was one of the terrible accidents that plague the human condition.

"He said I was the real victim... It was as if we were old friends, Michelle. In fact, he said we would be friends... for eternity. Can you imagine it?"

"This is incredible, Kirk. I don't know how to respond."

"Neither did I, didn't then, don't now. I suppose you can see why I've had so much difficulty talking about all this. You sure can't explain what you don't understand."

He disclosed the last encounter of the night telling her that it was the most joyous. The final experience brought his grandfather to the cliffs. He walked into his senses with Jack, the little horse he loved dearly during his boyhood. He smiled and scratched jack behind his ear. In the soft voice that Kirk remembered so well he told him that there was someone he wanted me to see. It was the little beagle he had given Kirk for his eleventh birthday. Kirk said she remembered him with the yelps and convulsive licks that he remembered so well. Papa explained that we are given animals so that we may have an inkling of absolute authority and a taste of unconditional love. He assured Kirk that human love creates for them a place in eternity.

"The next thing I knew, it was morning. I could see the first glow of dawn over the Golan Heights. At the same time Bill returned. He said he trusted that I had a good night. I was dumbstruck but I know he knew exactly what kind of night I had.

"So, there you have it; what can I say? You still want to go up there?"

"Yeah… I don't know why. I ought to be scared to death… but I do; I want to go."

25

FATHER BILL CASEY was nowhere to be found. Kirk thought he would catch him in the dining hall but he was not there. Neither was he in their room at the B&B. His scuffed brogans were under the cot but the bulging laundry bag he kept clove-hitched to the foot rail of the bed was gone. Kirk assumed he skipped lunch to get showered and changed before heading out. He didn't remember if Bill had told him what he was doing for the weekend.

He knew the footloose old priest was subject to pop into any Franciscan campus in the country at any time. Since the dirty laundry was gone, that's where he guessed Bill was headed—Laundromats being nonexistent except in Israel's major cities. He had hoped Father Casey and Michelle could talk before the trip to the Cliffs. But there would be plenty of time for that later.

On their way to the bus stop they ran by the office to get a phone card and change some large shekel notes for smaller ones. Joel LaRoche was on the pay phone outside. He raised an index finger asking them to hold up a minute. Michelle grinned at overhearing Joel recite an endless succession of assurances to his mother, back home in France.

"Oui Mama... oui... oui... adieu... adieu Mama."

Michelle could hear the woman still talking on the line as Joel gingerly placed the handset back into the cradle hook.

"Kirk, Michelle," he said, "Willy asked I tell you he and the father are gone for the weekend to Capernaum, to the monastery."

"Thanks, Joel. You hanging around here?"

"Yes. I sleep and read, nothing more."

Kirk looked at Michelle. "What did I tell you? I still can't picture those two hanging out together but Bill claims they've been friends for years."

"Maybe Bill just considers Willy a masterpiece in progress," said Michelle.

Kirk chuckled for the first few steps toward the main gate and the bus stop outside. As they walked, Kirk told Michelle Willy's account of being raised in the Louisiana brand of the Catholic Church and how he had lost no love for the institution.

"Willy says the only good thing the Catholic Church ever did for him was to put Ash Wednesday on the calendar; because without it, he says, there would be no Fat Tuesday. He also swears there's no way in hell he would have ever made it out of Vietnam were it not for the nuns at St Aloysius Junior High. Says he got better escape and evasion training in Baton Rouge than he did at Camp Pendleton."

Three hours later Kirk and Michelle were walking through the narrow streets of Moshav Arbel. The work week there had already come to a halt; Shabbat would begin at sundown. The only noticeable sounds were children at play and a few peafowl high in the ficus trees screaming the alert that strangers were in the village.

The odor of muck piles outside the dairy stalls and of burning feathers from behind the poultry houses fouled the air. Soon the stink was staunched by the piney scent of shredded wild rosemary rising from a freshly mowed fence row flanking the road.

Just beyond the last equipment shed a tractor road divided a vast grain field and climbed the mile-long slope up to the cliffs. Since Kirk was here weeks earlier, the barley had been combined and the stubble harrowed under. The harvesting and tilling had transformed the otherwise bad road into a kind of obstacle course.

The massive, dual-wheel tractors had made turn-arounds at the end of the rows leaving the rock strewn soil mounded in meter-high scallops in the middle of the road. The rest of the way up would be a difficult hike; it would be almost impossible for any vehicle but another tractor to drive up. But it meant they would probably have the cliffs all to themselves for the entire weekend.

Michelle was impressed; the breathtaking panorama at the top surpassed Kirk's description of the place and her expectations. The summit view was infinitely more than another grand vista; it was a window overlooking countless historical and biblical sites.

Below were battlefields spanning the millennia from Joshua's conquests three thousand years before down to the Six Days War triumph on the Golan Heights. Christianity was born around the shores of the lake below. Twelve hundred years later the battle that would evict the Crusaders from Islamic lands was fought a scant two miles to the West at The Horns of Hattin.

But this day no battles raged. It was impossible to smell the carnage, to hear echoes of the dying scream or to even to detect the scars of battle on the landscape. This evening the only sound other than a soothing breeze rustling a wild carob's wizened leaves was a far distant pair of F-16's en route to patrol the Lebanese and Syrian borders.

"Can you believe this place?" Kirk asked, breaking several minutes of silent appreciation. "How peaceful it is now, hard to believe how many thousands have died in, God only knows, how many wars down there. Ever notice, the most quiet and peaceful places on Earth are battlefield cemeteries?"

"Never thought about it; but you're right." Michelle answered. "Yeah, I could spend about a peaceful week here," she said, "that is, if you'd run back to town for wine and cheese. Gosh, the air smells so good up here!"

"Air's a lot cooler up here, too, especially at night. I forgot to tell you to bring a sweatshirt or something. We can harbor behind those rocks. They'll block this east wind but we'll still have a good view."

"I'll be fine," said Michelle, "I have my little micro fleece sleeping bag. Unzips into a nice blanket, too, might even share it with you." Michelle feigned a matter-of-fact posture and avoided looking at Kirk for a few moments until she turned, met his eyes and smiled.

"You got a sleeping bag in that little backpack?"

"Sure do; never leave home without it. Only weighs about a pound and it's better than any chintzy travel blanket."

When they first noticed, the sunset was a mesmerizing display of a hundred new, unnamed colors. And, as Kirk had also described, the first summoning moans were cranked out of the speakers atop a minaret in the small Arab village below. The chant, along with its several echoes, ricocheted up to their secluded ledge creating a haunting sound not unlike one of Enya's new-age overdubs. And, then, as the day dimmed on away, the village lights below flickered into focus until they themselves were dampened by a clear, lucent night sky which illuminated the whole landscape.

Michelle spread the unzipped micro fleece bag on the smooth rock surface. They sat close together with their backs relaxing into the comfortable contour of the wind-blocking boulders behind them. The peace of the night seemed to put the daylight world into its proper, trivial place. Soon the harsh schedule of before dawn wake up calls, heavy work and long hours in the sun took its weekly toll. Within minutes they were both sound asleep.

When Kirk opened his eyes, the late first quarter moon had arced far across the night sky. He pressed the tiny button to illuminate the face of his IndigloTimex. "Three thirty," he whispered to himself. The night was quiet and only a soft breeze remained of the early evening wind. Kirk tried to detect what had aroused him; he heard it again. From a short distance back down the path came the unmistakable sound of gravel crunching beneath shod feet. Someone was walking toward them.

Kirk sat upright, turning toward the approaching foot steps. He could barely make out a lone shape. It was backlit by the bright quarter moon but before he recognized the dark form he heard the voice.

"Kirk, don't let me alarm you two; it's only me."

"Father Casey? Damn!" Kirk was alarmed, relieved and a bit aggravated, too, all at the same time.

"Yes, it is I; hope I didn't startle you."

"Uh...no; we're okay. Michelle's not even awake."

"I am now!" Michelle sat up pulling the fleece blanket around her shoulders.

She squinted in the direction of Bill's voice.

"I'm sorry, Michelle. Please forgive me for arriving so unexpectedly, and in the middle of the night. Seems I have a knack for spooking folks, or so I'm told."

Father Bill didn't look to see but he knew Kirk caught his spooking folks comment. Kirk did pretend not to notice the remark. He searched his memory trying to recall who else he told about Bill's spiritual talk being so unsettling to him.

"Well, what on earth are you doing walking around up here at this hour?" asked Kirk. "Lucky you haven't plummeted to your death."

Ignoring the remark, Father Casey walked on over and sat on

a rock a few feet away. He pulled the hood of his cowl back off of his head, crossed an ankle over his knee and began tugging at a twisted sandal strap. Now Kirk could focus in on the old priest. It was the first time he had seen him in the thrush brown habit of the Franciscans.

Finally, without looking up Bill answered. "Didn't think you'd be on any schedule. Time just never seems to register with you up here, wouldn't you agree?"

"Yeah, I guess so," said Kirk. "Well, come on over and have a seat. I'll fire up my camp stove and make us some coffee."

"None for me thanks. I just came by so we could talk for a while. Sorry I wasn't around before you left yesterday afternoon. Oh, and don't worry; I'm not going to hang around here for long. Actually, I'm off on a trip I've been looking forward to for a long, long time. So the two of you will have the rest of the weekend together, all by yourself."

Neither Kirk nor Michelle had a chance to get in a question before Bill jumped straight into the message he had come to deliver. He began recounting the seminal events of Michelle's life; one hurt, one frustration, one perceived defeat at a time. The first few words of his review pooled her eyes with tears. Michelle couldn't believe she was caught up so quickly in so numinous an experience. Normally her alarm bells would be ringing her back to her safe old skeptical self. But this was like being caught up in some tabloid out of the body story, looking down at her own lifeless form but not wanting to go back. She accepted this strange old man's words without apprehension, as though they were a confirmation of the love from the departed father she worshiped.

To Kirk he repeated many of the same assurances he had given him that first day in the room at the kibbutz. It all seemed so familiar to Michelle. Had Kirk told her what he had said? She couldn't be sure. It was almost as if the old priest addressed them both as a single soul. Now she couldn't distinguish her portion of the revelation from his.

She had heard stories of people's lives flashing before their eyes in the moments before their death and she wondered if this was what was happening to her now. She was convinced she should be panic stricken but, instead, she felt a peace and protection she had never known and could not now grasp. Every fiber of her being told her that Bill's every verdict and absolution were true. And this time Kirk found the old priest's words a reassurance rather than a threat.

As suddenly as he had started the old man hushed. He rose and moved over close to the edge of the cliff. Stock-still he stood there gazing out over the plain of Ginnosar. For the longest time all three held their silence. It was evident that Father Bill wanted one of them to speak first.

"Father Bill?" Kirk was the first. "You remember telling me that it was no accident we were all over here together?"

Bill turned to face his friend and nodded. "Yes, I do," he answered.

"Well, is this what you were talking about, my coming up here and seeing the visions and the both of us...? I mean, I guess Michelle being here is no accident either?"

"No Kirk, none of us here are together by accident; you, Michelle or I. Neither is Jaclyn or Willy or any of the others we've encountered. All our lives are supernaturally entwined; they always have been. The difference is that now you are conscious of the connections.

"This is the first great spiritual truth: there are no accidental events. Even a seemingly insignificant ray of sunlight beaming into a stack of tea glasses is no accident and being there to see it is no coincidence. What there is, is wonder and woe, always has been, always shall be.

"The second great spiritual truth is this: wonders are more powerful than woes. For instance, I would venture to say that your love for each other—which you two just happened to find here—is a wonder that far outweighs any woes you've experienced here. Maybe even our new friendships outweigh most of the woes.

"In the short span of these past few weeks we have seen the best and the worst in man. None of it is new. It's as old as all the generations who lived and died below these cliffs. It's the essence of the most important message ever delivered to humanity. The message that we have little control over what happens to us but we have all power given to us to master our response to whatever befalls us."

"But Father Casey," Michelle interrupted. "I don't want to be rude or negative or... or whatever. But isn't that a terribly simplistic view of life or religion or... whatever?"

"Yes my dear friend, it is. The most simplistic message ever taught and I'm quite sure these are the most simple of all truths.

And because they are, they're comprehensible by us all regardless of intellect, culture, physical condition, our situation in life... History's great teachers taught nothing more or less than variations of these same simple principles.

"One of the greats said that of our lives are like the production of fine china: We're shaped, fired, removed from the fire and allowed to cool; the pieces that don't ring, when thumped, go back into the fire.

"And the founder of my Holy Order teaches that we should accept what we cannot change, change what we cannot accept and strive for the wisdom to know the difference.

"Simplistically put, we might have no control over our shape or the fire but we all have it within us to ring when we are thumped.

"Michelle, my beautiful friend, I know what you're thinking... Just like Kirk, you're too polite to come out and say it, don't want to hurt an old man's feelings. I know you didn't come up here to listen to me preach in the middle of the night. I know you didn't; I don't blame you. Just don't you worry; soon I'll be on me way and I promise I won't button-hole you again – at least not without you making a special effort to invite me. And I'm sure that's the farthest thing from your mind. But, before I go please hear me out. If nothing else I've said registers with you, please hear me now.

"This will be my last dig. In fact, yesterday was my last day at Kefar. You both will be returning over here for several dig seasons to come. Matter of fact, I think you two are – what do the kids call it – oh yes, an item. Yes indeed, I think you two are an item from now on."

"How..."

Father Casey cut him off. "Don't ask me how I know; I just know and because I know, I have a request of you. I want you to become locum tenentes in my absence."

"Become what?" Kirk asked.

"Become my replacements," said Bill. "I want you two to be fetchers, the ones who bring travelers here, to the cliffs.

When the time comes you'll know exactly who is to come, just as I knew you were to come. And I can tell you this. Many of the older folks who come to the digs are looking for more than a few old artifacts. Archaeology is just a way of escaping their own past... through the past of others, I guess. Why do I feel like you two know this?

"And I'll tell you something else. Archaeology is a lot like the rest of our spiritual pursuits. When you find exactly what you expected, you had best be very suspect of it.

"Everyone's so distraught about the effect our Ophrah's Gate tablet is going to have on biblical archaeology. The great irony is that, in the broader sense, it will have much the same effect as if it were as genuine as the Herodian Stones in the Western Wall."

"What on earth do you mean?" Kirk asked.

"I mean those who want it to be authentic will cling to it in spite of everything. They will allege a conspiracy to discredit it and they'll name a slew of likely culprits. And those who want it to be a fake would never have been convinced of its authenticity, regardless of any scientific evidence.

"But there is a potential for spiritual magic in this situation, you see, the magic of an epiphany. It can awaken us to another truth. If our faith needs tangible evidence of a material nature, then what we have is not faith at all. And it can teach us that spiritual truth has very little to do with human history. Above all else, it can teach us if we would only look to those whom we love, those who love us and within ourselves we will find our ultimate spiritual truth… or God, if you prefer."

"Father Casey," said Michelle. "I have about a thousand questions."

"I'm sure you do, darling, and that's just about the number of answers I'm short. Anyway, I must be on me way. All this will become crystal… well, maybe I ought to say, much clearer, in the days to come. In the meantime, I'm afraid I have to ask you to trust me. Oh my, it's getting light over the Golan. What time is it, Kirk?"

"It's… 5:20 Saturday morning, Bill."

"Well, as I promised, I have to be going now. You two have a wonderful weekend."

Father Bill raised his hand and made the sign of a blessing. Then he started toward the hewn stone steps which led down the face of the cliffs and to the zealot's caves. As he walked away he turned, smiled and waved one last time.

"One last thing." His voice had a reverberating, melodious quality through the morning mist. "In case I don't see her, please tell Sarah Bergman that she's right about the location of the copper scroll treasure. You'll find it in a season or two, right there in

Ophrah's Gate. Just remember that it, too, will be whatever you see in it and whatever it awakens within you."

Before either Kirk or Michelle could ask another question the old priest disappeared into the predawn dimness.

26

"COME ON, Kirk," Michelle coaxed. "If we hurry we can still make supper."

"Don't you think we ought to feel kinda stupid rushing to a pan of cold eggs and a big bowl of warm yogurt?" Kirk scoffed at the prodding. Refrigerated soft boiled eggs were not on the volunteers' list of most requested entrées. "All right, I'm coming," he said. "I'll meet you outside on the walk... soon as I throw my pack in the room."

The light dairy supper hour had passed but the kitchen staff was usually tolerant of stragglers returning from the weekend. The dining hall would still be open and, if they were lucky, food, such as it was, would still be out on the serving line.

When Kirk had dropped off their backpacks in his room he walked back outside, pulled the door shut and locked it. Michelle noticed that he had a white envelope in his hand.

"What you got there?" she asked.

"I don't know," he answered. "It's addressed to both of us. But I'm starving; we can open it at dinner."

"Oh, really?" Michelle gave him a playful, scolding look.

Kirk was right; when he and Michelle had entered through the poorly aligned double doors a huge stainless steel serving pan of boiled eggs was there to greet them. Neither had learned to read the Hebrew ink stamps on the eggs which indicated the soft from the hard boiled so they grabbed a couple of each.

Kirk sat down with his tray and stood the sealed envelope up against one of the pitiful little bud vases that adorned every Formica table top table in the dining hall. Michelle fixed herself a cup of hot chocolate. Trying to balance the too-full cup, she tiptoed on over and joined Kirk.

"How the heck can you drink that hot stuff this time of day?" he asked.

Michelle shrugged without trying to answer him. "Let's open this and see what it is." She carefully tore off the end of the envelope, pooched it open and removed a folded sheet of linen stationery. She held it up to her nose and then over to Kirk.

"What is that, sandalwood?" she asked.

Kirk took one whiff. "No ma'am; that's frankincense, the real stuff, too. That's one smell that won't stump an old Episcopalian acolyte. I probably put in more time holding an incense boat and thurible when I was a kid than I have hanging on to long neck Budweisers since then."

Michelle began reading the letter out loud. It was from Father Casey.

My Dear Friends,

As you may already know, I will not be returning to the kibbutz. And since I will not see you again in person before you return home, I am leaving this note which I ask that you read together. My intention is to plant an idea which I encourage the both of you to seriously consider. I am confident that you will recognize as pertinent what I am about to offer you.

During my early days as a priest I served as vicar of Sacred Heart Church in Haines, Alaska, a very small parish in a remote fishing village. One of my elderly parishioners, Victoria, was the only child of one of the area's early logging magnates. Victoria had never married, she was very wealthy and she took me in under her wing. She was my staunch defender against the usual snares that a fresh young priest always faces. She soon became much more like a trusted family member than a friend. Over the years we kept in contact and I was a frequent visitor to her home out on the Chilkat.

Victoria passed away in the early 1970s. Soon after her death I received a certified letter from an attorney in Juneau informing me that I was named as a co-executor of her estate. Her will stated that I was to have exclusive use of the property in Haines, that I was to use it as I saw fit, and that I was to be relieved of the duty of reporting and accounting to the probate department.

She directed that I be appointed to the board of a charitable foundation which was to be created using the bulk of her sizable estate. The foundation was to endow worthy Catholic organizations which met certain criteria. She also directed that I was to have unlimited travel and expense authorization in the execution of my duties among which were travel to and the discretionary use of her Chilkat Peninsula estate. In summary she directed that should there ever be any official objection by the Catholic Church to my serving in these capacities then all future income from the foundation trust fund was to be redirected to The Nature Conservancy and several other charities.

It is my wish to transfer this legacy on to the both of you. Within a few days you will be contacted by the law firm in Juneau which has handled these affairs since the beginning. The lawyers will explain everything including compensation for your services which I believe you will deem to be quite adequate.

I do not ask either of you to serve on the board of the foundation as I have asked my friend, Father Alimayu, to fill the position created by my absence. By the way, did I ever tell you that it was Father Alimayu who first took me to the Cliffs of Arbel? Well it was and he is perfectly aware of my wishes for the both of you and he will be available to assist you in any way.

I believe you will soon fall in love with the Chilkat Peninsula. Mr. and Mrs. Martin, the caretakers, will show you around the châteaux grounds and introduce you to the neighbors. You'll like all my friends. They'll soon have you digging clams and trolling for Chinook. And, by all means, make your way down town to the Fogcutter Bar and introduce yourself to Jackie the bartender. She'll handle the rest; soon you'll know everyone in town. But whatever you do, don't ring Gene Stewart's old bent-up propeller bell hanging at the bar or you'll be paying for a round. And do me one last favor; tell everyone in the place that Gene and I are both doing just great.

Take care, my dear friends. Perhaps I'll have the chance to visit with you on the cliffs again next year.

As ever,

Bill Casey

Kirk and Michelle were speechless. Michelle, at last, took a sip of her hot chocolate as Kirk began to clumsily peel one of the eggs. He guessed right; it was hard boiled. They had been so engrossed in the letter they hadn't noticed Jaclyn come into the dining hall or sit down at the table next to them. When Jaclyn's presence finally registered with Michelle she spoke.

"Hi, Jaclyn; I didn't hear you come in." she said.

"Perfectly all right," said Jaclyn. "I expected you two would be taken aback by Father Bill's letter. He told me what he was doing but we can talk about all that later. Right now I need to talk to you both in private. Why don't we walk outside; we can sit over in the playground."

Kirk was puzzled; no one was sitting anywhere near them. He didn't understand why this wasn't private enough but he went along with her suggestion. When they were all outside, sitting on one of the benches that flanked the children's playground, Jaclyn paused to gather her thoughts. A lonely palm dove hidden somewhere in one of the big ficus trees cooed away the afternoon heat. Jaclyn turned herself sideways on the bench to better face Kirk and Michelle.

"I've been waiting for you to return all afternoon," she said. "I'm afraid I have some shocking news. Father Casey and Willy are both dead."

"What!" Both exclaimed.

"The details are a bit sketchy but they both went up to Capernaum early Friday afternoon. From what I was told, they changed into their swimwear and went down to the lake. A grounds-keeper heard Willy shout something. When he looked up he saw Father Casey was floating motionless out in the lake. Willy swam out to him and was trying to keep his head above the water. They both just went under.

"I don't know who eventually answered the call – the gardener couldn't swim so he ran for help – but they found them both about three hours later. Willy was still clutching Father Bill's tee shirt with his good hand... didn't have enough strength in his other arm to swim for himself and hold onto Father Casey too, I suppose. The doctors say that Father had a massive heart attack. He was probably gone before Willy ever got to him."

Michelle sobbed softly. Kirk eyes were fixed into the playground sawdust while as they sat in stunned silence. When the details of the dreadful account began to sink in, Michelle realized that the time line Jaclyn had related didn't fit. When she could, she turned to Jaclyn.

"You said Friday afternoon but you meant Saturday, didn't you?"

Jaclyn gazed into Michelle's eyes with a look of compassionate understanding. But she answered by continuing with her message.

"Father Alimayu told me that Father Casey was laid to rest in the monastery's little cemetery on Mt. Tabor at sunrise this morning. Willy's remains are being sent home and he will be buried in the National Cemetery in Baton Rouge. Father Alimayu says that Willy was on the Marine Corps Rifle Team and that he was one of their top snipers in Vietnam.

"Oh, I'm sorry, Michelle; I almost forgot to answer your question. No, I didn't mean Saturday. Father Casey and Willy died around 3:30 Friday afternoon."

Printed in the United States
112344LV00001B/259/A